Tristan AND THE Majesteria

CORWYNN ROSEWOOD

Tristan and the Majesteria

Corwynn Rosewood

TRISTAN AND THE MAJESTERIA

Copyright © 2025 by Corwynn Rosewood

All rights reserved.

This is a work of fiction. All of the characters, organizations, and events portrayed in this novel are either products of the author's imagination or are used fictionally.

No part of this book may be reproduced in any form or by any electronic or mechanical means, including information storage and retrieval systems, without written permission from the author, except for the use of brief quotations in a book review.

No generative artificial intelligence (AI) was used in the writing, editing, marketing or publishing of this work. The author expressly prohibits any entity from using this publication for purposes of training AI technologies.

Cover Design: CRW
Developmental Editor: Parker Frost
Copy Editor: Jennifer Kinsey Bangley

First Edition 2025

Contents

Prologue   1
Chapter 1   13
Chapter 2   24
Chapter 3   39
Chapter 4   55
Chapter 5   71
Chapter 6   88
Chapter 7   103
Chapter 8   119
Chapter 9   137
Chapter 10   159
Chapter 11   181
Chapter 12   193
Chapter 13   207
Chapter 14   221
Chapter 15   240
Chapter 16   257
Chapter 17   270
Chapter 18   283
Chapter 19   296
Chapter 20   316
Chapter 21   333
Chapter 22   344
Chapter 23   359

PROLOGUE

Tristan Mulberry had a very unusual job. At first glance it didn't sound all that strange, but he always had some trouble explaining his job once he started getting into the details.

On the one hand, he worked for the Majesteria, some of the most powerful mages in the realm, assisting them with whatever they needed. It was a highly sought after position at Teakley Academy, a well respected academic institute, requiring expert use of complicated Starlight Magic and a near encyclopedic knowledge of herbs.

On the other hand, at least half the time his job consisted of tracking down an exceptionally small needle so that one of the Majesteria could embroider flowers onto a cloak, or procuring large amounts of cheese.

So much cheese.

He had not known much about cheese before he became a Majesteria Handler. Now he could tell you the origins of thirty different varieties of cheddar in his sleep. For you see, the Majesteria he worked for, those powerful mages of great renown?

Well.

They were mice.

Not your average field mice, of course. The Majesteria were a variety of mouse that was quite a bit larger, called a Hi-Mouse. They had slightly bigger ears, thicker fur, and were rather inclined towards walking on two paws and wearing clothes. Oh, and of course, they were almost always imbued with copious amounts of magical abilities.

Not all Majesteria were mice, Majesteria being the title of a larger group of magical animals, but quite a lot of them were Hi-Mice.

The three Majesteria Tristan worked for were Edwina, Marigold and Chica. They were wildly smart, very opinionated, vastly knowledgable and tremendously kind. They were also the most stubborn, gossipy and utterly ridiculous creatures he had ever met. Naturally, Tristan would have walked over hot coals to get them a wedge of cheese.

But right now, Tristan did not have to worry about such things. Right now, he was facing down something far worse than hot coals: middle management. He was sitting in the cold, empty waiting room of his supervisor, Lord Blanchard. They were about to have a meeting about the Teakley expedition to the Queen's Coronation to deliver the Royal Cinderflower.

Ah, the Royal Cinderflower. It had been the source of some excitement for Tristan and the Majesteria over the last few months. The Cinderflower was many things; first and foremost it was a rare and temperamental magical flower. It lived eternally, if properly cared for, and just one of its leaves would probably be enough magical power to instantly demolish an entire city. Or a very large village, at least. It was a relic of an ancient time when the authority of the Crown was established in these parts by means of magical force.

But mostly, it was a symbol. It represented the power and might of the Crown, and they put it on *everything*. It was on the flag, the coins, livery, cutlery, knight's shields and ornately embroidered gowns. Luxury furniture often featured a Cinderflower motif, but the cheapest matchboxes had the flower too. It was not just *a* symbol of the realm, it was *the* symbol and an essential part of the ritual for the new Queen's Coronation.

It was also just a flower that was very, very old.

It had old, dry, crusted soil; browned corners on the leaves, root rot, a little bit of pinkish mold, and a mysterious slime along the stem.

So, the Crown had sent it to the most expert magical botanists in the realm for examination and restoration to get it looking its royal best before the Queen's Coronation. Those experts happened to all reside at Teakley Academy.

The Royal Cinderflower had arrived at Teakley with an armed guard and a few dozen wagons, covered in gilded livery with bright flags flapping in the breeze. Tristan had watched with everyone else at the windows lining the courtyard as the Royal Guards brought the Cinderflower into the Academy, squinting to try to see the small, glittering flower in its gilded glass cage.

But that had been a few months ago, and they'd all gotten pretty used to looking at the Cinderflower by now. The flower had been attended to by many different mages with various specialties until it eventually ended up with Tristan and the Majesteria, who were tasked with putting the finishing touches on its restoration and maintaining its health with regular infusions of Starlight magic while they waited to return it to the Crown. It had spent most of the last month sitting on the Majesteria's living room table next to the kettle.

But now it was almost time to return the Cinderflower to its owners and all that was left to do was figure out how they would transport the highly dangerous and politically valuable magical flower to its destination, the island of Fairefeux, a popular trading city where the Coronation would be held.

"Tristan Mulberry, this way please," said a small and nervous voice.

Tristan looked up and saw a rather young Senior Apprentice in a royal blue cape with a Teakley brooch shining on her lapel. Apprentices often looked nervous, but she looked positively terrified. Tristan felt bad for her, working for Blanchard couldn't be easy.

He gave her a friendly smile and stood up to follow her into the office.

If the rumor mill was to be believed, Blanchard had been raised at Teakley South, the other branch of Teakley Academy on the Mainland. He was taken in as a young boy showing magical aptitude and raised by the professors instead of his parents, just like Tristan. But unlike Tristan, Blanchard's magical aptitude had drained over time, slowly ebbing away until he wasn't really magical at all. That's what they said anyway, Tristan wasn't sure he believed it.

What he did know was Blanchard certainly had a chip on his shoulder about something, so of course he'd ended up in middle management. When Tristan's previous supervisor, Professor Muggward, had retired to pursue his lifelong passion of mollusk breeding, Blanchard had transferred over from Teakley South to replace him.

Teakley South was far away in a major city, and people from there were...strange. At least, they felt strange to Tristan who'd spent most of his life with the friendly folks of Appleton Island.

Most of the people from Teakley South were just very different, they were often overly concerned with things like titles, prestige, rules and regulations. Whereas most people at Teakley were more interested in the idealistic gathering of knowledge and freeform exploration of magical possibilities.

Sometimes they didn't get along very well.

Tristan always tried to be helpful, to give new arrivals from Teakley South the benefit of the doubt and hope they adapted over time. Blanchard had not adapted. If anything, he'd gotten worse.

The Senior Apprentice opened the door and led him into the office.

It was painfully tidy and nearly empty, with minimal furniture full of sharp edges that made it feel cold and uninviting.

For a wistful moment he remembered the office as it used to be, packed with haphazard books and teacups, half-remembered academic projects, and small pots of herbs and flowers. He missed Professor Muggward immensely.

Blanchard was crouched at his desk with a quill in his hand, scribbling in a leather-bound ledger. He wasn't a handsome man; he had greasy hair, sallow skin, and the face of an angry stoat. He didn't look up when Tristan came in.

The Senior Apprentice led him to one of the chairs and Tristan sat down and waited. The only sound was the scratching of Blanchard's quill and the ticking of a small golden clock.

After a while Tristan coughed politely and said,

"Good afternoon, Sir."

Blanchard looked up from his writing, glaring at him with dull, tired eyes.

"What's wrong with you? Have you forgotten your manners? Do we not bow to our superiors any longer?" he said sourly.

Tristan hastily stood up and bowed deeply. He couldn't remember Professor Muggward ever expecting him to bow. Muggward had usually asked him to help repot some plants or organize scrolls while they talked.

"My apologies, Sir," Tristan mumbled.

"My name is not Sir," Blanchard said coldly.

"My apologies, Lord Blanchard."

"You will use my full title when addressing your betters, Mulberry," Blanchard said with a scowl.

"My apologies Lord Blanchard, Senior Liaison to the Grand Majesterium," Tristan said, wondering if he was supposed to bow again.

"And?" Blanchard said imperiously.

"My apologies Lord Blanchard, Senior Liaison to the Grand Majesterium *and* Collected Mages," Tristan said.

"Yes yes, we must not forget the little Collected Mages," Blanchard said. "I know you think you're better than everyone because you're a Majesteria Handler, but some of us respect *all* the magic workers at Teakley Academy, not just the famous ones."

Tristan tried not to sigh or roll his eyes as he sat back down across from Blanchard, who had returned to looking at the paperwork on his desk and ignoring Tristan.

There was a long, awkward silence. Tristan wondered if he should say something, but he was fairly sure that if he said anything Blanchard would just find some way to turn it against him. So he just waited, and waited, and waited.

Finally, Blanchard looked up from the paperwork and said,

"I see here that in the entire time you've been at Teakley you have not ever left the Fruitbasket Isles, in fact, you've rarely even left Appleton Island. Why is that?"

Tristan was momentarily taken aback by the question, and said,

"I thought we were here to discuss the trip to the Coronation?"

Blanchard narrowed his eyes, "Answer the question, Mulberry."

Tristan thought about it and realized he didn't really know why he hadn't travelled much, it just hadn't come up.

"I just go where the Majesteria go, Sir," he said honestly.

"You've been here nearly twenty years," Blanchard said, his tone accusatory. "You haven't been working with the Majesteria that whole time."

Tristan shrugged, "I was mostly training, and Apprentices rarely leave the island, and then I became a Majesteria Handler."

"Hmm," Blanchard said, somehow managing to convey disdain and distrust with the sound. "And *yet*, you expect to go to Fairefeux? It is a rather longer journey than a little jaunt across the river to *Pearsy*."

Tristan had never heard Pearsy, the name of the charming island next to Appleton Island, said with such disdain, like as though it was a dreadful country backwater of no importance.

"Of course, Lord Blanchard, Senior Liaison to the Grand Majesterium and Collected Mages, I will do anything the Majesteria need me to do," Tristan said, with just the tiniest hint of a smirk.

Blanchard gave him a resentful glare.

"For the course of this meeting you may call me simply Lord Blanchard," he said bitterly.

"Thank you, Lord Blanchard, your courtesy is graciously appreciated," Tristan said, enjoying the small amount of irritation he had brought the man who caused so much frustration to everyone around him.

Blanchard looked at his paperwork and sighed.

"While I have my doubts about your *limited* experience and questionable abilities, the Headmaster has made her decision. Despite the objections of her infinitely wise counsellors, she decided to send you to Fairefeux. So now it's left to me to wrangle you into shape for this mission, even though I made it very clear when the plan was devised that *I* would be a *far* more suitable companion for the Royal Cinderflower than a provincial mage with no experience."

Tristan could tell Blanchard was mostly talking to himself at this point, venting his frustration at the Headmaster's decision.

"I'm sorry Lord Blanchard, aren't you going to the Coronation?" Tristan asked, glancing meaningfully at the prominently displayed invitation sitting on Blanchard's desk.

Tristan remembered all too clearly the day the beautiful letter with gilded script had arrived at Teakley. Blanchard had carried The Official Invitation around for a week, mentioning it at every possible opportunity and leaving it conspicuously on the table near him in the cafeteria with the waxed royal seal on display.

"Of course! I will be *leading* the Teakley delegation," he said proudly. "But *you* will not be coming with us, we will be leaving a few weeks earlier."

"I'm very confused Sir, sorry, Lord Blanchard," Tristan quickly corrected himself, "if I'm not coming with you and the rest of the Teakley group, why am I here?"

Blanchard sighed and gave him a withering look.

"You and the Majesteria will be going separately from the rest of the group. With the Royal Cinderflower," he said slowly and deliberately, like he was talking to small child.

Tristan was momentarily rattled by this revelation.

"I'm sorry Sir? Why?" He asked, confused.

"Security, Tristan, Security," Blanchard said, standing up and beginning to pace, looking out the windows of his office at the vibrant herb gardens below, bursting with bright greenery. "The Crown is concerned about the possibility of thievery or political espionage as the Royal Cinderflower makes its journey to Fairefeux. It is a well known fact that the flower has been here at Teakley for restoration in preparation for the Coronation. We have only avoided being infiltrated by thieves and spies because everyone knows Teakley is well defended with powerful warding spells all over the grounds. But the group of mages travelling to the Coronation will be afforded no such luxury, making them an easy target for nefarious criminals. Thus, a plan was devised," he said, sounding quite proud of himself. Tristan was starting to develop a guess as to who had come up with this bizarre plan.

Blanchard returned to the desk and gave Tristan a pointed glare.

"Rather than sending the Cinderflower with the main group attending the Coronation it will be sent later, with a much smaller group of mages on a Registered Pirate Vessel."

"A pirate ship?" Tristan asked, clearly very surprised.

"A Registered Pirate Vessel," Blanchard said flatly.

"My apologies, I'm unfamiliar with that term," Tristan said.

Blanchard rolled his eyes,

"I forget sometimes how simple and unsophisticated you are, Mulberry. A few years back, in her infinite wisdom, Queen Aurelia, may she rest in peace, constructed a plan to deal with the pirating problem in the Evarian Sea.

Registered Pirate Vessels are a collection of reformed former pirate ships who have agreed to exclusively carry cargo and passengers, renouncing all illegal activity. In return they are allowed to continue sailing and have the freedom of the open seas."

Tristan took in this information, turning it over in his head and comparing it to his existing knowledge of pirates.

"What stops them from pirating?" He asked.

"Regular check-ins with the Royal Mariners who search the ship and arrest anyone who is not complying with the rules," Blanchard said.

"That doesn't sound very free to me," Tristan mused.

"When the alternative is jail, many find this to be a delightful proposition," Blanchard said crisply. "It has become so popular they say some ships even volunteer to become Registered Pirate Vessels."

"I see," Tristan said. "So I will be travelling to the Coronation on one of these...pirate ships–"

"Registered Pirate Vessel," Blanchard cut in.

"Right, sorry, Registered Pirate Vessel. I will be travelling to the Coronation with the Majesteria and...no one else from Teakley?"

"Secretly," Blanchard added.

Tristan raised an eyebrow "Secretly?"

"Yes, no one on the ship will know you are travelling with the Majesteria or the Royal Cinderflower, thereby dramatically lowering the chances of any possible intervention in the Cinderflower's journey to Fairefeux. Everyone will think you are just a solitary, unimportant mage on a personal journey to see the Queen's Coronation."

Tristan sat back in his chair, letting the information sink in. It was a terrifying prospect, hiding the Majesteria and the Royal Cinderflower. The thought of having sole responsibility for the Cinderflower's arrival at the Queen's Coronation wasn't one he was very excited about.

"Why a Registered Pirate Vessel?" He asked.

"Because it's the least likely place you'd ever find the Royal Cinderflower, isn't it?" Blanchard said proudly.

"I'm not sure this is the best idea, Lord Blanchard," Tristan said as his mind swam with the many things that could go wrong with this plan.

"Luckily, the decision is entirely out of your hands," Blanchard said, steepling his fingers and looking at Tristan severely. "Everything has already been decided, it must be the Majesteria because they can look after the flower's well-being and give it infusions of Starlight magic to keep it healthy during the trip. They need a Handler to move the flower and keep the Majesteria's existence secret. Now, if you feel that you're not *personally* up to the task, perhaps it's time I assigned someone else to be the Majesteria's Handler?"

Tristan's stomach dropped at his words. The idea was unthinkable to him, he loved being a Majesteria Handler and he couldn't imagine working with anyone else besides Edwina, Marigold and Chica. Doing magic and creating spells with them had easily been the highlight of his career, and possibly even his life.

"No Sir, um, Lord Blanchard," he said hurriedly. "I'm sure I can handle whatever the Majesteria need."

Blanchard frowned, "I thought you might say that. How unfortunate. I personally think you should be reassigned, but those mice won't let you go for some reason. Regardless, we're stuck with you now, so I must impress upon you the importance of this mission."

"It's very clear, Lord Blanchard," Tristan said seriously.

"Furthermore, I cannot emphasize enough how important it is that no one, and I mean *no one*, ever finds out that the Majesteria or the Royal Cinderflower are on board that ship. Understand?"

"Crystal clear, Lord Blanchard," Tristan said.

"Good. Let's start going over the specifics," Blanchard said, pulling a large envelope from a drawer of his desk and laying out paperwork on the table, while Tristan's mind whirred with activity as he absorbed this surprising turn of events.

The Royal Cinderflower, the Majesteria, and a Registered Pirate Vessel.

This was going to be a very interesting journey indeed.

ONE MONTH LATER....

Chapter One

Tristan woke to the sound of a loudly clanging bell. He shot up in bed and ran for the door, realizing just in the nick of time that he would need a bit more clothing before he stepped out into the hallway.

A few moments later he was running down the hallway his long, wavy blonde hair in a tangled mess and his dressing gown inside out. He burst through the door to the Majesteria's quarters, a large brass candlestick in hand.

"What's going on?" he shouted in a panic.

"Oh I'm so sorry Tristan!" Edwina said, "We didn't meant to scare you. We just wanted to make sure we weren't late for the trip!"

Tristan relaxed, loosening his grip on the candlestick as he realized his friends were not in immediate danger. He looked out the window at the bright morning sunshine and knew that he had slept far too long. He'd planned to wake at the break of dawn to give himself ample time to prepare for the journey but it looked a lot more like late morning.

No wonder the Majesteria had rung the alarm bell they usually only used for emergencies. Possibly missing the ship to bring the Royal Cinderflower to the Queen's Coronation *definitely* qualified as an emergency.

"It's quite alright Edwina, thank you for waking me," he said, taking a deep breath and setting down the brass candlestick.

"Were you going to use that to defend us?" Marigold said, her giggle barely contained behind her paw.

"I-I-well...you know, I was in blind panic, alright?" Tristan said, smoothing his long hair behind his ears. "Let me just get dressed and I'll be back in a moment."

"Don't take too long, we're already late!" Edwina said to his retreating back.

"And we might need you to defend us with a candlestick!" Marigold called as he closed the door.

He returned to his quarters and rushed to his bedroom, the anxiety building as he realized just how late it was and he wasn't even dressed. He ran past the trunks of his personal items he'd packed the night before, full of all his clothing, magical tools, and quite a few volumes from his large collection of pirate romance novels. He looked at his bookshelves and wondered briefly if he'd brought too many books. One row was almost entirely empty with only one tired volume clinging desperately to the side of the shelf. He wondered for a moment what the title was, he looked and saw it was *The Ethics and Study of Ancient Ferns in the Southern Hinterlands*. Ah, well, that can stay home then. He shook his head and returned to the task at hand, getting dressed for the day. His first day aboard a *pirate ship*, he realized with a shiver. This was going to be very interesting.

He quickly brushed out his dirty blonde hair and braided it behind his head just as he had every day for years, carefully tying the end with a small black leather cord. Then he put on a starched white shirt, which he buttoned carefully, and some well-fitted brown trousers with a matching waistcoat. He laced up his leather boots and went to pull a cloak from his closet, at which point he realized he'd already packed all his usual cloaks. There was one left hanging in the mostly bare wardrobe, it was a deep brown wool and too warm for this time of year. He considered the cloak, he would be overly warm but...he remembered one time at the local tavern a barkeep had told him that it made his shoulders look good.

He put it on and admired himself in the mirror, swishing the cloak back and forth. The barkeep had been right, the cloak *did* make his shoulders look good. But he felt that something was missing. What was it? He looked at his outfit in the mirror and felt that he simply wasn't dashing enough to travel on a pirate ship. He needed something more.

A little glint on his armoire caught his eye. He went over to his small collection of jewelry which he rarely wore. In the metal dish on the armoire was a stud earring set with a shiny pearl. He picked up the earring and looked at it, twisting the shimmering white orb in the bright morning light. It was certainly beautiful.

But...

Well, last time he'd worn it had been *a lot*.

He'd bought the earring at a holiday market in Sweetriel a few years ago, he had loved how the shining pearl looked on him, he thought it made him look more intriguing. He hadn't realized it when he'd bought it but...pearl earrings wasn't exactly the style at Teakley, which tended towards the drab. He'd worn the earring the next day and *everyone* had commented on it. At least a dozen people had mentioned his earring at some point throughout the day. The comments weren't rude, exactly, but there was definitely a few raised eyebrows. After that he'd put the pearl earring back on his armoire and only worn it on special occasions.

He looked at the little pearl in his hand and decided to try it. Even if he had to endure more commentary on his fashion choices that was better than being underdressed on a pirate ship, wasn't it?

He put on the earring and looked at himself admiringly, oh yes, that was exactly what the outfit needed. So much better! All that he needed now was his gloves to cover his Starlight tattoos. He grabbed his favorite pair of fingerless gloves, the soft leather worn in from years of use, and slipped them over his hands, carefully tying the laces.

He looked around his small bedroom, wondering if there was anything he'd forgotten to bring. There probably was but he didn't have time to figure it out, it was far too late now. Had he brought enough sweaters? How cold would it be on the ship's deck? Everyone in pirate novels was always wearing delicate linen blouses, but that was fiction, he suspected that in reality the ship would probably be windy and cold. Would he need a hat? Would they have tea? Okay, now he knew he was getting out of hand. Of course they'd have tea! He threw a couple more sweaters into the top of his luggage for good measure and began lugging the over-stuffed chests into the hallway.

A LITTLE WHILE later he arrived in the Majesteria's quarters to a flurry of activity. The three mice were running around their living area, scurrying up and down the ropes from the tables of their workshop. The sitting room was usually occupied by a few large tables full of papers, plant clippings, candles, tiny potion bottles, quills, and piles of books of all sizes. It was exactly like any mage's workshop except...smaller.

But at the moment, quite a lot of these items were being carried across the tables and ferried up ropes from the floor onto a growing heap of brown-paper wrapped parcels.

"What's all this then?" Tristan said, sitting down at one of the human-sized chairs near the Majesteria's tables.

Marigold, a slender grey Hi-Mouse in a pointy black witch's hat and deep green dress with floral embroidery stopped in front of him, a stack of tiny books in her paws.

"We're packing, Tristan!" she said.

"I thought we packed everything last night," he said, shooting a look at the trunks waiting by the door.

Another, somewhat larger grey-brown mouse walked up to him. Edwina was her name, and she wore short trousers, a thick sweater and a small sword the size of a toothpick at her hip.

"That was just the first round," Edwina said. "This is all the stuff we forgot yesterday."

He saw Chica, the third mouse, scurrying across the floor with a bundle of scrolls under her arm. Chica was the most traditional of the mice when it came to fashion, she almost always wore a Majesterial robe, which often had a celestial theme of moons and stars, usually made of shimmering fabrics or glittering beadwork. She began climbing the rope while gripping the scrolls under her arm and soon arrived at the top of the table, depositing her goods onto the ever-growing pile.

"This is nearly half the things you own!" Tristan said, looking at the heap, "Aren't we only going to be gone for a few weeks?"

"But what if we need this?" Marigold said, holding out a very small quill with a decorative pink plume.

"Why would you need that?" Tristan asked, examining the fancy quill. "Won't one of your other quills work?"

"I don't know why I might need it *yet*," Marigold explained, "which is exactly why I need to bring it!"

"If we're not sure, we pack it," Chica added, patting the heap affectionately. A few small books became dislodged and skittered across the table. Tristan sighed.

"Besides," Edwina said "you can just put anything that doesn't fit in your luggage!"

Tristan opened his mouth to protest but quickly realized it wasn't worth the breath. The Majesteria were formidable opponents when they set their minds to something, and the pile, although large, would probably fit in one of the trunks without too much trouble.

"Alright, I'll load it up," he said with a sigh.

"Oh, and Tristan?" Marigold said.

"Yes?"

"Don't forget to bring some cheese for the trip," she said.

"I would never forget the cheese," he said, his tone deadly serious.

~

He had just closed the lid of the last trunk when there was a knock at the door. His heart skipped a beat and his hands began to tremble. It wasn't that he was dreading the trip, in fact he was rather excited for it. It's just that his excitement didn't stop him being nervous. He had been worrying about all the things that could go wrong on this journey since that day in Blanchard's office a month ago. What if some enemy of the Crown found out they were on the ship? What if the pirates were awful and dangerous? What if someone found out about the Royal Cinderflower? What if something terrible happened to the Majesteria? It didn't bear thinking about.

The knock on the door was surely the Junior Apprentices ready with the wagon to take them to the Sweetriel docks, and that meant there was no going back now.

He took a deep breath and put on a confident smile as he opened the door. Standing in the hallway was a small group of people, he counted seven in total, their sizes, skin tones, and genders varied, but they were all younger than him. They wore the mid-length beige capes of a Junior Apprentice, their chests gleaming with their gold ink-bottle lapel pins. He smiled at them, remembering when he first became a Junior Apprentice, the burst of pride he'd felt to put that pin on for the first time.

"Good morning, Sir!" One of them said cheerfully, stepping forward with a bundle under one arm and a clipboard in her hand. "The wagon is ready to take you do the docks!"

"Yes, of course, come in," he said, opening the door wider for the apprentices to file in. He noticed a few of their eyes darting around the Majesteria's quarters with excitement, it was rare for a Junior Apprentice to get to see inside the Majesteria's workshop.

"Where are the trunks, sir?" a nervous apprentice asked him, looking around the quarters like he was trying to memorize every detail to share with his friends at the tavern later.

"There's a few in the hallway and more in the sitting room," he said, directing the apprentices who scurried off to look for the trunks.

The lead apprentice leaned in conspiratorially:

"Which trunk is the um, you know, the *special* one?" she asked.

"I will be transporting that one myself," Tristan said solemnly.

She looked aghast, "Of course, Sir, I would not have presumed such an honor for myself, I am terribly sorry for being so rude."

"It's fine, Ivy, you're doing great," he said with a comforting smile.

She looked relieved, and returned to examining her clipboard.

"Alright, I have some things for you," she said, handing him one of the items from the bundle, a package wrapped in parchment paper and tied with string.

"This is from the Tailor, she said you might need a heavy cloak for the journey," Ivy said. The next item was a small black lacquered box. "These are your new Academy brooches, please remember to wear them at all times. The Academy cannot protect you if you are not wearing your brooch." She sounded like she had memorized that part carefully.

She handed him the box and continued, holding up a small stack of paperwork and a jangling coin pouch.

"These are your maps of the region, your itinerary, travel ticket, and, of course, your travel money."

He took the items, feigning interest in the maps for her benefit. In reality, he had spent the last few weeks meticulously preparing for this trip. He'd memorized the route the ship would be taking to Fairefeux, and carefully looked up all of the surrounding islands and possible dangers. The only new information to him was about the ship itself, he noticed the travel ticket told him it was called *The Snapdragon*.

She handed him a small envelope.

"This is from Lord Blanchard, Senior Liaison to the Grand Majesterium and Collected Mages," she said, not pausing for breath as she said his full title. "He gave this to me before he left for the

Coronation and asked that you make sure to read it before you leave, he said it was of critical importance."

"Understood," Tristan said, nodding his head solemnly.

There was a loud crashing behind him.

Tristan and Ivy ran into the sitting room where the Junior Apprentices had dropped one of the trunks, apparently on someone's foot. One of the apprentices was crying and another was comforting them, while a third looked absolutely mortified. The three mice were standing on one of the tables looking at the activity with the interested sniffs of the staunch gossip fanatics he knew them to be.

"I'm terribly sorry, Sir," one of the Junior Apprentices said, "It's just that these trunks were quite a bit heavier than we were expecting."

Tristan shot a look at the Majesteria who appeared completely indifferent to this comment.

One of the apprentices looked nervous and nudged the one who'd spoken, whispering to them. Tristan thought he heard Blanchard's name at one point.

The apprentice looked back at Tristan nervously, then he bowed deeply and said,

"My apologies Lord Mulberry, Majesteria Handler to the Teakley Majesteria of the Grand Majesterium."

Tristan sighed and pinched the bridge of his nose. Blanchard was a plague and Tristan was dearly looking forward to some time away from his nonsense.

"Please, don't call me that," he said sincerely. "You can call me Tristan, and I'm definitely *not* a Lord."

"Sorry Sir," the apprentice said, looking more upset than ever.

"Don't worry Gerald, you're doing great," Tristan said, patting the young man on the shoulder and wondering if he had been this nervous when he'd been a Junior Apprentice.

He thought about it and realized he'd been worse.

"Tristan," Ivy said, "Do you think, um, you could possibly help us bring down the trunks? Matilda always says we're to ask you if we need help carrying heavy things."

Although he had a relatively narrow frame and spent most of his time reading books and carrying cheese, Tristan was not as frail as you might expect. A critical part of his job was as a conduit for Starlight, which was a massive strain on his muscles. To make this easier he worked hard to have strong muscles throughout his body, usually by helping out his friends in the gardens or chopping wood for the winters. After a while he became known around Teakley as a good person to ask if you needed to move something heavy.

"Of course," Tristan said, taking off his cloak and rolling up his sleeves. "I'll bring them down while you get Ash to the Healer."

"Thank you Tristan!" Ivy said, grinning with relief.

He nodded and got to work.

"OH LOOK, IT'S LORD MULBERRY!" Marigold said when he returned from loading the cart.

Edwina and Chica both started giggling. Tristan rolled his eyes.

"Alright, alright," he said. "Come on, let's get our brooches on, we're already late enough as it is."

"Yes, your Lordship," Edwina said with a dramatic bow.

"Did you read Blanchard's letter? What did he want?" Marigold asked as Tristan set the black lacquered case on the table.

Tristan sighed, "His usual nonsense, just trying to throw his weight around. Mostly the letter was just him telling me that I had to make sure I didn't tell anyone about you or the Royal Cinderflower, and that I was to remind you not to do magic."

"We're not supposed to do magic?" Edwina said, surprised.

"Apparently, he says it's too risky. He said you never know where a dangerous mage or nefarious criminal might be lurking who would feel the presence of your powerful magic."

"Hmph," Marigold said with a frown. "I thought the whole

point of taking this pirate ship was to avoid the mysterious, dangerous mages."

Tristan shrugged, "Me too. But you know how Blanchard is."

"Awful!" Chica declared. "Now let's get our brooches, I wanna be shiny!"

"You're already blinding me," Edwina said, looking at Chica's shimmering robes. "But I'm excited to see the brooches too!"

Tristan picked up the the black lacquered case and opened it carefully, feeling the weight of its importance. The inside was lined with red velvet, adding to the prestige of the jewelry. Inside was four brooches, one for him and three miniature ones barely bigger than his pinky nail, custom made for the Majesteria.

The brooches were shining gold with dark brass accents. They were beautifully crafted in the shape of a shield with a teacup on it, the symbol for Teakley Academy. He picked up his brooch and flipped it over, on the back etched in delicate script was his name, Tristan Mulberry. He carefully picked up the mice's brooches and was briefly awed at the craftsmanship of them. They were perfect miniature replicas of his own brooch, down to the tiniest detail, including the mice's names etched into the back.

He set the tiny brooches back down and the Majesteria scurried over to grab them and hastily affix them to their clothing, the gold glinting brightly in the morning sun.

"I'm *SHINY!*" Chica stated, twirling around in her sparkly dress.

Tristan smiled and pinned his own brooch onto his cloak and felt that surge of pride just like when he'd worn his first Teakley brooch as a Junior Apprentice.

"These are very nice," Edwina said appreciatively.

"Indeed, excellent craftsmanship," Marigold agreed with a knowing nod.

"They're so shiny!" Chica added.

Tristan looked around the half-empty room with a sinking pit in his stomach. All that was left now was to leave.

"I guess it's time for you three to get in the Boarding Trunk," he said, looking at the breadbox-sized box sitting on the table. It was the Majesteria's travelling abode, although they rarely spent much time in it once they arrived at their destination. The Boarding Trunk was mostly just a convenient way for them to travel without being observed by inquisitive humans. The box had mesh screens on one side to look out of and lots of small, soft pillows inside to make the journey more comfortable.

"I wish we could just walk there," Marigold said with a sigh.

"Yes but we're supposed to be going incognito," Edwina said.

"Like spies," Chica said.

Tristan laughed, "Alright, let's just get to the docks."

The mice all scurried into the Boarding Trunk, Tristan shut the lid, put the trunk under his arm, and headed out to the wagon.

CHAPTER TWO

A LITTLE WHILE later the wagon departed for the Sweetriel docks. The back of the wagon was loaded up with his chests full of sweaters, books, quills and parchment, an assortment of magical tools and all the tiny things his mice friends might need for their journey.

Then, of course, there was also that other chest.

The one with the priceless, highly magical, probably dangerous *Royal Cinderflower* in it.

But Tristan was trying very hard not to think about that.

Just keep your shoulders relaxed, your eyes forward and remember, you're from Teakley Academy, he thought.

He looked down at his bright new Teakley brooch, the gold teapot sparkling in the sunlight, and took a deep breath. He was from Teakley. He would be safe. He was just taking a little trip to Fairefeux, everything would be fine.

Probably.

Tristan was sitting at the front of the wagon, gripping the boarding trunk under one arm with sweaty palms. He didn't recognize the driver, but she wore the uniform of a Senior Apprentice. She was friendly enough but after the first few minutes, it was clear she didn't want to chat, which was fine by him.

Normally, Tristan enjoyed small talk and getting to know new people, but right now he was not in the mood. He had so much to think about, making sure the mice and the Cinderflower stayed secret and everyone got on board safe and sound. Secrets and subterfuge were not in Tristan's wheelhouse, and honestly, part of him just wanted to go home and curl up by the fireplace with a good novel and a cup of tea.

He remembered that he had a novel tucked into his satchel and breathed a sigh of relief, a little light reading would definitely help calm his nerves. He carefully wedged the boarding trunk into a spot on the wagon next to him where he thought it would be safe and rooted around in his satchel until he pulled out the book, *The Valor Of The Seas*. He felt himself relax just looking at the cover, it was like coming home.

You could say Tristan was a connoisseur of pirate novels. He had read and collected hundreds, and he had...*opinions*. He couldn't recall exactly when he'd started reading them, probably sometime in his teens, but once he read his first swashbuckling kiss under a moonlit sky, he was hooked. He remembered the day clearly. He had been reading stacks of pirate biographies, and one day the Academy librarian suggested he consider *A Pirate's Passion*, a romantic adventure novel inspired by the pirates he was reading about. Tristan brought the book back to his room and almost instantly a new obsession was born.

They were just so exciting! The danger, the romance, the adventure! He loved reading about the heroes standing at the front of the ship, the wind whipping their long hair around their faces as they stared into the misty horizon. The sweeping epic tales of exploration, forbidden love, daring escapes and magical monsters became his favorite pastime. He found them comforting, and in the last few weeks of stress leading up to this journey he needed all the comfort he could get.

With a dreamy sigh he cracked open the soft leather-bound

cover of *The Valor Of The Seas*, the first installment in his all-time favorite series, and began to read about Captain Santiago, his handsome boyfriend Alexander, and their merry crew of misfits and rogues. He turned the rough, well-worn pages and felt himself relaxing, his worries floating away on a pirate ship as he forgot the world around him, lost in a story of magic and adventure.

That is, until there was a bump in the road.

The wagon hit a large rock and jumped a foot in the air, jostling all the trunks loudly and knocking over the mice's boarding trunk. He yelped and dropped his book, grabbing onto the trunk frantically and clutching it close to his chest. He spared a glance to see that the Cinderflower's trunk was still held safely in place and then quickly opened the hatch in the boarding trunk and peered down into it.

The three mice, Marigold's knitting, and all of their tiny books were on the floor of the trunk in a big mess but they all looked unhurt. They peered up at him with small eyes and Chica waved.

"Are you alright?" he asked as he watched Edwina struggling to her feet in the shaky trunk.

"Of course, it was just a bump in the road," she chided him.

"Just a little dusty," Marigold added as she shook out her cloak and picked up her witch hat off the floor.

Relieved, he closed the hatch and focused on himself for a moment. His nerves were on edge already and everything was setting him off today. He took a deep breath, flexed his gloved fingers a few times, feeling the soft leather crunch as he made a tight fist.

"Don't worry Tristan, we're just fine. We're very capable," someone said. He jumped at the sound of the voice and looked down in surprise to see the mice had opened the hatch of their boarding trunk and all three were sitting on top of it, looking up at him with concern.

"I know, I know," he said, "You're right of course."

"I'm sure you'll feel much better once we get on the ship,"

Marigold added, gently placing a small paw on his finger. Chica nodded her head in agreement, wiggling her whiskers.

He smiled at the gesture, she was so sweet to worry about him like this. He took a deep breath and resolved to be courageous, to be stronger for his friends. To be the human handler they needed him to be.

"Yes, of course, I'll feel better once I'm on the ship" he said with the best smile he could muster. His eyes flicked to the Cinderflower, and he felt his heart flip-flop. This was going to be a long journey.

"What are you most excited for?" Edwina asked, trying to distract him from his nerves.

"Returning home," he said, with a shaky laugh.

Edwina laughed too.

"And probably seeing the Royal Library," he conceded.

"I bet you'll be wishing the trip was even longer soon enough," she said.

"I want to see The Ruins of Ahmet," Chica said wistfully.

"I'm looking forward to having a fresh strawberry!" Marigold said, clapping her paws with excitement.

"But you have strawberries all the time, what's exciting about that?" Tristan asked.

"Those are *imported* strawberries," she said disdainfully, "I want to try one fresh picked from the bush! They grow them on Strawberry Island, it's on the itinerary. When Bianca and her handler went to Fairefeux last year, she said they stopped there, she said they had strawberries bigger than a human's head!"

"I heard they make strawberry wine, strawberry pies, strawberry jam and even strawberry cheese!" Edwina said, nodding her agreement.

Chica opened her eyes wide in awe.

"Cheese?!?" Marigold could barely contain her enthusiasm. "That seems too good to be true."

"I hope it's true," Edwina said, "you'll have to find us some strawberry cheese if you can, Tristan."

"I'll do my best," he said absently. Tristan's attention wasn't on the mice anymore, but instead on the road ahead, because the wagon had just arrived at the Sweetriel docks.

~

THE SWEETRIEL DOCKS were loud and bustling. There were merchants hawking their wares to travellers, freelance sailors looking for ships to hire them, tourists filling their bags with tea from the Academy and other popular foods grown on the island. Importers were hauling large wooden crates off of big cargo ships, tiny dinghies were being hired by visiting academics to take them to other parts of the island. Witches were selling potions and enchanted amulets, and market stalls offered everything from maps to whiskey for the many different types of visitors.

Tristan was momentarily dizzy looking at the large crowds and frenzied activity.

"Where to?" the Senior Apprentice asked.

"Pardon?" Tristan replied.

"What dock?" she said sharply.

Tristan gulped. He realized he didn't know where they were going, and it was his job to figure that out. Where was that information? In all of his worry about the mice, the Cinderflower and the Registered Pirate Vessel, he'd completely forgotten to read the paperwork from Ivy. He cursed to himself quietly as he scrambled to find the papers in his satchel.

"Sorry, one second," he mumbled, frantically pulling things out of his overstuffed satchel and laying them next to him on the wagon. Finally, he found the papers crumpled in the bottom of his bag and smoothed them out carefully. He scanned them and then exclaimed,

"Thirteen!"

"Thirteen what?" the driver asked, bored.

"Sorry, of course, um, Dock number Thirteen," Tristan replied. "I believe the ship we are looking for is called *The Snapdragon*."

The driver nodded once and clicked to the horses, turning the wagon to go on the cobbled street along the water. Tristan piled all the stuff back in his bag, barely even noticing all the different sizes and shapes of ships in the port and the interesting looking people coming ashore.

He had just buckled the top of his bag again when he felt a little tug at his shirt sleeve. He looked down to see Edwina there, Chica was gone and Marigold's tail was just disappearing into the hatch of their trunk.

"We're getting back in the trunk now, we'll see you once we're in our quarters!" She looked around nervously, twitching her whisker. "Remember Tristan, you're just a regular academic going to the Queen's Coronation, nothing special, nothing weird. You got it?"

Tristan gulped and nodded his head.

"I got it, don't worry Edwina, I won't let you down."

She patted his hand firmly with her paw "I'm sure you'll figure it out, you're very clever."

"Thank you," he mumbled as he watched her clamber into her travelling home and heard the lid close with a definitive *snap*. It suddenly felt cold and lonely on the wagon. He'd thought he would be going on this perilous journey with his best friends, but he was starting to realize he would be spending a lot of it alone, pretending they weren't even there. He knew it was what the Academy needed him to do, but he didn't have to like it.

He held the Majesteria's boarding trunk close as the wagon carried on rattling across the cobblestones towards the docks. He looked out at the big ships bobbing in the shallow cove, the small waves lapping against their sides, and he began planning how he would explain himself to the crew of *The Snapdragon*. It wasn't going to be easy, he knew that much. Lying was very much *not* his strong suit. He wondered for a moment what his strong suit was. Brewing tea, probably.

～

It turned out to be rather a long trip to Dock Thirteen, as it was all the way at the other end of the port. He watched the painted numbers on the cobblestones get smaller as they travelled until, at last, he saw Dock Thirteen and he got his first glimpse of *The Snapdragon*.

He'd had a lot of ideas in his head about what a Registered Pirate Vessel might look like, most of them from Captain Santiago novels, and this certainly wasn't it. He had pictured something dark, brooding, ragged. With decaying wood and a scrappy sail with a skull on it.

This ship was not that at all.

But he had to admit, *The Snapdragon* was stunningly beautiful.

It put all the other ships to shame with it's deep green painted wood, which reflected teal shadows in the water around it.

The bow of the ship had a glorious carved masthead in the shape of a maiden with long flowing hair, a crown, and a dress made of swirling waves. The words *The Snapdragon* were painted in billowing golden script along the side. The sails were a bright teal color, and at the top of the masts were pennant flags painted with flowers, rippling eagerly in the wind.

The decks were a rich dark oak and some of the masts had ribbons of different colors hanging off them. The ship itself was quite a bit bigger than he'd been expecting, it had three levels with many windows and portholes all across the sides.

The long ramp leading down to shore was crowded with travellers and crew as people boarded and disembarked from the ship. As the wagon approached he got a clearer view of the people on the loading ramp and he saw a person who he knew immediately had to be the Captain.

His heart skipped a beat and his palms began to sweat in his tight leather gloves. The sight of her struck fear into his heart, but also something else. The fear was threaded with giddy excitement and hopeful trepidation.

Because Captain Wren Hawthorne looked exactly like a captain from one of his pirate books.

She wore black leather pants, sturdy boots, and a billowing black linen blouse. Her skin was a sun-kissed bronze and even from the wagon he could see she had fierce eyes that burned into your soul. She wore silver rings on all her fingers and a small cord tied around her throat. Her waist had a brown leather belt hung low, resting almost on her hips. Attached to the belt was a small curving knife, a telescope, and an ominous long scabbard with a shining silver sword hilt.

Her dark hair tumbled down her back in unkempt waves and for a moment he couldn't breathe. She looked mysterious, wild, and dangerous. He immediately felt under-dressed, and thanked the gods he'd decided to wear the pearl earring and his good travelling cloak today. Everyone always said his shoulders looked great in that cloak, so that was something.

The Captain was talking to a slender man with deep brown skin and tight frizzy curls in a meticulous waistcoat, he had long elven ears, small spectacles and well-tailored breeches. He held a leather bound ledger and a quill, and together they were meeting with passengers and burly people carrying cargo boxes to be loaded onto the ship.

Tristan frowned and looked away, a stunningly beautiful pirate captain who looked like she had stepped out of his daydreams was the last thing he needed to be thinking about right now. He had a responsibility to Teakley, to the Majesteria, to the *Crown*. This trip had to go flawlessly, and he had to make sure that everyone arrived safely, and secretly, to the Queen's Coronation.

Or there wouldn't *be* a Coronation.

Tristan tried to focus on the task at hand. The driver stopped the wagon and Tristan hopped off quickly to make sure that he carefully moved the Royal Cinderflower's trunk off the wagon and carried it cautiously to the dock.

His heart was hammering in his chest. Whether it was because of the Royal Cinderflower in his hands, his powerful magical mice friends hiding in the wagon or the beautiful pirate captain, he didn't know, but he was fighting with everything he had to stay calm and composed.

Together with the driver he unloaded the rest of his luggage and she gave him a brief wave before hopping back into the wagon and rolling away down the cobblestone street. He gripped the mice's boarding trunk in one leather-gloved hand and his travelling papers in the other and turned around. He squared his shoulders and prepared for battle.

~

WHAT ACTUALLY HAPPENED WAS A RATHER long wait. It turns out, boarding a ship where everything must be cataloged, tickets and travel itineraries must be checked and re-checked, and questions must be answered, is not a very fast activity. The queue of people waiting to get on the ship wasn't that long, but it moved very slowly. Every so often someone would finish and everyone would drag their trunks along the dock and resettle themselves to wait.

Tristan was the last in the line due to their rather late start this morning, so he settled in to wait and let his beating heart slow down to a steady rhythm. He sat down on one of his big wooden trunks and watched the picturesque pirate captain and her fastidious assistant. The Captain didn't talk much, she mostly leaned against the railing and spun a small gold coin in her fingers. She twisted and flipped the coin, it's bright gold flashing in the afternoon light, while she watched everyone and everything. Tristan guessed that very few things slipped past her.

Every so often she would move away from the railing, lean in towards someone, raise herself up to her full height, and pierce them with her gaze before asking a brief question. Once the terrified passenger had answered to her satisfaction, she would nod her head once at her assistant and resume her lounging. Tristan gulped. He suddenly felt very small and alone without the Majesteria or anyone from Teakley Academy. It was just him now.

He alone would face the formidable Captain of *The Snapdragon*.

Finally, after everyone else had boarded and the flow of foot traffic was slowing to a trickle, Tristan dragged his trunks up to the foot of the ramp and turned to face The Captain. His palms were sweaty as The Captain looked at him for the first time. Her searching eyes took him in, wandering over his sharp features, sun-tanned fair skin, and bold green eyes, his little pearl earring, his broad shoulders in his travelling cloak, and dusty blonde hair carefully braided back from his face. She looked at his perfectly pressed shirt and trousers, his fingerless leather gloves desperately holding on to the boarding trunk, and of course, the golden brooch representing Teakley Academy.

If she had a thought about his existence it did not show on her face. She kept her features impressively passive as she took him in, but he saw that she was sizing him up in some way he could not fathom. What she found he did not know, but he hoped that she found him appealing in some fashion. Well, that's not entirely true. He secretly hoped she found him impossibly handsome, but now was not the time for such thoughts.

After looking at him for a long time she didn't say or do anything, just kept flipping her coin and leaning against the railing, the telescope at her hip swaying softly in the sea breeze. Tristan let out a small sigh, he seemed to have passed the first test. For the moment at least, she was content to flip her coin and wait.

Her assistant moved in front of him, he was holding his over-sized ledger tightly with his brown hands and scribbling in it quickly with his quill. Up close, Tristan could see his nails were expertly manicured and he wore a few earrings in his long pointed ears. After a moment, he looked up and immediately stopped his scribbling, holding his quill in mid air.

He looked at Tristan, then looked him up and down in a way that could only be described as...*hungry*. It was an experience Tristan was fairly familiar with. He wasn't sure what the look was, but he'd seen it a lot when he met new people. They tended to stop looking at him like that after he talked at length about the intricacies of multi-generational herb splicing, or started ranking his favorite pirate novel villains. But the first look was always like this. He stood up a little taller and met the man's gaze.

After a second the assistant seemed to remember himself and cleared his throat, looking down at his notebook again with a low whistle.

"Don't see that everyday" he murmured, then in a more commanding tone he continued,

"Name?" he asked.

"Tristan Mulberry," he replied, holding his paperwork out for inspection. "I've paid in advance, I work for Teakley Academy."

"You don't say," the man remarked sarcastically, pointing the end of his quill at the brooch. "I never would have guessed."

The Captain smirked but did not say anything, she just fixed him with another appraising stare that made him want to apologize, though he couldn't figure out why.

The assistant flipped through pages on his ledger until he found Tristan.

"Ah, here we are," he said "going to the Queen's Coronation, how *original*." He rolled his eyes and scribbled more notes into his ledger before showing it to The Captain. Tristan suspected he'd written something disparaging in the margins.

"Anyway, I'm Emyr, first mate. This is Captain Wren, that's with a w," Emyr drawled in the dull tones of someone who said this many times per day. "This ship is *The Snapdragon*, and we are a dual passenger and cargo ship. We will likely make many stops before we arrive at your destination but it's not a cause for concern, this is just how ships function. You will find-"

"What's in the trunk?" The Captain asked suddenly, interrupting her assistant's pre-planned speech. Her voice was calm but it carried an edge as sharp as the blades she wore at her hip. Tristan looked at her nervously.

"I'm sorry?" Tristan said.

Her eyes narrowed "I need to know everything that's coming on my ship. You were marked down for five pieces of luggage. I count 1, 2, 3, 4, 5 out there on the dock and you are holding that trunk like your life depends on it. You work for Teakley Academy, known for mystical secrets and powerful mages. So, for the sake of the safety of myself and my crew, I ask you again, what's in the trunk?"

"I'm afraid that's Academy business, but I assure you I present no threat to yourself or your crew," he replied bravely. His words sounded even but his heart was beating fast and sweat was rolling down his back.

Wren pushed off the railing and moved closer to him, lifting herself up to her full height. She was quite tall, nearly meeting him eye to eye, and when she gave him the full weight of her dangerous stare he stumbled backward a little in spite of himself.

"I'll decide what kind of threat you present," she said in a tense, steady tone. "Now. What's in the trunk?"

"I-I-I...it's Academic business," Tristan said shakily.

"What business?" The Captain asked in a tone of quiet danger he was sure worked on most people. In fact, it was working very well on him and he was absolutely terrified. But that didn't matter because there was almost nothing Tristan would not do to protect the Majesteria, it would take a lot more than a steely tone to get him to admit anything.

"Academic business, for Teakley Academy," he said, looking up to meet her gaze. His stomach twisted in knots of fear as he looked into her fierce eyes, blazing with fire and confidence, warning him not to push his luck.

She tilted her head and gave him that appraising look again.

"I'm sure you get away with quite a lot walking around with a handsome face like that," she said cooly. "But I'm not easily swayed, and I need to know what's in the case."

Tristan's mind was whirring at high speed as he saw her hand trail down towards the sword at her hip. What should he say? What was his plan again? Had she just called him handsome? What would he do if she didn't let him on the ship?

He watched her hand settle on the hilt of her sword and blurted out the first thing that popped up.

"Have you killed a lot of people with that?" he said, before he could stop himself.

Her hand dropped quickly from the hilt and she eased her stance a little.

"No," she said crisply.

"It's just...aren't you a pirate?" he asked.

She frowned and seemed to get a little bit...softer.

"This is a Registered Pirate Vessel," she said smoothly, "we work for the Queen now. All passengers and cargo are accounted for and legal."

"Right, but you are a pirate, aren't you?" He asked again.

"That's really none of your business Mr. Mulberry", she said sternly. Her tone got a lot more pleasant when she said "Now, if you could just answer my question, what's your trunk Tristan Mulberry?"

She said his name in a whisper which sent shivers up his spine. Was that normal? Did ship captains always act like this? He searched his mind but the pirate novels he'd read did not teach him how to deal with this situation at all. Nor did they teach him very much about ships, mostly he'd just read a lot about long wild hair blowing in the wind, kissing under the moonlight and billowing linen blouses.

He tried to think about what Edwina might say in the situation, as she was the most confident and self-assured person he knew.

Never mind that she was a mouse.

He realized Edwina would fall back on the prestige and reputation of the Academy so he decided to try that next.

He lifted his chin and pushed his shoulders back, meeting her gaze.

"I am bringing my ticket, paid at a very handsome rate in advance, for the journey of one person and their luggage to the Queen's Coronation at Fairefeux, some of my luggage contains gifts for The Queen from Teakley Academy of a...discreet nature. I am not at liberty to discuss them, I'm sure you understand," he replied. He held up his paperwork like a shield and turned his body a little, just enough that the morning sunlight made his golden brooch shine brightly. The Captain glanced for just a second at the brooch on his cloak before drawing her eyes back to his and holding them there.

"Ahem." Her assistant coughed, and then put his ledger between their bodies, pushing them away from each other.

"We really need to finish boarding Wren, we were scheduled to depart two hours ago," he said firmly. He looked at Tristan's brooch and then back to The Captain, wiggling his eyebrows dramatically. She looked at her assistant and seemed to snap out of whatever mood she was in. Her shoulders relaxed, she stepped back and returned to her lounging Captain's stance.

"Of course Emyr, let's get Mr. Mulberry's paperwork finished and Ginger will show him to his cabin."

Tristan was so relieved he could barely contain his joy, but he tried his best to keep a stern professional face as Emyr stamped his paperwork with a large, official-looking stamp. He looked at the design of the stamp and recognized it as a snapdragon motif, just like the name of the ship. Emyr kept one copy and handed him the other. Tristan waved the papers in the wind briefly to dry them and then stuffed them back inside his overfull satchel.

A couple of muscular sailors standing nearby picked up his luggage and began moving it across the ship's deck. Tristan moved to follow them but The Captain stopped him, grabbing his arm firmly. She looked at him with her simmering eyes and said in a dangerous whisper,

"This isn't over Mr. Mulberry, be careful on my ship. If you get any of my crew hurt even the power of the Royal Crown won't be able to save you from *me*."

Then she turned back to Emyr and proceeded to ignore Tristan completely, looking over paperwork and quietly discussing their next order of business with her First Mate. Tristan looked at her for a long while but she never once turned around or acknowledged him again.

Once he had recovered his nerves enough to look away from the intimidating Captain, he turned to see a short, curvy woman with a huge smile waving at him cheerfully.

"I'm Gwen, Liaison To The Guests" she said with a grin, holding out her hand for him to shake. "Welcome to *The Snapdragon*, Tristan Mulberry!"

Chapter Three

The first moment he set foot on the ship Tristan felt something he wasn't expecting...*magic*.

It was subtle and relaxed but there was something there, a magical kind of...pulse, almost. Was it spells cast on the ship or was the ship itself magical, he wondered. Was it a powerful guest or crewmate somewhere else on the ship? He didn't know.

He reached out for a moment with his sixth sense but he couldn't sense anything more. All he knew for sure was that there was something magical about *The Snapdragon*.

As if this trip wasn't stressful enough.

"Well then Tristan, can I see your papers?" said a cheerful voice.

He looked down to see Ginger, Liaison to the Guests, before him. He shook himself out of his musings and nodded, handing her the carefully stamped copy of the paperwork Emyr had given him.

Ginger took it, attached it to a small clipboard, and gave him a big smile. The short woman had bright blue hair that curled out in all directions, brown skin, and large black horns which came up through through her hair. She wore sturdy leather trousers, big heavy boots, and had a thick belt around her hips with lots of jangling items hanging off of it. Large iron rings of keys, a few small potion bottles, a leather satchel and a quill.

After looking over his papers for a moment she looked up and met his eyes, flashing him another gigantic grin.

"Alright then, handsome," she said with a big wink. "Let's get you to your room. Oh-ho! Looks like it's the Luxury Suite, very fancy, very nice."

She darted off briskly across the ship's deck, motioning that Tristan should follow her. He could see his luggage descending onto the floor below ahead of them, so he hurried to catch up with the short Satyrborn woman.

"Now, this is the deck, you're welcome to come up here anytime you like, unless we're in a storm in which case we ask that the guests stay in the rooms or in the Canteen," she said over her shoulder as she walked.

"Speaking of the Canteen, it's at the end of the hallway off the guest rooms. There is also a shared washing room on the left of the hallway which you'll see on the map I'll give you in a moment here," she said, her large hips swaying as she headed towards a stairway to the level below. Tristan was only half-listening to her; his eyes were very distracted by the bustle and activity of the sailors as they lifted the sails and affixed the rigging, preparing the ship to set sail. Other guests milled about and various people were carrying cargo and luggage down the stairs and winding large ropes around sturdy iron hooks.

The movement around him was dizzying but as they ascended into the darkened hallway it got quieter and he found he could focus on Ginger's words better.

Which was good, because he realized she was asking him a question.

"Sorry, what was that?" he said quickly.

"I asked if this was your first time at sea?" she said, her cheerfulness not skipping a beat.

"No actually, I took a long journey by ship once when I was a boy, when they brought me to Teakley Academy."

"Oh yes, I saw your badge, very nice. You're not one of those terrifying mages they employ are you?" she said with a cheeky laugh.

Tristan was momentarily tongue-tied. He coughed a little.

"No ma'am, I like to think I'm not terrifying."

That got a big laugh from her, "I think we'll get along Tristan Mulberry," she said, resuming her bustling walk through the lower deck. "As I was saying, the Canteen is the main place to rest and relax outside of your room. There is a Breakfast and Dinner service, we've even got a bell for that! But you can always go down there any time and grab some snacks or ask Basel to cook you something. I'm quite partial to their omelettes. Ah, here we are, your room."

The door was ajar and Tristan could see his trunks piled up just inside the room. She grabbed the iron ring of keys on her belt and pulled a large key off of it. She handed the key to Tristan and pushed open the door to his cabin.

His first impression was that it was small but surprisingly warm and inviting. It had two rooms, a main living space and a bedroom, both of them with the same floral print wallpaper, deep blue velvet curtains and dark wood floors.

The main room had a writing desk, a small bookcase with some books, and a window made of many smaller panes. Tristan was delighted to see there was a tea station with mugs, a kettle and a portable stove with a few magicked coals for warming it, just like the one he had at home.

The most impressive feature was the centerpiece of the cabin and took up a large portion of one wall. Tristan was amazed to see the room had a Pixie Hearth. He'd heard about them, of course, but he'd never seen one in person before.

The Pixie Hearth was cleverly built into the wall exactly where a fireplace would go, but instead of a flaming grate there was a large pane of mottled glass with yellow and pink shapes dancing behind it, mimicking the look of flames. He could feel the subtle warmth coming off of it, and he found himself mesmerized, watching the magical flames dance up and down. He turned to Ginger,

"A Pixie Hearth?" he said, impressed.

Ginger put her thumbs in her belt and rocked back and forth, a big smile on her face.

"That's right, nothin' but the best for our guests," she said.

Tristan thought about this statement. Honestly, even with the Pixie Hearth the room wasn't what you would call luxurious. He could see peeling wallpaper in a few spots, a burn mark on the carpet, and the velvet curtains had seen better days. But the crew had clearly put some effort into making the space feel nice and he appreciated it. It would certainly be a fine place to spend time on his trip to the Coronation.

"It looks lovely," Tristan said truthfully.

He was more than ready to say goodbye to Ginger and flop down on the bed in the next room but Tristan's work was just beginning because he was a Majesteria Handler, and he had far more to think about than his own comfort when it came to accommodations. Surprisingly, this was not actually Tristan's first time travelling since he was a boy. He wasn't exactly a world-travelled adventurer, but he had taken trips with the Majesteria before. Albeit short trips. Very short.

They hadn't travelled far, but they had travelled plenty. Tristan had helped the mice catalog all the herbs and plants on Appleton Island and its sister island, Pearsy, while working on the mice's book *Flora and Fauna of the Fruitbasket Isles*. Pearsy was only a small ferry ride away from Appleton, and you could be back home in a few hours' wagon ride from the dock.

Nevertheless, it had given him some preparation for their grand adventure, which is to say, he had a plan for how the mice liked their room. Whenever they got to a tavern room the mice always wanted it *just so* and it was Tristan's job to make sure that happened. So, after taking a quick glance in the bedroom, he turned to Ginger and said,

"I'm going to need some more pillows."

"Your room has pillows already sir, if you'll–" Ginger began.

Tristan held up his hand

"I need about ten more," he said. "At least."

Ginger raised her eyebrows

"Ten more pillows?"

"Yes, and if you've got a few extra blankets or rugs that wouldn't go amiss," he added.

Ginger coughed awkwardly as she considered his request. After a moment she decided it wasn't worth it to rile up the extremely handsome guest staying the ship's most expensive room.

"I'll see what I can rustle up sir, but I can't make any promises," she said.

"Just do your best and I'm sure it'll be fine," Tristan said with a genuine smile.

"I'll be back in a jiffy," she said, her hips swaying as she dashed out of the room.

A few minutes later there was a soft rapping on the door and Ginger returned with an armful of pillows and a few large woven blankets.

"Here you are Mr. Mulberry," she said with a big grin. "It's not my policy to ask what our guests do in their cabins but I certainly hope you're *comfortable* with all these pillows," she said with an expectant look. She was clearly hoping that Tristan might give her more details, but his face remained impassive.

"Thank you Ginger," he said politely. He took the pillows and deposited them in a pile on the rug in front of the hearth. His eyes darted to the boarding trunk with the Majesteria inside and he turned to Ginger, hoping he'd be able to end this conversation quickly and let his friends out of their trunk.

"Did you have anything else you need or any questions?" Ginger asked, picking up her clipboard again.

"I believe you mentioned a map?" Tristan said.

"Silly me!" she said, ruffling the stack of papers on her clipboard. "I was so distracted by your mountain of pillows, I damn near forgot."

She handed him a small piece of paper, which he looked at briefly.

The map, if you could call it that, was very basic, to put it mildly.

It was a few hastily scribbled lines in the vague shape of the lower deck, with a few Xs marking locations. There was one which said 'LOO' and another that said 'FOOD.' There was also an arrow at one end, nearly on the edge of the paper, which said 'DECK.'

"Oooh hang on, I forgot to mark off your room," she said, snatching the map back hastily. She picked up her quill and looked at the map with a frown of concentration. She turned it around a few times and then drew a big X with a circle around it. She wrote "YOU" in big letters next to it.

"There you are!" she said, handing him back the map.

He looked at it with a carefully blank expression, sincerely hoping he wouldn't actually have to use it to navigate by.

"Thank you, uh, very much," he said.

"We're still working on the maps," she admitted, "they may not be up to the standards you're used to up at the fancy Academy." She leaned closer and lowered her voice, "Truth be told, I only joined the crew recently, but I'm doing my best to get our guest services up to snuff!"

"I think you're doing a great job," Tristan said, patting her on the shoulder and smiling. "I'm sure this will be very helpful."

Ginger stood back and gave him an appraising look, taking in his thick hair and taut, lean body, the cloak clinging to his shoulders dashingly.

She whistled and said, "Wowee, looks like that and you're nice to boot? I can't wait to see what happens when you meet the rest of the crew, now, I prefer ladies myself but from what I've seen of this lot they'll be fightin' over you and no mistake."

Tristan gave her an awkward little smile. He never knew what to do when people said things like this

"Thank you ma'am?" he offered.

She chuckled, "Alrighty, enough chit-chattin' let's get you all checked in then." She looked down at her clipboard for a moment then said, "Five large chests, one human man from Teakley Academy, and whatever this is," she motioned to the boarding trunk with her quill. "Is that correct Mr. Mulberry?"

He nodded, "Yes."

She handed him a piece of paper and the quill, "Fantastic, just sign here that everything was delivered as promised and was unharmed at the time of your arrival on the ship."

Tristan nodded his agreement and scribbled his signature on the papers.

"That looks perfect," she said. "Alright then, I think we're all done. Welcome aboard, and be sure to let me know if you need anything!"

~

He closed the door, turned the lock, and leaned his back against the sturdy wood for a moment, taking in gulps of air as he calmed his fraying nerves. He took stock of his surroundings and allowed himself a smile of relief. He'd done it! He'd made it onto the ship and kept all his secrets safe.

He was still worried about Captain Wren though. She didn't seem the type to let a possible threat to her crew drop that easily, but he could think about that later. Right now, he had his duties to tend to, and the first order of business was, of course, letting the Majesteria out of their trunk.

He looked around the room and saw a small wooden chair at the desk in the corner. He picked it up and wedged it securely under the door before he went over to the boarding trunk. He laid it down on the rug in front of the hearth and opened the side.

The mice tumbled out onto the carpet, their eyes wide and whiskers twitching eagerly.

"Are you alright?" Tristan asked immediately.

Edwina quickly stood up on the rug, straightened her vest and adjusted the sword at her belt.

"Of course we're alright!" She said, "are *you* alright?"

"Yes!" Tristan said with a laugh, "We're on the ship and I managed to keep everything secret."

"Is that a Pixie Hearth?" Marigold asked, scampering across the rug to warm her paws in front of the cozy magical fireplace.

Tristan nodded. "Indeed. This room is rather nice I think, much better than that tavern we started at in Pearsy."

"Velvet curtains and a Pixie Hearth, this place is so *fancy*," Marigold said, twirling her skirts around happily.

"Are you alright Chica?" Tristan asked. The mouse was laid out on the rug with her face down, her sparkly celestial dress splayed out around her.

"Mphmmph," she said without looking up.

"What was that?" he said.

"It's soooo soft," she mumbled, digging her paws into the plush rug.

Edwina bounced on the rug and nodded her agreement "Very soft, I like it. Very good."

"Oh my *STARS!*" Marigold shrieked.

"What? What's wrong?" Tristan said, looking around in alarm.

Marigold was scampering across the cabin floor at high speed, making a beeline for the writing desk in the corner.

"Is that a Smith & Porterson Automatic Quill Sharpener?!?" she squeaked.

"Wait, really?" Edwina said, looking around Tristan to peer at the corner. Even Chica raised her head from the cozy rug to squint at Marigold briefly.

Tristan stood up and went over to the desk to look at the item in question.

There was a small contraption nailed to the side of the desk with a few slots and a large hand crank. The words 'Smith & Porterson' were engraved in gold script on the side.

"It would appear so," he said with a smile. He knew this would delight the Majesteria who were *very* enthusiastic quill collectors. He'd had a rather long argument with them a few weeks ago about how many quills was appropriate to bring on this journey.

They had compromised at thirty-six.

Marigold ran her paws reverently over the device, her whiskers twitching with excitement.

"It's *beautiful*," she breathed. She examined the quill opening carefully and then looked up, beaming. "It's adjustable! It should even be able to accommodate quills as small as the Frederickson 15!"

"Are you serious?" Edwina shrieked, dashing across the floor. She quickly shimmed up the desk leg and clambered onto the desk top to examine the captivating device.

"Look at that, see that bolt?" Marigold showed her excitedly, "It can go as small as you like, we should easily be able to sharpen *all* of our quills here! Even the Frederickson 15."

"I didn't bring it," Edwina said, frowning. "*Someone* said we didn't need it because it was so small it was just a 'novelty item'," she said with a very pointed glare towards Tristan.

Tristan rolled his eyes, "you wanted to bring five hundred quills Edwina, what was I supposed to do?"

"I'm just saying," she said with a shrug, "That's why we don't have the Frederickson 15."

"Well...I'm sorry," Tristan said with a sigh. "This is still exciting though, isn't it?"

After a moment of continuing to glare at him, Edwina's face broke into a grin. "Yes, of course! I've always wanted to see a Smith & Porterson up close!"

"And also, you know, the whole journey across the sea to the Queen's Coronation..." Tristan trailed.

"Mmm, that too," Edwina said, thoughtfully turning the hand crank on the machine.

"Let's try some quills!" Marigold said, clapping her paws.

It was about twenty minutes before the mice could think about anything besides quills. Well, Edwina and Marigold at least. Chica had fallen asleep face down on the carpet and Tristan had carefully laid a small blanket over her.

Once Edwina and Marigold had sharpened every quill they had available, some of them twice, and marveled at the Smith & Porterson's accuracy and precision, they finally decided it was time to settle in and set up the room for Majesterial activities.

Spaces have to be designed differently when there are mice to consider. Especially when they are working and living in concert with their much larger and clumsier counterparts, humans.

So Edwina and Marigold set about directing Tristan with sharply squeaked opinions on how he ought to set up the furniture and unpack their luggage.

The human furniture was mostly stacked up against the walls.

The pillows were arranged in a cozy half-moon shape around the Pixie Hearth.

Favorite pillows, blankets and additional rugs were pulled out of their trunks from home and arranged artfully across the rug in front of the hearth.

The additional tiny bundles were retrieved from Tristan's trunk and placed on the rug.

Bundles were unfurled and miniature books, clothing, satchels of herbs, bottles of ink and scrolls were revealed and organized neatly.

The mice always liked things to be laid out tidily so they could make a mess of it themselves.

Finally, the Majesteria's area was set up and Tristan dragged his personal trunks into the bedroom and put the kettle on the portable stove to start heating for tea.

That only left one trunk unopened...

The Royal Cinderflower.

He knew they'd have to deal with the Royal Cinderflower tonight but he'd been putting it off. But as he searched through the piles of stuff for the mice's teacups he kept thinking about the Cinderflower, its trunk lurking in the corner of the room.

"We should um, probably take a look at the, um, Cinderflower soon," he said with a worried sigh. He'd tried not to think about it, but now that the other things had been dealt with he felt the weight of fear settle on his shoulders.

What if...he dared not even think it.

He couldn't get caught up in such thoughts, he must merely hope that the Cinderflower was in the same pristine condition it had been in when it left Teakley Academy.

"Oh dear! I completely forgot about it," Edwina said. She was holding a quill in her paws and admiring it's recently sharpened point.

Tristan was amazed, he couldn't imagine forgetting about the Royal Cinderflower even for a second. It loomed in his thoughts like a monster, worrying him to no end.

"Hmm, we should probably do the ritual right away, I think the tea will have to wait," Marigold said, putting down the tiny quill in her paws with a frown and dusting off her dress.

"You'd best turn off the tea kettle and wake Chica," Edwina agreed, then she climbed down the side of the desk and advanced on the waiting trunk.

Tristan nodded his agreement and removed the kettle from the warmer and crouched down on the rug to wake Chica. He nudged her gently.

"Hey Chica, we need you for the Cinderflower ritual," he said softly.

"Snrgflumphn?" she said, raising her head sleepily.

Tristan pointed over at the trunk, "The Royal Cinderflower, remember?"

Chica scrambled to her feet and sneezed loudly.

"There was some dust in that rug I think," she said, then scampered across the floor to join the other Majesteria.

Tristan followed them to the trunk and looked down at it, feeling the nervousness setting in as he contemplated opening the lid.

"Oh come on Tristan, don't make us do it!" Edwina said.

"Sorry," he mumbled, reaching for the lid of the chest.

"Best take your gloves off, Tristan!" Marigold added.

He stopped his hand an inch from the lid and nodded, quickly removing his fingerless leather gloves. He carefully watched the nine-pointed star tattoos on the backs of his hands as he opened the lid of the trunk.

As soon as it opened the tattoos began to feel warmer and they quickly turned from black...to grey...then light yellow...and eventually a blinding bright yellow-white light as they shimmered with the Starlight magic of the Royal Cinderflower. The effect was dazzling and Tristan was still awed by the magical tattoos' beauty even after all these years. It was truly an honor and a gift to be a Majesteria Handler.

He felt the warm magic pulsing through his hands as he pulled back the lid and looked at the flower, floating softly in it's gilded cage, bundled with blankets and sweaters inside the trunk. He breathed a sigh of relief.

So far, so good.

He carefully removed the items surrounding it until he could pull the flower from the trunk and lay it down gently on the floor of the cabin.

The Royal Cinderflower.

It stood encased in a glass gilded cage, sparkling with an otherworldly magic. Its petals drooped only slightly under the weight of its glittering magical power, the bright green leaves curling upwards along its stem shimmering with white Starlight.

For months the Majesteria had carefully tended its drooping leaves, snipping off brown bits with tiny scissors, mending and gluing it back together with magic siphoned from the stars in glowing silver vessels.

Now, it was finally healed and whole, ready to be presented to the new Queen, a critical part of the Coronation ritual.

All that was left was to make sure the flower got there in one piece.

Tristan and the Majesteria examined the flower and its golden cage carefully from all angles and finally he let out the breath he didn't know he was holding.

The flower was unharmed.

Edwina walked carefully up to the Cinderflower's cage and opened the hatch in the side. It was just big enough for her to walk inside and approach the Cinderflower. She set her paws on the stem and the flower began to shimmer brighter, the petals waving slightly.

"Do you need our help?" Marigold asked from outside the cage.

Edwina shook her head, "No, it's very healthy. We gave it so much Starlight yesterday it will be alright for a few days I should think."

Chica yawned, "Why'd I have to get up then?" she asked.

"Tristan's going to make us tea and a cheese plate," Marigold said.

"Alright then," Chica said with a little smile.

Tristan sat back and set his shaking hands on his knees, the tattoos still glowing faintly. He didn't want to admit how nervous he'd been. He watched Edwina close the door of the Cinderflower's cage and realized he probably wouldn't be able to hold a mug of tea without breaking it for a while yet.

It ended up being about an hour before Tristan made the tea. Right after the Royal Cinderflower was returned to its box, they felt a jolt as *The Snapdragon* pulled up the anchor. They heard shouting from the deck above and felt the ship wobble for a while as they finally set sail. The mice scrambled up to the window ledge and

Tristan stood behind them to watch as the ship pulled out of the harbor and their home, Appleton Island, began to get smaller.

Tristan felt a tugging at his heart as he watched the only home he'd ever known become just another speck on the horizon.

"I guess that's it then," he sighed. "We're really leaving."

"Of course we are, silly!" Edwina said, waving a paw cheerfully at the rapidly disappearing island in the distance. "Calm down Tristan, everything's going to be fine. Look how well it's gone already! We're on the ship, the Cinderflower is fine, and we're on our way to the Coronation."

"The cabin is quite lovely too," Marigold said.

"It's true!" Edwina agreed. "When I heard this trip was being arranged by *Blanchard*," she said his name like it was a piece of dirty laundry, "on a Pirate Ship, I don't mind telling you I expected the worst! But this cabin is really very charming. I guess it pays to travel with the Royal Cinderflower, eh?"

"It really does. The room's even got a tea kettle," Marigold added.

"Too bad we're never going to use it," Chica snipped.

"Sorry, sorry," Tristan said, turning away from the view of the bobbing blue waves. "I'll get started on your tea."

"And cheese!" Marigold added.

"And biscuits!" Edwina chimed in.

A little while later Tristan had assembled a small plate of only slightly squished bread, cheeses and biscuits they had brought from home. It was looking a little bedraggled after the trip on the wagon but he didn't have the energy to face the Canteen and meeting the crew tonight. Right now he just wanted a nice cup of tea and sitting in front of the Pixie Hearth with his friends.

He placed the tray in front of the mice and they began to eat, loudly and happily, while he poured the boiling water over the herbs and let the tea steep.

"Tell us about the ship," Edwina said around a mouthful of cheese.

"Ooh yes, did you meet anyone interesting so far?" Marigold asked. She was piling multiple pieces of cheese onto a square of bread that was considerably larger than her head. If Tristan hadn't seen her do it a hundred times before he wouldn't have believed she'd be able to eat so much.

"I only met a few people," he said as he unrolled the tiny mugs and teapot from their bag and set them on a small serving tray. "There was Emyr, the first mate, he was a bit...snippy, I guess, but nice enough. Then there was Ginger the Liaison to the Guests, she's a Satyrborn I think. She brought us the pillows, she was very friendly...and, then there was..." Tristan tried to think how to describe Wren. He stopped moving for a moment as he remembered the way her hair waved in the wind.

"Are you blushing Tristan?" Edwina asked, standing up with a cube of cheese in each paw.

"What? No!" he said hurriedly, looking away. He began inspecting the teapot, despite knowing full well the tea wouldn't be ready for another five minutes.

"He is blushing, Tristan has a crush!" Marigold shrieked.

"Mmphf," Chica said, her mouth full of cheese.

"What was that?" Edwina asked her.

Chica swallowed and said "Who is it Tristan?"

"I'm not responding to this," Tristan said haughtily. "However, I will say that I met the Captain when I was boarding and they were very suspicious about the Boarding Trunk."

"Ooooh, The Captain!" Marigold said.

"Tristan's aiming high, I like it!" Edwina said, nodding her approval. "Tell us about this Captain? What's their name? She, He, They?"

"Her name is Wren Hawthorne," Tristan said, and despite himself his voice sounded a little dreamy when he said it. "She wears all black, is incredibly dangerous and I think she kind of hates me."

"He's in love," Edwina said confidently.

Tristan pinched his nose and sighed. "Can we please just..."

"We're upsetting him," Marigold said in loud whisper. "Let's just get back to our cheese."

"Okay," Edwina said loudly, "I'm glad you met a not-so-nice Captain and definitely didn't fall head-over-heels for her!"

Tristan sighed.

He loved his job, but sometimes it was kind of a lot.

❧

THE MOON WAS high in the sky and his legs were already half asleep by the time Tristan finally said goodnight to his friends and stumbled into his bedroom.

He took a look around at the small space, illuminated by the moonlight streaming through the porthole. There was a small open closet for his clothing, which he'd hang up tomorrow, a map of the Evarian Sea pinned to the wall, and a big, fluffy bed begging him to lie down and fall asleep on it.

His shoulders relaxed as he put on a nightshirt, let down his hair, and lit a small oil lantern by the bed. The rocking of the ship was a strange sensation, one he wasn't sure he liked, but at least he was safe, his work was done and he could rest. At last.

He hung his satchel on the hook by the door and took out his novel, gliding his hands over the worn leather cover.

He crawled into bed, pulling the big blanket around him and opening *The Valor Of The Seas* to his bookmark. He planned to fall asleep dreaming of his favorite pirates, Captain Santiago and his handsome lover, Alexander. But he found, to his surprise, it was an entirely different Pirate Captain who filled his thoughts that night.

The last thing he thought of as he drifted off to sleep was a little gold coin, glinting in the sunlight.

Chapter Four

Tristan's first day at sea was a stormy one. He woke up groggy after a difficult night's sleep. Between the rocking of the waves, the creaking sounds of the ship, and the strangeness of a new bed he had spent most of the night tossing and turning.

He woke in the late morning to even more swaying and rocking and the sound of howling wind and rain pounding against the sides of the ship. He felt a gurgling in his stomach and knew he need breakfast immediately.

He hastily unpacked some of his clothing into the small closet, hanging up his cloaks and piling his sweaters neatly on the floor. He dressed in a buttoned shirt, well-fitted trousers, and a cozy brown sweater, affixing his Teakley badge to the rough wool with pride.

He braided his hair behind his head and tied it with a leather string before setting out to find some breakfast and see if the mice needed anything. When he entered the main room the Majesteria were fast asleep on the rugs by the glowing Pixie Hearth, they looked completely peaceful.

He envied their ability to sleep anywhere, anytime.

He tiptoed through the cabin and closed the door carefully, making sure to lock it with the heavy iron key Ginger had given him. As soon as he had finished locking the door the ship swayed wildly and he stumbled back from the door, steadying himself on the wall. He leaned over and felt the queasiness from before getting worse. He dearly hoped the nausea was only hunger.

He pulled out the map from Ginger and studied it for a moment before tucking it back in his pocket and deciding to wing it.

He wandered the long hallway with doors leading to other guests rooms and an assortment of large barrels, briny ropes, and piled up buckets and cleaning supplies. He heard lots of sounds from the deck above but the halls were surprisingly empty as he made his way to the other side of the ship.

As he passed the cabins he found the doors marked for Ginger, the washing room, and the healer's cabin. The end of the hallway opened out into a larger area encompassing about a third of the lower deck. The Canteen was split in half with a dining room on one side and kitchens on the other.

The dining hall had big tables with battered wooden benches and small stools with a couple of guests sitting on them reading books or eating pastries. Along the side wall were big windows providing a beautiful view of the stormy sea. Tristan took one look at it and felt his stomach roil, a wave of nausea hitting him nearly as hard as the ocean waves were hitting the ship.

He turned away to the other side of the room where the kitchen was separated from the dining hall by a long bar top with dozens of nautical maps encased under its glassy surface.

He walked up to the bar top and saw a few people in the kitchens busily stirring large pots. One of them came over when they saw him approach. The person was large in every sense of the word. They were very tall, with a wide chest and they had tattoos up and down their arms, mostly of herbs and plants used in cooking. They had unkempt reddish hair, a huge gold hoop earring in one ear, a large ladle tucked into their belt, and a smear of bright red rouge on their lips.

"Afternoon sailor!" they said, holding out a huge hand and

giving Tristan a wide, mischievous grin. "I'm Basel, with an E, I'm the Head Chef here on *The Snapdragon*. I'm more a theys and thems than a he or she, ya hear?"

"Absolutely," Tristan replied. Genderless folks were common in this part of the world; one of his good friends at Teakley was also a they.

He took the large person's hand and shook it.

Well, he attempted to shake it but mostly Basel just shook him.

Their grip was so strong that Tristan momentarily forgot his nausea. But a big swing from the ship happily reminded him and he leaned forward, bracing his hands on the bar top.

"Nice to meet you Basel," he said as his eyes started to water. "I'm feeling a…ah…a little queasy, do you have anything I can eat?"

"You bet I do! Basel's kitchen always has somethin' cooking!" they said happily, pounding on their chest and reaching behind the bar top. They pulled out a large crusty loaf of simple bread and began slicing off thick slices, they piled them onto a wooden plate with a large wedge of cheese and a cluster of grapes. They added a small golden pastry and a dollop of honey butter and slid the plate across the bar.

Tristan took the plate gratefully but before he could say anything Basel leaned over the bar top, dominating the space with their massive shoulders and bulging, tattooed muscles.

"Now, for the fun part," they said, winking. "I'll make you one of Basel's Fabulous Cocktails, all I need to know is your answer to one question. If you could be any kind of animal that lives in a swamp, what would you be?"

Tristan was finding himself overwhelmed by this person and his looming nausea. He got the strange sense that his answer to this question might be important, but all he could think was how delicious the fresh bread and cheese looked.

He picked up a grape and popped it in his mouth while he figured out what to say. He didn't want to be rude but he knew with the state his stomach was in he definitely didn't want to be drinking.

"I'm afraid I have a little bit of seasickness. I hope you're not offended, but I couldn't possibly drink any alcohol right now," he said with what he hoped was a friendly grin.

"A virgin cocktail is more fun to make anyway, I love a challenge!" Basel said, the giant grin never leaving their face. "Now answer the question," they said, their tone suddenly serious.

Basel was staring at him in a way he couldn't quite wrap his head around. Tristan didn't know if this was all in jest or if his response was important, and all he really cared about was eating something to hold his stomach together. He searched his mind for animals that lived in swamps and said the first thing that popped into his head.

"I guess I'd be a frog?"

"You *guess*? I need to know *for sure*," Basel replied sternly.

"I'm sure," Tristan said.

Basel clapped their hands together loudly, causing one of the kitchen staff to jump and nearly drop a tureen of soup.

"Well, *ALRIGHT*!" Basel whooped. "We got a FROG here BOYS! Let's GO!"

Basel spun around and disappeared into the kitchen.

Tristan leaned over the counter to look and saw them bustling around a table with an assortment of liquor bottles and small containers full of herbs, pickled fruits, and other strange things. Basel was whistling a tune happily while they worked, so Tristan decided to leave them to it.

He went over to one of the many wooden benches in the dining hall and sat down with his plate, devouring a slice of the bread in a few bites. As he'd expected by looking at it, the warm bread was delicious; he guessed it had probably been made fresh earlier.

He cut into the dry, sharp cheese and savored the tangy flavor with the crisp, sweet grapes. He was about to try the pastry when he heard a rustling and crunching behind him. He looked around for the source of the noise, and when he found it Tristan gasped in delight.

In the corner of the canteen was a giant tortoise. The tortoise was about the size of a large dog. It had a shiny bright green shell, a wrinkly little face, and a small collar with a golden bell on it. The tortoise was sitting on a bed of hay, munching on a large pile of lettuce leaves.

"Oh my stars!" Tristan said, excited. He loved animals of all kinds but tortoises were a particular favorite. He stood up and rushed over to crouch down next to the tortoise and gently pat its shell.

"Please do not touch my shell at this time," the tortoise said in a grumpy, monotone voice. Tristan stumbled backwards in surprise.

"Dear me, I'm so sorry, I didn't know you could speak," Tristan said, quickly yanking his hand away.

"Now you know," the tortoise said in a bored tone. He slowly ate a leaf of curly lettuce from a pile while glaring at Tristan.

Tristan hadn't realized that tortoises could glare.

Or that it would be so distressing when they did.

Tristan stood up "I'm...I'm so sorry, again," he said awkwardly. He wondered exactly what one should say to an angry tortoise.

"Head-scratches are allowed," the tortoise said blandly, lifting up his head pointedly.

Tristan was relieved, and he obliged happily, bending down again and scratching the top of the tortoises' head.

There was a loud clanging noise, and the door to the kitchen swung open wildly. The huge figure of Basel emerged with a strange looking drink in their giant hands.

"Oh ho ho, you must be someone special Frog Boy!" Basel said, their voice booming in the dining hall. "Ludwig usually hates newcomers."

"I did *not* say I liked him, I just like head-scratches," the tortoise corrected.

Tristan smiled, "I'm happy to oblige whenever you'd like more head-scratches, my friend."

"We're not friends," Ludwig said flatly. Then the tortoise stood up and ambled off down the corridor towards the cabins while munching on a leaf of lettuce.

Basel roared with laughter and clapped Tristan on the back. They said,

"Don't worry, that means he likes you. Now, time for your drink!"

Tristan returned to his seat and looked at the sparkling drink sitting before him. Basel was standing nearby, beaming proudly at their creation.

The drink was in a glass jar, gleaming with a green and yellow liquid. There were sprigs of bright green mint and a spiral of something that might have been a cucumber sticking out of the top. The whole drink glowed with sparks of golden light that he could only assume was pixie dust.

"Well?" Basel asked, leaning over the table. "Does it feel like a frog to you?"

Tristan gazed at the drink, wondering how he could possibly answer that question.

"I'll need to taste it first," he said.

"Naturally, naturally."

Basel loomed over him, watching Tristan carefully as he picked up the sparkling drink, which seemed to be making a fizzing sound, and lifted it to his lips.

He took a sip and his eyes went wide. Something in the liquid felt like tiny explosions on his tongue. It was sweet and crisp, it tasted like a cold spring morning when the dewdrops have just fallen on the leaves of the flowers. He found he wanted to jump up and dance for joy, but the emotion lasted only a moment, and then it was gone, the sweetness lingering in his mouth like a kiss.

"How did you do that?" he asked, marveling at the strange concoction.

"Well, did it work? Do you feel like a frog?" Basel asked breathlessly.

"You know, I did feel a bit like a frog," Tristan said with a grin.

~

HALF AN HOUR later Tristan finally left the canteen feeling sicker than ever. The rain and wind was battering the sides of the ship and rocking it from side to side. At first he'd thought the food and drink had fixed his nausea, but once he started walking around again he started to feel even worse.

He didn't know if it was from his frog-themed virgin cocktail or just the swaying of the ship, but by the time he had reached the door of his cabin he was woozy and wobbling.

He felt a rush of wind come down the stairs from the decks above and inspiration struck. Of course!

What he really needed was some fresh air!

So he walked past the door of his cabin and headed up to the main deck. As he walked up the creaky wooden stairs he felt the cold wind rushing past him and smelled the salty air. He breathed it in deeply, hurrying up the last few steps to emerge onto the deck in the stormy grey afternoon light.

He immediately wished he hadn't.

The rain pelted his face and the wind pulled at his hair, trying fruitlessly to unravel it from its tight braid. The swaying was far worse up here, and he immediately ran to the railing and clung to it, sure he would fall over otherwise.

He heard a strange sound and he squinted to see through the sleeting rain across the deck. It appeared that the majority of the crew were...singing.

The sailors were all in the middle of the upper deck, some of them were pulling on the rigging and guiding the sails. He could see The Captain in the distance at the wheel, but everyone else was clinging on to each other, singing, swaying, and dancing in the pouring rain.

Ohhh...
Our ship may strain, but our sails are strong!

There may be rain, But theres nothin' wrong!
What a perfect day for-a-singin' songs!
Now, come now, dance in the raaain!

Sky may be dark but our sails are strong!
We've been around this sea too looong!
A Sailor's Might and Bottle O'Rum,
And sing the song for the raaaain!
Ho!

The sailors had arms slung across shoulders as they sang, many of them holding half-empty bottles of whiskey and rum. Tristan gripped the rail tightly, feeling more woozy and disoriented by the moment. He could barely stand, the last thing he'd expected to see on the deck was a crew of drunken sailors singing sea shanties in the pouring rain.

He suddenly doubled over, trying to catch his breath as the nausea overcame him but there was nothing for it. Tristan leaned over the side of the ship and his lunch came pouring out of his stomach and into the sea. He vomited into the wind, the rain stinging his eyes, and then staggered backwards, wiping his mouth on his soaking wet sweater.

He moaned as he staggered across the deck, his hair finally escaping its bonds and tangling in a wet mess across his face.

"I–I–I'm not well," he said, before he fell down face first on the deck, his cheek pressed into the slick wooden boards.

TRISTAN WOKE up in the dimly lit stairwell, with fierce dark eyes gazing down at him in a beautiful mess of wavy dark hair. The Captain was leaning over him, a look of concern knitting her brows and a bottle of smelling salts in her hand. For a moment he sighed happily, thinking this was wonderful dream. But then another wave of nausea hit and he groaned.

"How are you?" Captain Wren asked sternly.

"I'm going to be sick," Tristan mumbled. He pressed his hand against his forehead. It was clammy and damp, his tangled hair clinging to it in clumps.

"We should take him to Bonnie," said a voice nearby.

He shifted on to his elbows to look up and he saw the speaker was Ginger, the blue-haired Liaison to the Guests.

"Aye," The Captain said, nodding her head. "I think it's just seasickness, Bonnie will have something. Help me lift him."

"*Lift him*?" Tristan said, alarmed. But before he could protest any further, Ginger and The Captain had hoisted his arms over their shoulders and pushed him to his feet. He staggered upwards, the vertigo threatening to cause more vomiting but he managed to keep it together enough to steady himself a little.

Wren heaved him up onto her shoulder, carrying most of his weight with Ginger only supporting his arm a little. Together, they pulled him down the long hallway until they arrived at the healer's cabin. Wren pounded on the door loudly, causing Tristan to wince in pain at the throbbing the sound caused in his head.

"Bonnie!" Ginger called, "We've got a seasick guest out here, can you help?"

The healer opened the heavy door with a loud creaking sound. Bonnie had dark caramel skin, a big crooked nose, and curling black hair with little blue flowers woven in it. She wore a long flowing dress in a soft blue color with floral embroidery around the neck. Tristan thought Marigold would probably love to have the same dress in mouse size. At her waist, she had a belt with lots of little bottles and satchels attached to it, and she wore leather bracers on her arms.

Bonnie looked him over and clucked her tongue before pushing the door back to allow them entry. The room was small with two cots on one side and the other half taken up with a large apothecary table and bookshelf. The table was piled high with open books, bottles of flowers and trinkets, small potions that glowed with an otherworldly light, piles of bandages, and littles tins of salves. There was a mortar and pestle, bundles of sharp smelling herbs, and jars of damp poultices.

One of the beds was already occupied by a slim, tanned woman who was knitting quickly and barely looked up when they came in. The Captain hoisted Tristan up on her shoulder and maneuvered him over to the other bed. She eased him down onto it before turning to Bonnie.

"He threw up over the side of the ship and then collapsed on the deck," Captain Wren said.

Tristan winced at the memory.

Not exactly the impression he had hoped to make on the beautiful Captain.

"We took him downstairs and brought him round with smelling salts," Ginger added.

Bonnie leaned around them to look at Tristan, then she turned back to Wren.

"Don't worry dearheart, I'll have him right as rain soon enough. You can get back to steering us out of this storm," Bonnie said, her voice light and airy. The Captain nodded her head to Bonnie and exited the room with Ginger on her heels.

Tristan's head was still spinning and the ship was still rocking as he laid back on the soft pillow, sinking into the bed with a sigh. He watched with bleary eyes as Bonnie moved around her herbalist's workstation, humming to herself. She pulled herbs from jars and mashed them with her mortar and pestle, adding little droplets from amber glasses and pinches of sparkling pixie dust.

After a moment he noticed he was being watched too. The tanned woman on the other side of the room was staring at him with wide eyes while she knitted quickly with her callused hands.

"Hello," Tristan mumbled, waving at her.

She jumped a little, she seemed surprised to have been noticed. She nodded at him once but didn't say anything.

Bonnie appeared in front of him with a warm compress.

"Don't worry dearheart, it's just the moon," she said, pressing the compress onto his forehead.

"Huh?" Tristan replied. He felt a bone-deep relaxation come over him when she pressed the warm compress to his head, his body melting into the bed.

"It's all in the movements of the moon," Bonnie repeated in her lilting voice. "The moon and stars have aligned across the Lion's Mane, and that just makes everything full of shadows today. It's a time of great magic and creativity, but danger will be heading our way soon as we head into The Sun Ferret's season."

As she said this she tucked a tiny yellow flower behind his ear and pressed a large crystal into each of his hands. Tristan wasn't sure what to do about this, but the warm compress felt so nice, he decided to just let it happen. He held onto the crystals tightly and waited. Bonnie turned back to her table and began humming again, pulling apart a small dried twig and lighting it on fire in a bronze bowl.

Tristan started to feel okay until the ship began to tilt sharply to one side. He rocked on the bed and watched in alarm as Bonnie's bottles and jars jangled on her desk. The woman on the other bed swayed with the ships movement, her knitting needles never stopping.

"Whooaoaaa," Tristan moaned as he felt the nausea rearing up again. He dropped the crystals and clutched his stomach "Oh no, not again," he groaned.

Bonnie steadied herself holding onto the side of her desk, then when the ship righted itself she smiled.

"Captain's taking us out of the storm, don't you worry dearheart."

"I'm gonna be sick," Tristan drawled, struggling to sit up and leave so he didn't vomit all over her cabin.

Bonnie was at his bedside quickly, she pushed him back down onto the bed with a surprisingly firm hand.

"You're not going anywhere, your potion is almost done, just hang on," she said. She pushed him down onto the pillow and put the warm compress back on his head.

Tristan gurgled but he didn't have the strength to fight her, his limbs felt like they were made of jelly. He just resigned himself to the deeply embarrassing possibility of throwing up all over her floor.

For her part, Bonnie seemed to have at last decided the situation required some urgency and she began flying around the room, grabbing herbs and tiny bottles and pouring them into her bronze bowl quickly. She didn't stop her humming though, if anything it got louder, and soon she broke into song.

After a moment Tristan recognized it as the sea shanty he had heard the crew singing upstairs. Soon she was singing with gusto and he noticed the other woman joining in as she continued knitting...

> *Our ship may strain, but our sails are strong!*
> *There may be rain, but theres nothin' wrong!*
> *What a perfect day for-a-singin' songs!*
> *Now, come now, dance in the raaain!*

On second listen he realized he rather liked the song, and he found himself wishing he knew the tune to sing with them.

As Bonnie finished the second verse of the song she stirred the bowl quickly, and little orange sparks flew out of it. The knitting woman on the other bed smiled at the sparks, looking delighted. Bonnie carefully poured the contents of the bowl into a large glass bottle, she scrawled a few words onto a small label and attached it to the bottle of glowing orange liquid before coming over to Tristan's side.

"Can you sit up to drink this?" she asked softly.

Tristan nodded and hoisted himself onto his elbows. He tried to take the bottle from her but his hands shook.

"No, no, let's not spill the potion everywhere, open your mouth," Bonnie chided. Tristan obliged and she poured just a few drops of the potion onto his tongue. Despite the potion's beautiful appearance, the taste was vile and he grimaced.

"Don't spit it out," Bonnie warned sternly.

He closed his mouth and nodded. For a moment he was sure he would vomit again, but within a few seconds he felt the nausea disappear and his senses cleared. He smiled brightly as he felt his vertigo slipping away and the room stopped spinning. Even with the ship rocking in the storm he suddenly felt he could weather it. Perhaps even join in a sea shanty or two someday.

"Thank you, you're a wonderful healer," he said, sitting up in the bed with still shaky hands.

Bonnie smiled and put a stopper in the potion, handing him the bottle

"That's for the rest of your journey, anytime you start to feel a little seasick have a sip. But never, ever drink the whole bottle at once."

"Why?" Tristan asked, intrigued.

"Because I'm the healer," Bonnie replied mysteriously. "Now that you're feeling better, wrap yourself in one of those woolen blankets to warm up from the rain and I'll go have Basel make you a cup of something warm."

"Please, nothing with mint," Tristan said frantically. "I had one of their cocktails right before I was sick and I don't think I ever want to have mint again."

Bonnie laughed, "Don't worry there will be no mint dearheart, now put that blanket on."

Tristan nodded and pulled the soft gray blanket around his shoulders gratefully as she opened the big, creaking door and slipped out, leaving him alone with the other woman and her feverish knitting.

"Hello, I'm Tristan. What's your name?" Tristan asked her.

"Birdy," the woman said, barely looking up from her knitting. She had dark, messy hair, shaved on one side of her head. Her hands were covered in scars and a few tattoos, and she wore a simple, sleeveless tunic. She didn't look like someone who fussed over their looks too much, most of her focus seemed to be on her deftly moving hands as she knitted faster than he'd ever seen someone knit before.

"Are you another guest?" he asked.

She shook her head "I work on the ship, I fix the rigging. When the riggin' don't need fixin' I do whatever needs doin'," she said.

He nodded, "Nice to meet you, I'm a guest from Teakley Academy," he offered.

"I don't think I've heard of that one," Birdy said with a shrug.

Tristan was surprised, "Really? You haven't heard of Teakley Academy? I thought everyone knew about it."

Birdy looked nervous, "I ain't been on land too much," she said, then looked back at her knitting.

The door opened and Bonnie returned with a large ceramic mug of steaming liquid and a plate piled high with small pastries.

"I got you a cup of warm broth, nourishing to your body and spirit. Sip it slowly and it'll set you right, dearheart. Basel also gave me this plate of pastries because...well, that's how Basel is. You can't leave their kitchen without something tasty to eat," Bonnie said with a shrug.

She handed Tristan the steaming mug and offered the plate to Birdy. Birdy looked at the plate for a moment before finally setting down her knitting with a reluctant sigh to take one of the delicious looking pastries.

"Can I have a pastry too?" he asked.

Bonnie shook her head, "Absolutely not, didn't I mention you can't eat for the rest of the day? Just let the potion work its magic, the broth is full of nourishment, it will sustain you dearheart."

Tristan sighed as he watched Bonnie eat one of the golden-brown pastries, her eyes closed as she savored the flaky crust.

He wrapped his hands around the mug and leaned back on the bed, closing his eyes and relaxing into the cozy environment of the healer's cabin. He took a big sip of the broth and let the savory liquid warm him from the inside out.

~

A FEW HOURS LATER, he returned to his room with a plate piled high with bread, cheese, pastries, and jam for the Majesteria. After he left the Healer's cabin he'd asked Basel for a big pile of food with extra cheese. The Canteen was already filling up with guests and crew, drinking and eating, but Tristan wasn't in the mood for socializing.

His stomach was still gurgling a bit and he wanted to check on the Majesteria and then go to bed early. Seafaring life had proved to be a bit more wobbly than he'd expected.

He unlocked the door of the cabin and opened it.

"Tristan!" Marigold shrieked happily when he entered.

"Cheese!" Chica and Edwina said in unison.

Tristan laughed.

"Sorry I haven't been back all day," he said, closing the door behind him. "I got seasick and had to go to the Healer's cabin."

"What was that like?" Marigold asked. "How are you feeling?"

Tristan walked over to where the mice were sitting by the Pixie Hearth. They were sitting on the rug with many open books and tiny scrolls strewn around them, and a very noticeably empty plate of food with a only a few crumbs left.

"She was lovely, a very capable healer," he replied. "Unfortunately, I did vomit over the side of the ship though."

"Oh no, I'm so sorry," Marigold replied.

Edwina and Chica seemed entirely focused on the plate of food in his hands. He picked up the empty plate and replaced it with the bountiful pile of cheese and pastries.

The mice jumped up and began excitedly cutting off chunks of cheese and pastry and stuffing them in their mouths.

"Mmmphmp," Chica said.

"What was that?" Tristan asked.

She swallowed "Tea?"

Tristan nodded, "Of course, what kind?"

There was some whispered discussion among the Majesteria and then Edwina said,

"Chamomile."

Tristan put the kettle on and began searching through the satchels of herbs for the Chamomile.

"Did you meet anyone else?" Edwina asked.

Chica was carefully taking an apricot apart with a large knife she had produced from somewhere, and handing wedges of apricot to the other mice.

"I met the Chef, Basel," Tristan said, "You would love them. They are loud and funny, and they make fantastic food."

"I can see that," Marigold said approvingly. She took a piece of pastry and closed her eyes, savoring the taste. "Mmmm, this is so good," she said.

"There's also a talking tortoise named Ludwig," Tristan said.

"Is he magical?" Edwina asked.

"I mean, he's a talking tortoise. Of course he's magical!" Tristan said.

"That doesn't mean he's magical," Marigold said. "There's lots of ways you can learn to speak with humans. A spell, a curse, a magical object, sheer force of will..."

"I've seen it happen," Edwina said sagely.

"Well, I didn't know that," Tristan admitted. "I didn't see anything else magical about him. I suppose we'll just have to see."

The tea kettle whistled and he poured the hot water over the herbs as he pondered this new revelation. The world was bigger and stranger than he had realized and his trip was only just beginning.

He could only imagine what new wonders tomorrow might hold.

CHAPTER FIVE

MARIGOLD COULDN'T SLEEP. She'd made the coziest spot she could, tucked in between two large pillows, wrapped up in blankets, the warmth of the dimmed Pixie Hearth washing over her. But she just couldn't seem to fall asleep.

They had only been on the ship for two days, but she was already restless. She'd heard the shouts and footsteps of the crew moving around all day long, the chattering and laughter in the hallway as people went to and from the Canteen. Tristan's reports of people he'd met had been nice, but it wasn't enough. Knowing there was a whole ship out there to explore and she was just cooped up in this room was starting to make her a little nuts.

She sighed and rolled over, pulling the blanket up to her snout, but she knew it was pointless.

Her paws were itching for adventure.

Finally, after about an hour of this, she threw off her blanket and stood up. To her surprise, Edwina and Chica both sat up too.

"You too?" Edwina said, standing up and stretching her arms.

"I can't sleep a wink," Marigold confirmed, getting up and pulling the warm blanket around her.

"Do you think it's the rocking of the ship?" Edwina asked,

pacing across the rug and picking up a small piece of leftover biscuit to nibble.

"No, its the excitement," Marigold said firmly. "I want to explore the ship, I want to see everything and meet everyone, don't you?"

"I do," Edwina admitted. "It's so frustrating."

"Me too," Chica agreed.

Marigold gave them a mischievous look, "I *mean*, who's going to see us? It's the middle of the night..."

"We can't!" Edwina said, but she looked excited and her whiskers were quivering.

"We shouldn't," Chica agreed, but she was standing up and putting on a warmer sweater.

"We can just hide if anyone sees us, we're *mice*," Marigold said. She knew it wouldn't take much to convince them.

"I can't argue with with that logic," Edwina said, twirling around with a little hop of excitement.

"Makes sense to me," Chica said.

"I'll get the Lantern," Edwina said.

"I'll get our cloaks!" Marigold replied, grinning widely.

A few minutes later the three mice were assembled in front of the Pixie Hearth, ready for adventure. They wore their long adventuring cloaks and sweaters. Marigold had left her witch hat on the clothing pile and Chica had replaced her star-themed robes with a more practical blue dress.

Edwina was holding a lantern no bigger than a thimble. Marigold whispered a few words of power and a small, warm glow appeared between her paws. The three mice blew on it softly and it grew bigger and brighter.

Edwina opened the door of the lantern and the bright spark travelled on the air slowly, sparkling in the dim light. It floated down through the open door of the lantern, and Edwina closed it quickly before the magical light could drift away. She held up the light triumphantly.

"Where are we going then?" she asked.

"Kitchen?" Chica asked, rubbing her paws together.

"The Deck!" Marigold said. "Don't you want to see the moon on the sea? It must be so beautiful."

"I had thought we'd just go down to the kitchens and sneak a little bit of cheese, but now that you mention it, I would love to see that," Edwina said thoughtfully.

"We'll get the cheese another night," Marigold said mischievously. "Tonight, *we see the moon*!"

"Okay, but I really want to go to the kitchens next time," Chica said, rubbing her stomach.

Marigold gave her a *look* and Chica looked down meekly.

"Tonight, we see the MOON!" Marigold said again, far more dramatically.

"THE MOON!" They all chorused together with excitement.

"Sorry Marigold," Chica mumbled.

The mice scrambled over the pillows and across the rug to the door of the cabin.

"Will Tristan be alright?" Edwina asked, sniffling her snout.

"Of course, he's a bit clumsy but I'm sure he'll be okay," Marigold said.

"What if he wakes up while we're gone?" Chica asked.

They stopped and looked at the door to Tristan's room, which had been closed for hours.

"Don't worry, we'll be back soon enough," Marigold said firmly.

The other two mice looked a little nervous but they nodded their heads in agreement. The allure of exploration was too great to be stopped by the possibility of worrying Tristan. There was adventure to be had!

They turned and looked at the large door, and Edwina began searching with her lantern for a small crack or opening they could squeeze through to get out into the rest of the ship. She ran her paw along the bottom of the door, her whiskers twitching with excitement. Finally, she let out a little squeak.

"I found a spot!"

She handed the lantern to Marigold and crouched down on the floor. There was a small gap, just a few inches across, where the door was slightly warped from age. Edwina was squeezing herself under the door, flattening her body into a pancake to get under it without ripping her travelling cloak.

Marigold watched until she was on the other side of the door, then she turned the lantern on its side and pushed it under the door.

"Come on through," Edwina whispered, the excitement in her voice palpable.

Marigold dropped to the floor and flattened herself just like Edwina before her, crawling forward under the door until she popped out on the other side. Immediately, she felt a cold breeze rushing up the long hallway, and the salty smell of the sea was even stronger out here. She stood up again and looked around. Edwina was hopping from foot to foot, anxious to get moving.

Chica came last, doing a little roll as she emerged from the crack under the door.

The hallway was long and dark with a few other doors along it, the sounds of snoring sailors and guests coming from them.

"Do you know which way to the deck?" she asked.

Edwina nodded, "Tristan got a map from the Liaison to the Guests, I got a look at it yesterday. It's this way!"

Moments later Edwina was moving down the hallway, the light from the lantern bobbing with a soft, cozy glow as she scampered across the smooth wood floors. Marigold and Chica followed behind, looking around nervously to make sure they were not seen.

But the hallway was dark and empty; no one saw the three small mice in their travelling cloaks scurrying down the hallway and up the stairs. They climbed the stairs slowly, hoisting themselves up onto the landing of each stair one by one. Edwina held the light up so Marigold and Chica could see what they were doing as they pulled themselves up the stairs, huffing and puffing as they went.

By the time they got to the last stair they could smell the sea and hear the waves lapping against the side of the boat, it made Marigold's fur stand on end.

"That smell, the sounds," she whispered.

"I know, it's wonderful," Edwina squeaked.

They emerged onto the deck and took their first deep breaths of the salty sea air, filling their lungs with the ocean breeze. Their paws landed on the smooth dark oak deck and Marigold felt excitement pulsing in her blood. They were really on an adventure, they were not at Teakley Academy any longer!

She looked at the ship's huge deck spreading out before her in all directions, the big teal sails and the small colorful flags flapping loudly in the breeze. Coiled ropes and briny barrels adorned the deck, and the ship creaked loudly in the quiet night. The moon was round and full, its soft white glow illuminating every surface. She breathed deeply and clapped her paws together.

"The moon, the stars, it's so beautiful..." she whispered. They all looked up and just stood there for a moment, standing on the landing of the stairs and taking it all in, their hearts bursting with joy.

"We're really on an *adventure*, I can't believe it," Edwina breathed.

"Let's climb the rigging so we can get a better view!" Marigold squeaked.

Edwina stepped back, surprised. "Really? You want to climb the rigging?"

"Yes, why not?" Marigold asked.

"I don't know, it's just you're usually the more reasonable one," Edwina said with a giggle.

"You don't know me, I'm Adventure Marigold, I do things differently than Academic Marigold!" she replied, putting her hands on her hips and puffing out her chest.

Edwina laughed, "Okay then Adventure Marigold, lead the way!"

Marigold squeaked happily and moved to the side of the ship so the three mice could climb along the railing and remain unseen if anyone was awake on the deck. The wind was stronger up here but the mice were talented climbers and clung to the railing expertly. After taking a moment to get their bearings they soon were scampering along the railing, the light from their lantern bobbing along like a firefly.

The ship was quiet, they couldn't see a human anywhere near them. The only sounds were the sails, the sea, the creaking wood, and the ropes hitting the side of the ship. Their cloaks flapped in the breeze as they made their way across the railing to the dangling ropes that led up to the mast.

"It's cold," Edwina said with a shiver, "I'm glad we brought our cloaks."

"Mhmm," Chica said, pulling her cloak tighter.

"Me too," Marigold agreed "I could go for a spot of tea right now."

"We'll bring some next time," Edwina replied. Marigold's heart soared at the thought...*next time.*

They really were adventuring now.

She looked up at the big mast, its teal sails rippling and flapping in the cold night breeze. The ropes hung down and twisted in all directions, knotted and secured in multiple places along the deck. Marigold spent a while looking over the ropes and planning out routes in her mind until she found the perfect one.

She picked her way over the ropes until she found the one she was looking for, and then motioned the other mice to follow her. Edwina came behind, lighting their way with her magical lantern. Chica came last, carefully picking her way over the route the other two traversed.

Marigold placed a paw on the rough hemp rope and grabbed hold of it tightly. She swung herself up onto it and they began climbing up the taut rigging, making their way towards the mast.

"Are you sure about this?" Edwina asked, looking down at the deck below as they climbed higher.

"Mostly," Marigold said, concentrating hard as she hopped onto a different rope to swing upwards towards the sail. "I just want to sit on the lowest part of the mast," she said, pointing to the spot she had in mind. "The view will be spectacular."

"Alright," Edwina said dubiously. But she didn't say anything else, just followed Marigold as she hopped to another rope and clambered ever higher into the night sky.

They barely needed the magical lantern on the deck since the bright light of the full moon provided plenty of illumination. The mood was quiet and eerie as they picked their way up the rigging to the bottom of the sail. Marigold pointed to the spot she wanted to sit and the three of them swung up onto the large beam and sat down, dangling their tiny legs over the side with the sail at their backs.

Marigold was right, the view was spectacular. The moon was hanging low in the sky, big, yellow, and full, casting a magical glow across the dark shimmering waters surrounding the ship on all sides. The stars sparkled in the dark night and the three mice felt the magic from them seeping into their tiny bodies and filling them up.

Their small capes flapped behind them as they sat on the beam, dangling their legs over the side. They took everything in, the moon, the stars, the sea, the dark wood of the ship's decks, the large ship's wheel, the Captain's quarters, and the beautiful maiden on the masthead.

Edwina sat back and sighed.

"It's so beautiful," she whispered.

"I love it here," Marigold agreed.

"I still want cheese," Chica said. "But, it's beautiful," she added hurriedly.

Then she let out a very loud squeak, almost like a wolf howling at the moon. She looked up at the big yellow moon and squeaked louder still.

Edwina smiled and lifted her snout high into the sky and squeaked at the moon. Marigold soon joined in the chorus.

For a little while they squeaked louder and louder, getting all their excitement out with their shrieking squeaks. After a lot of squeaking they fell silent and just sat on the beam in the kind of comfortable silence you can only have with friends you know very well. The soft sounds of the water lapping at the sides of the ship and creaking of the wood began to lull them into a cozy kind of sleepiness.

Edwina yawned, putting her paws up and rubbing her eyes.

"Are we ready to go back to bed?" She asked, yawning herself.

"Yes please," Marigold said sleepily. "I'm suddenly very tired."

She yawned and looked down at the ship.

"That's a long way down," she said.

"Magic?" Chica offered, her eyes looking sleepy.

"We shouldn't," Edwina said. But her heart wasn't in it.

"Oh it's just a little Starlight, there's plenty around," Marigold said.

"Okay then Adventure Marigold," Edwina said with a laugh.

The three mice grasped paws and looked up at the stars.

They whispered words of power in unison, watching with wonder as little wisps of Starlight drifted into their hands and began to create a small, swirling light around them. Within a few moments the three mice were standing on air.

The Starlight moved them in a gentle swirl of light and wind across the sky and slowly down onto the deck, carefully depositing them onto the dark oak floor, right by the stairwell to the lower decks.

"Just a little magic," Marigold said with a cheerful whisk of her tail.

"Let's get to bed," Edwina said, before disappearing down into the lower deck.

The other mice followed the bobbing light of her lantern into the dark stairwell.

~

WHEN TRISTAN CAME out of his bedroom in the late morning he didn't notice that they'd fallen asleep in their travelling cloaks or that the Starlight lantern was leaned carefully against the wall.

Humans never noticed things like that.

He just saw the three mice sleeping peacefully in front of the hearth and he smiled, happy to see them safe and sound.

Because Tristan was far too busy worrying about the day ahead of him to notice the fashion choices of the Majesteria. Because today he was going to have to do something difficult and he wasn't looking forward to it.

One of his duties as Majesteria Handler was catching Starlight. It was a simple ritual that only required clear access to the sky and a skilled Starlight worker. He would usually go and stand out on the balcony of his quarters back at Teakley and perform the magical ritual, pulling down the magic from the stars using the magical tattoos on the backs of his hands. He'd siphon the tendrils of bright silver light into a small vial that he wore around his neck. He kept it hidden under his shirt but it was always there, glowing softly and making sure that the Majesteria would have a little bit of Starlight whenever they needed it.

If the mice were working on a big magic he would spend hours late into the night siphoning even more Starlight until he was so exhausted he couldn't stand up anymore. Luckily, he didn't usually have to catch that much Starlight though, the small vial was usually enough.

The thing about Starlight was that the magic faded in a few days, which meant even if the stored Starlight didn't get used he'd still have to fill up his vial every couple of days. He usually did it every night to make sure it was as potent as possible.

He hadn't collected Starlight since they had left home, and when he checked on his vial this morning he'd seen that the light had dimmed completely.

So now he'd have to figure out how to do the Starlight magic ritual on a ship full of people who couldn't know he was a Majesteria Handler.

What could go wrong?

He had been pondering how to solve this puzzle for a few days and he'd finally decided his best course of action was to ask Ginger, the Liaison to the Guests if there was somewhere private he could do the ritual. He didn't like admitting to her that he did magic, but he couldn't see a way out of it. The mice would be needing some Starlight soon for the upkeep of the Cinderflower, and the small vial was already empty.

Tristan left the mice sleeping peacefully and headed to Ginger's quarters. Luckily for him he'd found the ship very easy to navigate, and Ginger's scribbled map was not at all necessary. Within a few moments he was knocking on a door with a small golden plaque on it that said 'Liaison To The Guests.' The door creaked open, and the short Satyrborn woman greeted him with her usual sunny disposition.

"Hello there Mr. Mulberry," she said, opening the door wider. "What can I do for you?"

"You can call me Tristan," he assured her as he stepped into her office. The room was small, with an overcrowded desk on one side and what appeared to be linen storage on the other. She motioned him to sit on one of the wooden stools clustered around her desk. It was obvious the cabin was used for working, not socializing.

"No problem Tristan," she said smoothly, "what can I do for you?"

"Um, this is a bit of a delicate situation," he began.

Ginger adjusted herself in her chair and moved closer, giving him the full attention of her bright stare.

"That's quite alright," she said.

Tristan smiled a little awkwardly.

"As you know, I work for Teakley Academy," he said.

Ginger nodded, eyeing his brooch. "Mhmm," she said.

"You remember when you made a joke about our mages?" he said. "I am in fact...a magical sort of person, I guess you could say."

"Ah, I see," Ginger said, leaning back in her chair and picking up a quill on her desk.

"Yes, so anyway," Tristan continued, "For um, magical purposes, I need somewhere I can...perform a..."

"Ritual?" Ginger filled in.

"Yes, exactly," Tristan said with a sigh of relief. "I need to do it at night, outdoors...every few days."

Ginger raised her eyebrows, "That's rather a lot of specifications, Tristan."

"I know, I'm terribly sorry," he said sincerely. "If there was any other way, I wouldn't be asking you. But I'd rather not sneak up onto the deck in the middle of the night, you know?"

"Yes, we'd rather you didn't do that either," Ginger confirmed. "What else can you tell me about this ritual?"

"Nothing," Tristan said dismally, "Except I can promise that it won't harm the ship or anyone on it."

"You can't tell me what tools or magic you'll be using?"

"Unfortunately, I'm not at liberty to say," Tristan said.

"Ah, I see."

Ginger twirled a piece of her bright blue hair around her finger while she thought about his request, the corkscrew curl bouncing wildly when she let it go. After a minute, she leaned forward.

"I'm afraid I can't help you," she said. Tristan noticed it was the first time he'd seen her without a grin on her face. "It's just not something I can agree to without more information."

"I understand," Tristan said. "But I absolutely need to do this ritual and the rules of Teakley Academy prohibit me from explaining more. What other options do we have?"

"Hmmm, I suppose you'd best ask The Captain," Ginger said with a sigh. It was obvious she hated disappointing guests.

Tristan felt his stomach drop out from under him. He'd suspected it would come to that, but he'd been dearly hoping it wouldn't. He tried not to to think about the racing of his heart as he said,

"When can I see her?"

~

TRISTAN LEFT Ginger's office a few minutes later and headed for the Canteen. Ginger had told him that Wren was always busy, and she didn't know when The Captain would be able to meet with him, but she promised it would be later today. She suggested he spend the afternoon relaxing in the Canteen and try not to stress about it. Since his stomach was already growling at him, he decided to take her suggestion.

He followed the hallway til it opened into the larger room of the Canteen. Now that he wasn't so seasick he could finally take a look around the space. The wide windows gave breathtaking views of the sea, the deep azure waves sparkling in the bright afternoon sunlight. He turned around to look at the wall behind him, and nearly jumped in alarm.

Dominating the space was a large tapestry in bright colors with a rather garish scene of a Harpy descending upon a flaming mountaintop. He was surprised to realize he'd failed to notice the gaudy tapestry before, the seasickness must have been remarkably distracting.

Along one wall was a tea station with a few baskets of pastries and a sign indicating these items were available at all times of day, even when the kitchen was closed. He looked over at the kitchen area and saw that a small placard had been placed on the countertop indicating they would be closed until Dinner Service. Basel and their small army of sous chefs were busily chopping, stirring and boiling. Tristan watched their busy motions for a moment; he always found it a delight to watch experts at work.

Tristan poured himself a cup of coffee from the large pot on the counter and piled a small plate high with a variety of pastries.

Today a few other guests were seated at the benches, some of them writing in notebooks, a few playing chess quietly in the corner were Ludwig was munching on what looked like the remains of a watermelon.

Tristan wound his way through the seats, nodding politely at the other guests until he got to a spot by the window. The bench here was covered in a soft padded cushion and the view of the ocean waves was stunning. He sat down and settled into the cozy seat, pulled his book out, and began to read.

As he sunk into the story he felt a calm wash over him, a sort of different calm than he was used to. It was strange to be so far from home and yet have the comforts of a big warm cup of coffee and a favorite book. The sensation of being safe and comforted but also full of excitement and adventure at the same time was a new one.

Huh. He thought as he settled into the bench and sipped his coffee, putting his legs up and leaning back against the row of windows. Maybe being on an adventure wasn't that different than being at home after all.

It was about an hour later when The Captain arrived. Tristan heard the clicking snap of her boots in the hallway and glanced up as he saw her walk into the Canteen, all dark leather and cascading hair. He looked around to see if anyone else saw what he did, but the handful of other guests in the Canteen seemed to pay her no mind, continuing their games of chess or scribbling in notebooks. None of them looked like their hearts were suddenly racing and their stomachs full of butterflies.

They all just sat around acting as though wildly beautiful glamorous Pirate Captains in black leather pants walking into the room was the most normal thing in the world.

Tristan pretended to keep reading, but he knew there was no way he'd be able to focus with Captain Wren nearby. He watched her as she walked across the room and hailed Basel in the kitchen. After a quiet conversation Basel disappeared for a moment, then returned with a big steaming bowl of soup, a mug of something, and a few large slices of bread with butter. Wren took the food with a hint of a smile, nodding her head appreciatively, and turned to find a place to sit.

Tristan saw her look around the room and eventually her gaze fell on him. He looked up ever so slightly and saw she was making her way across to room to exactly where he was sitting.

He started to sweat. He chided himself. What are you doing? he thought. You're acting like a teenager! You need to talk to her about catching Starlight anyway, why are you acting like this?

But his emotions didn't care about any of that. They were entirely focused on the sway of her hips and the heart-pounding feeling of her penetrating gaze.

A moment later she sat down a few seats away from him and set her food on the table. She swung her legs over the bench in a movement that brought to mind the word 'swashbuckling' and looked at him in that terrifying way she did.

Up close, he could see that Wren had a scar across her face, a jagged line cutting from her eyebrow to her chin. The scar did not, however, make her any less devastatingly beautiful. In fact, it had quite the opposite effect. From her hard leather boots to the long sword at her hip, Wren effortlessly communicated that she was the type of person who took no shit from anyone, and her scar was like a little exclamation point on that fact.

"Hello," he said nervously, setting his book down.

"Ah, Mr. Mulberry," she said, entirely unperturbed. "Have you finally decided to tell me what's in your strange little trunk?"

With just a few words she woke him from his dream of sailing across the seas with a beautiful pirate captain and sent him crashing back into reality.

She wasn't his friend and she definitely wasn't his lover. She was an obstacle to his job and he had an important job to do and secrets to protect.

For Teakley, for the Majesteria, for the Queen.

"Not today Captain," he said firmly. "I'm afraid I'm still not at liberty to share that information."

She nodded and looked down at her food, taking a large piece of bread and dipping it in the soup. She took a bite thoughtfully and looked out at the sea, ignoring him completely.

The silence grew as she ate, making Tristan feel even more nervous. He yearned to fill the space with conversation, but he didn't trust himself not to spill his secrets if he let down his guard.

After a while of quietly eating her soup, Wren pulled out a flask and poured a generous amount of liquor into her drink.

"So what was it you wanted to see me about?" she asked abruptly.

"I couldn't possibly disturb you while you're having lunch," Tristan said.

Wren looked amused,

"A Captain is always working Tristan, what do you need?"

He set down his book and took a deep breath, something about her just made him so damn nervous.

"I realize this may be overstepping my rights as a passenger, but I'm afraid I don't have a choice," he began.

Wren looked up and cocked her eyebrow with interest.

"Do go on," she said cooly. "This sounds interesting."

"I need somewhere to um, do a...a...a ritual. A magical ritual. For my work," he said. "Ginger said I would need to ask you."

Wren returned to looking at her soup, her face inscrutable.

"Let me guess, you can't tell me what kind of ritual."

"No, I can't."

"Mmm, and can you tell me what it's for?"

"I'm not at liberty to say," he said.

"I'm sure you're not," she said. Another piece of bread dipped into the soup. "This ritual, it needs to be private?"

"Yes," he said, shifting nervously.

"Is it dangerous?" she asked, her eyes suddenly locking onto him.

"No," Tristan said. He didn't want to lie but he knew he had to.

"*Really?*" She asked with a note of surprise.

"Not to the crew or the guests," he amended. "It only poses a danger to me."

"Interesting," she said, leaning back and taking a sip of her spiked drink. "What if something happens to you?"

"It won't," he assured her.

"Why not do this...*ritual*, in your cabin?"

"It requires that I be outside, in the...moonlight," he said carefully. He doubted that Wren was aware of the intricacies of Starlight Magic but he figured it was better not to mention it.

"I see," she pulled out her golden coin and began flipping it absentmindedly in her hands again as she thought. She looked him over, his handsome face, the book on the table and the remains of his food. She seemed lost in thought, but then he saw something change in her eyes.

Her attention caught on something and a look of surprise moved quickly across her face before she returned to her unreadable expression. Her hand moved across the table and she picked up his coffee mug.

"How long have you been here?" She asked, looking at the mug, wisps of steam rising from the top.

"About an hour?" He said.

She tilted her head to the side.

"Is this your first cup of coffee?"

"Yes," he said, confused. "Why?"

She looked at the mug for a while, her hands gripping the warm ceramic. Finally she let it go and put the mug back on the table, seemingly coming to some kind of internal decision.

"No reason," she said, suddenly brisk and casual. "I know a place you can do your magic, privately. Meet me on the deck when it gets dark and I'll show you."

"I'll see you later then," Tristan said, grabbing his book and practically bolting out of his seat. He didn't want to to sit there sweating under her gaze any longer than he had to.

He was halfway down the hallway before he remembered the Majesteria and jogged back to Basel's bar top.

"Can I have a platter with at least six different types of cheese?"

Chapter Six

Tristan went up to the deck at sunset just to be sure he wasn't late. He leaned on the railing and watched the sky become painted with bright umber and streaks of gold while the sails flapped in the breeze. Finally, when the first stars were starting to peek out of the blanket of darkness above, Wren tapped him on the shoulder.

"This way," she said.

He followed her across the long deck, she tipped her hat or waved lightly at the sailors as she went. Wren was a Captain fully in control of her domain. Wren led him across the ship and towards the helm. The ship's wheel was in a section raised above the rest of the deck, right behind the Captain's Quarters. A gate closed off a short stairwell leading up to the small deck for the steering wheel.

Wren opened the gate and Tristan slipped in after her, feeling the sudden quiet in this part of the ship. He noticed that magic feeling again; he could sense it more here. He stopped and closed his eyes for a second, trying to sense the magic better and discern its source. But he couldn't seem to find it, not exactly. The magic felt like it was everywhere, but that couldn't be right.

"What's wrong?" Wren asked.

Tristan opened his eyes and saw her standing right in front of him, her piercing dark eyes searching his face. He suddenly felt just how alone they were, how private it was up here. His pulse quickened as he tried to focus.

"Nothing, sorry," he said. "Please, go on."

She searched his eyes for a moment, then nodded and continued up to the small landing where the ship's wheel was stationed. She turned around and leaned against the railing, the little gold coin twisting in her fingers again.

"This is it," she said. "Emyr and myself are the only people allowed up here. You won't be bothered while you're doing...whatever it is you're doing."

Tristan looked around at the railed-in area, so much quieter than the bustling deck below.

"Thank you, this should work," he said. He paused for a moment then added, "I'm sorry I can't tell you more. I would if I could."

Wren looked at him, her eyes sharply calculating.

"You know, I believe you," she said, with a note of surprise.

With a nod she turned around and headed back down the stairs to the ship's main deck. Right before leaving she stopped, turned her head, and looked back at Tristan, her hand lingering on the latch of the gate.

"How did you...know you were magical?" she asked.

"I blew up a well," Tristan replied.

"What?"

"When I was twelve, I got in a fight with my brother and I blew up a well," he explained. "It was an accident, of course. After that, my parents wrote to Teakley and someone came out and tested me. Then I moved there to train and learn more about my powers."

"You can blow things up?" Wren asked.

"No, not anymore," Tristan said with a chuckle. "Magic is much more volatile when you're very young, that's why training is so important."

"And, after you train, they...make you stay at Teakley forever?" There was a note of something strange in her tone, but Tristan didn't know why.

"No, I chose to stay," he said. "My basic training took a very long time, but I did very well and they offered me an apprenticeship, and eventually I became a Majesteria Handler. It's quite an honor."

"Hmm. Do you like it there?"

Tristan paused. He realized he hadn't ever thought about that. Teakley just was. He'd never considered if he liked it.

"Yes...mostly."

"Alright," she said, her usually piercing gaze seemed to be looking elsewhere, lost in thought. "Thank you."

"Um, sure," Tristan said, not quite clear on what he'd done.

"Do you need anything else?" she asked absently.

"No, this should be fine, thank you," he replied, wondering what she could be thinking about to make her act so strangely.

Wren nodded and walked away, lost in her thoughts.

THE VIEW of the ship from up on the steering deck was breathtaking. The moon was gleaming silver, making dark outlines of the ship's rigging against the sky. The crew were moving about in the darkness, hanging lanterns in the rigging, their warm yellow glow casting ethereal pools of light against the shadows.

He looked up at the sky full of sparks of light and breathed deeply, letting the cold wind from the sea wash over him.

This was a life he could get used to.

He opened the satchel he had brought with him to begin the ritual for catching Starlight. Inside were the assorted magical instruments he used to make things easier, though mostly what he really used were his tattoos and his own magical abilities.

He set down the satchel on the counter in front of the wheel and pulled out a rolled up cloth containing his kit. He unrolled the cloth, revealing his instruments, which gleamed in the soft light of the moon.

He reached into his shirt and pulled out the necklace with its empty vial that he would be pouring the Starlight into. He took the necklace off and unscrewed the lid of the vial, turning it upside down to clear out any impurities. In his kit was a small brush and a cleaning cloth, which he used to carefully clean the vial, inside and out, preparing the vessel to receive the Starlight.

Next, he prepared the channelling batons. The small metal sticks with pointed quartz crystals on the end made wonderful conduits to draw down the Starlight using his magic. He picked one up and twirled it in his hands, getting the metal warmed up, and putting his mind in the right mental state for catching Starlight. He needed to clear his mind of worries about their trip or thoughts of beautiful pirate captains with mysterious eyes. He needed pure focus, all that mattered was the vast field of stars spreading out above him.

He took off his leather gloves, the nine-pointed star tattoos on his hands were still the dark black of ink. He picked up the baton and twirled the small metal rod between his hands again, warming it up more and connecting his skin with the conduit. He looked up and stared at the bright dots in the dark night, twinkling with promises of magic and power. He whispered a few of his favorite words of power and soon began to feel the heat in his hands growing.

The tattoos began to get brighter and lighter, turning from black to gray to pale pure white in a matter of moments.

Suddenly, he could feel the Starlight flowing into him, filling him up with magic. He tried not to let too much in, he knew from experience that would create an awful hangover. But it was always hard, once you turned on the faucet Starlight wanted to pour into you like water crashing through a dam.

Finally, he saw what he was waiting for. Bright little tendrils of light twisting down from the sky, like hanging cords, just waiting for him. He plucked at them gently like they were delicate silken ribbons, pulling them out of the night sky and twisting the glowing strands around the metal rod.

He felt the tension of the magic growing in his body as he kept pulling the threads of glowing light out of the darkness. His muscles began to ache with the strain of holding back the magic, stopping it from overtaking him. He kept winding the whisper-fine threads until the baton glowed with a bright white light. Finally, when he knew he had enough to fill the vial, he set the channelling baton down on the counter and whispered a few more words of power to end his connection to the Starlight, making sure to push the magic out of his body with his intention at the same time.

The magic whooshed out of him, disappearing into nothing in a few seconds. The sudden loss of tension and magic in his limbs always sent him reeling and today was no different. He keeled over, head between his knees, gasping for breath, his whole body shaking.

He placed his hand on the counter and took deep breaths to steady himself as he acclimatized. He took a few more panting breaths and felt the energy draining out of him. He looked around his kit until he found a nut bar, full of honey, dried plums, and almonds, wrapped up in a little piece of brown paper. He always kept a few in his Starlight catching kit for times like this. He ripped open the wrapper and bit down hungrily, the sturdy food giving him a burst of energy.

After a few moments of thoughtful chewing, he started to feel the blood coming back to his limbs and his head stopped spinning. He would have very much liked to sit down for a cup of tea, but he knew he wasn't done yet, so he finished his nut bar in one huge bite and wiped his hands clean. He picked up the glowing rod and the vial and began the painstaking process of slowly siphoning the Starlight off of the baton and into the small glass vial.

He was almost done pulling the last threads of the shining white light into the vial when he heard a loud bell in the distance, the kind of bell you'd use to bring all the cows in for the evening. He jumped a little and then remembered that Ginger had mentioned there was a bell for the Canteen's dinner service.

Perfect. A nice dinner would be just the thing to get his energy back.

~

THE CANTEEN WAS ALREADY full of people by the time Tristan arrived. He heard the sounds of laughter and merrymaking drifting down the hallway as he made his way to the dinner service. When he arrived the Canteen it was busier than he'd ever seen it before. Nearly every bench and stool in the room was full and many people were chatting and laughing loudly. He saw many people he recognized, and lots of crew and guests he'd never met before. People were eating, drinking, telling stories, and playing cards.

The kitchen countertop was piled high with food and he drifted over to it hungrily. After all the other delicious food he'd had, Tristan had expected the Dinner Service to be exceptional, but he was still impressed.

Mushroom-stuffed rice balls battered and fried, stacks of little pot pies with golden crispy edges and gravy oozing out the sides, a large pot of what looked like a creamy leek soup, candied yams, and vegetables roasted with fresh sprigs of rosemary. Small mountains of soft dinner rolls, toasted sesame crostini and spiced apple tarts. At the center of it all was a large pan of a cheese and onion lasagne bake, although there were only a few servings left of the popular dish.

Behind the scores of mouth-watering food, Basel and their chefs were busy refilling tureens and roasting more vegetables. The kitchen was a bustle of activity with Basel standing proudly at the counter helping the guests.

"If it isn't Froggy!" they boomed cheerfully when Tristan approached and began loading his plate with gold-crusted pot pies. "That's some appetite you have there, fella, it was only a few hours ago I gave you, what was it, *nine* different cheeses?"

Tristan paused in the middle of ladling a heaping pile of candied yams onto his plate. He set the ladle back down in the bowl gently and coughed awkwardly.

"I...um...sailing makes me hungry?" he offered.

"Aye, I can understand that," Basel said, nodding sagely and piling a few rolls on Tristan's plate. "Don't let me stop you lad, I love a hungry guest!"

"Sailing always makes me so hungry too, especially when the food is this good," said an elderly woman next to him. She wore a bright pink sweater and was carefully piling rice balls in a dangerously wobbling tower on her plate.

"It is delicious, isn't it?" Tristan agreed.

"Mhmm, best I've ever had on a ship," the woman said. "Emilia Waltingham." She held out a hand. "I'm a Horse and Pony Breeder."

Tristan took her hand and shook it, "Nice to meet you, I'm Tristan."

"Come sit with us dear," she said, motioning him to follow her over to one of the crowded tables. She ushered an older gentleman to make space and Tristan squeezed in between them.

"So what do you do then, Tristan?" the self-professed horse breeder asked.

"I work at Teakley Academy," he said.

"Goodness me, isn't that fancy! What do you do there?" she said, spearing her rice balls furiously.

"Um...academic things, mostly," he said.

"Ah, I heard about Teakley," the older gentlemen on his left said. "Heard they have these mice that work for them, who do all sorts of magic and so on."

"Don't be ridiculous dear," the elderly woman said, shaking her head with laughter.

"Why's that ridiculous?" he replied.

"Because they're tiny!" she said.

"I don't see how bein' small would prevent 'em from doin' magic," Basel said, joining the conversation. They sat down at the table with a plate of food as the rest of the kitchen crew began to put away the large platters.

"Last call for food!" one of the kitchen staff called out, and a few people scurried over to fill their plates one last time.

"How can they do magic with those little paws?" the woman

persisted, shaking her head. "I'm sure you need to do all kinds of strange incantations with your fingers."

"That's a good point," her husband admitted.

"Now then, Froggy," said Basel, tucking into their plate with vigor, "You ready for a *real* cocktail tonight?"

"Umm," Tristan stalled, trying to find a way to let them down politely. After vomiting the frog-themed drink off the side of the ship the idea of drinking something similar sounded highly unappealing. "I think I'll just have some ale tonight."

"Dammit, not another one!" Basel said, throwing their napkin down on the table. "No one on this bloody ship appreciates a good cocktail!"

"I'm sorry Basel," Tristan said, "maybe tomorrow."

"Fine, fine, I can't make ya," Basel said shaking their head. "What about you Mrs. Waltingham?"

"I'm afraid we really must be going dear," she said, standing up hurriedly, "it's just getting so late for us older folks."

"It's barely nine o'clock," her husband said, but she was pulling on his shirt and he quickly got the hint.

"Nice meeting you Tristan," she said, waving goodbye as they left the Canteen. As they walked out Tristan's eye was drawn again to the most unusual tapestry along the wall. He stared at the bright red flames and the Harpy's gleaming eyes for a while, trying to remember where he had seen the image before.

"Ah, you lookin at Ole Gertha?" Basel said, grinning widely. "She's my pride and joy, my mum made her as a going away gift for me. Ain't she a beaut?"

"Your mum made this tapestry?" Tristan said, eyes wide.

"Aye, embroidered it herself," Basel said, a small tear coming to their eye.

Tristan suddenly went silent because he finally remembered where he'd seen the gaudy tapestry before.

It was in a catalog.

The Majesteria often made their own clothes since the type of things they liked to wear could be challenging to find in mouse size.

Marigold was particularly fond of embroidering her dresses with flowers, and he was often tasked with ordering her various supplies from embroidery catalogs.

It was all coming back to him now. Ole Gertha, as Basel had called the tapestry, was one of many pre-made embroidered tapestries you could buy from *Enchanting Embroidery: Embroidery Essentials For The Discerning Stitcher.*

For a fraction of a second Tristan considered mentioning this fact, but one look at Basel's misty grin looking at the garish tapestry, and he knew that he would be keeping Basel's mum's secret forever.

Over the next few hours many of the crew and guests retired to their rooms or other parts of the ship and the Canteen emptied out into a smaller group, mostly crewmates playing cards at the big table by the window.

After he'd finished his food Tristan drifted over and sat down near Emyr, the very well put together first mate with pointy ears. He was in the midst of a very serious card game with Wren, Ginger, and Birdy. Bonnie and Basel sat nearby, drinking ale and chatting.

Tristan looked with interest at the card game, after watching them put down a few cards, he recognized the game. They were playing Find The Cherry Basket In the Wolves Den, more commonly called Cherry or Cherry Basket.

Tristan was *very* good at Cherry Basket.

Most people chased after having a lot of Cherries but Tristan knew all that really mattered was finding The Lady. If you didn't have someone to carry The Basket, you were nowhere. He'd once even won with only two Cherries because he had The Lady.

Edwina had not been very happy about that, but a thorough examination of the rule book had come down in Tristan's favor.

After that they played Word Salad instead of Cherry Basket.

Much less drama.

He looked over the board with interest. It was obvious that Ginger and Birdy weren't very good and would probably have to fold soon. To his eye, Emyr and Wren had the signature movements of talented players and he expected their games probably got rather heated. Especially when you considered the pile of coins and trinkets slowly growing in the middle of the table.

Tristan sat back drinking his ale, watching the game, and listening to the chatter around him.

"It's going to be strawberry everything all week," Basel was saying to Bonnie who was nodding her head. "Strawberry scones, strawberry blintzes, strawberry jam, strawberry ale-"

"Strawberry ale?" Bonnie said, surprised.

"Well, maybe I'll just put some strawberries in the ale," Basel conceded. "But those fresh strawberries from Strawberry Island are the best in realm and I'll be damned if I'm not going to buy as many baskets as I can I fit in the store room."

"As you should, as you should," Bonnie nodded the slightly wobbly nod of someone who'd had quite a lot of ale.

Tristan had also had a lot of ale, and thus he found himself drawn into intently watching the Cherry Basket match.

"You might not want to play that," he said suddenly. Ginger looked up, her hand in the air holding a card.

"What?" She said.

"It's just...if you put that Hedge down now, you'll never be able to get The Basket."

"Damn it, you're right," she said, setting her card down. "Gah! I'll never get the hang of this game."

"Please refrain from giving advice, it's a violation of the rules," Emyr said primly, holding his cards close to his chest.

"I didn't think of that, I'm so sorry," Tristan mumbled.

Wren gave him that look again. The calculating appraisal.

But the drink was getting the better of him, so he waggled his eyebrows at her and said,

"What's wrong?"

She took a sip of her drink and didn't say anything for a while, long enough that Tristan started to feel nervous again, in spite of the ale.

Finally she said, "Where'd you learn to play Cherry Basket?"

"From a book," he said promptly. "You can learn everything from a book."

A few of the pirates snorted with laughter.

"I'd have to disagree," Wren said cooly. She played a Cherry and turned over a Basket.

"Aww man!" Birdy said, throwing her cards down.

"I doubt you could learn much about our life from a book," Bonnie said thoughtfully.

"I don't know, I read a lot about pirates when I was preparing for this trip," Tristan said without thinking about it.

"We're not pirates," Wren said, her eyes dangerous.

"I'm sorry...I didn't mean...I just-" Tristan stammered.

Suddenly all the crew started laughing, even Wren.

"She's just joking with you Froggy," Basel said. "We may be Registered but we'll never stop bein' pirates!"

"Ah," Tristan said, feeling his cheeks turn pink.

"If you've learned so much, pray tell us something useful about pirate life you learned in a book Tristan," Emyr said, carefully pulling a card off of the pile and sliding it across the table.

"Umm, I don't know how useful what I've read is," Tristan said, eyeing Wren nervously. "But I learned about how ships are constructed, the materials and processes of sail production, common rope and knot types, and waterproofing ship repairs."

"What about in those novels you read? *The Valor Of The Seas* I think it was? Anything useful in that?" Wren said, her eyes dancing.

Tristan met her gaze and felt his cheeks warm again, but perhaps it was just the alcohol.

"No, um, not really. Mostly there is lots of fighting and um... kissing."

Everyone at the table laughed at this.

"Oh-ho, not too inaccurate then," Ginger said.

Bonnie rolled her eyes, "You're giving him all the wrong ideas about us," she said.

"Hardly," Ginger said with a wide grin. "I've not been here long but I already know what this crew is like. They're a real wild bunch."

"It's true," Wren agreed with a chuckle. "Emyr's got a man in every port."

"People in glass houses shouldn't throw stones," Emyr said with a sassy glare. "Especially when we'll be at The Wild Berry Tavern tomorrow."

"What's special about The Wild Berry? Tristan asked.

Wren glowered at Emyr but didn't say anything.

Emyr leaned in conspiratorially,

"Well you see, The Captain here," he said, waving his drink at Wren, "had a woman once, her name was Willow, they were together for quite some time. When they broke up, oh boy the fights, you should have seen it. But soon The Captain found someone else, a handsome dark-haired man, Calryn. He was mooning over her for ages but it never quite worked out right. When they finally broke up, Calryn was devastated. But he met a beautiful woman on Strawberry Island and they bonded over having both had their heart broken by a moody Pirate Captain..."

"Yes, yes, thank you Emyr," Wren said, glaring at him and throwing a card onto the pile. "Let me just summarize: my exes married each other and bought the Tavern where they met and renamed it The Wild Berry. Your play Emyr," she said, throwing a few more coins on the pile and laying The Lady down on the table.

Emyr gaped at her, while he'd been busy gossiping Wren had quietly been working to win the round of Cherry Basket. Emyr cursed and threw his cards down. Wren was grinning like a cat as she pulled the pile of coins and trinkets towards her.

"Damn you!" Emyr said

"It doesn't pay to gossip darling," Wren said with a self-satisfied smile.

~

AT LAST THE day had come for their first stop. They had been at sea for quite a few days now, and even with his potion for seasickness Tristan was growing weary of the ceaseless bobbing of the ship and yearned to put his feet on firm ground.

Naturally, he was thrilled when Ginger slipped an itinerary under his door letting him know they would be docking at Strawberry Island overnight while the crew got supplies. The note informed him that he was welcome to join the crew, explore the island alone, or stay on the ship. Of course, the Majesteria had insisted on adventuring onto the island.

Shortly after the letter arrived the three mice had scrambled up to the window ledge and Tristan had stood with them watching the smudge on the horizon get larger and larger until it finally became an island, and eventually they could see a small seaside town clinging to the side of rolling, bright green hillsides.

Now, he had just finished getting dressed and was packing the Majesteria's Travelling Satchel for their day trip to Strawberry Island. He had put on his best cloak and Academy brooch, braided his hair, and taken a small amount of the travel money and put it into the satchel. All that was left was the Majesteria.

The Travelling Satchel looked just like a regular leather bag but it had a special compartment for the mice to sit in should they want to travel with Tristan without being seen. It was separated from the rest of the bag and even had a fine mesh screen, which they could use to view the world around them. It wasn't a very comfortable way to travel, as the mice had loudly informed him on many occasions, but it would do in a pinch.

Today, the three mice did not even squeak once in irritation as they hopped into the satchel. They just waved at him and smiled, chattering to each other about strawberries.

He laid the satchel gently over his shoulder, making sure that the mice were safe and protected. He felt them move around a little, so he knew they were okay, and then he opened the door to his quarters and headed up to the deck, squinting and blinking in the sunlight.

The deck was bustling with activity, the sailors were adjusting rigging and preparing everything for landing. A small crowd of crew and guests had gathered at one part of the ship to watch them land, and he joined the group, peering over the railing of the ship with interest.

Tristan held his hand over his eyes to shield them from the bright morning sun so he could get a glimpse of the famous island. The island was far smaller than where he'd come from, but it was beautiful, the lush green hills covered with vibrant plants and dashes of red poking out from between the leaves.

The docks they were approaching were small with space for no more than a dozen ships to anchor. Right behind the docks was the village, an assortment of faded, sea-worn buildings. Although varied the buildings all had one thing in common, they were painted various shades of pink. He guessed they were once vibrant red or fuchsia, meant to remind you of the island's famous berries, but they had become shades of pale pink over the years. Some of the shops and businesses also had strawberries painted on their buildings or signs.

The sun beat down on him as the ship began its long journey into the port and he felt warm sea air pulling at the laces of his braid. He had never found the tight cuffs or collar of his shirts constricting before, but suddenly in the sun on the ship, he felt... wrong. His woolen waistcoat itched him and his perfectly pressed shirt felt tight around his body.

He looked around him and saw he was the only one dressed this way. The crew and other guests all looked far more comfortable in their billowing blouses, flowing dresses, and soft robes. He wondered for a moment if perhaps he should buy such a shirt for himself. He imagined himself in voluminous linen blouse, his hair blowing in the breeze like Captain Santiago.

He couldn't imagine what people back at Teakley Academy

would say if he walked into an academic meeting dressed like that, but it was...certainly something to think about.

Soon enough the ship pulled into the small docks and put down its anchor, a moment later Captain Wren was standing at the front of the ship on top of a crate. Her first mate Emyr stood nearby, ringing a large bell with both hands.

"Attention! Attention!" He shouted so loudly that Tristan was sure everyone on Strawberry Island had heard it. The crew and the guests all crowded around to listen to what The Captain had to say.

She stood tall, her long hair tumbling in waves around her, dark leather breeches clinging to her hips, her face commanding authority.

"Within the hour we will be landing at Strawberry Island," she began. There was a small cheer from a few of the guests, which earned a glare from the Captain. They immediately fell silent.

"As I was saying, when we arrive at the Island you are free to go where you choose for the evening. However, you must return to the ship by high noon tomorrow. There will be no exceptions, if you are not back at the ship by NOON EXACTLY, you will be staying on Strawberry Island. Understood?"

"AYE!" Came the answering call of the crew. Tristan and the rest of the guests all nodded their heads in understanding. Wren gave a nod of acknowledgment, then jumped off the crate and walked away with Emyr to work with the crew lowering the ramp down to Strawberry Island.

CHAPTER SEVEN

THE MICE HAD BEEN VERY clear about the need to purchase many types of strawberry-related foods and other tourist items to bring back home, so Tristan's first order of business was to explore the village.

It seemed some of the other guests had the same idea, so he followed the crowd into town and wandered the through the pink-hued shops, taking in all the sights and sounds. The village was fairly small, with one main street with a few dozen shops and food stalls along it.

Many of the shops had prominently displayed strawberries painted on their signs, and quite a few hand berry-themed puns for their names. Dotted among the shops were various food vendors, some were in carts on the cobbled street with bright red candies hanging off the sides and gold-crusted pies piled high.

Tristan followed the flow of traffic, tagging along behind the other guests from *The Snapdragon* as they dipped into stores and purchased items. Every now and then he'd hear a little squeak and he'd know he needed to purchase something. After a little while he came out of a shop and saw the rest of the guests clustered around a wall, talking quickly and looking around nervously.

He walked up to them and craned his neck to get a look at the subject of their attention. It was a large, black and white Wanted Poster pasted to one of the pink walls of the village. He read:

WANTED: Mad Richard
aka 'The Mage Stealer'
Pirate of Dangerous Repute
Murders, Torture, Abduction and Crimes of Depravity
If found DO NOT APPROACH
Alert the Local Authorities
REWARD FOR INFORMATION

It also included an illustration of a scruffy looking man with a scraggly beard, scars, and eyes that bore into Tristan with a look of pure evil. He stepped back a bit as he felt a cold knot of dread turn in his stomach. 'The Mage Stealer?' What did that mean? Pirates were one thing, but this man...this sounded like a villain from one of his favorite books.

Which wasn't someone he wanted to meet in real life at all.

A FEW HOURS later the group of guests finally left the village and began the winding walk up the hillside to the Strawberry Forest. Tristan was struggling, his arms were loaded down with shopping bags from the town, full of every strawberry-themed item a very small tourist could desire.

Although the village was small it truly had every item you could imagine with a strawberry on it (and quite a few you would never think of). Much to the mice's delight he had found a shop with a large dollhouse collection, so they were able to acquire numerous mice-sized strawberry items, including a teapot shaped like a giant strawberry.

For himself Tristan had purchased a large ceramic tea mug with strawberries painted on it, a tea towel, and a bookmark with a little strawberry charm dangling off it.

They had bought postcards and books for friends back home, but mostly they had bought food. Cheeses, jams, pies, wines, tea, biscuits and toffee. He kept thinking he was done shopping, and then he'd hear a little squeak, hold the Travelling Satchel up to his ear surreptitiously, and one of the Majesteria would ask him to buy more things.

So now he made his way up the hillside with the rest of the tourists, his strong arms just barely managing to carry the shopping bags. They walked under a big sign which declared this to be:

STRAWBERRY FOREST
Home of the Ogreberry

Everyone drifted over to the small wooden booth at the entrance with painted strawberries on it. The booth was manned by a dwarf with long plaited red hair and a constellation of freckles across her face.

"Good afternoon everyone," she said with a big grin. "My name's Pollywolli and I'll be helping you today! Entry to the forest is ten coins per person. The entry fee is only for observing and does not include berry picking. Our price list for berry picking is to my left, and baskets to my right. We have a large assortment of baskets, bags, and sacks, something for every style and need, each with our signature Strawberry Forest logo to commemorate the occasion. We also offer these pamphlets about the history of Strawberry Island and the Ogreberry, and of course, an assortment of Strawberry foods. If you have any questions about our selection or Strawberry Forest, please feel free to ask."

"Why does it say Ogreberry?" someone asked.

Pollywolli pulled at the straps of her suspenders and smiled as she answered, "That's what we sell here, these giant berries you see are actually a different breed of strawberry, unique to Strawberry Island, called Ogreberries."

"So they're not strawberries?" a disappointed voice asked.

"They are," Pollywolli assured them, "but they're also not. I mean, have you ever seen a strawberry this big?" She reached under her counter and pulled out a strawberry about the size of a watermelon. There was oohs and ahhs from the guests and she looked quite pleased with herself. "No, this ain't your regular strawberry. It's *better*."

This seemed to satisfy the guests who all clustered around the Strawberry Stall and began buying baskets and sacks with much enthusiasm. Tristan heard a squeak and lifted the Traveling Satchel up to his ear.

"Get us a Large Basket!" Marigold's voice said, "I want to go strawberry picking!"

"Didn't you hear what she just said? They're Ogreberries," Edwina's voice said.

"Don't be silly, those are strawberries and I want to eat a fresh one!" Marigold's voice countered.

"Can you get a pamphlet too?" Chica said. "I want to know the history."

"No problem," Tristan whispered, resting the satchel back on his hip while Edwina and Marigold argued about Ogreberries inside it.

When he approached the counter to buy the basket and pamphlet he noticed that Basel was there, negotiating with Pollywolli to get a few crates of berries delivered to the ship. Tristan didn't want to interrupt so he left a few coins on the countertop and took his basket and pamphlet.

He shouldered the bags and began making his way towards the trees, still struggling under the weight of them.

"Excuse me! Sir!" said a voice behind him. "Your change!"

He turned to see the dwarf woman with her bright red hair pushing coins into his hands.

"It's fine, don't worry about it," he said, shaking his head.

"Please sir," Pollywolli insisted, "you must take your change."

Tristan looked at his loaded-down arms helplessly, trying to figure out the complicated process of putting things down in order to put the coins away.

"Er,...can't you just keep it?"

"It's against our policy," the dwarf insisted. "However, if you'd like to store your packages while you explore the forest, we've got a lockbox over here."

Tristan's shoulders sagged with relief so much he nearly dropped a bag full of strawberry pies on the ground.

"Thank you, that would be amazing," he said gratefully.

Ten minutes later and Tristan was already lost in a forest of strawberries. After making sure he was well away from the rest of the tourists he had opened the Travelling Satchel and the mice had happily scampered away through the strawberry plants, leaving him wandering through the strange jungle of giant strawberries alone.

The tourist trap at the entrance had led him to believe the Strawberry Forest would not be very interesting, but he had to admit it was an incredible experience. In all the illustrations of strawberry plants they were usually small and low to the ground, but these were nothing like that. The ogreberries grew from tall stalks rising into the sky like corn, with the juicy red berries growing from them at all angles. The berries were unlike any strawberries he'd seen before, ranging in size from as small as his thumbnail, to larger than his head. They varied in color, from a light pink to a dark crimson. However, he sampled one of the smaller ones and confirmed that they tasted mostly the same as any strawberry he'd had before.

In fact, they were just a little bit better.

After a while of wandering around in awe, he began filling his basket with berries of various sizes and colors. The berries were easy to pick, coming off the vine with just a gentle tug, snapping off with a small bit of green at the top. The basket was almost full when he heard it.

A small squeak of fear, followed by many louder squeaks.

He dropped the basket and ran.

"Marigold? Edwina? Chica?" He called out, bending down low and frantically searching through the damp grass, littered with fallen berries. His heart hammered in his chest as he heard more squeaking, getting louder this time. He ran down the rows of strawberry plants, listening to the squeaking until he finally found them. Edwina was sprawled out on the grass, twisting around and squeaking. Her travelling cloak was trapped under a strawberry at least five times bigger than her. She was struggling to get out from under the large berry while Marigold and Chica were trying to get her to calm down.

Tristan ran forward and knelt down, rolling the strawberry off of her.

"Edwina, I'm so sorry, I should never have left you alone!" He exclaimed, fear and worry clouding his face. "I'll take better care of you in the future."

Edwina staggered to her feet, shaking out her cloak and dusting off her breeches. Then, she turned to Tristan and gave him a look that could wilt roses.

"What's that supposed to mean?" she said, her tone angry.

"I-I-I just mean, I'm supposed to protect you," Tristan stammered out.

Edwina raised herself to her full height, about six inches, held up her head and pulled out her sword, brandishing it at Tristan.

"Just because I am small doesn't mean I need you to take care of me, Tristan," she said.

"Yes, you do!" he replied before he could stop himself. "You almost got crushed by a strawberry!"

Edwina tsked at him, "Don't be silly, you just rushed over here too fast. I could have handled that just fine."

Marigold rolled her eyes, "Humans think they're so special cause they're tall."

"Mmmphf," Chica said, her cheeks bulging as she ate a strawberry with both paws.

Tristan pinched his nose.

"You're right, I'm so sorry, next time I'll just let the strawberry kill you."

Eventually, Edwina put her sword away, and after about ten minutes of frosty silence, Tristan finally made amends by finding a nice spot for them all to eat their basket of strawberries out of sight from the rest of the tourists.

He laid a blanket on the ground and set out some of the juiciest looking strawberries on it as well as a few of the cheeses and breads they had picked up in town.

"At last, I will taste a fresh strawberry!" Marigold said dramatically.

"Someone got started a little early," Edwina said, looking side-long at Chica.

"I was hungry," Chica said with a shrug. Her face and paws were bright red from strawberry juice and she looked tremendously proud of herself.

"Ahem." Marigold gave them a meaningful look and began again, thrusting her snout into the air. "*At last!* I will taste a fresh strawberry!"

Tristan tried not to laugh as Marigold cut herself a piece of the berry and held it up to the air like a valiant hero. She raised the piece of berry to her lips and nibbled thoughtfully.

"It is, as I had expected, far superior to *imported* strawberries," said Marigold in the knowing tone of one who has instantly become an expert on strawberries. "The fresh bite, the depth and richness of flavor. It's incomparable. I'm afraid I'll never be satisfied with an *imported* strawberry again," she said woefully.

"Isn't it an Ogreberry though?" Edwina said.

Marigold glared at her.

"Can't I just have a strawberry in peace, Edwina?"

"I'm just saying, you can still enjoy strawberries at home," Edwina said with a shrug.

Tristan could sense the tension in the air as Marigold stood up with her paws on her hips and he decided to intervene.

"I've got the, er, pamphlet here about the history of the Strawberry Forest if anyone would like to read it?"

The effect was immediate; all three mice scurried over to him, ready to learn more about the history of the island. It made sense, they were academics after all. Chica, the historian of the group, took it upon herself to read the pamphlet aloud to the group.

"Strawberry Island was founded by Dee Dee Berry of the Berry Explorers, sometime in the Reliacian Era. It is part of the Berry Galapagos, situated just North of the Fruitbasket Isles. The island known for its wide variety of berries and the noted giant strawberry plants, or Ogreberries as they are known regionally.

The main economy for the island is based around tourism, and the export of strawberries and strawberry-related goods. There are less than a hundred residents on the island, but the annual visitor count is well in the thousands, with hundreds of ships stopping at its port every year on the popular Spicer's Trail shipping route.

The history of the plants themselves is the source of some dispute. Some say that the Ogreberry trees were cultivated by an ancient civilization, created as an experiment by a magical botanist. A popular theory is that Ogres the size of mountains lived in the region thousands of years ago and left their berries behind. Others say the berries simply grew that way.

No one knows for sure how they came to be, but all can agree, they taste delicious!"

"That is absolutely true," Marigold said, hacking away at the giant berry and stuffing more into her bulging cheeks.

"Please go on Chica," Edwina said, taking a piece of strawberry from Marigold.

"That's it," Chica said, dropping the pamphlet with a frown. "The rest is just illustrations of strawberries and Dee Dee Berry."

"Huh. I'm not sure that was really with worth three coins, but it's alright I guess," Edwina said.

"Maybe our standards are just higher than most for historical research," Marigold said primly. "At least the berries are good!"

THE MOON WAS RISING high in the sky by the time Tristan brought the mice back to their cabin and unloaded all their strawberry-themed goods, setting the teapot down carefully in their boarding trunk. The gifts for back home were carefully put away in their luggage and the food was stacked on a blanket in the corner where the mice could easily reach it themselves when Tristan was away.

He retired to his bedroom with a cup of tea to rest after the long day adventuring with the Majesteria. His gaze fell on the itinerary from Ginger on the nightstand. It included information about the island's beloved tavern, The Wild Berry, and directions for how to get there from the ship.

Tristan looked at the paper for a moment and considered.

The conversation from the evening before had drifted into his mind many times that day. Wren's ex lovers...a man and a woman.

Did that mean, perhaps, he had a chance?

He dismissed the thought. A romantic interest in people of his gender did not indicate in any way that she would be attracted to a Majesteria Handler with a large pirate romance novel collection who didn't get out much.

He wasn't woefully inept in the romance department, thank goodness, but...it had been a while. Over the years he'd had lovers here and there; much like Wren he was attracted to many genders and had enjoyed the company of a select few. The past few years though, his job had kept him very busy and he rarely left Teakley, generally spending his evening reading or working on projects with the Majesteria. This state of affairs was just fine by him, most people he'd met weren't nearly as wonderful as the dreamy characters in his favorite books anyway.

At least, until he'd met Captain Wren.

He looked at the paper again.

Then he stood up and began pulling clothes out of his trunk.

Twenty indecisive minutes later and he was heading out across the deck in the moonlit night. He'd done his best to find something tavern appropriate among his rather bland wardrobe he normally wore at the Academy. He had worn his pearl earring, of course, and a dark shirt with no vest and black leather gloves. He'd pulled his hair out of its braid, letting the dirty blond waves fall around his shoulders. He had added his good cloak to complete the look, although he still felt that he was lacking that special something. He thought of the loose linen shirts the pirates all wore and realized that would be perfect.

But that didn't matter now because he didn't own one, and really, did he need to? He'd be back at Teakley in a few weeks where sweater vests and drab brown shirts just made sense. He didn't need to be dreaming of black leather pants and linen blouses billowing in the breeze.

He looked around the empty deck, the dark wood creaking under his boots and the soft breezes pulling at his clothes. The lanterns were swinging in the rigging again, their warm glow giving him a sense of comfort. Something about them made *The Snapdragon* feel like home.

He meandered across the deck, taking his time and feeling the breeze in his long hair as he headed towards the ramp down to the dock. He was about to ascend down it when he heard a thumping and someone said,

"Shhh!"

"Don't worry, there's no one around," a voice whispered.

"Even so, Captain said no one's to see us," the first voice said.

"Alright, well we'd best hurry then eh?" the other one said.

Tristan felt an unease come over him as he realized he was not supposed to be where he was. He looked around frantically and in a moment of panic decided his best bet was to duck behind a nearby barrel. He ran over and crouched down behind it, his heart pounding in his chest, and then peered cautiously over the top.

He saw a few crew-mates dragging some large crates up from the docks and onto the ship. The crates made a clinking, jangling sound as they moved. They were wearing very dark clothing and one of them was looking around suspiciously, making sure no one saw them moving the clattering crates.

Tristan held his breath until all the crates had been moved into the belly of the ship and the crew had disappeared inside. He sat there for a while, nervously wondering what to do. Were they smuggling illegal goods? Would they get into trouble for that? Could this endanger the Majesteria and the Royal Cinderflower?

He didn't know the answers to any of those questions.

So he did the only thing he could think of.

He stood up, shook out his cloak, and walked down to the tavern like nothing had ever happened.

THE WILD BERRY TAVERN was on the far end of the village. It was painted the dark red-purple of a berry wine, and had a motif of brambles and berries painted on the trim around the doors and windows. The lattice-covered windows were bright with warm glowing light spilling out into the dark night, and Tristan felt a tingle of excitement as he opened the door.

It was a cozy and warm tavern, clean and well kept with bouquets of wildflowers and baskets of fresh strawberries on all the tables. The Wild Berry was lively and busy, with a three-piece band playing a jig in the corner and many sailors and visitors drinking and chatting. Tristan watched the band for a moment, the lyre player swaying his hips back and forth as the drummer beat a rhythm on a large drum. There were a few people dancing to the music, including one person who seemed particularly enthusiastic. The slender woman was clambering onto a table and soon was standing on it and kicking her legs high into the air. Tristan watched her for a moment before he realized it was Birdy, the rather quiet woman he'd spoken to in the Healer's cabin. He saw the rest of the crew of *The Snapdragon* clustered around a large table towards the back.

When he looked towards them, Ginger waved and ushered him over.

He walked over to the table and waved awkwardly at the assembled crew.

"Ay, Frog Boy is here!" Basel said, cheerfully clapping him on the back so hard he nearly fell face-forward onto the table.

Tristan coughed as he recovered from the clap.

"Hello," he said.

Captain Wren was seated at the table, leaning her chair back against the wall and flipping her coin lazily. She wore her usual black leather pants, an assortment of silver rings, and a large black hat that came down over one of her eyes. Tristan felt his pulse quicken when she looked at him with her icy stare and tipped her hat in his direction.

Tavern socializing not being his forte, Tristan decided it was best to stick with a classic that no one would object to.

"Can I buy you all drinks?" he said with a smile.

A large cheer of "AYYYE!" went up from the pirate crew, and even Wren gave him something resembling a smile.

"Are you sure?" Ginger asked him quietly. "There's quite a lot of us."

"It's on the Academy's dime," Tristan assured her.

"Alright then, maybe a few pitchers of ale for the table then?"

Tristan nodded, "I'll be right back," he said, with one last look at Captain Wren.

He walked up to the bar and waited while the bartender attended to someone else. After a moment, the man turned and Tristan was momentarily speechless. The man had warm brown skin, dark hair, cheekbones that could cut glass, and eyes you could drown in. He wiped the bartop and nodded to Tristan

"Evenin," he said.

Tristan gulped. "Er, hello, could I get a four pitchers of beer for that table over there?"

"Of course," the handsome man said with a grin, "crew o' *The Snapdragon*, eh?"

Tristan was briefly lost in his dazzling smile.

"What? Oh, yes."

"How's my ex-girlfriend then?" The gorgeous man asked cheerfully as he poured the beer into the pitchers.

"You're..." Tristan suddenly realized who he must be talking to.

"Calyrn, yes," the man said turning around and giving Tristan a wink that made him weak in the knees.

"She's good, I'm um, I'm a guest," Tristan said awkwardly.

"How's *MY* ex-girlfriend you mean," said a woman's voice. Willow stepped out from behind Calryn, and Tristan found himself in what is known to some as a bisexual panic. She had short dark hair, tattoos up and down her arms, and was heart-stoppingly beautiful.

Wren certainly had good taste, you could say that much.

Her husband laughed and gave her a peck on the cheek. He set one of the pitchers on the bartop and began pouring another.

There was a little hiss from beside him. Tristan looked down and saw a small Dragonling curled up in a basket on the counter. It had bright blue scales and was about the size of large cat.

Tristan gasped in surprise.

"A Dragonling?" he said. He knew how rare and expensive the tiny house-trained dragons were. He'd often dreamed of owning one himself, but they were way out of his budget.

"Aye, that's little Pretzel, ain't she a sweetheart?" Calryn set another pitcher of beer on the counter and came over to scratch the back of the dragonling's head. The tiny dragon made an adorable chirp of happiness.

"They're dreadfully expensive, of course," Calryn said with a sigh, "but she's the best friend a barkeep could have. Can't run a bar in these parts without a Dragonling. They keep all the pests away, and the tourists just love 'em. Plus, she roasts the chestnuts like nobody's business."

He held up a small bowl of chestnuts and the Dragonling opened one sleepy eye and then huffed a small burst of flame over the bowl, cooking the chestnuts instantly.

Tristan was delighted.

"I think I've got to get a bowl of chestnuts now," he said with a grin.

"See? She pays for herself," Calryn said, laughing.

Tristan took the nuts while the charming man returned to pouring beer. He munched on a way-too-hot chestnut and tried to look anywhere else besides the arrestingly beautiful couple behind the bar.

His eyes fell on a poster on the wall, and he felt a chill go down his spine.

It was the poster from before of the wanted man, the mage stealer, Mad Richard. There was something about his eyes, Tristan felt like they were following him.

"What about this Mad Richard, should we be worried?" he asked, attempting a casual tone, though he felt a cold fear stirring inside him.

Calryn brought the other pitchers of beer up to the counter and handed Tristan his bill. He frowned and said,

"He's definitely a menace, I know I certainly wouldn't want to find myself alone with him. These posters don't even begin to do justice to the chilling stories I've heard about him. I expect you'll probably be alright at sea with Wren at the helm, but I'd make sure to keep your wits about you when you're on land."

Tristan handed him some coins and said, "But what about the Royal Mariners? Won't they find him and bring him to justice?"

"Ha! Good one. I can see why Wren likes you," Calryn replied, pocketing the coins.

"Oh, it's not like that, I'm just a guest..." Tristan trailed off but Calyrn was already halfway down the bar helping another customer.

Tristan brought the pitchers back to the table, still thinking about Mad Richard. Birdy hadn't stopped dancing on the table to the band, but she was now joined by a few of the bar's other patrons.

There was a cheer from the crew as he put the drinks down, and Emyr began pouring glasses for everyone

"I knew you were a good one Froggy!" Basel said, raising a glass of ale in his direction.

Tristan poured himself a mug of the ale and looked for a place to sit. He moved away from Basel, hoping to avoid more heavy claps on the back, and ended up between Ginger and Emyr.

"Is that Birdy?" he asked Ginger once he was sitting. The riotous dancer looked nothing like the quiet woman he'd met on the ship.

Ginger laughed, "Aye, she loves a good jig."

"She's usually so quiet," Tristan said.

"Not after she's had a few drinks," Emyr said, with a snicker.

The band picked up a new song, this one a livelier number which many of the crew seemed to know. Basel let out a howl and jumped up from their chair to do a little dance around the tavern. Most of the crew laughed and went back to chatting.

"I was wondering about something," Tristan began, noticing as he spoke that Wren had turned to look at him, her intense gaze making him swallow nervously. "I saw there was a, um, wanted poster? For a, er, pirate who...steals mages?" He suddenly realized this might be a tricky subject.

"Aye, Mad Richard," Wren said, nodding.

"Yes," Tristan said, "he seems...quite dangerous."

"He is, you'd do well to be cautious when you're on land," she said firmly.

"But what about The Royal Mariners? I know they patrol this part of the sea-"

Wren snorted "Mariners? They won't be helping anyone."

"Why not?" Tristan asked.

"The Mariners don't do anything but scratch their bums, polish their badges, and take the Queen's wages for doin' nothing. I thought everyone knew that," she said.

"Oh," Tristan said. He found that hard to imagine, and he wasn't sure he believed her. In fact, he wasn't sure what to believe, especially after what he'd seen on the deck earlier, but he knew one thing for sure. He was certainly glad that the only pirates in The Wild Berry were Wren and her crew.

Chapter Eight

Tristan woke to a hammering on the door. He opened one bleary eye and realized he had a pounding headache. He stumbled out of bed, glancing briefly out his porthole and noticing that it was just barely after dawn, and the sun was beginning to peek out on the horizon in the grey morning light.

The hammering continued.

Tristan groaned.

He wrenched open the door of his bedroom and shouted, "I'm *COMING!* HANG ON!"

His outburst caused Marigold to jump and drop her quill.

"Calm down Tristan," she scolded. "I'm sure it's not a big deal."

She was already dressed for the day and happily scribbling academic notes on a large scroll in front of the hearth.

"Ehhh??" Edwina said, sitting up groggily under a pile of small blankets.

The face-down lump on the rug that he knew to be Chica did not move. Chica could sleep through a hurricane.

The hammering continued.

"What should I do?" Tristan asked the mice helplessly. He was too tired and hungover to figure it out.

"See who it is!" Marigold said. "We'll jump in the boarding trunk if we need to."

"Oh. Okay," Tristan said, yawning.

He pulled open the door and finally, finally, the hammering stopped.

"Yes, hello?" he said.

Standing on his doorstep was Ginger, her bright blue hair shiny and fresh, she looked for all the world like a person who had slept calmly for eight hours after a relaxing day indoors. You would never have guessed she'd spent the night drinking ale, playing Cherry Basket, and dancing on the tables with Birdy. Tristan was totally confused by how incredibly calm and put together she appeared.

Clearly, he was not cut out for pirate life.

"Mornin' Tristan," Ginger said with a cheery grin, "The Captain would like to see you in her office."

"Now?" Tristan said, rubbing his face and trying to get his hungover brain to work. "Can it wait a few hours?"

"Yes, now," Ginger said sternly, her face still in a big grin.

"Okay, umm, I guess I can," Tristan mumbled.

"Great!" Ginger said cheerfully, taking his mumbling as an affirmation. "I'll just wait out here while you get dressed, but please make it snappy."

Tristan looked down and realized he was wearing his nightshirt and nothing else, his hair a tangled mess after last night.

"Okay, right. Yes," He said, closing the door. He leaned his back against it and took a deep breath. He really didn't want to see The Captain right now when his head was pounding and his vision was swimming, but really, what could he do?

"I guess I'd better go," he said.

"Seems like it," Marigold said, dipping her expertly sharpened quill into a pot of ink nearly as big as she was. "I think you'd better hurry or Ginger might start pounding on the door again."

Tristan shuddered at the thought.

A few chaotic minutes later and he was being bustled down the hallway by Ginger, trying to ignore his aching head. Her boots clicked decisively on the polished floors as she steered Tristan past the cabins and up to the deck. It was quieter than usual as they crossed the ship, most of the crew was not awake yet, and the few that were looked miserable to be there. He could relate.

He squinted at the brightness and shielded his eyes from the evil sunshine as Ginger led him to the windowed cabin on the upper deck and knocked briskly on the brass-handled door.

There was a mumbled sound from within, and Ginger opened the door for him. Once he was inside, Ginger left and shut the door firmly behind her, leaving him along with The Captain and his hangover.

The Captain's office was beautiful but messy, which was to be expected. The walls were a dark wood with a teal carpeted floor. In the middle was a desk scattered with paperwork, maps, and mostly-empty bottles of rum, with a few leather chairs clustered around it. In a corner was an over-stuffed wardrobe full of rolled up maps and dark leather map cases.

Oh, and of course, there was the weapons.

So many weapons.

Swords, knives, crossbows, throwing axes, brass knuckles.

They were scattered around the place like dangerous knick-knacks, stuffed into piles of paperwork, resting against the wall.

Tristan had seen weapons before, of course, but they were usually for display, beautifully polished and carefully hung on a wall beside a plaque.

These were not like that.

Wren was holding one such weapon, a long, small-bladed rapier with a large ornate handle. She had a polishing cloth in the other hand and was wiping it along the blade, which gleamed in the sunlight streaming through the small windows.

"Good morning Mr. Mulberry," she said when he walked in. "Do take a seat."

For her part, The Captain looked almost as fresh as Ginger. She had on her usual black breeches and linen shirt, though today she had also added a brown leather vest. She was sipping from a large mug of coffee and Tristan could smell its enticing aroma from across the room.

Tristan walked over to a dark green chair and sat down, his wobbly legs grateful to no longer be burdened with attempting to hold him upright.

"How are you this morning?" Wren asked with a level of brightness he would not normally associate with the moody Captain. If he'd been a little more awake he would have sensed something was strange about this.

"Tired," Tristan said, gazing longingly at the large pot of coffee sitting on her desk. Her eyes followed his gaze but she did not offer him any.

"I'm sorry to hear that," she said calmly, wiping the shining, sharp blade. "Did you not have a good time at The Wild Berry?"

"A little too much of a good time, I think," Tristan said with a laugh, running his hands across his tired face. "That coffee smells delightful, did Basel make it?" he asked hopefully, his eyes focusing again on the mug.

"No, I made it," Wren replied solemnly.

She did not offer him any coffee.

"Oh, well, um, it smells great," Tristan said.

She still did not offer him any coffee.

She cleared her throat and took another sip of the coffee. She seemed to savor the taste as she leaned back in her chair and resumed cleaning her sharp sword edge.

At another time Tristan might have been intimidated by the razor-sharp blade in her hands. Or he might have found it seductive and dangerous.

But right now, he wasn't thinking about any of that.

Only one thing was calling to Tristan's heart in this moment.

Coffee.

Finally, Wren set the sword down on the table and leaned towards him, putting the glistening blade between them.

"Tell me Mr. Mulberry," she began, but he interrupted her.

"Tristan is fine," he said, automatically.

She nodded, "Tristan then, how has your journey been so far? Would you say you're having a good trip?"

Tristan's brain was still half asleep but he had just enough awareness to catch the dangerous edge to her voice, the glinting of the sword, the powerful grace of her movements. He wasn't sure what was happening but he started to feel like he was out of his depth.

"It's been very...good," he said cautiously, careful to remain neutral as he tried to figure out what she was angling towards.

"Wonderful, wonderful," she said, leaning back again. She pulled a small dagger from somewhere and twirled it in her hands, the metal catching the sunlight brightly. After a moment she set it down on the desk between them, but it was unmistakably within her reach.

Tristan gulped, he didn't know what was happening but he really wished he'd been able to have some of that coffee before this conversation began.

"I think it could be improved by some, um, coffee. Perhaps a pastry?" He ventured.

"Ah yes, all in due time," she said firmly.

She took another sip from her mug of coffee and then placed it down on the opposite side of the table only a few inches from where Tristan was sitting, the smell filling his senses.

"I'm just wondering," she said, softly, dangerously. "Now that you've enjoyed our hospitality, do you think we could perhaps come to a truce, you and I?"

"A truce?" Tristan asked, confused. "What do you mean?"

"I mean, I just think friends...tell each other things. Like what kinds of magical items they are travelling with," she said smoothly.

With those words his brain finally woke up and Tristan realized this was a set up. Wren knew he would be hung over, she knew he'd be desperate for the steaming mug of coffee so tantalizingly out of reach, she knew he'd be more likely to answer her questions.

Immediately, Tristan put up his defenses and changed his attitude.

"I think *friends* let each other have their secrets," he said. "Like, say, when people carry a bunch of jangling crates onto a ship in the middle of the night."

Wren frowned, but she looked the tiniest bit impressed. She picked up the knife and twirled it in hands.

"What my crew does in the night is no business of yours," she said sharply.

"Fair enough, but the contents of my trunks are no business of yours," he countered.

He leaned back in the chair, his shoulders stiff, his hands shaking a little.

"Oh, but they are," she said, spinning the glittering blade. "Because this is *my* ship. Are you sure you don't want to be friends Tristan?"

"I think friends give each other coffee, and don't wake up people after a night of drinking," he said coldly.

There it was again.

That little quirking of her lip.

She was frustrated, but just a little bit impressed.

"I'm sorry, I didn't realize you couldn't hold your liquor," she said.

"It's only been a few hours! How are you not hungover? How did you get enough sleep?" he said, a little desperately.

"Who said I slept?" Wren asked.

He wasn't sure if she was serious or not, but it didn't matter. Not really. He wasn't going to tell her what she wanted to know.

Especially not like this.

He felt the frustration and anger rising above his throbbing headache to take over. How dare she try to manipulate him like this!

"The Academy paid you, above market rate I believe, to take me to my destination, keep me safe, and treat me well along the way. I really don't think you want to upset them. Now. Do you actually need anything from me or can I go back to my cabin?" he said bitterly.

Wren stood up, her eyes flashing with that same fierceness he'd seen the first day they met. She stabbed the dagger's point into the desk, and leaned back against the wall with her arms folded.

"You're not my enemy, Tristan. But you must understand, this crew is my family. Teakley Academy is well known in these parts. Magical books and artifacts, ambitious mages, and the terrifying Majesteria; there are any number of strange things that they might want to transport. Personally, I don't mind transporting dangerous goods, but I *need* to know what they are. How else can I keep my crew safe?"

Tristan calmed down a bit at her words. He could see she was sincere and he believed her that her only concern was the security of the crew. Over the past few days, Tristan had started to become very attached to the crew of *The Snapdragon*.

He could see her point.

But he had made a promise.

"I'm sorry Captain," he said. "But it's Academy policy. I've made a promise, and I can't break those rules."

She was quiet for a while, looking him over, assessing him.

He knew she was trying to read in his eyes how dangerous he was.

How honest he was.

He hated to think about what face she might make if she knew what he was hiding in his cabin.

She sat back down and reached under her desk. She pulled out a mug and a small plate of pastries. She handed them to Tristan and then poured some coffee into the mug.

"Thank you," Tristan said, relief washing over him as he took a sip of the warm liquid and let the coffee work it's magic on his aching head.

Wren put away the swords and pulled out her gold coin to flip while she talked.

"My old Captain, the woman who ran this ship before me, she was an incredible person. She had a saying that I always found quite useful."

"Mphm?" Tristan said, his mouth full of pastry. It was exactly what he needed to get this hangover out of his system.

Wren leaned back and put her leather boots up on the desk.

"She used to say *'if the rule is rotten, it's our duty to break it'*. Sometimes, the people who make the rules may not have a good heart, or a sound mind, and they might make a rotten rule. So tell me Tristan, is the rule rotten?"

Tristan immediately thought of Blanchard with his weaselly little face and obnoxious opinions. There was no question.

But then he thought of the Majesteria and he knew that Wren had no chance to get him to reveal his secrets, no matter how many blades she waved in his face.

~

AFTER TAKING a long nap in his cabin to recover from the morning's interrogation, Tristan woke again at the sound of a bell. He sat up in bed, realizing he had fallen asleep in his clothing, and rubbed his face as the bell kept on ringing.

He suddenly remembered Wren loudly declaring to the assembled guests that they would ring a bell at noon when it was time to depart from Strawberry Island. He decided he wanted to watch them leave from the deck this time, so he made himself a cup of tea and grabbed a fluffy pastry from the Canteen and wandered up to the top deck.

The air was warm but breezy when he arrived on the deck of the ship, and bustling with activity as people prepared the ship to leave. He spotted Ginger's bright blue hair standing at the railing and went to stand next to her and look down at Strawberry Island.

"Good afternoon," he said.

"Aye Tristan," Ginger said with a grin. "Sorry about this mornin', Captain's orders."

"I understand," he said, taking a sip of his tea.

Ginger gave him a nod before returning to looking at the beach below.

Tristan followed her gaze and then raised his eyebrows in surprise.

On the warm, sandy beach to the left of the docks, a few people seemed to be having an argument. A man he recognized as one of the other guests was standing there with a few chests at his feet. Captain Wren was a few feet away and screaming loudly at him while brandishing her sword. Emyr was holding her back and vaguely trying to calm her down.

"What's going on?" Tristan asked, surprised.

"That man there, Mr. Werthers," Ginger said, pointing to the man who was currently flinching as Wren shouted more obscenities at him. "Some people have been having their valuables go missing, coin purses gone from their pockets, that kind of thing. We did a lil investigating this morning and found out he's been pickpocketing. I think he'll be staying on Strawberry Island for the time being."

"Goodness" Tristan said. "Should I be concerned?"

"Don't worry, Wren has it handled," Ginger said, "just enjoy the show."

Tristan leaned back and took a bite of his pastry, savoring the sweet strawberry jam Basel had filled it with. Captain Wren was advancing on the man now, shaking her fist in his face while Emyr tried to get her attention. The man looked terrified and was stumbling backwards down the beach, looking desperately from side to side for help.

"Is she going to cut him to ribbons?" Tristan asked, thinking back to the weapons in the Captain's cabin.

Ginger looked appalled, "Captain Wren? Goodness no, her bark is far worse than her bite. She's just a little bit overprotective of the ship and her crew."

"But she has so many swords..." Tristan said.

"You've been reading too many pirate novels," Ginger said, laughing.

A moment later they heard a door open nearby and a devilishly handsome man walked out onto the deck from the door of Emyr's cabin. He looked very tired, and was slowly buttoning up his pants. He presumably had a shirt but he hadn't bothered to put it on; merely draped it over one shoulder, leaving his toned and muscular chest shining in the afternoon sun. He wandered up to Ginger and Tristan and said,

"Pardon me, have you seen Emyr?"

Tristan's tongue was tied, so all he did was point down to the beach below. The handsome man leaned over the railing for a moment, his shoulders rippling, and took in the scene. He turned around and ran a hand through his shiny dark hair.

"I see," he said. "I really must be going, can you give him a message for me?"

"No problem," Ginger replied, looking like she was about to crack up. Tristan suspected the crew would be teasing Emyr about this at the Canteen tonight.

"Just tell him thank you, I had a lovely evening," he said demurely, before adding "and morning."

He started to turned away and then his gaze fell on Tristan. He stopped and

looked him over for a moment, studying him, taking in his sharp jawline, mussed clothing, and lightly tanned skin. Then he gave a loud whistle and said,

"You should come by the Wild Berry next time you're on Strawberry Island, sailor. I'm the dishwasher there, but don't let that fool you. I can show you a *very* good time, handsome."

He gave Tristan a saucy wink, which caused him to choke on his pastry.

The man smiled and wandered down the ramp and off the ship, whistling to himself while Tristan coughed violently.

Ginger slapped him roughly on the back, "Keep it together, Froggy," she said with a laugh.

"My stars, is everyone who works at the Wild Berry hot?" he asked after he'd regained his breath.

"Seems like it," Ginger said with a laugh. "I guess Emyr really does have a man in every port."

Tristan laughed, took a sip of his tea, and returned to watching the scene on the beach. It looked like Emyr had finally managed to calm Wren down a bit. She was now opening the man's chests and pulling items out while Emyr stood between the two of them as a mediator.

Just then, a figure emerged from the other side of the beach, running sort of weirdly, stopping every now and then to hop on one foot and shake their hands.

"Who's that?" Tristan asked, squinting to see the figure in the sunlight.

"Oh boy," Ginger said, shaking her head. "Never a dull moment on *The Snapdragon*."

As the person came into view he realized it was Birdy. She was running down the beach with only one shoe, burning her other foot on the hot sand. She was waving her arms in the air trying to stop the ship from leaving without her.

Eventually she spotted Wren on the beach and slowed to a walk.

"You're quite a wild crew aren't you," Tristan observed.

Ginger chuckled, "You don't know the half of it."

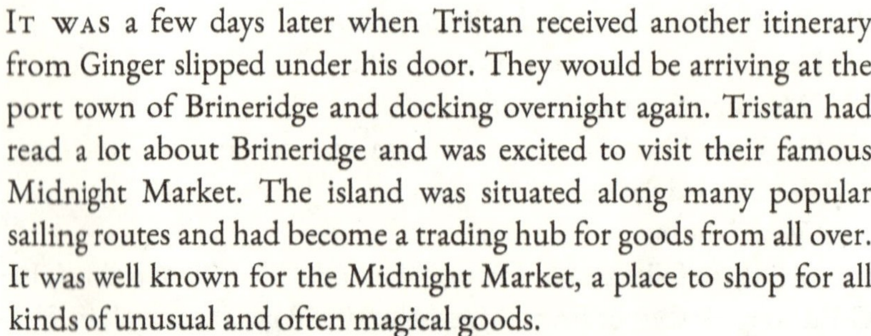

It was a few days later when Tristan received another itinerary from Ginger slipped under his door. They would be arriving at the port town of Brineridge and docking overnight again. Tristan had read a lot about Brineridge and was excited to visit their famous Midnight Market. The island was situated along many popular sailing routes and had become a trading hub for goods from all over. It was well known for the Midnight Market, a place to shop for all kinds of unusual and often magical goods.

The Market, which began at dusk and ended at dawn, was a

large marketplace where vendors from all over came to sell their wares to merchants, travellers, and tourists alike. He'd heard it was beloved among the chefs of the realm for its incredible selection of ingredients from across the islands, with many travelling to Brineridge to source specialty foods and spices.

Tristan wasn't much of a cook but he loved a market with interesting things to buy, particularly when it meant he could hunt for a good bargain or an unusual object. There were a few smaller markets back home, and he had found some of his favorite books and trinkets there, so he was very excited to explore the Midnight Market.

The ship arrived at Brineridge in the early morning. He had just finished his breakfast and decided to head up to the deck to get a view of the new island.

Tristan emerged on the deck to a hubbub of activity. He saw lots of passengers he recognized from dinners in the Canteen: Mrs. Waltingham the pony breeder and her husband, a witch named Maggie, Milo De Nilmon, and quite a few others. All were gathered around Ginger and Emyr, with an ever-growing pile of luggage and trunks.

Ginger was shouting out names and scribbling them down on her clipboard, the big feather of her quill moving furiously. Wren stood off nearby, casually leaned against the railing, wearing her Captain's Hat. She twirled her coin and nodded her head approvingly from time to time. Tristan noticed she did this a lot, he wondered briefly if perhaps merely the presence of a Captain was all that was needed to lend authority to her crew.

He walked up and stopped next to her,

"Morning Captain," he said.

She tipped her cap at him but maintained observing the crew with her shrewd dark eyes.

"What's going on?" he asked.

"All these folks are leaving us," she said. "They'll be taking The Great Magick Carpet from Brineridge. It will get them to Fairefeux a few days sooner so they can experience more of the Coronation

festivities. They can't take their luggage with them though, so they're leaving it with us and we will deliver it to them at Fairefeux when we arrive."

Tristan was surprised. "But...why would they do that?"

"Arrive at the Coronation early and get to take a ride on a giant magic carpet? Seems pretty obvious to me. But your ticket was *very specific* that you not be separated from your luggage under any circumstances."

She turned her piercing gaze on him.

"Now, why was that?"

Tristan coughed. "Academy business," he mumbled glumly.

"Right, Academy business, of course," she sighed and returned to watching the guests. Tristan thought about what she'd said for a minute and then realized something.

"But they'll miss the Ruins of Ahmet!" he said, aghast.

Wren chuckled.

"You'd be surprised to know that most people aren't as interested in looking at a pile of dusty rocks as you are, Tristan," she said, her lips quirking up at the sides.

"It's not just a pile of rocks! It's the sacred temple where the great warrior Duchess Xavier took her last stand!" He paused. "I'm being...academic again, aren't I?"

"Just a little," she said with a low laugh. She turned to him with playfulness sparkling in her eyes, "but it's cute."

Tristan felt his stomach do a somersault at her words. But before he could figure out what to do about it, there was a crashing from the deck as one of the trunks finally wobbled off the precarious pile.

There was a stunned silence followed by a cacophony of shouting and running around.

"Duty calls," Wren said, and pushed off the railing and into the fray.

~

Tristan was just finishing getting dressed for the Midnight Market when he heard shouting from the deck. He finished putting on his Teakley Academy brooch, and paused when there was a loud thump on the roof of his room. He dashed out of the cabin and up the stairs where he saw a very unexpected scene.

A few dozen bedraggled looking men in Royal Mariner uniforms were milling about the ship, with a cluster of them up by Wren's office, yelling at her and the crew. He drifted across the deck while observing the shouting men.

Tristan had been raised to believe that Royal Mariners and Queen's Guards were the kind of honest, upstanding people he could trust with his life and his safety. Nothing about these men suggested they were like that at all besides their gold-buttoned jackets.

They were dirty and loud, they walked with bored arrogance and sneered as they poked at the ship. They leered at the crew and turned barrels over for the fun of it.

In short, they were bullies.

He arrived at the other side of the deck where he could finally hear the conversation.

"Come on Frisk, I already gave you the coins," Wren said. She was backed up against the door of her office, guarding the entrance with her body. She was full of fiery rage, but it was the first time Tristan had seen her look anything but supremely confident.

One of the officers picked up a large barrel of oranges and dumped it out across the deck, sending oranges rolling in all directions.

"Oops!" he said with a laugh.

The leader of the group, a man who looked like he'd never said no to a bad idea in his life, picked up a nearby stool and slammed it onto the deck, breaking it in half and sending splinters flying.

"I told you, we need more. You're a *pirate*, remember?" He spat the word like it disgusted him. "If you recall, there's a rather dangerous *pirate* going about these parts, Mad Richard. How do I know he's not here?"

Wren folded her arms and glared at him, "Don't be stupid, I hate him as much as anyone else. Probably more."

"Mmm, but that's what you would say, isn't it beautiful?" The man said, leaning over her and trailing a small knife along her neck. She grimaced and her eyes looked at him with pure hatred, but she didn't stop him. "No, I think we're definitely going to need some more *proof* that he's not here."

Tristan suddenly remembered the jangling crates stored below the deck and realized that it could be a very big problem if the men searched the ship and things took a turn for the worse. For a start he'd have to find a new way to get to the Coronation. But more than that, he knew whatever Wren was doing with those crates wasn't something she deserved to be put in prison for.

He decided it was time to take a stand.

He took a deep breath, clenched his fist, and squared his shoulders.

"Excuse me, good sir," he said in the haughtiest voice he could muster.

The man turned around and looked at him with his cruel eyes. He moved away from Wren and walked towards Tristan. Fisk wore a bright blue uniform with gold buttons, the jacket hanging open over a dirty shirt. His big shoulders strained at the edges of the woolen jacket, and his close-cropped hair was pushed back with grease. As he approached, Tristan noticed he had an overpowering smell of stale beer.

"What's your name, Officer?" Tristan said politely.

"Lieutenant Fisk," the man said, tapping the badge on his lapel with a dirty fingernail. "Who might you be?"

"Tristan Mulberry," he said with a gracious bow. "I'm sure there's just been a misunderstanding, Lieutenant, there's no need for conflict. As you can see by the brooch I have here, I'm a representative of Teakley Academy. This vessel is transporting me to the

Queen's Coronation. I can assure you on my honor as a Scholar that there are no hidden pirates on this ship, and there is no need for any of this strife."

Tristan rocked on his heels while the men gaped at him after he gave his little speech.

Wren groaned and pinched her nose.

After a minute of staring, they burst into laughter.

It was not fun laughter. There was no joy to it. It was the kind of laughter that often precedes blood.

One of the Mariners advanced on him, he had a wiry beard and foul breath. Before Tristan knew what was happening, the man ripped the brooch off his cloak and threw it to one of the other Mariners. Tristan watched with horror as the men looked at the brooch, laughing, and tossed it to the Lieutenant.

"How do we know you didn't steal this off some poor academic loser?" said one of the Mariners, earning him a chorus of laughter.

A small greasy-looking man next to the Lieutenant said,

"I ain't never seen no Scholar as looks like him."

"Too good looking by half," another man added.

"Hair of flaxen gold," someone else said.

The Lieutenant held his hand up for silence.

"We're at sea precious, your little trinkets don't mean anything here."

He threw the brooch down on the deck with a clatter.

"How dare you!" Tristan said, but before he could continue the Mariner nearest him pushed him, hard. Tristan stumbled a few feet and fell, sprawling onto the smooth wooden deck at Wren's feet.

Lieutenant Fisk looked him in the eyes for just a moment, his gaze steely. "Don't be stupid," he said and turned his attention back to Wren.

Tristan looked up at her and their eyes met. He wasn't sure what to do, but she motioned with her hands for him to stay down. He decided to trust her, so he stayed where he was and watched.

Wren handed a small bag tinkling with the sound of coins to the Lieutenant.

"That's all I can spare," she said. "You know I'm not hiding Mad Richard, I'm a Registered Pirate Vessel and they checked me. I'm clean Fisk, let it go."

Lieutenant Fisk took the bag and peered inside it.

"I don't know," he said, "I'm not sure this is enough, we might need to search your cabin Captain, how do we know you're not hiding Mad Richard in your *bed*?"

Some of the Mariners sniggered.

Wren looked disgusted but she pulled herself up and said,

"How much, Fisk?"

He smiled. Tristan could see he was toying with her like a cat and he loved to watch her dangle on the string. He peeked in the bag again.

"Oh, about double this," he said.

Wren's mouth dropped open.

"You can't be serious," she said.

"I'm *deadly* serious," Fisk said, letting his dirty fingers linger over the large cutlass at his hip. "Of course, there are other ways you could pay," he said, leaning against the door frame and towering his body over hers.

Tristan thought he might vomit.

"No thank you," Wren said crisply, holding his gaze firmly, even as her body recoiled away from him.

One of the men came up and whispered something to Lieutenant Fisk who raised an eyebrow and then shrugged. He turned to look Tristan over again, but this time the appraisal was not the same, he was making a very different calculation.

"We'll take the pretty boy instead if you're not...available," he said.

Tristan scrambled back across the deck involuntarily, trying to put as much distance between himself and the disgusting men as possible.

Wren glared at the Lieutenant.

"He's not for sale, I'll pay the coins," she said.

The Lieutenant looked over Tristan and then Wren with a

hungry look in his eyes that made Tristan's skin crawl. He seemed to think it over for a moment, twirling his knife in his hands.

"Fine, but make it another hundred just for being cheeky."

Wren looked at him, her face seething. For a moment, Tristan thought she might strike him. She was obviously thinking about it.

But eventually she gritted her teeth and nodded, dipping into her cabin to get the money. She came back a few minutes later and threw another bag at Fisk's chest.

"There you go, now get the hell off my ship."

"Mmm, I love a feisty woman," Fisk said. "Makes her more fun to bring to heel. Don't worry Wren, we can have some fun next time. Alright boys, on to the next ship!"

One of the Mariners handed Wren a stack of papers before he left and said,

"These are for your guests, make sure everyone gets one."

One of the papers drifted down onto the deck where Tristan was still sitting, dumbfounded. He picked it up and looked at it.

It was a Wanted poster for Mad Richard.

CHAPTER NINE

"Hmm, he does look quite terrifying," Marigold said. Her paw was on her hip as she looked down at the Wanted poster of Mad Richard. "You said he's been terrorizing these waters?"

"Yes," Tristan said with a sigh. He was on his second cup of tea after returning to the cabin, but he still wasn't feeling right.

The Majesteria had helped him sew up the hole in his cloak and he'd put his brooch back on, but he was still on edge after the experience with Lieutenant Fisk.

He'd felt so...helpless.

It was an awful feeling, and remembering the experience gave him a gnawing feeling in his gut.

He was starting to see that the world at sea was more than a little different from Teakley Academy.

One thing that was really worrying him was Mad Richard.

Because if *this* was what the Royal Mariners were like, how bad was the guy they were chasing?

"Don't worry Tristan we won't let him steal you," Edwina said, pulling out her miniature sword and waving it around. "I'm not scared of him, I'll take 'em on! He won't know what hit 'em!"

Tristan looked at the little mouse with her sword and laughed, she looked ridiculous but he knew that, in fact, she probably *could* take him on.

The thought lifted his spirits.

He had been so helpless today because he was in Wren's world, just a bystander to a terrible situation he knew very little about.

But when he was in *his* world, the world of Majesteria and magic, he wasn't helpless. The Majesteria could have magically blown Lieutenant Fisk and all his stupid men off the ship and out to sea if they'd wanted to.

He had to remember what he was doing and what really mattered.

Getting the Royal Cinderflower to the Coronation.

That was what they were here for.

But still...

He wished he could have done more.

"HANG ON, I'M ALMOST READY!" Marigold called from inside their Boarding Trunk. "I just need to find my hat."

The door of their Boarding Trunk opened dramatically and the three mice strutted out onto the rug, twirling around in their outfits for the Midnight Market.

Edwina wore her usual suede trousers and tiny sword, but she had added a black velvet waistcoat embroidered with stars.

Marigold wore a bright green dress she had embroidered with strawberries, an ode to her experience of a truly fresh berry, and her black witch hat which she had adorned with tiny flowers.

Chica came last in a deep blue robe carefully embroidered with small silver beads in the shape of constellations.

Tristan applauded their outfits and they took dramatic bows.

"You all look so dashing," Tristan said. "It's a shame no one but me will get to see you."

"What do you mean?" Marigold asked. "I think the market should be busy enough we can wander around freely."

Tristan looked surprised, "How would that work? I'll be with some of the crew from the ship."

Marigold twitched her whiskers in distress, "What?! Why is the crew coming with us?"

"They invited me yesterday," Tristan said, "they're familiar with the market and are doing some shopping for supplies. I thought it would be great to go with someone who knows their way around."

Edwina frowned "But...what about us?"

"What about you?" Tristan asked, confused. "You're coming too, aren't you?"

He held up their Traveling Satchel.

"Yes, but...I want to *really* explore the market!" Edwina cried. "We want to go to Quincy Quint's Quill Emporium. If you'll recall, Bianca got one of their quills when she visited with her handler last year, and it was of exceptional quality."

Tristan frowned, "I think the crew are going to be buying food and herbalist supplies, I don't know if we'd have time to go to Quincy Quint's. Do you really need to get another quill?"

As soon as the words were out of his mouth, Tristan knew he'd made a mistake.

Edwina looked horrified, "*How dare you!* Quincy Quint makes unique, hand-crafted quills of exceptional quality, the best in the realm. We *can't* go to the Midnight Market and not get quills! Why can't you just tell the crew you can't go with them?"

"But...I want to go with them," Tristan said. "I was really looking forward to it, I'm sure they know all the best spots."

"Well, *I* want to go to the quill maker and wander the market in my fabulous outfit, not be cooped up in a little bag all day," Edwina replied, hands on her hips.

Marigold stepped between them and said, "Calm down you two, I think I have a solution."

Tristan looked relieved, Edwina looked skeptical but she flicked her tail and waited for Marigold to continue.

"Why don't we split up?" Marigold suggested.

"WHAT!" Edwina and Tristan both said at once.

Marigold giggled, "You two are far more alike than you realize. Really, it's not that crazy an idea. Edwina, Chica, and I will go to the Quill Emporium, and Tristan can go with the pirate crew."

"What if something happens to him?" Edwina asked.

"What if something happens to you?" Tristan asked.

"Us?" Edwina scoffed. "*We'll* be fine, we can handle a market. It's you I'm worried about Tristan. A market like this is a dangerous place full of scoundrels and rogues."

"I can handle myself *just fine*," Tristan said tartly.

"Don't you remember what happened when you went to buy those magic beans on Pearsy?" Edwina reminded him.

"Yes, I remember I didn't have the coin purse I was supposed to. Who's fault was that?" Tristan countered.

Edwina glared at him and put her paw on her sword hilt.

"Okay, okay, settle down," Marigold said. "I think it's decided then, we will each explore the market on our own, and meet up back at the ship."

"I don't like this at all," Tristan said, folding his arms with a sigh.

"Me either," Edwina said, pacing around the rug with her tail whisking back and forth.

"Do either of you have any better suggestions?"

Edwina and Tristan opened their mouths to speak but before they could, Marigold held up a paw.

"Ahem. Suggestions that are not just you getting your way?"

Edwina closed her mouth and glared.

Tristan sighed and rolled his eyes.

Neither of them said anything.

"There we go then," Marigold said, clapping her paws together. "You're both miserable, which means we've reached a compromise."

~

It was just after sunset when Tristan finally left the ship with Basel, Bonnie, and Emyr. After helping the mice prepare their bags for the journey he'd met the crew on the deck, and they set off together down the ramp, the way lit by large lanterns, swaying in the warm sea breeze.

Bonnie was wearing a dark green dress with lacing up the front, her curling black hair pinned up on her head with a jeweled comb. She carried a large burlap bag on her shoulder and an empty woven basket over her arm, ready to fill with herbal supplies from the market.

Basel wore their usual sleeveless tunic of cream-colored linen, which showed off their collection of herbal tattoos, tan colored breeches rolled up to their knees, and sturdy leather boots. They had big gold hoop earrings in both ears and an extra sparkle of something glittery on their eyelids.

Basel was dragging behind them a large wooden wagon, it was a dark green color with a few vegetables painted on the side. Tristan imagined that by the end of the night the wagon would be full and overflowing with all kinds of unique ingredients and spices, which would make trips to the Canteen even more delightful.

Emyr came last, dressed in his dark, perfectly-tailored waistcoat, a midnight blue cloak, and trailing his own wagon like Basel's, although his was painted black.

When they reached the bottom of the ramp Tristan saw a familiar shadow in the gathering darkness; her large Captain's hat an imposing shape in the blue evening light. She nodded at them as they approached, and after a few simple greetings she fell into step next to Tristan.

He felt the magnetic pull of her presence next to him, he wanted to say something but he didn't know what. He kept thinking about what had happened with the Royal Mariners, how it had all gone so wrong. He felt like he needed to speak to her, but he figured since she was coming with them, he could wait a while to figure out what he wanted to say.

The crew walked in amiable silence as they wandered through the busy and crowded docks and up the main road towards the

Midnight Market. The lights, sounds, and smells coming from the market were enticing, even at a distance. As they approached the market they saw street performers and food vendors lining the way. Jugglers throwing flaming batons, belly dancers spinning wildly to a hand-drummer, artists painting swirling floral patterns on visitor's arms and legs.

There were small carts selling candied apples, little baskets of freshly roasted potatoes and nuts, golden brown dumplings stuffed with spiced vegetables. Tristan was dazzled by the entertainers and food already, and they hadn't even entered the market properly.

They reached the top of the sloping hillside and the cobbled street opened up into a massive, pulsing marketplace. The vendors had tables, tents or covered stalls with brightly colored fabrics, hung with decorations and lights. The ground was hard-packed dirt, worn down from thousands of feet passing over it.

Above the stalls were tall posts set with hanging lanterns that lit up the market with an ethereal glow in the deepening night, making everything feel like it was touched with otherworldly magic.

As they passed through the entrance Tristan saw a vendor selling maps of the market for a copper coin, so he quickly darted over to them and bought one. He jogged to catch up with the rest of the crew, trying to get a good look at the map. He saw from the map that he would be going to the far eastern side of the market where the food and herb vendors were located, while the quill and book makers were on the western side. For a moment his brow knitted in worry as he thought about the Majesteria, so small and alone in this sea of people. They swore they could handle themselves, but sometimes he wondered if they weren't a bit more naive than they realized.

"I'll be off then," Wren said to them and Tristan felt a jolt of surprise.

"What? You're leaving?" he said.

"Aye, I've got work to do," she said. "I've got to go find us some new clients in the Trader's market. Hopefully someone wants some cargo sent to Fairefeux."

The rest of the crew nodded at her and waved their goodbyes. Tristan began to follow them, but he felt a lurching in his stomach at the thought of leaving Wren without saying something.

"Can I catch up to you? I want to talk to The Captain for a moment?" He asked.

"Don't take too long Froggy, we got lots to do tonight!" Basel said, giving him a clap on the back that sent him stumbling.

"I'll be quick," he promised and dashed after Wren's rapidly disappearing shape.

"Wren! Wait!" He called.

She turned around and stopped, all tangled hair and fierce dark eyes. The soft glow of the Market's lanterns did something magical to her bronze skin that made him feel a little dizzy.

"Yes?" she said, her eyes darting around and foot tapping. She was obviously itching to go to her destination.

"Oh, I, um, er," Tristan found himself even more tongue tied than usual.

She arched an eyebrow, "Out with it Mulberry," she said sharply.

"Earlier, er, with the Royal Mariners," he began.

Her shoulders sagged and the fire drained from her eyes. A look came over her that he couldn't quite understand.

"What about it?" She said sharply.

"I just...I'm sorry," he said, moving a little closer to her and meeting her gaze with as much strength as he could muster. "I shouldn't have said what I did, I know I made a bad situation worse and I'm terribly sorry. Can I give you some money to help cover the costs of the, um, incident?"

He reached into his bag and pulled out his coin purse, pulling out coins to hand to her. "I'm not sure what the right amount is, but um..."

He trailed off when he saw her face.

She had pulled away from him, grimacing and looking anywhere but at his eyes. Her hands were balled up in fists.

"I don't need your damn money," she said, through clenched teeth. "Put your stupid coins away Tristan."

"But those men, the Mariners..." he said, trying to understand what he'd done wrong.

She folded her arms "I can handle my shit, I don't need some *scholar* to come save me," she said, spitting the word scholar.

"I'm not trying to save you," he said stepping back. "I'm just trying to make amends."

"You don't need to make amends, and you don't need to help me. I don't want your money Tristan, you don't know what you're doing. Lieutenant Fisk is just like that, Royal Mariners are a fact of life. It's what I signed up for when I agreed to become a Registered Pirate Vessel."

"But...it's not right! They're supposed to help people," Tristan said.

"That's not how the world works," she said. "I'm sorry everyone isn't as friendly as at Teakley Academy. The rest of us have to deal with pieces of garbage like Fisk all the time. I'm used to it. Now please, let me go? I need to do my job."

"Of course," Tristan said, standing back and looking down at the bag in his hands. "I'm...sorry for bothering you."

She nodded once and turned away, she started to walk away and then stopped. She sighed, her shoulders drooping and turned back to look at him.

"Thank you for...trying," she said, reluctantly. "But it's not your world, you are a guest on my ship. Just go and have a good time at the market, and don't worry about this stuff, okay?"

Tristan nodded, "Okay, I'll try," he said.

～

Tristan wasn't thrilled about what had happened with Wren but he wasn't really sure what to do, so he decided to do as she'd asked and try to have a good time at the Market. He followed his map towards the foodstuffs vendors and caught up with the crew fairly quickly. Basel's big shoulders and bright red hair was hard to miss, even in a crowd this interesting. When he found them Basel was eating a spiral of fried potato on a stick while Bonnie was buying an assortment of small glass bottles, corks, and different colors of wax for her healing potions.

As for Emyr, well, he was living up to his reputation.

Somehow, in the fifteen minutes Tristan had been gone, Emyr had managed to pick up an extraordinarily handsome man with pointed ears and pale hair. They were standing a little ways away from the booth, holding hands and gazing dreamily into each other's eyes.

"Ayeee, Froggy's back!" Basel said with a grin. "We was about to send out a search party, thought maybe Mad Richard got ya."

"Is that...a possibility?" Tristan asked, alarmed.

"Here? Not likely dearheart," Bonnie said over her shoulder. "But the Midnight Market gets all types, so you'd best stay with us."

She paid the vendor and put her purchases in the big burlap bag on her shoulder.

"On to the next!" She said cheerfully and the crew re-entered the crowds along the walkway. Tristan stopped to look at his map, turning it around to try to figure out exactly where he was.

"This way Tristan!" Bonnie called. He looked up and realized they were making a turn, and they had stopped to wait for him.

"Sorry, I was just looking at this map of the market," he said.

"You won't need a map Frog Boy, you've got ME!" Basel boomed cheerfully. "Nobody loves the Midnight Market more than me!"

"It's true," Bonnie said with a laugh.

"Alright, I'll just follow your lead then," Tristan said, carefully tucking the map away inside his waistcoat.

They made their way slowly through the crowded marketplace. They passed flower vendors selling fresh potted plants and bouquets overflowing with brightly colored blooms.

After that was the crystal and jewelry stalls with sparkly gems dug from the Briarwood mountains, dwarven gold pendants, and elvish steel diadems set with moonstones.

Then it opened out into more varied vendors: everything from maps and compasses, to adventuring clothes, mushroom-farming equipment, magical potion-making supplies, and horse tack.

Before they even got to to the cooking ingredients they had passed more mouth-watering food and drink than Tristan could keep track of.

Eventually, his growling stomach could not wait any longer, and when they passed a cluster of food vendors he asked if they could stop for some food. They agreed and everyone got some food and brought it to sit on some small tables and stools nearby.

Basel got a large plate piled high with rice and mushrooms, with tempura-fried squash on top, a cup of roasted hazelnuts, and a huge mug of spiced mead. Bonnie bought a very large dough pocket stuffed with cheese and onions, and an Elderflower cordial.

Emyr and his man, who Tristan had learned was named Guy, bought a large basket of sweet potato frites to share, although they didn't pay much attention to the food.

For his part, Tristan bought a massive mushroom-on-a-stick with a dark brown liquid to dip it in, and a round bread stuffed with brie and figs, roasted over an open fire.

He could not decide on a drink so he got two: a spiced orange-apple cider and something called a Firebreather's Revenge, which Basel swore was the best drink at the market.

Once they were seated Tristan tucked into his food which was every bit as delicious as it had looked. While he was eating he spotted another Wanted poster for Mad Richard on the table under some sauce bottles. He shuddered as he looked at the scraggly bearded man staring up at him.

"Ain't ya gonna have some of that drink?" Basel asked.

"Huh?" Tristan said, lost in thoughts of terrifying pirates attacking the ship.

Basel nodded to the glass on the table, the Firebreather's Revenge.

"Oh, um, well," Tristan said. He had been questioning if buying it had even been a good idea.

It looked...strange.

The drink came in a long, tall glass and had liquid that faded from red to orange to yellow at the frothy top. It sparkled with gold dust and was making a fizzing noise. Basel and Bonnie looked on with interest as Tristan raised the glass and looked at the glittering concoction for a moment.

"What *is* it?" he asked.

"Firebreather's Revenge," Emyr said, pausing his canoodling to watch.

"Go on then Frog Boy!" Basel said, stuffing a fried squash in their mouth and glugging their mead with a loud burp.

Tristan took a deep breath and decided to go for it. He raised the drink to his lips, taking a large sip.

At first it was pleasant and familiar.

Flavors of orange, cherry, and cinnamon.

Then slowly, from the back of his throat he felt a numb, tingly feeling that burned his mouth as it moved towards his lips.

It felt like there were a dozen tiny fairies dancing across his tongue in shoes made of liquid fire. He raised his eyebrows at the strange sensation, but a moment later the spicy tingling was replaced by a violent, fiery assault on his senses, filling every part of his mouth, throat, and sinuses.

His nose began to run and his eyes watered as he felt the dragon fire slide down his throat.

"Wa-wa-*water*," he managed to croak out, signaling frantically to the crew as he felt something akin to molten lava take hold of his chest.

Bonnie rushed to a nearby booth and returned with a cup of water, which Tristan poured down his throat gratefully.

But...it wasn't over yet.

He felt a strange sensation in the pit of his stomach when the cool liquid met the lava-like drink, and he felt a strange roiling begin inside him.

He stood up and began to cough and wretch.

As he did this something strange began to happen.

He started to smoke.

Through watering eyes he saw large plumes of glittering smoke pour out of his nostrils, engulfing the table in dark clouds. At one point he was sure he saw a tiny flame escape his mouth.

A handful of onlookers began to clap at this performance.

After a minute he finally stopped breathing smoke and he wiped his eyes, taking another sip of water as his mouth returned to normal.

"AYE! Firebreather's Revenge!" Someone cheered.

"Nothin' better!" Someone else added with a chuckle.

"Hang in there!" A shout from across the way.

Tristan took another massive gulp of water and breathed in the cool night air, fanning his face as his body started to recover from the drink.

"Why didn't you warn me?" he asked, glaring at the crew.

"I thought the name was pretty self-explanatory," Bonnie said with a shrug. "I figured you wanted a *fiery* good time, dearheart."

Basel nodded their agreement, then they looked at the drink.

"You want the rest of that?" they asked.

"It's all yours," Tristan said with a laugh.

～

AFTER TRISTAN HAD RECOVERED from the Firebreather's Revenge they got back to wandering the market. It wasn't long before Tristan found himself alone again.

They had arrived at Gerard & Co. Spices and Herbs, the largest herb and spice vendor at the market. Basel and Bonnie were both thoroughly engrossed with examining and shopping for herbs. As for Emyr and Guy, they had finally moved on to the kissing portion of the date and had very little interest in the world around them.

So Tristan began to wander away from the group, taking everything in and just enjoying the sights.

Suddenly a young girl appeared before him. She was slim and pale, with a long white dress trailing on the packed dirt ground behind her. She wore an elvish silver diadem set with gemstones, and had flowers braided into her long hair. She held up a hand for him to stop.

"*Hello there traveller,*" she said in a strange, otherworldly sounding voice. "*You look like a wanderer who is seeking answers.*"

"Oh no, I'm just here with a some friends," Tristan said.

"*The question answers itself,*" the young girl said solemnly, then bowed her head slightly. "*I have the answers you seek.*"

"I don't understand," he said, genuinely confused.

The girl pointed to a stall nearby and it all became clear. The stall had a long table covered with velvet fabric and all manner of fortune-telling supplies.

Scrying crystals, little stones with symbols carved in them, many different types of tarot and fortune cards, and spirit boards. Behind the table was a small tent with a door of jangling beads, and a sign which offered an expert fortune teller inside the tent.

Tristan didn't know much about fortune tellers. It was a mysterious art that was generally disregarded by Teakley as too erratic. But he found that curiosity got the best of him as he looked at the little tent.

"You know, I think you may be right," he said to the girl, but when he turned, she was gone. He spun around looking for her, but he didn't see the girl in the white dress anywhere.

Strange.

He shook his head and walked to the tent, pushing aside the jangling curtain. The air hung heavy with thick scents of sandalwood and myrrh, Tristan coughed a little at the dense, hazy air.

Inside the tent was a small, low table covered in a shimmering cloth set with candles, crystals, and incense burning slowly. The floor was full of embroidered pillows with long silky tassels.

On the other side of the table was an older man in simple white cotton robes. He had black horns and pointed ears with silver earrings.

"Welcome traveller," he said serenely. "The price for answers is twenty copper pieces, half paid in advance. Sit down, and give me ten copper pieces."

Tristan grabbed the coins from his wallet and placed them in a small bronze bowl on the table. He sat down on one of the embroidered pillows and waited, his heart pounding faster in his chest.

He suddenly felt nervous and afraid, what if he hated the answers he got?

"You may not like the answers you receive, but that doesn't mean you don't need to hear them," the man said calmly, as though he could read Tristan's mind.

For a terrifying moment he wondered if he could.

"Don't worry, I can't read your mind," the man said with a wink that Tristan did not find at all reassuring.

But he didn't have time to ponder this because the man was already busy with the work of fortune telling. First he dropped rose petals and pixie dust into a small glass decanter and shook it around, before pouring the glimmering liquid onto a spirit board. Tristan didn't sense any magical changes in the air, but the fortune teller seemed very intrigued to watch the droplets of water roll across the board.

"Interesting, very interesting," he mumbled. Then he wiped the board with a silk handkerchief. "Let me see your eyes."

Tristan leaned forward across the table and the man held up a pink-hued candle and examined his eyeballs.

"Mmmm, mhmmm," he said, nodding his head. Tristan leaned back, and the man pulled out a velvet pouch full of throwing stones with little symbols on them. He threw them a few times, tilting his head and making little notes in a small ledger. Finally, he closed the book and looked up at Tristan.

"Tell me, is there a dark, dangerous, raven-haired person in your life?"

Immediately Tristan's mind went to Captain Wren.

"Yes," he said. "Although...probably not for long."

The man waved this away with his ring-covered hand, jangling with all the bracelets and jewelry he wore.

"That matters not, we don't know how it will end yet."

Tristan wasn't sure if he should respond, so he just smiled.

"This raven-haired person, this dark figure. You must tell them the truth as soon as possible."

Tristan raised his eyebrows, "The truth about what?"

The man nodded but did not elaborate.

"Now, the next order of business is the bad omen."

"What?" Tristan said. That didn't sound good.

"This is only what I learned from the spirits, how you interpret it is up to you," he warned. "The spirits told me: *beware the falling moon, it will bring a fiend from the realm of death.*"

His voice was whispered and chilling. Tristan felt a cold tingle go up his spine.

"What does that mean?" he asked.

"How you interpret it is up to you," the man reminded him sagely.

"But I don't know how to interpret it!" Tristan said.

"I have one more piece of advice for you," the fortune teller continued, completely ignoring Tristan's complaints. "Are you ready?"

"I suppose so, though I'd really like to know about the realm of death thing," Tristan replied.

The man shook his head

"That's for you to interpret. But there is more you need to hear, young man, and it is this: Some run brazenly into danger, thinking little about the consequences. Others live for safety and comfort, burying their true selves for the promise of a safe tomorrow. These people do not know their own souls. They don't know that their heart yearns for magic and adventure, they just think that's a funny feeling in their stomach. But it's not. It's a wild spirit, longing to be free."

Tristan's sat back, stunned. It felt like the man had cut into something deep inside him, something he hadn't even known himself.

"That's beautiful," he said, his voice barely a whisper.

"That'll be ten copper pieces," the fortune teller replied, holding out his hand.

"Right, of course, thank you," Tristan said, handing him the coins and standing up awkwardly, trying not to hit his head on the top of the tent. The man pocketed the coins and then motioned Tristan to leave.

He took the hint and ducked through the jangling beaded curtain and returned to the market. But the fortune teller's words stayed with him, lingering in his head for a very long time indeed.

BY THE TIME Tristan finally returned to the group he saw they had arrived at the ingredients and cooking supplies.

Everywhere Tristan looked, he saw vendors selling anything a chef could wish for: dwarven iron frying pans, steel woks from the western isles, towering mountains of bright orange and yellow spices, overflowing vats of chilies and peppers.

Giant mushrooms as big as watermelons were hanging from the roofs of stalls. There were carts of dried fruits and berries, apples and oranges in wooden barrels, freshly baked breads piled high on covered tables.

Stacks of cheese wheels and heaping mounds of fresh soft cheese, malted vinegars, pickled onions and gherkins in sea-brine, walls of carefully selected rare herbs and spices in tiny jars, dozens of flavors of salt, and barrels of mead, ale, and wine.

Tristan was dazzled but nowhere near as excited as Basel who was humming a sea shanty loudly and buzzing around the stalls like a hummingbird. They bought bread and cheese, root vegetables and fruits unfamiliar to Tristan, and piled them in the wagon.

Tristan meandered behind them, falling into step with Bonnie.

"How are you liking the market, dearheart?" Bonnie asked as they walked while Basel sampled plums and argued with vendors about the price of spring onions.

"It's wonderful," Tristan said, his eyes lighting up. "Like nothing I've ever seen."

"You've not travelled much?" she asked.

"No, I don't leave the Academy very often," Tristan admitted. It felt weird to say it now, it had never bothered him before but suddenly it felt like an odd thing to do. "But, perhaps I should."

"Aye, travelling is good for the soul, dearheart," Bonnie said sagely.

"Yes, I rather think it is," Tristan said.

They stopped while Basel crouched on the ground and stuffed a large bundle of parsnips into the wagon. It was now full with so many strange fruits, vegetables, and cheeses it was hard to see where the wagon ended and the food began.

"I think that's it for me today," Basel said, a little sadly. Then they smiled with a roguish grin. "Unless I buy another wagon!"

Tristan and Bonnie laughed.

"I suppose you could do that, dearheart," Bonnie said, patting them on the arm.

"Wait for us!" Emyr called. They were sprinting down the aisle hand-in-hand with Guy and lugging the black wagon.

Tristan looked down at the wagon and raised an eyebrow.

It was completely full of bottles of rum.

"That's...a lot," he said.

Emyr shrugged, "I'm a pirate, what do you want?"

Tristan laughed, "Fair enough."

"If you're done getting your rum, I've got to get a few more things," Bonnie said. "Follow me!"

~

While Bonnie collected more herbalist supplies the rest of them strolled off in different directions. Emyr and Guy found a romantic spot to sit and watch a bard playing love songs. Basel found some chefs to argue about cumin and coriander with, and Tristan decided to do some shopping.

The first thing he knew he wanted to buy was a gift for the Majesteria. He hadn't liked their fight earlier and thought a little gift would be a nice way to apologize.

He stopped at a few clothing stalls but struggled to find anything that would fit a mouse. But something did catch his attention, though not for the Majesteria. He was looking through a booth of clothes, when he saw a white linen blouse billowing in the breeze. He walked to the shirt and looked at it, the soft, light fabric was exactly what he pictured the pirates in the books he read wearing. It had Captain Santiago written all over it.

He held up the blouse, it was his size. Voluminous and flowing, the gauzy fabric felt like adventure and wonder. The fortune-teller's words came back to him. A wild heart yearning to be free. Or something like that.

The shirt stirred something indefinable inside him, and he knew he had to have it, even though he didn't know where he'd wear it. He bought the shirt and quickly stuffed it in his satchel and then returned to browsing.

For a moment he entertained the idea of buying Wren a gift.

It was a passing thought when he saw a sword-cleaning kit at one of the booths and imagined it on her desk.

But he quickly shook this thought away.

He was a guest, *and* he was lying to her.

He definitely shouldn't be buying her gifts.

After buying himself a few reading candles, an interesting dangling silver earring he wasn't sure he had the courage to wear, and a first-edition copy of *The Glory Of The Storm* (signed by the author!), he finally figured out what to get the Majesteria.

Along the back edge of one aisle there was a small booth of specialty teas. Each tea came in a little metal tin with a gold-embossed label on it. They even had a tea for the Midnight Market called "Midnight Delight."

Tristan picked up three of the little tins and added them to his satchel, now bulging with purchases, and kept on wandering through the aisles as the darkness of the night began to deepen in earnest.

Wandering through the lantern-lit aisles, he noticed the light got dimmer as he moved farther into the market. Past the tea vendor's stall there were some weapons vendors and potion sellers, with fewer and fewer lanterns at every turn. He started to feel a little nervous as he moved through the stalls, the darkness seeming to creep up around him like a cloak. He looked around for his friends; he saw Basel towering above the crowds a few aisles over, red hair sticking out wildly in all directions. He wasn't lost or anything, it was just a little darker over here. He breathed a sigh of relief and continued to walk through the shadowy stalls.

Soon he could barely see the merchandise, the night was brooding, darkness enclosing this part of the market. He noticed as he kept walking that the goods on offer were starting to be a little bit... different.

Potion bottles had black ribbons and painted eyeballs instead of golden charms.

Books on tables had names like *The Dark Art of Necromancy*.

There were quite a lot of weapons.

Not the gleaming swords and decorative knives he'd noticed on the other aisles, but flails and axes made of dark, heavy iron.

It was starting to occur to him that this part of the market might be the home of some of those 'scoundrels and rogues' he'd heard were frequenting the Midnight Market, and that he ought to get back to the crew before one such nefarious character found him.

But...

He saw someone selling gloves.

Beautiful thick leather gloves in all shapes and styles.

Tristan wore gloves all the time to hide his Starlight tattoos. Gloves had become a big part of his wardrobe after becoming a Majesteria handler, and he had never seen such a large and interesting selection. He paused for a moment.

What was the harm in it, really?

It was just gloves. Sure, maybe the vendors in this part of the market were a little...unsavory. But he was just buying some gloves.

He decided it would certainly be fine and made his way over to the stall.

He looked around the table and examined all the different colors and styles, admiring the craftsmanship.

"You lost, lad?"

He looked up to see a burly woman with scars criss-crossing her face and a patch over one eye.

"Um, no, I was just looking for some gloves," he said.

"Well, we've got those," she said, taking a gulp from a flask and folding her arms.

He nodded and picked up a pair. They were gorgeous, fingerless leather gloves, purple so dark it was almost black, silver stitching, and a moon clasp at the wrist.

"Can I try these on?" he asked.

"Mhmm, but I'm watching you," the woman said forcefully.

"Of course," he said, unbuttoning his gloves and setting them down on the table.

"My my, I ain't seen tattoos like that in a long time," said a gruff voice nearby.

Tristan jumped a little and turned to look at the man next to him.

He was tall and broad shouldered with long, tangled hair and inquisitive dark eyes. Most alarming though was the tattoo on his face, a cutlass with three drops of blood. Tristan stepped back a little, nearly dropping the gloves.

"Oh-ho, ain't you one of those star magic types from up at them witches school?" said the glove-seller.

"These are the markings of someone who works with *Majesteria*, if I'm not mistaken," said the brooding man, looming over Tristan to get a better look at his hands. "I know a buyer if you'd like to sell them."

Tristan was confused.

"Sell what?"

"The Majesteria," the man said, his cold gaze fixed on Tristan's hands. "Such creatures would fetch a very fine bounty."

"Absolutely not!" Tristan said, horrified.

The man got a devilish glint in his eye and Tristan felt his stomach drop.

He hadn't meant to admit that he was a Majesteria handler.

Tristan hastily put on the dark purple gloves, desperate to cover his hands as quickly as possible. They fit perfectly, the soft supple leather molding to his hands instantly.

"I'll take these," he said hurriedly, handing the woman some coins and stuffing his old gloves into his satchel. "Have a good evening!"

"He ain't even gonna tell us what it's like workin' with them magic animals, some people are *so rude*," said the glove-vendor, shaking her head.

Tristan ran out of the dark stalls and into the light, finding Basel's head bobbing through the crowd like a lifeboat. His heart began to beat normally again as he blended back into the flow of traffic, and within a few minutes it was as though he'd never met the intimidating man lurking in the shadows.

Bonnie, Emyr, and Guy rejoined the group, and they all went

off to find some mead and get a few drinks in before the night ended.

Tristan never noticed the man with the cutlass tattoo on his face following at a respectable distance, lurking in the shadows.

He didn't follow Tristan for long.

Not long at all.

Just long enough to see which ship Tristan returned to.

Chapter Ten

There are things that only a mouse can know. Ways of moving through the world that cannot be understood by humans, at best they can only be observed. These mysterious ways of mice and tiny creatures is how Edwina, Marigold, and Chica would travel through the Midnight Market.

They began their journey the same as Tristan, travelling down the ramp from the ship under the lanterns swinging gently in the sea breezes. But that was where the similarities ended. When the mice arrived on the busy and crowded docks, they hoisted their heavy backpacks full of coins and supplies onto their shoulders and looked around for a place to hide.

One of the first and most important steps for moving through the world as a magical mouse is hiding. Humans didn't really know how to cope with mice that wore clothes and talked. They had all kinds of strange reactions, so most of the time it was simplest to just avoid them wherever possible. Luckily, the Majesteria were familiar and comfortable with humans, but even so, it was always easier to move in the animal world than the human world.

A good hiding spot was ideal for making plans and looking at routes, and one thing mice are very very good at is finding a place to hide. It wasn't long before Marigold spotted somewhere good, a small trash bin behind a tavern on the pathway up towards the Midnight Market.

Marigold pointed out the spot, Edwina agreed it would work and instantly, the three mice were moving. Their tiny feet scurrying over the cobblestones, cloaks brushing along the ground, they wove through the human legs and carriage wheels expertly and at high speed. In only a few minutes they had arrived at the large trash bin and were scampering into the small, dark alcove behind it.

They sighed with relief, taking their packs off and sitting down with their paws up to catch their breath for a moment.

"This is so exciting," Edwina said, her eyes sparkling. "We haven't done this in so long."

"I know!" Marigold exclaimed, "Adventure Marigold has returned! It's high time we got out of that stuffy Academy and let our paws run loose."

"Mmm, I don't know, they have very soft rugs at the Academy," Chica said thoughtfully.

"And excellent cheese," Edwina added.

"Argh! Can't you two just let me have fun for once?" Marigold snapped.

"Sorry, Adventure Marigold," Chica said.

Edwina peered out of the crack in their hiding spot to see what or who was around. There was a cat across the way but they didn't look magical. Nearby a few seagulls picked at scraps of food but everyone knew seagulls were rude. Then she saw what she was looking for, sleeping in the flower box of the tavern was a Dragonling, a tiny dragon no bigger than a house cat.

She let out a little squeak and pointed to the Dragonling. Marigold and Chica squeaked too as they peered out at the Dragonling.

She let out a little squeak and pointed to the Dragonling. Marigold and Chica squeaked too as they peered out at the Dragonling.

"How fortuitous!" Marigold said dramatically, "a wondrous Dragonling in our hour of need."

"You should go talk to it," Edwina said.

"Me? Why me?" Marigold said.

"I mean, aren't you Adventure Marigold? I shouldn't think a Dragonling would frighten Adventure Marigold," Edwina said slyly.

"Plus, everyone likes you," Chica said.

Marigold smiled despite herself. "Fine! I'll go talk to it, you two stay here with our packs."

"Aye!" Edwina said.

Marigold gave her a look.

"What? Why can't I talk like the sailors?" Edwina asked defensively.

Marigold shrugged and turned to the task at hand. She took off her witch's hat and laid it carefully on her pack. Then she checked the area quickly to make sure it was clear, and began climbing up the scaffolding on the side of the building.

Marigold was an expert climber and found her way up the wall quickly. Then it was just a matter of crawling across a very narrow ledge until she could hop down into the flower box, all in a day's work for an adventurous mouse. When Marigold landed in the flower box she startled the poor Dragonling who woke with a start and blew a little puff of smoke out of its mouth.

"I'm so sorry to startle you!" Marigold said as sweetly as she could. When she spoke it was in a different language than the one she used with humans, she instead used a common regional animal language.

"We are travelling from out of town and want to go to the Midnight Market," Marigold continued, "do you know any way we could do that?"

The Dragonling blinked slowly for a moment, taking in the small mouse in her embroidered dress and travelling cloak.

When it spoke, the Dragonling's voice was high-pitched and squeaky.

"Who is *we*?" she asked.

"Myself and two other Hi-Mice, Edwina and Chica. I'm Marigold by the way," she replied, bobbing her head.

The Dragonling nodded its small, scaly head wisely, "I'm Diamond."

"An honor to meet you," Marigold replied, bowing deeply.

This seemed to please Diamond who puffed a few clouds of smoke happily.

"There are many ways for one such as you to visit the Midnight Market," she said, "what do you wish to see?"

"We are hoping to go to Quincy Quint's Quill Emporium and buy some custom quills," Marigold said. "We'd also like to have some tasty food."

Diamond snorted at this, "Tasty food will not be a problem anywhere in the market."

"I'm not surprised to hear that," Marigold said.

"Hmmm, Quincy Quint's is far away, on the western side of the market. You will need transport."

"I expected as much, we are able to pay in whatever ways are needed," Marigold supplied.

Diamond looked impressed, "I wish I could take you myself, but alas, my human would worry."

Marigold nodded wisely, "Of course, I understand. I know how humans can be."

"They worry so much, when the one who needs help is *them*," Diamond said with another puff of smoke. "They are terribly silly and very bad at taking care of themselves. But they mean well and they have good food, you know?"

"My human is *exactly* the same," Marigold said with a laugh. "Do you know someone who can take us there?"

Diamond curled her shiny tail around her body and flexed her claws in the dirt before she replied.

"There is a dog, his name is Marcus. I think he can help you, he lives with the map vendor at the entrance to the market. His favorite food is carrots, I'm sure if you brought him some he'd take you to get your quills."

Marigold clapped her paws together. "Thank you so much, that sounds perfect! Do you perhaps know where I could get some carrots? I could trade you some cheese and a pinch of pixie dust."

Diamond raised her head at this "Cheese? What kind of cheese?"

"Strawberry Cheese from Strawberry Island," Marigold said confidently.

As expected, Diamond sat up very straight at these words and began licking her lips, "I can get you the carrots from the tavern kitchens. Where should I bring them?"

Marigold pointed to their hiding spot behind the trash bin and Diamond nodded.

"Give me a few minutes," she said, and with a last big puff of smoke she disappeared inside the open window.

As promised, Diamond appeared a few minutes later, swooping down on her leathery wings with a bunch of carrots clasped in her mouth. She laid them on the ground next to the mice and Marigold handed her the wedge of cheese wrapped in waxy paper and a small packet of pixie dust. Diamond thanked them and made off with her loot back to the flower box, while the mice set about tying the large bunch of carrots to a stick to make it easier to carry.

Once the carrots were secured they crawled back into their hiding place to figure out their route. They discussed and planned and after a few minutes they began their journey. They put their packs back on and hefted the large bunch of carrots, Edwina and Chica holding one side of the stick with Marigold scurrying ahead to clear the path and look for obstacles. The carrots would make it harder to travel, so they had decided on a route that didn't require too much running around in busy human areas.

They waited until the foot traffic was slow, then they quickly hefted the carrots into the air and ran across the street to the dense underbrush on the other side. They scurried under the bushes and began picking their way up the hillside through the rocky dirt. It was tough going. Their cloaks caught on the thistles and the carrots kept snagging on branches, but eventually they made it up the hillside and arrived at the entrance to the Midnight Market.

They set down the carrots and spent a moment looking at the view of the market. The lanterns lighting up the night with a warm glow, the jugglers and dancers, the food carts, the humans and animals from all walks of life and parts of the realm.

"It's so beautiful," Marigold breathed, her eyes wide and glittering.

"I love it," Edwina agreed, her whiskers twitching happily.

"Wowee!" Chica said.

After a moment of reverie it was time to get back to their journey, so they heaved the bunch of carrots again and began the perilous task of crossing the road, weaving through the humans' feet until they arrived at the map vendor's stall. They made it to the other side unharmed, and, as usual, not a single human noticed them at all.

The map vendor had a small stall of maps of the market as well as the surrounding islands. It was a small table and one chair where the vendor sat with their dog napping at their feet. The dog was medium-sized and scruffy, with a big bushy forehead and floppy ears.

"I like him," Marigold said immediately.

Edwina rolled her eyes "You like *all* dogs."

"They're just so sweet," Marigold said, her eyes big.

"Except the scary ones," Edwina said.

"They just need extra love," Marigold replied, undaunted.

Luckily, Marcus was not a scary dog at all, and he opened his big, soft eyes happily when he saw the mice approach.

"Hello!" Marigold said cheerfully, running up and giving him a pat on the nose. "My goodness your nose is so wet."

"Yes!" Marcus said, he was clearly excited. He looked from the mice to the carrots and back again. "Carrots for me?"

"Yes," Marigold said. Marcus stood up and began wagging his tail quickly.

"But- we need your help," Marigold said.

"You need a ride?" Marcus asked, sniffing around the carrots.

"Yes, Diamond said you could help us."

"Sure, I don't mind," Marcus said, pawing the carrots in frustration. "Why are they on a stick?"

"We put them on that so we could carry them, don't worry, we'll take them off the stick," Marigold said.

"Can I have the stick too?" he asked with a little whine.

"I don't see why not," Edwina said. She began untying the knots to free the carrots from the stick, and then backed up as Marcus jumped around the carrots excitedly.

"Can you take us to Quincy Quint's Quill Emporium?" Edwina asked.

"Yeah, yeah," Marcus said, his tail wagging happily. "But I gotta have carrots first!"

While Marcus ate his carrots, Marigold climbed up the leg of the table to look at the maps. There were all kinds of maps of different sizes and shapes, colors, and languages. She scrambled over the table, staying out of sight of the map vendor while she searched for one that was a little more manageable for her.

Finally, she found a bunch of "novelty maps" that were a few inches tall. The sign said they were for "Silly Gifts and Tiny Friends." Marigold twitched her tail and looked through the maps, finding one of the market and one of the surrounding islands.

She looked around and found the price sign, it was three maps for two copper coins. Well, in that case, she'd better find one more.

She looked through the maps and found one of somewhere called The Otherwilde Seas. She'd never heard of it before but it sounded mysterious, she figured it would be nice to hang on her wall when she got home.

She pulled off her backpack and found two copper coins, which she placed on the table next to the maps. She then rolled up the maps and stuffed them inside her pack before she clambered down from the table again.

"I got maps!" she exclaimed when she got back down to the ground.

"Do we need maps?" Edwina asked. "Isn't Marcus just going to take us there?"

"I mean, it seems useful to me," Marigold said. "Plus, we can always put them up as decor when we get home."

"That would be so pretty," Chica said wistfully.

Edwina twitched her tail. "Are you ready Marcus?"

The scruffy dog looked at the carrots sadly. He'd already eaten two and there were four left. He looked like he very much wanted to eat all of the carrots right now, but he nodded his head.

"Yeah alright," he said and crouched down so the mice could clamber onto his back. Edwina got up first and then reached a paw down to help Marigold swing onto his back behind her. They both reached down to help Chica who scrambled awkwardly up and then flopped on Marcus's back like a pancake. Chica wasn't particularly good at climbing, but she never seemed to mind.

"Don't you want to sit up to ride Chica?" Marigold asked.

"Mmmph," Chica said, face buried in fur.

"Let her do what she likes," Edwina said, shrugging.

The other two dug their paws into his fur, grabbing fistfuls of it tightly, and then Edwina whistled to Marcus that they were ready.

He leaned back to gather momentum and then...they were off.

Marcus leapt forward and began to trot through the aisles, his well travelled paws familiar with every inch of the Midnight Market and its stalls.

The ride was bumpy and a little windy, but a lot more stable than the mice had expected. In fact, it was pretty fun riding on the back of a dog. After a while Marigold thought she heard Chica snoring behind her.

Marcus's fur was soft and cushiony, and he kept his pace reasonable so they didn't have to fight to hold on. They particularly enjoyed the experience because a dog's height provided a very interesting view for a mouse. It was not as high up as riding on Tristan's shoulder ,but Marcus was a lot taller than a mouse so riding on his back afforded them a wonderful view of the marketplace.

The market was a swirl of colors, voices, smells, sounds, and movement. They saw all kinds of humans from the all the realms they could think of, and many animals as well. They were not the only animals wearing clothing, though they might have been the best dressed.

They saw a badger with reading glasses and a waistcoat in a bookseller's stall, a hare in a dashing pink dress, a mysterious fox in a long woolen cloak, and many more Dragonlings, dogs, and cats.

The stalls they passed were as interesting and exciting as they had anticipated. They passed vendors selling fried foods wrapped in warm tortillas, soups full of chunky vegetables, and long sticks of crystallized berries dripping in honey and toasted nuts. They passed cobblers with rows of neat shiny leather shoes and hard-working adventuring boots. Milliners selling wild and extravagant hats with vibrant feathers and bejeweled brooches. All the supplies sailors could need from sails and rigging to ledgers, barrels, lanterns, compasses, maps and spyglasses.

Finally, Marcus started to slow down as the stalls started to have more books, stationery, and paper supplies. He stopped in front of a stall selling inks in dozens of colors and styles, including some with magical properties.

"This is the main book area, you'll find all the quill vendors here," he said, before sitting down to let the mice clamber down gently.

"Do you know where we might find a snack?" Edwina asked him while Marigold helped a rather groggy Chica off his back.

Marcus grunted, "You can't have my carrots," he said.

"I don't mean carrots," Edwina said. "I mean, do you know a

food stall nearby where they wouldn't mind selling food to...our kind."

Marcus scratched his ear with his paw. "Selling? You're not gonna beg?"

"No," Edwina said firmly, "we have coins for the humans."

"Probably Stormy, the kebab vendor. Her bullfrog is named Fish, he's a bit weird but he'll help you."

"Her bullfrog is named...Fish?" Edwina asked.

"Yes," Marcus said. Then he began to whine a little. "Can I go back to my carrots now?"

"Of course, thank you Marcus," Edwina said, patting his paw with her much smaller one.

Marcus howled happily and ran off at high speed, wagging his tail as he darted through the market.

AFTER WANDERING around for about twenty minutes and reluctantly agreeing that there was no way they could carry a box of fifteen different colored inks back to the ship, they finally found Stormy and her kebab stall. The stall was small but cozy; there was a smoldering fire with an iron grate where Stormy was cooking the kebabs. Potted plants and flowers were tucked in any available corner, and a little string of tiny lanterns was hanging above her while she worked. Edwina and Marigold could smell the kebabs from far away and already their whiskers were twitching.

The scampered up to the front of the booth looking for Fish. They found the bullfrog perched on top of the stack of wax papers, handing one to Stormy whenever she was ready to wrap up a finished order. Stormy had short brown hair, kind eyes, and an embroidered apron tied around her waist.

They climbed the small table and hopped up next to Fish. The bullfrog looked surprised for a moment when they arrived, but he adjusted quickly.

"Good evening," he croaked.

"We'd like to buy some kebabs," Edwina said, stepping forward with more confidence than she felt. "Marcus, the map seller's dog... recommended you."

Fish's eyes narrowed, "We don't sell to...*rodents*," he said.

Edwina stepped back, aghast. She turned to Marigold and Chica, twitching her whiskers, unsure what to do.

"Really?" Marigold asked him.

"Of course not!" Fish said, with a loud croaking laugh. "But you should see your faces!"

Edwina breathed a sigh of relief, noticing her paws were shaking just a little. She was starting to realize just how much bigger the world was than what it seemed back at the Academy, and it was just a little bit unnerving.

"Alright, get in here you three," Fish continued, motioning the mice further into the booth where there was a small, cloth-covered table with the vendor's supplies and personal items. "We've got lots of choices, here's the menu," he said, pointing to a piece of paper on a wooden board. "I recommend the Cheese & Squash Kebab, it's the best at the market in my opinion. Roasted Chestnuts are always very popular. If you're feeling frisky, we've got three different spice levels, for whatever your palette prefers. We've also got drinks: Peach Nectar, Raspberry Lemonade, and Water."

"Thank you," Edwina said, reading the menu and looking around the booth. "Can we set up a blanket and eat here?"

Fish looked around to see if Stormy was watching but she was busy spreading brown liquid over raw kebabs.

"I don't see why not," he said. "But you might want to duck out of sight if any strangers come too close. Stormy is good people but you get strange sorts in the Market."

"We understand," Marigold said. "Are we ready to order?"

Edwina and Chica nodded, their whiskers twitching at the enticing smells of the kebab stall.

"What'll it be then?" Fish asked, handing a waxy paper from his stack to Stormy without even looking up.

"One Cheese & Squash Kebab, spice level Medium, and a Peach Nectar" Edwina said.

Marigold squeaked, "Medium? I don't know about that."

"Medium is more like Extra Spicy anywhere else," Fish added.

"I don't mind spicy," Chica said.

"I want *mild*," Marigold said firmly.

Edwina sighed, "Fine, we'll get two. One Mild, one Medium."

Chica nudged her and pointed a paw at the menu.

"And a Roasted Chestnuts," Edwina added.

Fish croaked loudly, "Coming right up!"

He hopped over to the counter where Stormy was pushing vegetables onto sticks and began talking to her quietly. She glanced at the mice for a moment then nodded her head and looked away.

Marigold set her pack down on the table and began searching through it until she found their picnic handkerchief. She pulled it out of the bag and together with Edwina they laid it out on the table, and they all sat down to await their dinner. Chica laid out on her belly and kicked her legs up in the air behind her.

They watched the humans walking past the stall; the miniature lanterns swaying in the breeze cast a warm glow over everything.

They saw all kinds of people, and animals, walking past the market but one in particular caught Edwina's attention.

A woman with long dark hair, a big black hat, and leather pants walking swiftly through the market carrying some ropes under one arm.

Edwina motioned to the other two excitedly.

"I think that's her!"

"Her who?" Marigold asked, peering suspiciously into the crowd.

"Captain Wren, the one Tristan is swooning over."

"Where?" Marigold asked, standing up to get a better view.

Even Chica vaguely peered into the crowd with lazy interest.

Edwina pointed to the woman who was stopped at a booth nearby buying a small leather-bound notebook.

"Goodness, she's beautiful!" Marigold said. "I'm not sure that Tristan could romance someone like her."

"Why not? He's quite good-looking too," Edwina said.

"Is he?" Marigold looked surprised. "I've never thought about it, really."

"Oh yes, all the humans say so. He's *very* attractive, for a human, you know."

"Fascinating," Marigold said. She stood on her tip-toes and peered at the woman. "She certainly does match his description."

"I'm sure it's her," Edwina said confidently. "How exciting!"

Marigold sat back down and leaned back, looking up at the stars.

"I wonder..." she began but stopped.

"Mmm?" Edwina said.

"Hmm, nothing," Marigold replied. "Just thinking about... things."

"Like how fun it is travelling on a ship? Like what if our Handler meets a beautiful pirate captain and she likes him too?" Edwina asked.

"How did you know?" Marigold said.

"Just something I've been thinking about myself," Edwina said.

"I like the ship," Chica said. "Good food, good rugs."

"ORDER UP!" Came the call from across the stall and Fish hopped over to the grill with a fresh piece of wax paper. Stormy leaned down and whispered something to him before handing him the kebabs and a small wooden cup. Fish wrapped up the food and hopped over to the table where the mice were relaxing.

He placed the sizzling kebabs in their wax paper down on the blanket, and the wooden cup full of nectar next to it. The smell was overwhelming and the mice hopped up quickly, excited to taste the special food.

"There's extra sauces over there if you need more spice," he added to Edwina. "Also, this is a bit weird but Stormy has a message for you."

Edwina whisked her tail, "What kind of message?"

Fish sighed, clearly uncomfortable. "Well, Stormy is um, she's a little bit *friendly with the spirits* you could say, you know what I mean?"

"She drinks a lot of alcohol?" Marigold asked, confused.

Fish croaked a laugh, "While that is true, that isn't what I mean. I mean she sees into the future, talks to ghosts, that sort of business."

Edwina looked over at Stormy, her head bobbing in the lantern light as she threw another sizzling kebab onto the grill.

"What does that have to do with us?" she asked.

Fish licked his eyeball with his long tongue then said,

"Sometimes she feels certain people, or mice, need to hear certain things."

"What do we need to hear?" Marigold asked, slightly distressed.

"She said *beware the falling moon*," Fish replied.

"What does that mean?" Edwina asked with a frown.

"No clue, I just deliver the news and the food," Fish said.

"Did she say anything else?" Marigold asked.

"Nope, that's it, just the moon thing. You need anything else?" Chica nudged Edwina.

"Roasted Chestnuts?" Edwina asked.

"Hang on!" Fish said.

A moment later the bullfrog was back with a small wooden bowl full of very hot chestnuts.

"Give 'em a minute to cool down. Anything else?"

"I don't think so," Edwina said. "We've brought our own utensils. Thank you Fish!" She grinned and handed him two silver coins.

"This is more than you need," he said with a croak.

"Keep the rest for yourself," Edwina said, twitching her whiskers.

Fish croaked loudly, "You let me know if you need *anything* else, okay?"

"Absolutely," Edwina said.

Then she turned to the challenge before her. The kebab was

piping hot and bigger than she was. Cutting pieces off of it for her dinner would be tough, and probably messy, but with the delicious aroma filling the area she was more than willing to put in the work.

She had pulled her tiny sword out of its sheath, looking for the best angle for carving the toasty kebab. She approached from the side, going first for a piece of the halloumi cheese, from past experience she knew it would be easier to cut into than the squash. Edwina dug the sword into the hunk of warm cheese, her paws already covered in the brown sauce that slathered the kebab. She sawed at the cheese for a moment until a large piece of it came free, and she stuffed it in her mouth, her eyes lighting up at the delectable flavor.

"You have to try this cheese," she said. But when she looked over, she saw Marigold was already bowled over on the blanket, half of one of the cheese chunks in her paws and a look of absolute bliss on her face.

"Oww!" Chica squeaked, dropping the piping hot chestnut back into the bowl with a frown.

"Mhupmphhh," Marigold said.

A BIT over an hour later the Majesteria finally clambered down the table and waved goodbye to Fish. Their bellies and hearts were full from the delicious meal and good company. They had ended up talking to Fish for a long time and he had regaled them with fascinating tales of the Midnight Market and the strange things that happened there.

He'd warned them to be careful at the market, you never know who you might meet, but the mice didn't worry too much about his warning. After all, they were Majesteria.

So they resumed their journey having fulfilled one of their missions already: the quest for a tasty meal. Now, they were ready to find Quincy Quint's Quill Emporium. As expected, no one took much notice of them at the market, especially the humans. At first they were careful, darting between feet and hiding under stall tables, but soon they realized there was no need; no one was looking at the ground anyway.

After a while of wandering around and being distracted by looking at fine paper goods, they eventually consulted Marigold's map of the market and saw that they were, in fact, very close to Quincy Quint's.

"I'm so excited, my whiskers are tingling!" Edwina said as they made their way towards the end of the aisle to see the quill booth.

"Me too! I can't believe we're really going to see Quincy Quint's in person."

"Did you know they were the first Quill Maker in the Evarian Sea?" Chica said.

"Really? I didn't know that," Marigold said.

"Mhmm, they have been making luxury quills longer than anyone else."

"Bianca said they make the quills there, I want to see that!" Marigold said.

They reached the end of the aisle where Quincy Quint's dominated the back corner with a huge booth. Finally, the booth came into view and the mice let out little squeaks of awe.

The sign for Quincy Quint's Quill Emporium was large and lit with gold and pixie dust, the name in swirling script. The booth had red velvet rugs and was buzzing with activity, dozens of smooth leather boxes with embossed golden logos were laid on carefully turning displays with warm lights above them. A few craftspeople in smart purple uniforms were sitting at worktables carefully assembling quills with delicate tools.

"It's so beautiful," Marigold breathed.

"I could live here forever," Edwina said.

"Those rugs look really cozy," Chica said.

They climbed the leg of one of the tables to peruse the merchandise. The boxes of gilded quills were shining in the soft light like gems from the sea, glittering and majestic. They carefully

tiptoed across the table, looking at all the boxes on their way to see the craftspeople.

"Do you see any quills in our size?" Marigold asked, pulling up her skirt as she jumped over a large quill box.

Edwina peered out across the tables.

"Over there?" she asked, pointing.

"I think that's it!" Marigold squeaked.

They scrambled down the table and dashed across the rug and up the other side.

Laid out before them on the elegant tablecloth were dozens, *nay*, hundreds of quills in niche sizes. Mouse sized, badger sized, fox sized, dwarf sized, Dragonling sized, there was even a giant quill as tall as a human leaned longways on the back of the table.

If you could hold a quill, you could buy one in your size here.

They tiptoed through the small quills section, picking up the boxes and examining the beautiful craftsmanship, comparing various feather types and complicated adornments.

Unfortunately, the fun came to a stop when Edwina checked the price.

"Fifty gold coins!" she shrieked, dropping the box she was holding like a hot potato. "That's highway robbery!"

"I'm sure they can't all be that much," Marigold said, picking up another of the tiny quills to check the price on the bottom.

"Oh."

"What? How much?"

"It's more." Marigold frowned and carefully placed the quill back with a little pat.

A quick examination of the quills determined that they were all in this price range.

"Oh dear, what are we going to do?" Edwina asked woefully. "We only brought eight gold coins, we can't even buy *one* with that!"

"Maybe these are the super luxury ones?" Marigold suggested. "Perhaps they have some, um, less luxurious ones somewhere."

"But I *want* a luxury one!" Edwina wailed.

"I want more Roasted Chestnuts!" Chica said.

"I'm sure some of the, um, lower-end ones would be just lovely," Marigold said, ignoring her. "Let's go over to where they make them and see if we can learn more."

Edwina looked like she didn't believe that at all but she agreed.

They scampered across the rugs and climbed up onto the table on the other side onto the quill-making workstation. There was an older man with white hair and pointed ears wearing a purple uniform with gold trim and looking down through a big magnifying glass. Under the glass his expert hands were carefully winding a piece of leather ribbon around a quill. When he finished, he paused for a second and looked up.

"Hello!" Marigold said, waving at him.

The man jumped back a little

"Oh dear, you scared me little mouse," he said.

"My apologies sir," Marigold said with a little bow. "My friends and I are just shopping for some quills."

"Namely, why are they so bloody expensive!" Edwina said, stepping forward with a hand on her hip.

The man frowned at her and said,

"Every quill is carefully handcrafted by a select group of artisans who have trained their whole lives for this task. If you'd prefer to find something *cheap*, there are plenty of other quills in the world. You come to Quincy Quint's when what you want is *quality*."

"Are you saying the quills I have at home are bad quality?" Edwina said, brandishing her sword. "How *dare* you!"

"Hold on there, calm down Edwina," Marigold said, bowing again to try to mollify the man. "I'm terribly sorry about my friend, she just gets rather excited about quills."

The man looked down at the angry mouse waving her sword, no bigger than a toothpick, violently in his face.

"We have a bin of irregulars over by the cash register?" he offered.

Suddenly, there was a loud crashing sound.

"Oh no!" the man shouted.

Marigold had a bad feeling. She turned to look and saw Chica sitting on the table under a pile of ribbons, holding a small feather in her paw.

"I'm sorry, it looked really soft," she mumbled.

Marigold put her head in her paws and groaned.

AFTER A LOT OF APOLOGIZING, and helping the quill maker to roll up all the ribbons, the mice finally made their way over to the irregular bins and bought themselves two slightly bent quills with their eight gold coins. They also took a mail-order catalog for later.

"I can't believe we couldn't even get three quills for *eight* gold coins," Edwina said, still fuming even though they'd left the booth some while ago.

"At least we got quills!" Chica said cheerfully. "Maybe we could get some more Roasted Chestnuts now?"

"I'm not sure, we're almost out of money," Marigold said with a frown. "I was really hoping to buy some clothes and a gift for Tristan too."

"Humph. If Quincy Quint's hadn't been such a rip-off, we could have bought a quill for Tristan too," Edwina said, whisking her tail back and forth angrily.

Marigold rolled her eyes, "Please, Edwina, can't we just enjoy the rest of the market?"

"I agree," Chica said. "I would really enjoy getting more roasted chestnuts."

"Okay, *fine*," Edwina said, folding her arms. "I'll try to move on and we'll look for clothes...and chestnuts."

"Thank you," Marigold said. "Look over there! It's a cloak vendor, let's see if they have our sizes."

The mice made their way across the aisle, Edwina still fuming about Quincy Quint's and Chica still dreaming of roasted chestnuts.

They crawled under the long cloaks, momentarily lost in a sea of fine silks, wool, and velvet. Eventually they found their way out and clambered up onto a countertop to look at a small rack of doll clothes. Marigold squeaked happily and began skimming through the clothing, checking the prices carefully.

"These are very cheap, I think we could afford to all get something, maybe even two things," she said, her face brightening.

"Really?" Edwina said, surprised. She took a look at the clothing. There were beautiful velvet cloaks with satin ribbons and a few soft flowing dresses. "These are gorgeous, maybe even enough to make up for the lack of quills."

Chica pulled out a long black velvet dress and twirled it around.

"This would look so pretty if I embroidered some stars onto it," she said. "I might even be able to give up the Roasted Chestnuts."

"Don't worry, we're getting those chestnuts!" Marigold said firmly. She set her backpack down on the counter and counted her coins. "We've got just enough, as long as Tristan's gift isn't more than a few copper coins."

"What could we get him that is that cheap?" Edwina asked.

"Tea," Chica said, still twirling in her black velvet dress.

"That's perfect!" Marigold squeaked. "Now I just have to narrow it down to two dresses and one cloak."

"Hey! I thought you said we were each going to only get two clothing items," Edwina said.

"I don't remember agreeing to that," Marigold said, tying the silky ribbons of a cloak around her neck and admiring herself in a nearby mirror.

~

It was almost dawn by the time the Majesteria returned to *The Snapdragon*. The night had been long and eventful but they were happy by the end of it. After they bought the clothing and Tristan's

tea, they wandered for a while more, buying some very cheap embossed stationery and a candied orange slice to share. They ended the evening with another round of Roasted Chestnuts and a small cup of Peach Nectar.

Eventually they found a friendly Dragonling at a barbecue stall who flew them back to the docks for the price of Marigold's last piece of strawberry cheese.

Their paws were aching and their hearts were full as they scampered up the ramp to the deck and onto *The Snapdragon*. They felt a sense of calm and comfort as they walked across the deck with its big lanterns swinging in the breeze above their heads, the sounds of the waves lapping against the ship's sides.

"I like it here," Marigold whispered. "Is that weird?"

"No, I like it too," Edwina said quietly. "It's a good place, it feels like...home, somehow."

Marigold's eyes went wide "You feel it too?"

"Mhmm, there's something special about this ship."

"Yeah, I think so too," Marigold replied.

"It's *magic*," Chica said.

"Huh. Perhaps it is, I hadn't thought of that," Edwina said. "You think the ship itself is magical?"

"Oh yes, 'tis quite obvious," Chica said. "It's so *friendly*."

"*Arrgahhh-fwush*," Marigold said, falling over on the deck with a thump.

Edwina and Chica were startled and turned to look at her, but all they saw was a wriggling piece of paper. After a few moments Marigold emerged, slapping the paper away from her.

"It *attacked* me!" she squeaked, angrily.

"It's a piece of paper," Edwina said, looking down at it. "How could it attack you? It's one of those Wanted posters for that pirate guy, it was probably the wind."

"Or *magic*," Chica said, dramatically.

"Either way, I don't like it," Marigold said, glaring at the poster. "He's dreadful! Just look at that stupid tattoo on his face. Who does that?"

Edwina peered at the poster, "A cutlass with some drops of blood, tattooed on his *face*. Goodness, how ridiculous."

"Maybe it's *magic*," Chica said again.

"That doesn't even make sense," Edwina replied.

"Sorry, I'm tired," Chica said, yawning. "Can we go to bed now?"

"Yes, please!" Marigold said.

Thus the three mice trooped off to bed, leaving the Wanted poster flapping in the breeze behind them.

CHAPTER ELEVEN

TRISTAN AWOKE to the sound of shouting. He sat up quickly and rushed to the door. The last time he'd heard the sound of shouting on the ship had been the visit from the Royal Mariners, and that wasn't something he wanted to repeat. He went into the main room of the cabin in his pajama shirt with bare feet and unkempt hair.

As it was most mornings, Edwina and Marigold were busy writing notes and reading from complicated spellbooks. Chica was asleep and snoring loudly, her pudgy mouse body splayed out on the plush rug in front of the Pixie Hearth.

He realized the sound was coming from the hallway, not the deck above.

"What's going on out there?" he asked.

The mice shrugged, "Not sure but it sounds...*interesting*," Marigold said.

"I'm going to see what it is," Tristan said.

He approached the door and opened it a crack, peering out into the hallway.

What he saw was...quite something.

Emyr and Guy were in the narrow ship's hall, in various states of undress, though they were both wearing pants. Mostly.

"What about all those letters you sent me? Did you mean *any* of it?" Guy said, his angry voice a surprisingly deep bellow for such a slender man.

"I meant every word!" Emyr said. He moved towards Guy but he backed up, shaking his head.

"You said I was the only man for you, I was the sun to your moon," Guy shouted.

"I was being poetic, saying what I felt in the moment," Emyr replied, raising his voice to be heard.

"What about *THIS* then? Huh?" Guy said. Tristan saw Guy waving around a bright red item that was, most likely, some very small undergarments.

"What about it?" Emyr asked, folding his arms and glaring.

At this moment Tristan heard a door creak, and he noticed one of the doors down the hallway opening just enough that two heads could poke out of it and look at the scene taking place in the hallway.

The people peering at the scene in the hallway were Ginger and Birdy, from behind the same door. They were looking very disheveled and not wearing much clothing. He squinted to make sure what he was seeing was true, but there was no mistaking Ginger's bright blue hair.

Oh my. This ship really does love drama.

Tristan closed the door quietly and turned around.

Marigold and Edwina, always the gossip hounds, were now inches away from his feet, listening intently at the door crack.

"Goodness, humans are so weird," Marigold said.

"You can say that again," Edwina chuckled.

"I should've known better than to fall for a bloody *sailor*!" Guy shouted, his voice muffled through the closed door.

"Don't let him worry you Tristan," Marigold said sweetly. "Not all sailors are like that I'm sure."

"Wren seems lovely," Edwina added.

"Wren and I aren't dating," he said flatly.

"Whatever you say," Marigold said cheerfully.

Tristan sighed and pinched his nose.

"Tea?" he asked.

"Yes please!" Edwina said.

"My goodness, I almost forgot! We got you a gift at the market," Marigold said.

Tristan brightened as he poured water into the kettle and set it on the portable stove.

"That reminds me, I got something for you as well, hang on," he said.

He dashed into his room, poured the contents of his satchel onto the bed, grabbed the tea tins, and returned to the living room.

When he arrived he saw that Marigold, Edwina, and a just-barely-awake Chica were presenting him with a tin of tea that was identical to the ones he was crouching down to offer them.

"Great minds think alike I guess?" He said with a laugh.

"One Midnight Delight for everyone!" Edwina said with a grin.

"Thank you kindly," Marigold said, bowing as she accepted her gift.

"Hey, isn't that what we bought you?" Chica said with a yawn.

"Yes, yes it is," Tristan said, taking his tin carefully and bringing it to the tea station with a smile.

Ten minutes of steeping and a lot more shouting from the hallway later, and Tristan finally poured the tea. He put his in a large mug, and then filled up the Majesteria's teapot and brought it on a small tray over to the hearth, along with a little plate of biscuits.

He sat down on the rug next to them and held up his mug

"Cheers!" He said, then took a sip...and made a face.

"To the Midnight Market!" Edwina said, holding her mug of tea in the air.

"To Adventure!" Marigold said.

"Can we get some cheese to have with this?" Chica asked.

Marigold glared at her.

"Oh, um, I mean, cheers?" Chica said, taking the mug of tea Marigold handed her.

All the mice took a sip and then made the same face Tristan had made.

"Ye gods, that's horrible!" Edwina said.

"I think I'm gonna be sick," Marigold moaned.

"I've had worse," Chica said, taking another sip. "It is quite bitter though. Some cheese might help."

"Is that Anise?" Edwina asked.

"With notes of...Oregano?" Tristan said.

"*I* think it has notes of horse dung," Marigold said, putting her mug down reproachfully.

"I'll just brew us something else," Tristan said, picking up the tray gingerly. "I think the kettle still has some water."

~

THE SHIP WAS a lot quieter after they left Brineridge. Tristan had watched the crew loading crates of cargo from the docks, and then they'd pulled up anchor and moved out into the open sea. Afterwards he'd wandered down to the Canteen to get some lunch.

When he entered the room, he was once again taken with a momentary shock when he saw the Harpy tapestry, or 'Ole Gertha' as Basel called her. The violent harpy's scowling face as she flew towards the flaming volcano was unsettling to put it mildly. But he recovered quickly, his stomach grumbling as he made his way to the countertop.

He noticed immediately that it was a lot quieter than he'd ever seen it before. In fact, there seemed to be no one in the Canteen besides himself and Ludwig, the tortoise.

Even the kitchens lacked their usual bustle, there was one person putting some bread in the oven quietly, and another sitting on a stool reading. Basel was at their cocktail station, chopping up strange things and labeling jars. They got up when Tristan approached and came to lean over the counter, resting on their giant arms covered in herbal tattoos.

"Wow, it's quiet in here," Tristan said, looking around in surprise.

"Aye, all the guests left to take that Magick Carpet thingy, everyone on the ship is crew now," Basel said.

"I'm not crew," Tristan said.

"Bah! Says who?" Basel boomed. "You're practically family now, feels like you've been here forever Froggy."

Tristan found himself smiling broadly at this. It was a nice thought, being a part of a crew like *The Snapdragon*, one he wouldn't mind at all.

But then he remembered his job. The Majesteria and the secrets he was keeping. Staying on *The Snapdragon* wasn't likely.

"Anyway, um, I'd like some food. When is dinner service?" He said.

"Ah, not doin' that now it's just crew," Basel said. "Just come on by whenever ye want something, I've always got a few pots stirring. Mostly strawberries, mind you. Might have overbought there if I'm being honest, didn't know everyone would be rushing off so soon. What'll ye have then Frog Boy?"

"Hmm, I think something light," Tristan replied, "I ate so much yesterday at the market, some kind of soup and salad would be nice."

"No problem, no problem at all." Basel said. "How about some strawberries on that salad?"

"Er, I don't know," Tristan said, trying to be polite.

"I can put some candied walnuts too, and some goat cheese. You know, one of them fancy sweet salads. Come on Froggy, don't let me down!"

"Alright then," Tristan said amiably. Basel was hard to say no to.

"You won't regret it!" Basel said cheerfully, turning away towards the kitchen. Suddenly, Tristan was struck with a horrifying thought and he stopped Basel in their tracks.

"Basel, there's not going to be...*strawberries* in the soup is there?"

Basel turned around but wouldn't meet his eyes.

"Why would ye ask that Froggy?"

"I just want a regular soup," Tristan said.

"It tastes better than you'd think!" Basel said. "Why not give it a try?"

"I'll pass just the same," Tristan said firmly.

"Fine, I'll get ye the mushroom," Basel muttered and walked away, shaking their head.

After Basel had given him a big bowl of mushroom soup, a large salad, and side of strawberry slices ('just in case'), Tristan went and sat down in his favorite spot by the window.

"Ahem," said a sardonic voice by his foot.

"Oh, hello Ludwig," Tristan said.

"I see you're having salad," the tortoise replied.

"Yes."

"I'm not having salad," Ludwig said sourly.

"Okay," Tristan ate a spoonful of soup.

"I like lettuce."

"Would you like a strawberry?" Tristan asked.

"I have had enough strawberries," Ludwig said, his monotone voice tinged with bitterness.

Tristan looked down and saw there was a huge bowl of strawberries nearby. It looked entirely untouched.

"Ah, I see." he said.

Tristan took about half of his salad and put it carefully on top of the strawberries.

"There you go buddy, some lettuce for you," he said.

"We're not buddies," Ludwig said, moving towards the bowl with surprising speed.

"Right, of course," Tristan said.

"This doesn't make us friends."

"I know."

"But you can scratch my head."

"Okay."

Tristan smiled and scratched the tortoise's head while Ludwig munched on the salad.

∽

THE MOON WAS RISING into the sky, its shimmering light catching on the waves as Tristan emerged onto the deck with his toolkit in hand, ready to catch Starlight.

He stopped when he saw a familiar figure hunched over a large copper telescope, peering into it, and then standing back to make notes in a small leather notebook.

"Evening Captain," he said, walking over to her.

Her body tensed momentarily and he thought perhaps he had spooked her, but whatever she felt, she didn't show it on her face. By the time she turned around to look at him she was as relaxed and confident as ever.

"Evening, Tristan," she replied, nodding her head.

"Anything interesting in the sky tonight?" he asked. He was already feeling nervous, just being close to her in the romantic moonlit night, with no sailors nearby. It felt intimate, in a way that made his skin tingle.

"Actually, yes. Would you like to take a look?" she said, standing aside so he could use the telescope.

"The stars look beautiful, but I don't see anything different," he said.

"Hold on, let me move it to the right spot," she said.

She leaned around him, positioning the telescope carefully, her body heat in stark contrast to the cold night air. For a moment he couldn't breathe when he felt her brush against him, but he tried to stay focused on the stars she was pointing him towards.

"I see it!" he exclaimed. "Is that a falling star?"

"Sort of, I think it's quite a bit more than one," she said. More and more little white streaks were starting to cross the the sky. More were arriving every second, after a moment, he didn't need a telescope to see the barrage of light.

"A Star Shower, yes I've read about this," he said, standing back. "They're quite magical, are they not?"

She nodded, her face a knot of worry.

"I've heard that too," she said. "Beautiful, but dangerous. Terrible timing as well."

"Why's that?" He asked.

"We're heading into The Straights of Stormrock, it's a narrow channel where...well, nevermind."

"Where what?"

"Nothing, it's just that..." she sighed. "It's the most dangerous part of the journey to Fairefeux. It's a straight between two outcroppings of rock, the water is choppy and the waves are big. The weather is often strange and magic is a little more wild in The Straights. A lot of things can go wrong through there, and if you don't navigate it correctly...all kinds of things could happen. Let's just say, it's not a nice place to make a mistake."

"What happens if something goes wrong?" he asked.

"Don't worry, I'm just thinking out loud," she said. "It'll be fine. We travel through The Straights all the time, nothing's ever gone wrong before."

"Oh no!" Tristan said, alarmed.

"What?" she asked.

"That's what everyone always says in adventure novels right before everything goes horribly wrong!"

Wren scoffed at this, "You need to get your head out of those romantic books you're always reading, life on a ship is nothing like that."

"I beg to differ. It's been *exactly* like the books so far," Tristan countered. "I've seen strange islands, there's been drinking and sea shanties, criminals and danger, billowing blouses and kissing. Pretty much exactly like the books."

"Kissing?" Wren said, raising an eyebrow.

Tristan suddenly felt their closeness, the expansive deck faded into the background as he looked into her eyes. Her dark eyes shimmered with the light of the stars, and something else. Something he wasn't expecting at all, something quite a lot like...longing.

"Ahem, well, I mean, I have seen...some people on the crew are very..."

"*Very?*" She asked, taking a small step towards him, her leather hips swiveling ever-so-slightly in his direction. Her gaze locked on his, and the gold coin stilled in her fingers as the tension in the air grew.

"You know...um...adventurous," he said.

He didn't really know what he was saying, he was too lost in the deep pools of her eyes and the way she kept inching forward with her body.

He leaned towards her without even realizing he was doing it, placing his hand right next to hers on the telescope.

"Adventurous?" She said the word very differently than he had.

Sensuously. In a way that made him think of very different things than swords and sorcery. "I like the sound of that," she said.

Their fingers touched on the telescope and he felt the warmth of her callused finger on his soft hand. The coldness of her silver rings.

She didn't move away.

She just kept staring at him, fixing him with her glittering gaze.

He felt his heart pounding in his chest, like a bird trying to escape.

He leaned towards her, his breath coming in short, ragged gasps...

"Hey look! The sky is falling!" a cheerful voice shouted.

Suddenly the crew was filling the deck, Wren hastily removed her hand and the spell was broken. She backed away quickly, but her gaze still lingered on him for a moment. She looked at him with something unmistakeable.

Desire. She didn't try to hide it.

Soon everyone on the ship was up on the deck watching the

stars falling. The streaks of white light got bigger and brighter, filling up the sky. The sight was awe inspiring and Tristan felt his tattoos tingling as the air began to feel thick with magic.

He wasn't sure but he could have sworn he felt the ship leaning towards the Star Shower, almost as though it wanted to be closer to the magic.

As the night got colder Ginger brought big rough wool blankets up to the deck, and Basel brought around a tray with cups of warm broth. They put the blankets around their shoulders and watched the stars flash across the sky. Tristan felt a tangle of emotions. First and foremost, he wished the Majesteria could have seen the Star Shower. As a Starlight mage it felt wrong to not be sharing this experience with them, he knew they would have loved it. He also felt a knot in the pit of his stomach at the knowledge he'd been lying to Wren for so long. She had no idea that right below her feet was the Royal Cinderflower and three Majesteria.

Then there was tonight.

He couldn't stop thinking about the moment they'd shared before the crew showed up. The look, the touch, the heat. It was a different kind of magic, one he was desperately yearning to feel again.

All these thoughts were swirling around in his head as he stood on the deck watching the glittering stars arc across the darkening sky.

"Wren! Come see this," Emyr shouted. He'd been looking through the telescope at the area where the stars were falling.

"What is it?" she asked, hurrying up to the telescope.

"I think it's a whirlpool," he said.

There was a gasp from the crew.

"What does that mean for us?" Tristan asked.

"Nothin' good," Birdy said, shaking her head.

There was more muttering and worried gasps.

"Those can sink a ship in seconds!" a sailor nearby said.

"What if it pulls us in?" someone asked.

"That's how my mam died," another sailor said.

Wren looked up from the telescope, her face stern.

"Calm down everyone," she said, pitching her voice so it could be heard across the deck. "It's alright, we've avoided plenty of whirlpools before, and this one will be no different."

"Ain't we goin' into the Straights of Stormrock?" someone asked.

"Aye, we are," Wren said. "But we will be fine, we will idle here for a while until the sea calms down. I'll turn the ship West, and we'll make for calmer seas and wait it out."

Another gasp went up from the crew.

"What? What is it?" Wren asked.

Everyone pointed to the sky.

Tristan looked up and his mouth dropped.

Suddenly, the fortune-teller's warning appeared in his mind.

Beware the falling moon.

The moon was hanging in the sky, full and bright, its light glistening on the churning waters. But something was...moving. The moon seemed to be getting bigger and redder, and heading towards them rapidly.

"*The Falling Moon*," Tristan breathed, anxiety creeping up his spine. "It's happening, the prophecy."

The crew, as one, moved towards the railing to get a better look at the moon and the whirlpool.

Wren was already running to the wheel, her boots tapping loudly on the wooden deck. Emyr was right behind her, a smaller telescope in his hand.

The crew started shouting to each other and cursing as they caught sight of the bright red moon growing larger every moment. Tristan watched as the "falling moon" separated itself from the real moon and became a ball of light, soaring across the sky. The light seemed to be headed for the ever-growing whirlpool, getting bigger and bigger as it flew, all the while the ship was rocking wildly from side to side in the suddenly choppy sea.

"CAPTAIN!" Birdy shouted.

"What!" Wren shouted back, wasting no time on extra words when she had a job to do.

"We've got company!" Birdy called back.

"WHAT THE HELL?" Wren shouted.

Emyr ran down the ship's side to where Birdy was pointing. The crew crowded around to see.

Tristan gasped along with everyone else.

Birdy was right.

A very large ship was bearing down on them at high speed.

Chapter Twelve

"EMYR!" Wren shouted. "TAKE THE WHEEL!"

"AYE!" he called back and ran to take her place.

Wren came barrelling down the deck to where everyone was watching the ship come in. The crew parted to make room for Wren to pull the spyglass from her hip and look out at the ship.

"Who is it?" Birdy asked nervously.

"I don't know, but they're headed straight for us," Wren said, sparing a glance for the shower of stars falling into the sea. "At the worst possible time."

"Maybe they're friendly?" Ginger suggested cheerfully.

"Yeah, maybe," Wren said with a frown. "Birdy!"

"Aye, Captain?" Birdy said, throwing off her blanket and standing to attention.

"Raise the Queen's Flag," Wren said promptly. "Quickly."

Birdy didn't say anything, she just nodded and dashed away.

"Ginger, do you know where the solid color flags are?"

"In my office, Captain," Ginger said.

"Get the Red one as fast as you can. If they are friendly, we want to make sure they know not to come this way."

"What if they're not friendly?" someone asked.

Wren didn't reply.

"What's going on?" Tristan asked, almost to himself. The whirlpool and the star shower he could understand, that threat was obvious. But why was everyone more concerned with this other ship?

Then he remembered his pirate novels.

How the evil pirates would always come up on the heroes in open waters and board their ship, fighting them for their cargo and treasures.

"The Captain is raisin' the Queen's Flag so if they're friendly, they'll know we are too," Basel said.

"The Red flag is so they'll know there is danger ahead, dearheart," Bonnie added.

Birdy returned, and together with some of the deckhands, attached the Queen's Flag to the ropes. Then she hopped up into the rigging and began climbing, pulling the flag with her as she ascended to dizzying heights.

She affixed it to the mast and unfurled the flag, its bright fabric flapping in the wind. Tristan couldn't help noticing the the Queen's Flag depicted the Royal Cinderflower with crowns on either side.

He felt a trembling in his hands as he realized the many possibilities of what could go wrong tonight: that very same flower was on this ship.

Birdy climbed back down and grabbed the Red flag from Ginger's hands and then returned to the rigging, affixing the flag slightly below the Queen's Flag.

Then, everyone waited, holding their breath.

The ship didn't slow its pace at all; it kept heading towards them, the dark shadows of its sails looming larger every moment.

Finally, the ship raised a flag.

It was the Queen's Flag, the same as theirs.

But...it kept coming towards them just as fast.

A ragged cheer went up from the crew as they relaxed a little. But Wren's expression didn't change, she was still wound as tightly as a bowstring as she peered through her little spyglass at the oncoming ship.

"What is it?" Tristan asked her.

She frowned and began to pace the deck.

"They're still coming at high speed, even after the Red flag," she said, thinking fast. "Sometimes pirates raise a false flag so that they can get close enough to shoot before they tell you who they really are."

"Maybe something is wrong on their ship and they need our help, even if it's dangerous?" Ginger suggested, but she didn't sound very confident.

"Maybe," Wren said with a sigh. "Ginger, take some of the crew and get some weapons from my office. Birdy, prepare the sails to fly at high speed. Regardless of what happens with this oncoming ship, we still need to get out of range of the whirlpool. Basel take your chefs and Tristan below decks and–"

Wren's command was cut off by a gasp of horror from the crew.

Tristan looked out at the oncoming ship and saw that they were firing a catapult, sending a wave of pixie-dust-laced explosives across the sea.

"That ain't friendly!" Ginger shouted, sprinting away to Wren's office to grab the weapons.

"*EMYR!*" Wren shouted, looking at the ship through her spyglass again.

"Already steering us out of range Captain!" Emyr called.

Basel ran downstairs to take cover with the chefs, but Tristan couldn't seem to get his feet to move. He knew Wren had asked him to get out of the way but he was locked in place, still reeling from everything that was happening around him.

"*FUCK!*" Wren shouted suddenly. The blast had hit the side of the ship, but thanks to Emyr's steering had only grazed them. That wasn't why Wren was cursing.

Tristan followed her gaze to the oncoming ship and saw that the Queen's Flag was gone and replaced with an entirely different symbol.

A black flag with a large cutlass and three red droplets of blood.

"What does it mean?" He asked.

"Mad Richard," Wren said. "That's his symbol, haven't you seen it on all those posters? He's got it tattooed on his face!"

Suddenly, a vision of a strange man in a darkened aisle of the Midnight Market came to Tristan's mind.

A man who showed a lot of interest in Majesteria and had a very unusual tattoo on his face.

"What are we going to do?" Ginger asked, dumping a pile of crossbows, swords, and axes on the deck. "We're not prepared to fight off someone like him. Hell, I've only ever been on passenger ships!"

"It might not come to that," Wren said, looking worried. "Our cargo is fairly low value compared to what he's used to, he's fired a warning shot so he's obviously hoping we'll surrender without a fight. Which I suppose we might do, if it comes to that, but first I need to figure something out."

"What's that, Captain?" Ginger asked.

"*Why* is he chasing us?" Wren said, her expression cloudy as she tried to work out the puzzle. "He would know what a Registered Pirate Vessel has on board. People like him don't usually waste their time with ships like ours, especially with the Royal Mariners on their ass. So, why us?"

Tristan felt his stomach drop as it all became crystal clear.

Mad Richard, *the Mage Stealer.*

And just like that, his feet could work again.

~

TRISTAN BARRELED down the stairs to his cabin, his heart feeling like it would rip out of his chest. The tension in his body made his breath shallow and quick as he ran, panic growing inside him. He turned the door handle and was momentarily shocked by the scene of the Majesteria cheerfully eating cheese and scribbling academic notes on their scrolls.

He had completely forgotten that only an hour before things had been cheery and calm, he'd wandered up to the deck to catch Starlight in the cool night breeze.

"Tristan, are you alright?" Marigold said, laying down her tiny quill when she saw the look on his face.

Tristan shook his head, leaning over and gasping for breath, trying to get control of himself.

"What is it? What's happening?" Edwina asked, scurrying over to him.

Tristan told them, explaining how Mad Richard had seen his tattoos at the Midnight Market while he was trying on gloves, and inquired about the Majesteria. He explained how he hadn't known at the time that Mad Richard had a tattoo of a cutlass on his face, and hadn't realized the strange man was a wanted pirate, a pirate known for abducting mages. He briefly told them about the Star Shower, the magic whirlpool, and that Mad Richard was now firing on the ship, most likely because he wanted to abduct the Majesteria.

The mice were silent for a while, looking at him and adjusting their outlook to the new circumstances.

"I think we should put it to a vote," Edwina said solemnly.

"What?" Tristan asked, confused.

"If we should tell Wren we are on board and use our magic to help, or if we should stay hidden and not use our magic like we're supposed to," Edwina said, her tone suddenly taking on the air of a powerful, well-respected mage. "Revealing not only ourselves but the existence of the Royal Cinderflower is an incredibly *serious* thing, and should not be taken lightly. I propose a vote."

Marigold and Chica both nodded their agreement.

"All those against say NAY," she said.

"NAY," Chica said. "I think we should tell them!"

"All those *for* say AYE," Edwina said, giving Chica a withering look but not dropping her serious demeanor.

Tristan, Marigold and Edwina all said "AYE"

"The AYEs have it," Edwina said formally, "we shall tell the Captain and offer our assistance in this serious matter."

"Wait, AYE meant we wanted to tell her? Can I change my vote?" Chica asked.

"We already decided to do it," Edwina said.

"Yeah, but I still wanna change my vote," Chica said.

"We really don't have time for this," Marigold said, "Tristan, please get our supplies and we'll get in the Boarding Trunk for you to carry us up. Let's meet Wren in her office."

"Of course," Tristan said, standing up and hurrying to their luggage to find the Majesteria's magical toolkit.

The mice ran off to their Boarding Trunk where he knew they would be changing into their ceremonial robes.

"I still don't see why I can't change my vote," he heard Chica saying as they scurried into the trunk.

~

THE SHIP WAS in chaos when Tristan emerged, clutching the Boarding Trunk tightly to his chest. People were running and shouting everywhere, Birdy was trying to show some of the newer deckhands how to use the weapons. Ginger was swinging an axe around wildly in the way that only someone who didn't know how to use it could. Wren was steering while Emyr was looking through his spyglass and shouting things. The ship was starting to rock and sway from the waves created by the falling stars.

But all Tristan could think about was his mission.

He stalked across the deck purposefully and ran up to the steering wheel. Wren caught sight of him and said,

"Tristan, I told you to get down below. It's not safe up here!"

"I need to talk to you, *NOW*," Tristan shouted. "In your office."

He held up the Boarding Trunk.

"Now? You want to show me what's in the trunk *now*?" She said, never taking her hands off the wheel.

"Yes! It's very important can you please come with me?"

"Tristan there is a mad pirate coming and–"

He cut her off.

"*NOW CAPTAIN!*"

His tone was firm, harsh, and unyielding.

Wren took notice.

"Okay fine," she said. "Emyr take the wheel, I'll be right back."

Emyr nodded and seamlessly took the wheel from her, stuffing his spyglass inside his waistcoat.

Tristan didn't check to see if she was coming. He just started barrelling down the little staircase to her office. By the time he got there Wren was right behind him and opened the door to let him in.

She walked over to her desk and turned to him with folded arms and angry eyes.

"I've got the most wanted pirate in the realm bearing down on me and a flaming star falling into the sea, so this better be *damn* fucking good Tristan," she said.

Tristan nodded and put the box down on her desk. He turned to pull the little hatch open and hesitated for a fraction of a second.

He knew she would be furious at him, she might even hate him. The rest of the crew might, too. But really...what could he do?

If Mad Richard caught them she'd find out anyway, but this way he'd have a chance to stop them. Plus, the Majesteria had already voted so it wasn't like he had a choice.

He pulled open the hatch and the Majesteria ran out, their ceremonial robes sweeping along the paperwork on Wren's desk.

Wren gasped and sat down with a thump.

"Oh *gods*," she breathed. "You're those, those...special magic mice aren't you? The really powerful ones."

The mice all bowed very dramatically, sweeping their robes around them.

"We are Majesteria, madam," Edwina said in her most pompous

tone. "We currently reside at Teakley Academy, but we are a part of The Grand Majesterium of Magical Creatures."

"And you've...been on my ship...this whole time..." Wren said weakly.

She looked up at Tristan helplessly.

He coughed nervously.

"There's more, I'm afraid," he said, frowning. "I'm so sorry."

"We are on an important Mission," Marigold stepped forward, lifting her paws in the air with all the drama of a stage actor. "We are bringing The Royal Cinderflower to the Queen's Coronation."

"*WHAT*!?" Wren stood up violently, sending her chair flying across the room.

"You...you can't be serious?" She said, pointing a shaking finger at Tristan. "Is this some kind of horrible joke? *The Royal Cinderflower*?"

"Yes, we've been travelling from Teakley Academy, to bring it to the Coronation, it's very important-" Edwina started.

"I know it's fucking *important*! It's on the gods-damned *flag*!" Wren shouted. She yanked open a drawer on her desk and Tristan flinched, unsure what she might pull out of it.

It was a bottle of whiskey, which she began to drink in large gulps.

She wiped her mouth clean, her eyes wide and breathing shallow.

She stared at the wall and then turned back to Tristan with a fire blazing in her eyes that made him stumble backwards til he hit the wall.

"*HE KNOWS, DOESN'T HE*!" She shouted, pointing a trembling finger out towards the general direction of the approaching ship. "*That's* why he's here."

"Yes, well, sort of, he doesn't know about The Royal Cinderflower, thank the stars," Tristan was babbling at high speed, "it was an accident really, I was trying on these gloves and..."

"We don't have time for this," Edwina said primly, stepping

forward. "We have chosen to *reveal ourselves*, despite it being *against the rules*, in order to offer you our help."

Wren looked down at the three mice standing boldly before her and took another sip of her whiskey.

"What?" she croaked.

"As you noted so sensibly before, we are powerful mages, and since our circumstances are part and partial of this grave situation, we would like to offer our assistance in resolving this matter," Marigold said in her best professional voice

Wren just stared.

"WHAT?"

"We do magic. We're gonna do magic at the bad guy," Chica said helpfully.

Wren tried to sit down again but her chair was gone so she just stumbled backwards. She nearly fell over but managed to steady herself. Tristan watched with absolute awe as Wren began her emotional journey back from total shock to the confident Captain he knew. Within a few minutes, and quite a few more sips of whiskey, she had composed herself. Wren looked at the mice with the face of someone who's just remembered that it's their personal responsibility to save the lives of everyone on their ship.

"Alright, what do I do?" she asked.

As it turned out, Wren didn't need to do that much. Mostly, she just needed to listen. Once she understood the situation it became clear that, no matter what, they absolutely could not surrender and let Mad Richard on their ship.

After a brief conversation with the Majesteria she stalked briskly out of the cabin with Tristan trailing behind her with the Boarding Trunk.

"*ATTENTION!*" she shouted, pitching her voice til it was booming across the ship, full of command and authority. Despite the chaos and noise all the crew stopped whatever they were doing and turned to give her their rapt attention.

"Birdy! *Do not* raise that flag," Wren said, noticing in the nick of time that Birdy had been about to unfurl the white flag of surrender.

"We're not going to surrender?" Ginger said, her voice trembling.

"But we have to!" someone called out.

"We've got no chance against Mad Richard!" someone else said.

"Isn't is safer to just surrender?" another sailor asked.

"We have some *extremely* important...cargo, that we cannot let Mad Richard get his hands on under *any* circumstances," Wren said severely. "Tristan and his mage friends will be helping us fight him. *Do not* disturb them, no matter what strange magic you see. I promise you, this is the right decision. We will have a meeting after we are out of danger and I'll explain everything. For now, help however you can and get our rigging ready to *fly*, we are sailing out of here."

A few of the crew murmured surprise but they shrugged and nodded their heads in agreement.

"AYE!" came the call of the crew, and then Wren was away, dashing up to take the wheel again while Tristan was suddenly left alone.

He looked at the dreadful ship, nearly upon them. He could see the Captain standing at its prow, grinning like a cat while his crew prepared to fire on *The Snapdragon* again.

Not today, Mad Richard.

Tristan set down the Boarding Trunk in the middle of the deck and sat down beside it. A few of the crew looked at him sidelong but no one said anything, they would not disobey Captain's orders at a time like this.

He pulled open the hatch and the Majesteria came out onto the deck, their long ceremonial robes sweeping along the slick wood.

"What now?" he asked them.

"Do you have any Starlight?" Edwina asked.

Tristan shook his head, "I had been about to catch some when all this happened, I'm sorry."

"That's okay," Marigold said, patting his hand with her paw. She caught sight of the falling stars and gasped. "I think Starlight should be easy to come by tonight!"

"The air is thick with magic," Chica said, licking a paw and putting it in the air to feel the wind.

Tristan nodded, "I can feel it too."

"Let's use the channelling batons," Edwina said thoughtfully, "and we will set up a Binding Circle. Please tell one of the crew that we will need to be hanging near the railing when our spell is ready."

Tristan nodded and quickly set about following their orders. He handed them chalk and their metal instruments to make the Binding Circle, and pulled out the channelling batons from his own toolkit. He set them down and went to find a sailor to help him while the mice marked up the deck with magical symbols.

It didn't take him long, Ginger was standing very nearby trying desperately to pretend she wasn't staring at the Majesteria.

"Ginger, my friends-" Tristan began.

"The mice?" She asked, peering curiously around his shoulder.

Tristan cleared his throat "Yes, they are mages. They will be helping fight Mad Richard with magic, but they are going to need to be hanging near the railing when their spell is ready."

Ginger gulped and nodded her head as she digested all this information.

"Okay, I can get something ready I think. How soon do you need it?"

"A few minutes," Tristan said, turning away without even waiting to hear her answer. There simply wasn't time.

A couple seconds later he was back with the Majesteria and pulling off his gloves. The star tattoos on his hands lit up almost instantly in the powerful magical energy coming from the Star Shower. The mice were almost done marking out their binding circle with occult symbols, soon they would be ready for the Starlight.

He picked up the channelling batons and focused his mind.

He gasped as the Starlight poured into his body instantly, the magic filling him so intensely he guessed he must be glowing like a star himself. He pushed back with all his strength, trying to wrestle and contain the powerful magic of the Star Shower. He only needed a little bit for this spell, so he pulled the tendrils of Starlight out of the air as quickly as he dared, winding the strings around the channelling batons. As soon as they were brightly glowing he broke the connection, staggering backwards as he tried to get ahold of himself.

He stumbled in a dizzy haze towards the mice as he felt the Starlight clambering around him, trying to soar through the channel that was his body again. He tried to ignore it and focus, but it wasn't easy with so much magic in the air.

He sat down and placed the channelling baton next to the Majesteria as he tried to steady himself on the shuddering deck. After a brief glance to make sure he was alright the mice began to pull at the threads of Starlight on the channelling batons with their paws, funneling the light into their circle and lighting up the chalk like it was made of liquid fire.

The circle glowed brighter and brighter; then the Majesteria lifted it up off the deck, holding it hovering in the air with their outstretched paws. Then they moved towards each other and the glowing circle got smaller and smaller until it was the size of a pocket watch.

"Okay Tristan, it's ready!" Edwina called out. The glowing circle was humming and jittering as the mice held it in place.

There was a horrible sound, a crash and a splintering, followed by a scream. Tristan glanced up and saw that Mad Richard's mages had loosed another catapult blast at the ship again, this time it landed in some of the rigging, setting it on fire.

The crew was shouting and running around, trying to put the fire out. He looked to the stern and saw Wren's determined gaze as she immediately began pulling the ship away.

Tristan noticed a strange sensation as the ship changed course.

The ship was moving way faster than it should be and big sprays of water were coming up onto the ship and splashing over the crew.

He turned back to the Majesteria, he didn't have time to think about crashing waves, he had to focus on the task at hand.

A moment later Ginger appeared at his side.

"Will this work?" she asked, holding up a small bucket stuffed with a towel, ready to be tied onto the rigging near the railing so the mice could easily lean out of it to cast their spell.

"This is perfect," Tristan said, taking the bucket and lowering it to the floor. He turned it sideways so the mice could hop in, carefully holding the shaking spell between them. He gently picked up the bucket and handed it nervously to Ginger who took it cautiously.

They moved to the rigging, Tristan watching with worry at every step. Ginger tied the bucket low on the ropes, holding the bottom in place at an angle so the mice could get a clear shot of the other ship.

For its part *The Snapdragon* was careening fast now, gliding through the water at strange angles, while the wind was getting louder and stronger, pulling at Tristan's hair and cloak. But he paid all of that no mind, all he could think about was getting the spell released before Mad Richard's mages could load their catapult again.

The Majesteria moved carefully to the edge of the bucket and with one fluid motion they flung the spell into the air. Tristan, and most of the crew, watched with wonder as the small shimmering circle of magic flew across the dark night, expanding in size as it crashed over its destination.

The spell exploded above the ship in a massive wave of blue-white fire, shooting across the ship and pouring down a rain of starlight not dissimilar to the Star Shower they had witnessed a little while before.

For a moment Tristan saw Mad Richard, his eyes alight with anger and shock, and then his ship was blown wildly backwards by the blast. Tristan watched as the pirate's ship got flung out to sea, far away from them, just as their own ship was rocked by a massive wave.

He quickly ran up to the rigging and untied the bucket, hugging it close to his chest as a huge wave crashed over the side of the ship, pouring water over everything and everyone.

Tristan looked up and saw dark rocky islands loomed on either side of the ship, and when he looked out to sea all he saw was choppy waters and waves getting ever larger as they crashed into the sides of the ship.

Suddenly, a horrifying thought crept into his mind.

He'd forgotten about the whirlpool.

Chapter Thirteen

WHAT HAPPENED NEXT WAS a bit of a blur to Tristan. Ginger bustled him down the stairs to his cabin in a daze, clutching the bucket of Majesteria tightly to his chest with white knuckles. He stumbled along behind her as she carried the Boarding Trunk and his magical tools into his room.

All the while, the ship swayed and shook wildly.

She laid down the tools in his room and muttered,

"So *that's* what all those pillows were for," before dashing out again to rejoin the rest of the crew on the deck.

"Too...Much...Starlight..." he mumbled.

Tristan made it into the room and set down the Majesteria's bucket before he collapsed, falling forward onto the pile of cushions, intermingled with scrolls and quills.

When he woke up the ship was rocking and the wind was howling. Edwina, Marigold, and Chica were standing in front of him looking very concerned. Marigold was holding one of his nut bars under his nose, hoping he would eat it to regain his strength. Edwina was pacing back and forth, throwing her hands in the air and mumbled to herself. Chica seemed to be attempting to lift one of his eyelids.

He sat up, shaking off Chica, and took the nut bar from Marigold, biting into the nourishing food.

"You're awake!" Marigold cheered. Edwina didn't stop her pacing.

Tristan nodded numbly. "There was...so much magic," he said.

"But *where* are we going?" Edwina whispered to herself, scratching her head.

"She's been taking Starlight readings," Marigold explained. "It's very strange, she thinks the whirlpool has turned into a portal to another realm. I don't know how likely that is, but we'll see I suppose."

"I hope they have good cheese there," Chica said. Tristan noticed she was poking him in the leg with one of the channelling batons.

"Ow!" he said. "What are you doing?"

"Tryin' to get the extra Starlight out," she said. "You got too much."

"I know I did but I don't think- Ow!- Poking me with a channelling baton is doing anything."

"It's making me feel useful," Chica said, poking him again with grim determination.

"Ow!" Tristan said.

Before they could continue this conversation the ship swayed furiously, sliding so sharply in one direction that all of them went tumbling across the floor in a whirlwind of pillows.

When they settled the cabin was on a serious slant, but Edwina struggled to her feet and said,

"I *knew* it! Look at the window! We're in the whirlpool now!"

Tristan looked up at the window, horrified. All he saw was water.

The ship lurched again and they went sliding further across the floor along with most of their trunks.

"The Royal Cinderflower!" Marigold squeaked, hurrying over to its trunk. Tristan crawled along the floor to the trunk, not daring to stand and risk falling over again. He carefully lifted the lid and peeked inside the trunk, breathing a sigh of relief.

"It's alright," he whispered. "Although it's looking a little droopy."

He shut the lid carefully just as the ship lurched again, sliding them all crashing into the back wall. Luckily, Tristan's body broke the fall of the Cinderflower's trunk and it was undamaged. Unfortunately, Tristan couldn't say the same for himself.

In addition to his wooziness from conducting too much Starlight through his body, he now appeared to have cut himself on the Cinderflower's box and was bleeding in a few places.

But he barely noticed because the ship was still rocking and swaying and the sound of rushing water was getting louder.

He looked around for the mice; they had all landed in a pile of pillows. That was something at least.

"Are you all okay?" He called out.

"Yes!" Marigold called back. "Tristan, you're bleeding!"

"I know," he said, raising his voice to be heard over the terrifying sounds coming from outside the ship. "But the Cinderflower is unharmed, so it's going to be okay."

It had to be.

Tristan held tightly to the Cinderflower's box, the corners cutting into his chest, as the ship wobbled and rocked frantically and the swirling water got louder and louder. The mice clung onto each other, scrunched into a corner between a mountain of pillows.

"But *where* are we going?" Edwina said.

"WHAT?" Tristan shouted over the sound of the raging waters.

"WHERE ARE WE GOING?" she yelled back.

"I DON'T KNOW!" Tristan shouted.

And then, it was silent.

The ship veered back to normal with a thump, sending them all swinging wildly across the floor in the other direction, sliding over to the Pixie Hearth again. After a moment of scrambling, they saw that the ship appeared to have righted itself and was now bobbing along in the water softly.

Tristan ever-so gently let go of the Royal Cinderflower's box and staggered to his feet to look out the window.

He gasped.

"What is it?" Marigold asked, scrambling to stand up and running towards him.

"I think Edwina was right," he said. "We're somewhere new."

"But where are we? *That* is the question!" Edwina said, scurrying across the floor to climb up to the window.

Chica climbed up too and looked out at the view.

"Why's the sea like that?" she asked.

"We're somewhere new!" Marigold said, her voice awed.

The sea had a bright green color. Not bluish-green like the sea often is, but green like an apple, with hints of sparkling emerald cresting the waves.

Beyond the strange color of the sea there was nothing else to see in the moonlit night of the strange realm. Just a big green sea stretching out to the horizon.

"Let's go up on the deck," Tristan said.

"You might want to eat another nut bar first," Marigold said, noting the way in which Tristan sagged when he stood.

"You should really get those wounds patched up," Edwina added.

"One thing at a time," Tristan said with a sigh.

When they arrived on the deck everyone was as battered and confused as they were. The deck was in chaos, broken barrels and knotted rope lay everywhere, seaweed and seashells tangled in the wreckage. Many of the crew were laid out on the deck, bleeding or holding their heads. Absolutely everyone and everything was soaking wet.

He looked around for Wren when he saw she wasn't at the ship's wheel. She didn't need to be any longer, the ship was floating along peacefully as though they hadn't just been in a colossal whirlpool a few minutes before.

Tristan finally found her, crouched over the shattered remains of the telescope with Emyr.

As Tristan and the mice walked across the deck only a few people raised eyebrows. Most of the crew had far too many other things going on to worry about some strange magical mice.

When they arrived Tristan watched while the mice scurried forward to speak to The Captain.

"Do you know where we are?" Wren asked them, sounding dazed.

"Another realm," Edwina said firmly. The other mice nodded their professional agreement.

"Right, I noticed that. But, um, which one? The stars are not the same," Wren said, glancing upward nervously.

Tristan and the mice looked up at the stars and saw she was right. All the constellations were completely different, though they still glowed just as brightly and he could still feel the little pulses of the stars' magic under his skin.

"Not sure I know, Captain," Marigold said with a small salute.

"Thank you anyway," Wren said, picking up a piece of bent metal with a sigh. "It's gonna be a lot harder to figure out without this thing."

Edwina scurried over to the telescope and began peering at the broken pieces with a professional eye. Marigold and Chica soon joined her, speaking to each other in hushed tones.

Wren sat back on her haunches and thought for a while.

"It seems we are safe...for the moment," she said. "I believe Mad Richard is still in the Evarian Sea. For now, we should tend to wounds, get some food, and try to figure out where we are before the dawn."

"I think we can fix this!" Edwina said cheerfully.

Wren looked surprised "Really? With magic?"

"Magic? Why would we use magic?" Chica asked, confused. "It's just a telescope."

"Mhmm, it's just got these components that are twisted here," Marigold said pointing, "that's your real problem, the glass is easy enough to replace but we're gonna need to bend those back into shape."

"We'll need to get some wire and something to solder it with," Edwina added thoughtfully.

"Um, yeah, okay," Wren said, looking at Tristan with a raised eyebrow.

He just smiled. He knew soon enough the other shoe would drop and all Wren's justified rage would come boiling up to the surface, but for now he was just enjoying seeing his friends stomping around the deck like they owned the place.

It felt good to have the Majesteria finally out of their cabin.

IT WAS about an hour later when Wren called everyone into the Canteen for a meeting.

Tristan and the other injured had been carefully administered to by Bonnie, who dressed his wounds with a foul-smelling poultice.

Wren had set up an area for the Majesteria to work on repairing the telescope in a corner of the Canteen with Birdy running back and forth getting them supplies.

Basel had brought out a large pot of potato soup and a basket of rolls for everyone.

Ginger had made a big pot of tea and most of the crew were sitting around looking exhausted holding a cup of tea or bowl of soup in their hands.

Wren stood on the side of the room where everyone could see her and whistled to get their attention. The murmured conversations of the tired sailors ceased as they all turned their eyes to look at their Captain.

"I'm sure you all have a lot of questions, as do I," Wren began. "Here's what I know so far. Tristan Mulberry," she pointed at him when she said his name and Tristan's cheeks went red, "is from Teakley Academy and is travelling to the Queen's Coronation in Fairefeux."

The crew was nodding along so far, all this was not new information.

"He is bringing with him three Majesteria, for those who do not know they are some of the most powerful mages in the realm, possessed of incredible capabilities."

The mice had stopped their work to listen and puffed up their chests proudly.

"Did you hear that?" Edwina said. "I didn't know I was *that* powerful."

"I guess we'd better live up to it," Marigold said.

Wren continued,

"The mages he is working with are named Edwina, Marigold, and Chica. They are seated over by Ludwig repairing our telescope."

"Who's Ludwig?" Chica asked, looking around.

"No clue," Edwina said.

The crew turned to look at the mice. Some had not noticed them before and craned their necks trying to find the mages.

"Where are they?" one of the deckhands whispered.

"It's those mice!" one of the cooks said.

"What in the hells?" the deckhand replied.

"Shhh," Birdy said, giving them a reproachful look.

Wren continued her speech,

"Mad Richard pursued us because he got information that the Majesteria were aboard our ship. Of course, we could not let him come aboard, and the Majesteria kindly agreed to help us fight him off. Unfortunately, while we were busy fighting, we got swept into the whirlpool which, due to the Star Shower, became a magical portal to another realm."

Some of the crew looked out the windows, but no one looked very surprised to hear this, all it took was one look at the water to know they weren't in the Evarian Sea any longer.

"We are currently trying to find out where we are, how

dangerous it is, and how we can get back to the Evarian Sea," Wren continued. "The Majesteria are repairing our telescope and we will be able to map the stars soon."

There were a few more curious looks at the Majesteria, but mostly the sailors just waited for Wren to continue.

"While we wait for more information, take this time to rest, eat, and recover," she said. "If you are able please return to the deck and help in the effort to get us ready to sail again. I don't know yet where we are and how fast we might need to leave. I'll let you know as soon as we have a plan, probably in a few hours."

She clapped her hands to let the crew know she was done speaking and they all nodded or murmured their agreement.

Tristan couldn't help but notice that Wren didn't mention the Royal Cinderflower at all.

It was shortly before dawn when the Majesteria finished their work on the telescope and marched it confidently up the stairs to the deck. Well, Tristan carried it up the stairs, and the Majesteria marched nearby with a lot of confidence. They brought it to the deck and then sat back to watch as Wren and Emyr began their work.

Using a collection of books, charts, and star maps Wren had brought from her office, they looked through the telescope and measured with their compasses and astrolabe. Finally, after a while of this, they stepped back and Tristan saw Wren's shoulders sag with relief as she said,

"I know where we are."

"Thank the stars!" Edwina said, clapping her paws together.

"We're in The Otherwilde Seas," Wren said, carefully closing her books and rolling up the star maps.

"Where's that?" Tristan asked.

"It's um," Wren thought about how to answer this. "Where we are."

"Oh. I see, one of those kinds of places," he said.

"Indeed," Wren said.

"But there's a way back, right?" Marigold said nervously.

"I'm sure there is," Wren said, "let's go to my office and get the map."

Tristan and the Majesteria followed Wren and Emyr into her office. Emyr lit a lantern and the mice clambered up to sit on the desk while Wren began to look through the messy assortment of maps and scrolls rolled up in the big cabinet. There were hundreds of them, and suddenly Tristan got a sense of just how strange and difficult Wren's job actually was. He wondered how many of them she'd actually used before.

After a short search she triumphantly pulled out a long brown leather tube with a small dangling tag on the end. Tristan got a glimpse of the tag as Wren moved the tube, which read *The Otherwilde Seas* in small, tight script.

Wren removed the cover of the map tube and tipped it out onto the desk. A copper coin and a few pieces of lint fell out. She turned it over and peered inside, putting her hand in to feel around.

"Well, shit."

Marigold suddenly got up and started whispering to Edwina and Chica. They huddled for a while, discussing something. Wren didn't notice, she was busy looking for another map, but Tristan did.

At some point Edwina looked up and caught his eye. She give him a *look* and a nod. He nodded back and said to Emyr

"We'll be right back."

Then he held the door open for the Majesteria who were already running across the floor. He followed them across the deck and down the stairs back to their cabin.

"What's going on?" he asked.

"I might have a map, but I'm not sure," Marigold said as they ran.

Tristan digested this information, rubbing his eyes.

"How?" He asked.

"I bought some novelty maps at the Midnight Market, one of them was for The Otherwilde Seas," she said as Tristan opened the door for them and they began searching through the chaos that was their cabin after the whirlpool.

"How did you possibly know we'd be stuck here?" Tristan asked, taking a pile of sweaters and putting them back in their trunk.

"I didn't, it was just luck, I thought it was pretty," Marigold said with a shrug. She was carefully stacking quills to get them out of the way.

After a few minutes of searching, which often involved the Majesteria asking Tristan to move heavy things out of their way, Marigold dove into a pile of scrolls and came out triumphant.

"Ah-ha!" she squeaked, clutching a few tiny papers in her paw.

She scurried over to Tristan and the other mice and spread out the map on the carpet.

Tristan looked down it.

"It's rather...small," he said quietly.

"It is pretty though," Edwina said.

"I love the gold detailing," Chica added.

Marigold looked proud.

Tristan held the map up to his face, it was barely bigger than a biscuit. But the detail was incredible. To his untrained eye, at least, it looked exactly like any other map. Just quite a bit smaller.

"Let's just hope Wren has a magnifying glass," he said.

When they returned to Wren's office she was cursing loudly while sorting through the map cabinet with Emyr, piles of rejected maps and leather tubes lay at their feet.

"We have some news," Tristan said.

Wren stood up and turned around, with her hands on her hips.

"We have a map!" Marigold said cheerfully.

"Of what?" Wren asked.

"The Otherwilde Seas, of course," Edwina said.

"What?! How?"

"It was a bit of an accident really," Marigold said.

"But a happy one," Tristan added.

"You see, when I was at the Midnight Market I bought some maps-"

"You went...shopping? At the Midnight Market?" Wren looked surprised.

"Yes, why wouldn't I?" Marigold asked, a paw on her hip.

Wren looked down at the tiny mouse in a ceremonial robe with a little pointed witch hat perched on her head.

"No reason, sorry, please go on," Wren said, sitting down at her desk wearily. Emyr followed and perched on a stool nearby.

"Anyway, as I was saying, I bought a few maps at the market and one of them happened to be a map of The Otherwilde Seas," Marigold said triumphantly.

Tristan gently laid the miniature map on the desk in front of Wren.

She stared at it for a moment.

He had to admire her poker face.

She barely had even the tiniest hint of a grin.

"That is um...wonderful news," she said tactfully.

"You may need a magnifying glass," Marigold acknowledged, "but it looks like a solid enough map to me."

"Of course, you're the expert," Tristan added.

"May I?" Wren asked, hands hovering over the map.

"By all means," Marigold said.

Wren carefully picked up the tiny map with both hands, holding it up to her face and scrutinizing it with the careful eye of a professional.

"It certainly *looks* like an authentic map," she pondered. She set it down and reached into her desk for a large bronze magnifying glass and held it up to the map closely.

Everyone held their breath while she examined it.

She pursed her lips and moved closer to the map

"Emyr, the lantern," she said, motioning with her hand. Dawn was starting to arrive over the horizon but the shadowy dim blue of night still clung to her office. Emyr hurried over with the lantern and placed it carefully beside her, the warm yellow glow casting a ring of light across the desk.

She examined the small map for a while, no one making a sound, and finally she looked up.

"Well, there's good news and bad," she said. "The good news is, there is a way to return to the Evarian Sea, a portal through a place called The Dragon's Neck. It looks like some a narrow straights, not dissimilar to the ones that brought us here."

"Hooray!" Chica said, clapping her paws.

Tristan put a hand to his chest and breathed a sigh of relief.

"The bad news?" Emyr asked, not missing a beat.

Wren leaned back in her chair and sighed.

"If I'm reading this map correctly, the portal is about six days sailing from here."

"Oh no!" Marigold squealed. "We have to be in Fairefeux in only *three* days!"

"Exactly."

"Are you sure about that timing?" Emyr asked. "Do you mind if I take a look?"

"Be my guest," Wren said, handing him the map and the magnifying glass. "I'm not entirely sure, the main problem is I'm making a guess based on these distance lines over here." She pointed at the map and Emyr nodded his head thoughtfully.

"I see," Emyr said. "Those would suggest six days but, of course, it's a novelty map. There's really no way to know how accurate it might be."

"That's what I was thinking," Wren said with a frown.

"We could compare it to the other maps I bought?" Marigold offered.

Wren looked up, surprised. "You have more?"

"Yes, one of the Evarian Sea and one of the Midnight Market," Marigold said. "Tristan, could you get them?"

"Of course," he said.

He ran back to the cabin and returned a few minutes later with the other tiny maps. After Wren and Emyr studied them for a while they came to the conclusion that the maps were impressively accurate. Including, unfortunately, when it came to distances.

"Why is it so much further away?" Tristan asked, turning the small map of the Evarian Sea around in his hands.

"It's another realm Tristan," Edwina said reproachfully. "The rules are different!"

"Space, time, dimensions, colors, and magic, it's all different," Marigold added.

"It's weird," Chica said, nodding.

"Hmm," Tristan said, setting the map down. "So what do we do?"

They all looked at Wren.

He realized there was not a single person on the ship who didn't trust Wren's judgement. Himself included.

Wren looked like she wanted to sleep, cry, and punch something all at the same time. She ran her hands down her face and took a sip of her whiskey as the bright dawn light filtered through the cabin's windows.

"I don't know," she said. "We don't have the ability to row, we rely on the winds to carry us. If we get lucky with a lot of wind we could knock off a day, maybe two. But that will hardly matter when the Crown finds out it was our fault they couldn't Coronate the damn Queen."

"But it's not your fault," Marigold said, placing a paw gently on Wren's hand.

Wren looked down at the tiny paw, the whiskey bottle hovering at her lips. Tristan could see that working with Majesteria was probably a very unusual experience for her.

"They won't see it that way," she said darkly.

"Well, I'll *make* them see it that way," Edwina said, pulling her sword out and shaking it angrily at the sky.

Wren and Emyr both looked slightly taken aback at this sight.

"Ahem, settle down Edwina," Tristan said out of the corner of his mouth.

"Wren's right," Emyr said with a frown, "the Crown won't care about the who's and why's. They'll just strip us of our Registered Pirate Vessel status and throw us in a dungeon."

"Probably take the ship too," Wren said miserably.

The mice all gasped in horror.

"They wouldn't!" Marigold said.

"I won't let them!" Edwina shrieked, raising her sword in the air.

"We can make it in time," Chica said solemnly. "I have a plan."

The other two stopped their exclamations and stared at her.

Chica didn't talk much. So when she did, you listened.

Chapter Fourteen

Chica's plan was a simple one.

Using Starlight magic the Majesteria, with Tristan's help, would cast wind spells into the sails. The powerful magical winds would be able to accelerate the speed of the ship as it travelled across the Otherwilde Seas.

But, it had a few problems.

"It's against the rules!" Tristan said.

"It's incredibly dangerous!" Marigold added.

"Is it even possible?" Wren asked.

"Blanchard will hate it," Edwina said firmly. "I vote AYE!"

"Oh no, we're voting again?" Chica said mournfully. "I haven't even changed my vote from the last one."

"Sorry, but I have to ask again, is it even possible?" Wren asked. "How would this work?"

"We can only do magic with Starlight," Edwina explained, "so we'd have to work at night and sleep during the day. Basically, Tristan will be a conduit for the magic, and we will then draw the Starlight into our Wind Casting Circle and send it up to the sails, creating small whirling balls of wind. Then we'll just repeat the process after the spell diminishes."

"If we cast all night we should be able to cut the travel time in half," Chica said proudly.

"The wind spells should be able to push the ship far past its normal capacity," Marigold added. "They certainly did previously."

"You've tried this before?" Wren asked, sounding relieved.

"We've tested the theory extensively," Edwina said sagely.

"We've done plenty of experiments," Marigold said.

"The boats were a bit smaller though," Chica admitted. "But it should work, theoretically."

"How much smaller?" Wren asked shrewdly.

Tristan pinched the bridge of his nose.

"Wait, you're saying you want to try to do that game you play in the duck pond with the little wooden ship with *The Snapdragon*?"

"It's not a game!" Edwina said reproachfully.

"It's a professional experiment!" Marigold said.

"I remember last time you did it Chica refused to come out of the boat, and she went around in circles shouting 'wheeee!' for three hours straight!" Tristan exclaimed.

"Yeahhh," Chica said, "that was so fun."

"Do you have any better ideas?" Marigold said, glaring at him.

"You're making us look bad in front of The Captain," Edwina whispered loudly. "Can't you just say yes?"

Wren sighed.

"I don't have any better ideas either, I'm afraid," she said. "My suggestion would be that we try it for one day, and then we'll check the stars to see how far we've gotten. If we think we can make it, I'm willing to help manage the...risks."

"That's very reasonable Captain," Marigold said.

"I believe...it's time for a vote," Edwina said dramatically.

"Not again," Chica moaned.

"I don't think it will be necessary," Tristan said with a sigh. "Have we even got another choice?"

They all sat in silence for a while, contemplating this fact.

Finally, Edwina stood up and raised her sword into the air.

"*THE AYES HAVE IT!*" she declared.

~

AFTER WORKING out some of the finer details of what would be needed from the crew, the meeting ended and everyone began to file out of Wren's office.

"Tristan, a word?" Wren said, her tone suddenly a lot colder than when she was making plans with the Majesteria.

"We'll just go down to the Canteen with Emyr," Edwina said.

"I could really go for some tea," Marigold said, scurrying behind the first mate with the other mice.

Emyr closed the door behind them and Tristan turned to face Wren, a feeling of dread stealing over him. He looked in her eyes and everything got so much worse.

He had expected her to be angry, to yell at him...he hadn't expected her to look so sad.

"I'm so sorry," he said, the words tumbling out of his mouth before he could stop them. "I'm sorry for lying to you, so many times. For putting you and your crew in danger, for...everything. If I'd had any other choice, I promise you I would have taken it."

Wren sat at her desk looking strained. The night's activities seemed to be catching up with her. If he hadn't been so stressed Tristan might have felt honored that she'd allowed him to see her looking so vulnerable. But right now he was just worried.

"You always have a choice," she said quietly. "As my old Captain used to say, if the rule is rotten, it's our duty to break it."

"I remember," Tristan said. "It's a good saying, but not everything fits into a nice little box like that, you know? You put your crew at risk too. I saw them smuggling those crates back on Strawberry Island."

Her eyes flashed fire,

"You seriously think me running some crates of semi-legal Elderbough Sap to sell to the junior mages in Fairefeux is *at all* the same as you bringing three Majesteria and the gods-damned *Royal Cinderflower* onto my ship in secret?"

Tristan thought about that for a while. It hadn't seemed that reckless or harmful when he'd agreed to the journey. He was just doing his job, helping the Majesteria, like he always did.

"No, I suppose it's not the same. But we're not the same Captain, we have different responsibilities."

"Who's idea was it to lie to me?" she asked.

Tristan met her eyes with surprise. He hadn't expected her to care.

"My superior, Lord Blanchard," he said. "He's...dreadful, honestly. I can't stand him, none of us can."

"I see," Wren said.

"Does it matter?" he asked. He wondered if maybe it did. Maybe it mattered for reasons that had nothing to do with her crew and everything to do with the look she had given him earlier when the two of them had looked at the Star Shower through the telescope.

Had that happened *today*? Everything had been turned upside down completely in such a short amount of time.

"You lied to me," she said in a small voice, and he knew in that moment that it wasn't about the crew. She looked like she wanted to throw something, but she didn't, in fact she barely moved at all. She just stared at him, which was significantly worse.

"Yes, and I'm sorry," he said softly.

They were both quiet for a long time, the only sound the creaking of the ship as it drifted along peacefully in the strange green sea.

Finally, Tristan said,

"I couldn't help but notice that you didn't tell your crew about the Royal Cinderflower."

"The less people that know the better," she replied. "If they don't need to know, why put them in danger? I wasn't going to burden them with knowledge that could put them at risk."

"But you lied to them," Tristan said, his voice firm, but kind.

"I just did what I needed to do to protect my crew," Wren said, without thinking about it.

Tristan didn't reply, he just let the words hang in the air.

After a minute Wren said,

"Oh. I see. Yes." She sighed, "That's what you were doing too."

He nodded.

"The Majesteria are...your crew. You didn't have a choice, not really."

"No. But even so, I wish I hadn't lied to you. I shall endeavor not to do it again," he said earnestly.

She looked at him, with a glimmer of brightness in her tired eyes.

"You know, I think I believe you."

THE MORNING HAD BEGUN in earnest by the time Tristan and Wren made their way down to the Canteen.

The Majesteria were already there, seated on one of the tables on a pillow, a plate of cheese and pastries nearby. Some of the sailors were asking them things, but most of them looked too exhausted to care about anything, even talking mice in fabulous outfits.

But everyone straightened up a little when they saw Wren, the conversation dying down before she even spoke. Once she had their full attention Wren explained the situation and their plan.

After the initial round of shocked gasps at the words *Royal Cinderflower*, the crew quickly turned to planning what would be needed for the task at hand.

"How are our supplies?" Wren asked. "Without the stop for provisions at The Ruins of Ahmet?"

"We're not going to the Ruins of Ahmet?" Edwina said, looking stricken. "I hadn't even thought of that!"

"Oh, I was so looking forward to it," Marigold said miserably.

"Me too, Duchess Xavier is one of my favorite historical figures," Chica added.

"Ahem," Tristan said to the mice, nodding his head to the crew who were looking at them like they were more than a little mad.

"Right, of course, sorry," Marigold said, "please go on, Captain."

Marigold gave a little salute and then sat down.

"Our supplies?" Wren asked again, ignoring the mice's outburst.

"All's good on our front," Ginger said cheerfully. "Plenty of lamp oil, candles, rope, pixie dust, parchment, we could last for weeks on most things I believe."

Her chipper spirit didn't seem dimmed at all by her torn clothing and the large bandages around her hands.

"Basel?" Wren asked. "How about food?"

"No problem Captain, we've got plenty of strawberries," Basel replied confidently.

Wren blinked.

"Er, do we have...anything else?" she asked.

"Rum!" Emyr said cheerfully.

"Well, I suppose that's alright then," she said with a shrug. "I think I've covered everything. Ginger will ring the bell when it's time for us to wake up and prepare for the night's sailing. For now, let's all get some rest."

"AYE CAPTAIN!" Edwina said, standing up and saluting.

"Edwina's really getting into this sailor thing," Marigold said quietly to Tristan.

"Indeed," he replied.

WHEN THE BELL rang to wake him the next day, Tristan immediately felt the gravity of the situation. This wasn't a cheerful dinner bell you could listen to if you were interested. This was a summoning, a call to arms, a loud bell screaming across the ship that it was time to wake up.

Do not ignore this bell, it said, you are needed.

He got up wearily, feeling a chill in his bones. He peered blearily out the porthole and saw a smattering of snowflakes floating past the window and falling into the bright green sea. He dressed quickly in the dim blue evening light, wincing in pain as he put on a sweater and a woolen cloak. His chest still ached from protecting the Cinderflower during the whirlpool, though Bonnie's healing salves had improved his wounds immensely.

When he emerged in the main cabin he found the Majesteria getting ready. Tristan had hastily cleaned up from the whirlpool the night before, and now the mice were sorting through their bags of magical tools and arguing about which ones would be the most useful for casting wind spells.

"Good morning Tristan," Marigold said. Then she looked at the sky. "Er, good evening, I guess."

Edwina pulled a large metal spindle with a crystal on the end out of a velvet bag and held it up to the light. The crystal glittered as she turned it from side to side.

"I think we're going to need a bigger one," she said firmly, putting it back in the bag. "There's no way this can hold enough Starlight."

"What is the plan, exactly?" Tristan asked them.

Marigold tapped her paw on her lips as she thought.

"I think you will be up by the ship's wheel drawing Starlight onto the largest spindle we've got," she said. "Then you'll run the spindle down to us and we'll move the Starlight onto the channelling batons."

"I think we should use the smaller spindles instead," Chica said, folding her arms.

"No, no, the Starlight holds better on the channelling batons," Marigold said, frowning.

"There's also the weather to consider," Edwina said, glancing up at the window. "I believe it's very cold out there."

Tristan nodded "It's snowing a bit, so I think the channelling batons are best. They hold the Starlight better in cold weather."

Chica sighed, "I don't know why I bothered, I should've just stayed in bed."

"I wouldn't mind that myself," Tristan said with a yawn.

Once their magic toolkits were all sorted out Tristan headed out into the hallway with the Majesteria where they joined the crowd of tired sailors making their way to the Canteen for food and coffee. The moon was just peeking over the luminous green sea as they arrived.

There was a nervous energy he'd not experienced in the Canteen before as everyone prepared for the magical journey to come. He saw a few sailors shooting him strange looks, and quietly keeping their distance.

He was used to odd glances and unusual comments like 'goodness he's handsome' but these were different. There was a mix of fear, wonder, and curiosity. He was reminded of just how rare and special his job and the Majesteria were, even though magic and mice had become mundane for him.

He tried to put these thoughts out of his mind and focus on the task at hand: breakfast. Or, dinner, depending on how you looked at it.

Basel had set out a large array of food and drink for everyone along the countertop. In a nod to the strange time of day Basel had made an assortment of breakfast and dinner foods, all with generous helpings of strawberries added in creative ways. Strawberry scones and strawberry jam sat next to a cheesy tart topped with strawberry slices. There was plenty of other food as well: hearty potato soup, baskets of rolls (although quite a few had some suspicious red chunks baked in them), a big metal platter of scrambled eggs with onions and mushrooms, and a heaping mountain of hotcakes.

Tristan had just finished ladling a large bowl of potato soup when Wren appeared at his side, looking like she'd barely slept at all. Her eyes were sunken and her face was somber as she looked over the array of food.

"Quite a lot of strawberries today," she said.

"Aye Captain, we got all the strawberries you could want," Basel said firmly.

Tristan did not doubt this fact.

"What if I don't want strawberries?" she asked.

"You'd be missin' out, I'll tell you what," Basel said, shaking their head. "This fruit and cheese tart right here is the very best, my mam used to make it for me when I was small. It's her own original recipe."

"This is the same one who made that tapestry herself?" Tristan asked, looking up at the flaming harpy known as Ole Gertha.

"The very same!" Basel boomed cheerfully.

The mice looked at the tapestry.

"Hey, wait a minute," Marigold said.

"I've seen that before," Edwina said with a gasp.

"*Enchanting Embroidery,*" Chica said, nodding.

"Shhh," Tristan said to them.

Wren raised an eyebrow as she watched Tristan trying to hustle the Majesteria away.

"We'll just take the whole tart," he said, grabbing it and walking away. "I'm sure it's as lovely as your mother's embroidery!" He said over his shoulder.

"You bet it is!" Basel said cheerfully.

Tristan hurried across the room with the Majesteria scurrying behind him. He found his spot in the corner and plopped down.

"What was *that* about?" Marigold asked.

"Basel's mother didn't make that tapestry," Edwina said.

"I know!" Tristan said with a sigh, "I recognized it too."

"*Enchanting Embroidery,*" Chica said, again. "*Embroidery Essentials For The Discerning Stitcher.*"

"Yes, yes, I remember," Tristan said. "But Basel loves it so much, I didn't want to tell them the truth. I mean, what's the harm right?"

"Hmm, I suppose so," Marigold said.

"I don't care, I just want the food," Chica said, approaching the tart with a hungry look in her eyes.

"I guess we can keep the secret too," Edwina said.

"That's very sweet of you," a voice said.

Tristan looked up and saw Wren, standing nearby with two

mugs in her hands. He was momentarily awed by the way the soft light landed on her bronze skin and the jagged scar crossing her face.

"You forgot your coffee," she said handing him a mug.

"Thank you, please don't tell Basel about the tapestry," he said.

"Your secrets are safe with me, Tristan Mulberry," she said, her sharp eyes twinkling with amusement. She held his gaze just a little too long and then turned, her long dark tangle of hair swishing behind her.

Tristan forgot to breathe for a minute as he watched her walk away to talk with some of the sailors about the plans for the day.

"Tristan's got it bad," Chica said, holding up a pawful of cheese and strawberries and shoveling it into her mouth.

"It's true, but I can't blame him," Marigold said.

"Shhhh, please!" Tristan said, his cheeks burning. "She'll hear you."

"I wouldn't worry about that," Edwina said, "did you see that look she gave him?"

"Shh, we're not supposed to talk about it," Marigold said.

"Right, right," Edwina said while cutting into the tart with her sword. "Sorry Tristan."

He just sighed.

THE COLD WAS SNAPPING at their heels as Tristan and the Majesteria followed the crew out onto the deck under a blanket of stars, their cloaks flapping in the chill winds. There was a small awning over the doors to the Captain's Quarters and the Majesteria decided it would be best for them to set up under it to hopefully get some protection from the elements.

Tristan set down their Boarding Trunk by the door in case they needed to rest or take cover inside it, as well as the bag of their magical instruments.

The mice barely looked around them, so intense was their focus on the task at hand. They removed and organized their tools carefully, debating in small squeaks which tools would be most useful.

"I hope I'm not intruding," said a voice quietly near Tristan's shoulder. He looked around to see Ginger hesitantly holding a glowing red cylinder. She had a nervous quality he wasn't used to seeing from her as she peeked at the Majesteria assembling their implements. "I thought, since it's so cold, the mages might like to use one of these portable Pixie Hearths."

Tristan felt the heat radiating off the object in Ginger's arms and he took it from her gratefully.

"Thank you, I'm sure they'll appreciate it," he said.

Ginger took one last look at the mice and then moved away quickly. As he watched her walk across the deck he noticed the crew were all looking at them. Some were pretending to do another task, like coiling rope or tying knots, but many of them were just quietly watching and waiting to see what would happen next. He gulped, feeling an anxiety building in his stomach, and turned away, focusing on setting up the little portable Pixie Hearth where the Majesteria would be able to use it.

A little while later he saw Wren walking up the stairs, a large tray in her hands. Earlier in the Canteen, after she'd given an encouraging speech to the crew she had come over to the Majesteria and quietly asked them,

"Is there anything else you need?"

"Welll, since you asked," Chica had said with a mischievous smile.

"There is one thing that would be very helpful," Edwina had said.

To her credit, Wren took the Majesteria's request very seriously.

Tristan was truly impressed when he saw the Captain solemnly carrying the large tray with its towering mountain up onto the deck.

Camembert, Gouda, Cheddar, gooey Brie, round balls of Mozzarella, tangy Blue Cheese, Aged Asiago, Havarti, briny Feta, crumbling Pecorino Romano, Gruyere, a soft Herbed Goat Cheese and a wedge of Strawberry Cheese from Strawberry Island.

Barely squished on the side of the tray next to the mass of cheese were some crackers, strawberry jam, and a large pot of tea.

She set the tray down next to the Majesteria's boarding trunk with all the grave seriousness of a foot soldier bringing a shining sword to a heroic warrior.

The mice halted their work for a moment, bundles of herbs and crystal batons stopped moving in their paws as their eyes bulged at the sight before them.

"Is that...all for *us*?" Chica breathed.

"It's beautiful," Marigold said.

Wren smiled, and pulled out her little gold coin to twirl it in her fingers.

"It's all yours," she said. "I shall be up at the wheel. If you need me, just ask any sailor, okay?"

"Mhmm," Edwina said, lost in a dream of cheese.

"Ahem," Tristan said to the mice. "I believe we've got work to do."

"Oh, right, right, yes, mhmm," Marigold said, sniffing the air and wiggling her whiskers.

"We musn't," Edwina said, looking at the cheese mournfully.

"Mmmphgh," Chica said, her round cheeks already stuffed with gouda.

After the other two had pulled Chica away from the cheese mountain with a firm scolding, the Majesteria returned to their work. They enlisted the help of a few sailors to assist them in drawing a massive circle in chalk across the middle of the deck. They began to walk around the giant circle with one of the sailors holding a book up for them to copy down the magical symbols and shapes, adjusting them to fit the scale of the casting circle and the purpose of their spells.

Tristan turned away and left the Majesteria to their work,

heading up the small staircase to the deck with the ship's wheel where he would be catching Starlight.

"Evening," he said softly to Wren when he arrived on the landing, noting how the little snowflakes landed like fallen stars in her dark hair.

She looked up from where she had been staring out at the sea through her spyglass.

"Did you need something?" she asked, clearly surprised to see him.

"No, I'm just going to be working up here," he said, pointing to the little counter nearby. "I'll be catching Starlight up here and then bringing it down to the Majesteria below to use in their spells. If that's alright with you?"

"Of course, I just didn't realize," she said with a nod. She gave him a strange look that he couldn't quite place, but didn't say anything more.

As the Majesteria finished drawing their circle they began strengthening the charms with incantations, burning little bundles of herbs and waving them around the symbols. Meanwhile, Wren took to the wheel and Tristan laid out his instruments. He realized, with a knotting in his stomach, that suddenly everyone down below was looking at him.

He wasn't used to having an audience and the idea made him feel a little faint. Usually, he would catch Starlight alone on his balcony overlooking the gardens at Teakley. He didn't know how he was going to focus with a bunch of sailors who knew nothing about magic staring at him.

He looked around helplessly, his cold hands shaking a little with nerves as he pulled off his gloves and set them down on the counter.

"Everything okay?" Wren asked behind him.

"Hah, not used to an audience," he replied.

"SAILORS! BACK TO WORK!" Wren called out, her tone firm and authoritative.

Tristan watched in awe as the crew all began scurrying about the deck, coiling rope, tightening knots around the pulleys and preparing the lanterns.

"Thank you," he said softly, breathing a sigh of relief.

"Aye," she said, returning to the wheel.

With the crew distracted Tristan finally relaxed a little and could turn his attention to catching Starlight. He reached into his mind, focusing his thoughts and emotions on the little threads of magic that only he could feel in the vast expanse of glittering stars above. His fingers were brittle with cold but the nine-pointed star tattoos on the back of his hands soon began to glow with the light of the stars above.

He felt its warmth and power flowing through him like a wave crashing into his body, the Starlight pulsing and pulling at his muscles and his mind. He quickly picked up the channelling batons, using them to ground himself in the world before he got carried away by the powerful magic.

He set the large metal spindle on the counter, it had a bulbous shape and was about the size of a wine bottle. The Majesteria only used it when they were doing very large spells and needed a lot of Starlight, which was fairly infrequent back at Teakley where their magic was largely theoretical.

Out here though, with the frigid winds whipping his woolen cloak around him, everything felt different. Magic meant something. He was doing something important and useful. He felt a new kind of power as he pulled the strands of glowing light out of the air and wound them around the spindle, the light jittering between his fingers.

He wound and pulled the threads from the sky, on and on, not seeing or hearing the sounds of the crew below, the creaking of the ship or the spinning of the Captain's wheel behind him. His eyes glittered as he looked at the shimmering threads and pulled them into tangible existence, winding them around and around. For a moment he forgot everything and everyone, he was nothing but Starlight.

But then he hit the end of the spindle, it had reached capacity, and somewhere in the back of his brain he remembered what he had to do, that he could not let himself drift away into ethereal light, no matter how appealing a proposition it was. He deftly tied the end of the Starlight around the spindle and broke the connection, slamming a wall down in his mind. He pushed and pulled at the Starlight inside him, yanking it out of his limbs with the force of his willpower.

Then it was gone, and he was keeled over, gasping and aching from every part of his body. His muscles throbbed with a deep, dull pain that stretched all the way to his bones. His skin was tingling and sensitive, the cold wind cutting across it like a million tiny knives.

He fell to his knees and fought for breath.

Wren dropped the wheel and ran to his side.

"Are you alright?" she asked, putting a warm, comforting hand on his arm. He looked at her hand, and for a moment he didn't know who she was, but then it all came rushing back and he sat back on his heels.

"Aye, it's alright," he said, smiling weakly. "I'm sore but I'll manage."

He staggered to his feet, almost falling over a few times but Wren steadied him, subtly supporting his weight.

His hands were shaking as he took hold of the nut bar and gobbled it hungrily, the food anchoring him and filling up his depleted energy.

Once he could stand on his own Wren's gaze fell to the large glowing spindle sitting on the counter, casting a blinding light upon the deck.

"I didn't know it would be like that," she said softly, "it was so beautiful."

Tristan smiled and nodded.

"But...what happened to you? Is that normal?"

Tristan shrugged, taking another bite of his nut bar and breathing deeply of the cold night air.

"Yes, it's a natural part of the process. I am using my body as a channel, like filling up a well, and then I pull the magic through me into the threads. But when someone has a strong connection to Starlight like I do, the magic...wants to stay, I guess you could say. The experience can be very draining, and if I'm not careful it can do terrible things to my body."

"Do the Majesteria do the same thing?" she asked.

"Sort of, their connection to Starlight is much stronger than mine. But for obvious reasons I do most of the Starlight catching," he explained.

"Not obvious to me," Wren said.

Tristan laughed, "Their bodies are a bit on the small side for channelling."

Wren looked tremendously curious, and opened her mouth to ask more questions, but Tristan held up the spindle.

"I really need to bring this to the Majesteria now," he said.

"Of course, right, sorry," Wren said, turning back to the wheel.

She watched him thoughtfully as he carried the spindle, glowing as brightly as if he'd plucked a star from the heavens, down the small staircase to the deck below.

He found the Majesteria surrounded by cheese.

They had finished their preparations and were now taking a cheese break while they waited for the Starlight.

"Mphmgh," Edwina said, pointing at him with bulging cheeks.

"Mrgphm!" Marigold exclaimed.

"Ahem," Tristan said, gently lowering the brightly glowing spindle onto the deck.

The Majesteria hurriedly swallowed their cheese, dusted off their robes, and ran across the deck to the spindle. They walked around, looking at the Starlight with the appraising eye of a professional mage.

"Hmm, will it be enough?" Edwina said.

"I think so, it's very good," Marigold said, nodding her approval.

"There's only one way to find out," Chica said.

The other two nodded their agreement.

"Do you need anything else?" Tristan asked.

"I don't think so," Edwina said.

"You should rest," Marigold added.

"You can have some of our cheese if you need it," Chica said, in the tones of someone making a very grave sacrifice for the greater good.

"I'm alright, but I'll let you know if I need it," Tristan said with a grin.

The Majesteria began by pulling the Starlight off the spindle and onto three channelling rods. They formed a chain of mice, feeding the Starlight through their glowing paws as they pulled the cords of light off the spindle. Next, they each took one of the channelling rods and marched it to a spot along the circle, forming a triangle. They set the rods down and each Majesteria began slowly pulling the threads of Starlight and feeding it into the giant circle they had drawn on the deck.

The light travelled through the lines like liquid fire, lighting up the circle and the symbols inside it with glowing light. Whenever it filled up a new line, the Starlight would flare brightly for a moment as it made the connection to the spellwork, and then fade out to a dim glow.

Tristan decided to give his wobbling legs a rest and he sat down by the door to Wren's quarters. He wouldn't dare touch the Majesteria's cheese, no matter what Chica said, but he did pour himself some tea. He dropped a cube of sugar in and held the warm mug between his freezing hands, noting as he did that the tattoos on the back of them glowed faintly with the remnants of Starlight still inside him.

The Majesteria were doing the spell now, pulling the glowing symbols off of the deck to hover in the air, then bringing them together into a bright ball of light, made entirely of threads of

Starlight. It swirled and shimmered in the dark night, rising up above the sailors who stared at it with wonder.

Tristan sipped his tea and watched the Wind Casting with a smile. It was beautiful to watch, but even more fun was watching the faces of the crew, their unblinking eyes following the Majesteria's movements with reverence. After a few moments the Majesteria lifted their paws into the air and called out their incantation, releasing the Wind Spell and sending the glowing balls of light twirling towards the sails.

And then they were off!

The spells hit the sails, which instantly filled to capacity with a loud snapping sound. Immediately the ship was hurtling through the sea, the waves flying up on either side of it, the rush of motion causing the ship to shudder wildly. Tristan gripped his mug tightly as the tea splashed around while Wren pulled at the wheel and the ship settled into its new position.

He heard a sound and looked up.

The crew was cheering, hollering, and jumping, leaning over the sides of the ship and whistling at the roaring waves.

He looked to the stern and saw Wren grasping the ship's wheel with both hands. She cut a dashing figure in her black billowing blouse and leather pants, her dark hair flying out behind her as the ocean spray crested at the back of the ship sending drops of water everywhere. Next to her was Emyr, his dark skin dusted with moonlight, he was looking through the spyglass and yelling out directions to Wren while she steered.

He looked back to the deck and saw Birdy climbing the rope ladders of the rigging at staggering speed, leaping from one loudly snapping sail to the next, examining the pulleys and checking the straining ropes.

"All clear!" she called out to the crew below who cheered their approval.

Then she found a spot on the mast and curled herself around it to sit and wait, ready to call out to the Majesteria to prepare the next spell as soon as the wind started to fade.

Tristan looked at the silver spindle sitting on the deck, the bright light of the moon reflected on its shiny silver surface. He finished his tea with one gulp and picked up the spindle, realizing even as he winced at the pain in his aching muscles that it was already time for him to start preparing the next batch of Starlight.

But he was not alone in his struggle, everyone's skills would be needed tonight. The crew would be pulling the sails in the right direction, so the intense winds wouldn't send them careening off course. Other people would be replacing the ropes when they snapped and the sails when they frayed beyond use from the heavy strain of the magical wind. Basel and Ginger would be making sure everyone had food, drink, and woolen blankets as the freezing night wore on. The Majesteria were already on the deck, sketching out the next batch of chalk symbols for the spell, and Wren's constant steering would be needed to keep the ship on course.

So, he made his way up to the little deck to begin casting again, reveling in the unique joy of being part of this strange crew and their magical journey across the Otherwilde Seas.

Wren gave him a nod as she slowly turned the wheel.

He took up his spindle and they sailed on, into the cold, dark night.

CHAPTER FIFTEEN

Tristan woke to the sound of the horrible bell, the clanging vibrating through his weary head. Every part of him was aching and sore but he knew that somehow he had to go on. After spending all night catching Starlight he had staggered into bed at dawn's light without enough energy to change into his pajamas. He'd simply keeled over on the bed and closed his eyes.

The sun was riding low in the sky and painting it shades of purple as he changed into fresh clothes, the dull ache of his muscles making his movements slow and careful. He pulled a stippled brown sweater over his shirt and added the rather damp woolen cloak he'd worn the night before since the cold was even worse now.

He pulled on his leather gloves and tied up his boots, his fingers trembling with exhaustion. As he carefully repositioned his Teakley brooch on his cloak, the little golden teapot gleaming in the dim light from the porthole, he realized with horror that he would be catching Starlight for two more nights. The pain didn't bear thinking about. He just hoped his body could manage it.

He yawned heavily as he went into the main room but the Majesteria were already gone. He made his way slowly to the Canteen and saw the mice were there, sitting on a flat pillow on one of the tables.

He waved to them as he headed over to the countertop to get some breakfast. Immediately, he could sense that something was different. The crew stepped aside carefully as he walked by; some of them even seemed to bow a little. They looked at him with a sort of awed respect, and maybe just a hint of fear.

Basel, on the other hand, was as brash and straightforward as ever.

"AYYY! Frog boy! More than just a pretty face!" Basel said, clapping him on the shoulder cheerfully as he stepped up to countertop. Tristan staggered back a little from the blow but managed a smile.

"Morning Basel, or, evening, or...good to see you?" Tristan laughed.

Basel laughed loudly and took a big gulp of something out of a large wooden mug, Tristan was pretty sure it was very alcoholic.

"Heard you was messing around with the stars Froggy, they've been telling me all kindsa things about ye today," Basel said shaking their head, their gold earring jangling. "Tonight I'm gonna see it for meself, I wanna see those precious little dumplins' do their funny magic spells."

Basel was looking across the room at the Majesteria with soft eyes.

Tristan wasn't surprised that Basel was already charmed by them, the Majesteria had a way of easily winning most people's affection.

"We'd love to see you on the deck Basel," Tristan said.

"Now how bout it, what ya eatin' Froggy? Maybe another one of my famous cocktails?"

"I couldn't possibly, I've got to keep my focus," Tristan said firmly.

"Damn, that's true," Basel said with a sigh. "All this magic business keepin' ya busy, well, if you change your mind?"

"I know where to find you," Tristan said.

He looked over the spread of food, it looked a little less elegant than the day before, but no less delicious. Today, there were little round strawberry cakes with a whole berry baked in the middle. A whipped strawberry cream cheese was provided to slather on top. The remains of a massive quiche occupied a large area of the countertop, along with spring salad and roasted potatoes with rosemary. More eggs, hotcakes, and freshly baked rolls were there too, and of course, a nearly overflowing tureen of strawberry jam, a bucket of carefully cut strawberry wedges, and a carafe of strawberry lemonade.

Tristan took some of the quiche, a mug of coffee, and a strawberry cake, and made his way to his favorite corner by the window. Some of the sailors were already working, a few of the sails were spread out on one of the tables, and a bunch of people were sewing up the holes. They were chatting and humming cheerfully, Tristan thought of joining in but he was too tired for much socializing. He sunk into the pillow and curled his legs up under him, hoping no one wanted too much from him right now.

He stared out the window, noting that there were chunks of ice floating in the strange green waters now. He looked out to the horizon and saw a little island in the direction opposite to where they were headed. A light pink mist lingered over the water, and strange glittering shapes like dolphins dipped in the waters by the shoreline. A small cluster of bulbous houses with bright blue roofs and round doors clung to the cliffside. As he looked at the unusual island he felt a little pang to realize he wouldn't be going to see those rolling hills and meet whoever lived in those little houses. Once the Coronation was over, they'd just head back to Teakley like nothing had happened at all. It was strange to think about, and Tristan realized it was a thought he did not care for.

"Good evening," Wren said, sitting quietly down near him with a mug of coffee in her hands. "How are you feeling?"

Tristan turned to look at her, "I'm alright, I'll be ready to get back on deck soon."

He didn't bother to tell her how exhausted he felt; he knew they were all tired.

"That's good to hear," she said, sipping her coffee, "I just finished checking our position with Emyr, it looks like the Majesteria's plan has worked."

Tristan sat up and grinned, "Really? We're going to make it in time?"

Wren smiled too, "Yes, just barely, if we can keep up this pace we should get there the night before the Coronation."

Tristan leaned back and sighed, "Well, that's a relief," he said.

"Don't I know it," Wren replied.

They looked out at the sea for a while and sipped their drinks. Tristan felt a warm, companionable silence growing between them. Sitting quietly with her stirred something inside him, there was just something he found so comforting about her presence.

She cleared her throat.

When he looked at her, she was looking at him with another one of her inscrutable expressions. Some people are like an open book; you can know everything they're thinking just by glancing at their face.

Wren was the exact opposite.

He could never tell what she was thinking unless she wanted him to.

He suddenly remembered that look she had given him on the night of the Star Shower, and held his breath.

"I wanted to ask you," she began, her voice a low, soft sound, nearly drowned out by the sound of the crew nearby. Tristan leaned in to hear her better, his eyes lingering over her delicate fingers spinning her favorite gold coin.

"I don't know if I can ask this," she continued.

Tristan felt his pulse quicken, he leaned closer, meeting her eyes.

He couldn't read her face, but he hoped maybe she could read his.

"Yes?" he said, his voice a husky whisper.

"I was just wondering how you came into possession of the Royal Cinderflower?" she asked.

"Oh. Ahem. *That*," Tristan said. He quickly leaned back in his seat, his cheeks burning with embarrassment. He chided himself for thinking she had been about to declare her desperate infatuation with him like a character in one of his favorite romance novels.

"If you can't answer, I understand," she said.

"No, it's fine," he said, recovering quickly. "It was brought to Teakley for repairs and-"

"Repairs?" She looked confused. "I thought it was a plant?"

"It is, but those need repairs too," Tristan said with a wry grin. "Leaves need trimming, soil needs replacing, sometimes they need to be repotted, all kinds of things. Magical plants are even more temperamental and require very special care. Naturally, they wanted the Royal Cinderflower in its best possible shape before the Coronation."

Wren leaned back, contemplating. Eventually she said, "That makes sense, it's both a symbol and a powerful magical weapon. It's a show of strength and power having it on display to help crown the new Queen."

She flipped her coin thoughtfully.

"Why my ship though?"

"I believe the idea was to bring it secretly on a Registered Pirate Vessel with a small crew in order to make it less of an obvious target. A lot of people would like to get their hands on it, and who would suspect that it would be sent with a lone scholar on a Pirate Ship of all things?"

"I can see how they'd think that," she said, her expression unreadable.

"I don't know why they chose your ship specifically, I had no involvement in that process. They just gave me the ticket and told me where to go."

She nodded, "I know why they chose *The Snapdragon*," she said, frowning.

"You do?" Tristan said.

"Yes. My crew was the only one desperate and foolish enough to take such a risk. The ticket order was clear that it was for someone from Teakley Academy, and they would not be answering any questions. Everyone knows about *mages*," she said the word in a way that Tristan had never heard before. "How dangerous and arrogant they are." She looked at him. "I mean, most of them."

Tristan just nodded. He didn't know what to say.

"But we are a newly Registered ship, we're desperate to prove to the Crown that we can be counted on to reliably transport whatever and whoever needs moving. Not to mention, the money was good, very good. So when I got the ticket request I accepted it, even though I knew it was risky. I couldn't afford not to. Maybe I was naive to think that they'd just be sending a mage with a magical artifact or something."

"That's what they did," Tristan said.

"Ha! There's magical artifacts and then there's the bloody Royal Cinderflower. From what I hear that thing is like a bomb of condensed magic. One wrong turn and it could blow us to bits, and that would just be a warm up."

Tristan didn't say anything for a while.

She was right, of course. He'd never thought about it that way, but it was true. Truthfully, back at Teakley he hadn't thought about the crew of the ship at all. They were just a Registered Pirate Vessel which was needed for the Academy's purposes. It wasn't Wren and Ginger and Basel and Birdy and Bonnie and a bunch of other sailors, all with their own lives and stories. They weren't putting *Wren* and her crew at risk, they were just...hiring a ship.

"I never thought about it like that," Tristan said. "I'm so sorry. I hope...I hope it all works out." He searched his mind for what else he could say but he didn't know how to bridge the gap.

"Thanks," she said, standing up. "I appreciate your honesty, I'm glad to understand a bit more. Anyway, it's time to get ready, I'll see you out there."

Tristan just nodded as she walked away.

He watched the crew for a while and started to find his energy returning. Birdy seemed to be leading the group, directing different sailors in what to sew and how, occasionally teaching them new techniques. Ginger sat at her side, her bright blue curls bouncing as she sewed. Every now and then Tristan saw them share a secret smile or a knowing glance, and he remembered seeing them poking their heads out of Birdy's room before they left Brineridge.

The Majesteria, for their part, seemed to have blended in with the crew rather quickly. Edwina was playing Cherry Basket with a rotating cast of sailors, Marigold was learning how to tie complicated knots from one of Birdy's crew and Chica...well.

Chica was sleeping on the pile of finished sails.

Tristan smiled and laughed a little when he saw her little lump with her paws splayed out across the sails. Chica really could sleep anywhere.

He stretched out his legs and decided to read for a bit while he waited for the crew to finish the sails, allowing his body time to relax and recover before he began to torture it again up on the deck. He had finished reading *The Valor Of The Seas* earlier in the journey and was now re-reading the second book in the series, *The Glory Of The Storm*.

He cracked open the yellowed pages of *The Glory Of The Storm* and fell into the story, with the sounds of the creaking ship and the chattering crew fading into the background.

Everything was harder on the second night. All the crew were tired, the sails were worn, and Tristan's muscles ached through to the bones. Not to mention the freezing wind which found every tiny hole in his clothing and sliced through it, biting at his skin like icy daggers. He could see his breath winding up into the dark night in bright white clouds as he made his way across the deck to begin his first round of casting.

Wren was on the deck when he arrived, looking at the stars through her spyglass and making little notes in a small leather-bound notebook.

The snow was starting to fall in earnest; little flurries of white landing on the deck and dusting Wren's dark shoulders. Tristan shivered under his cloak, his hands shaking as he set up his tools to begin catching Starlight. The cold air nipped inside his collar and under his trouser legs, anywhere it could find an opening. He looked out at the crew, pulling the sails into position, winding the rope around the pulleys, and sketching symbols in chalk with the Majesteria. Everyone was moving sluggishly under a cascade of slowly falling snow, pulling their cloaks tight and hoods down over their eyes.

He could tell this was going to be a very long night.

AT FIRST, things went well. The crew were more accustomed to working with the magical winds, and knew how to adjust the sails and rigging to accommodate the sharp tension added by the fierce wind spell. As for Tristan and the Majesteria they were more familiar with the practical aspects of their work as well. After spending many hours casting the night before, they all knew their jobs well and executed them better and faster than the night before, even with the icy conditions.

A side benefit of everyone's growing expertise is that it left a little more time for socializing. Basel, Ginger, and the rest of the crew from downstairs came up and brought steaming bowls of soup, roasted chestnuts, and warm cups of tea and coffee. Some of the crew played cards or told stories, and at one point Tristan was sure he saw Birdy knitting while she was sitting on the mast.

But Tristan's favorite part was the songs.

After a little while, and a few good chugs of rum, the crew launched into some of their beloved sea shanties as the ship zigzagged through the icy waters.

Oohhhh
Their once was a fearsome Pirate Queen
Her flaming eyes, they must be seen

She sailed the seas on her floating steed

She brought to heel a bold gale indeed
From the North it came to frost and freeze
Tore through the sky with frightening ease

And nowwww
In our sails it blows with greed
The night is dark we must take heed
Though its frosty breath blows on our backs
In this frightful wind our sails won't go slack

Do not fret this ship is strong and boooold
Our rum is good, our sails will hoooold

We'll weather the stoooorm!
Our rum will keep us warm!
The ice may bite and cold might cut
The wind will nip and the snow will gut

Buuuut
We'll weather this stoooorm!
And our rum will keep us warm

The sound was warm and comforting, much to his surprise
Tristan found the singing didn't bother his focus when he was
catching Starlight, in fact, it improved it. He felt...comfortable and
safe, when he heard the crew singing. It felt like no matter how bad
things were, they couldn't be *that* bad if you could sing a song
about it.

A few hours into the night Tristan was resting on the small deck
by the ship's wheel when Wren sat down next to him. She put her
knees up, resting her arms across them, a bottle of rum in her hands.
Tristan saw Emyr gripping the wheel tightly on the other side of the
small deck.

"Want some?" she asked, waving the sloshing bottle in his

direction.

Tristan shook his head.

"I'm basically already drunk from this," he said, waving his hand in the general direction of his magical tools.

"Got it," she said, taking a swig of rum and leaning her head back. She pulled her hand across her shoulder, massaging the sore muscles there.

"Long night for you too?" He asked.

"Huh, yeah," she said. "The tension with the magical winds, it's like nothing I've felt before. I have to grip it so tight just to keep hold of the ship, it's tearing up my arm muscles. But, I'll be alright. I've had it worse."

"I'm sorry," Tristan said, leaning his arms across his legs.

"For what?"

"That you've had it worse," he said simply.

Wren laughed, a hollow, sardonic sound.

The rum sloshed as she took another gulp.

"Thanks Tristan," she said. "Sorry about what I said earlier, about mages and stuff. You're...not like what I expected at all."

"I'm not?" Tristan said.

"No. I'd heard that mages were controlling, power-hungry, egotistical–" She stopped when she saw his face.

"But I realized you weren't like that when I saw she liked you," she finished.

"She?" Tristan asked.

Wren rapped her knuckles on the deck.

"*The Snapdragon*," she said.

Tristan put his hand on the deck, palm resting against the cold, wet, wood. It made sense now, that feeling he'd had when he first stepped aboard. A feeling that never really went away, even after all the other guests had left. He'd tried to figure out where it was coming from, but it just felt like it was a little bit magic everywhere. It was so obvious when he thought about it.

The ship was magic.

"She...likes me?" he asked.

"Oh yes," Wren said, laughing.

"How do you know?" he asked, fascinated.

"Your tea is always warm."

Tristan looked down at the slightly steaming mug by his side. The snow was falling into it with a soft crackling sound but that didn't seem to change its temperature at all.

"Huh. I didn't notice," he said. He picked up the drink and sighed as the hot liquid warmed his chest. He felt a twinge of something where his hand was touching the deck, it was almost like... satisfaction.

"Maybe you're just used to everyone liking you," Wren said very quietly.

Tristan's heart began to race. But he wasn't sure what she meant at all.

"Everyone likes me?" he asked tentatively.

"Certainly everyone on this ship, she said. Basel's already fretting about you leaving us."

"They are? I didn't know," Tristan said, touched.

"I'm more worried about you making it through today," Wren said, peering at him through the softly falling snow. "You're looking drained. You may be closer to your limits than you realize, it happens to all of us sometimes. Maybe you should go rest?"

Suddenly Tristan felt himself become part of her domain. She was Captaining at him, checking on him the way she would any member of her crew, making sure everything was functioning properly.

"I can't rest, we won't make it," Tristan said with a sigh. He ran his hands across his face and felt the deep strain on all his muscles. "But I believe I can do it. I have to."

"Promise me you won't do anything stupid," Wren said. It wasn't a question, it was an order.

"Aye, Captain," he said with a quiet smile.

She laughed softly and sipped her rum.

~

AS THE NIGHT wore on things just got harder. Every time he Caught Starlight was more painful than the time before, his muscles felt like they were full of lead, dragging him down. At first when the spindle was full Tristan would nip down to the deck to eat some food and warm up, sometimes chatting with some of the sailors and relaxing under the awning while the Majesteria did their spell.

After a while though his energy wasn't coming back, and the few steps down to the deck started to feel like a very long walk indeed. He began asking the crew to bring the spindle down so he wouldn't have to use extra energy, saving every scrap of strength he had for the next spindle. As the hours wore on he felt the exhaustion taking hold of him and he started to think maybe Wren was right, maybe he was pushing himself beyond his limits.

And then there was the storm.

It came in a swirl of snow and sleet, battering the sides of the ship with freezing sleeting rain and pellets of hail. The ship's deck turned shimmering white with snow, and the sounds of the crew below were soon drowned out by the hammering of the hail and wailing of the wind.

The icy wind whipped and lashed across Tristan's face as his stiff, frozen hands fumbled to pull the threads of Starlight, their bright glowing light barely visible under the barrage of snow, sleet, and hail.

On the deck he saw the crew struggling to keep the sails upright in the piercing wind. Birdy was picking her way down from the mast across the rope ladders of the rigging to help the rest of the sailors as they dislodged chunks of ice and built-up snow from the masts. Ginger was leading some of the crew in sweeping the snow into piles and hauling it over the side, while the kitchen staff walked around holding lanterns high to help with visibility.

Behind him he saw Wren and Emyr were both holding the wheel now, sharing the task to maximize their chances of success against the powerful elements. They were both hunched down with thick woolen cloaks around them, gripping the wheel with grim determination.

The sound of the wind howling that night was something Tristan wouldn't forget for the rest of his life. The hail peppering the deck and the ice cutting across his face like a knife as he wound the threads of Starlight onto their spindle.

As the storm wore on he started to feel himself slipping. He paused the casting to pull his cloak tight and rub his hands together to get some feeling back into his numb and freezing fingers. After a while he realized he couldn't see very well, but more worrying than that; he didn't know why.

His vision was full of blotching bright spots, shimmering in and out like twinkling stars. It was possible that it was just the storm, that everyone's visibility was like that. But maybe he had just moved too much Starlight through his body and his spent muscles were crying out to be relieved of their duty. He didn't know, and his brain was far too tired to figure it out.

As Tristan spun his last batch of Starlight onto the spindle, he felt himself falling. But he knew he couldn't, not yet, he had to get the Starlight out. As his body crumpled to the deck he used the last of his energy to push the Starlight out of his bones, beating it back with the force of his willpower, the remembrance of the people he'd seen who were consumed by Starlight, the hard determination that he would never be one of them.

When he eventually felt his body returning and remembered where he was, lying facedown on the cold, wet deck of *The Snapdragon*, he finally let himself close his eyes.

He didn't remember what came next very well. He knew that he'd felt arms lifting him, that someone had supported his weight as he'd staggered down the stairs to the main deck. He'd mumbled something to the person who was holding him, and then he'd fallen down into warmth and softness, and he'd drifted off to sleep in pure bliss.

It's too bad he didn't remember what he'd said that night because it had gone a little something like this...

"Whoa there sailor," said a voice, as firm hands stopped his stumbling fall down the stairs.

"Mmm...not a sailor..." he mumbled, "*but* I think I'm in love with one..."

"Okay, let's get you inside, the night's nearly over anyway," the kind voice had said, dragging his body along the deck.

"In loooove with a sailor, it's like a song, a pirate song," he said, his voice a drunken mumble as his mind was a muddy soup of exhaustion and the remnants of Starlight.

"We'll sing songs tomorrow, right now, you rest," the voice promised, pulling his slack feet through the drifts of snow and ice.

"The sailor, she's...She...she's the most beautiful person I've ever seen...inside *and* out, you know? Oh, Captain Wren, jewel of the seeeea," he said wistfully.

The person hauling him across the deck didn't say anything, they just kept on pushing his barely working legs.

"What do you think Ginger? You think I've got a shot?" Tristan asked.

"I'm not Ginger," the person holding him said.

"Yes, yes, you are, I'm sure you are," he said, waving his hands in front of her face. "I would know if you mrgphfmp..."

"Come on Tristan, we're almost there," Captain Wren said.

WHEN HE WOKE many hours later his body was burning with pain, but he was warm and dry, which was a considerable improvement. Whatever he was lying on was impossibly soft, and for a moment he thought he could quite happily stay like this forever. He opened his eyes and peered at the dim glow of a Pixie Hearth flickering before him, and saw he was lying in front of it on a fluffy white rug with a downy blanket around him. His cloak and sweater were laid out on a chair nearby to dry in front of the hearth, but he was still wearing his undershirt, pants and shoes. He dug his hands into the warm fluff of the rug, feeling the soft fibers between his fingers.

Suddenly he sat up, realizing he had no idea where he was.

This wasn't any room he recognized from anywhere on the ship.

He looked around, bewildered.

There was a large bed with a big puffy comforter, a small desk with some bottles and a few nautical tools on it. Chairs with piles of black clothing, and a dressing table with a battered mirror and a messy pile of jewelry. At last his gaze fell upon a large black wide-brimmed hat and he realized where he was.

HE DIDN'T KNOW how he'd gotten to Wren's room or what had happened, all he knew was that someone had brought him here to let him rest in safety.

He didn't see the Captain anywhere, including the bed, even though the sun was well into mid-day. He stood up slowly, his muscles protesting at every tiny movement, and held on to the chair for stability on his wobbling legs. He picked up his sweater, and as he was pulling it on, his gaze fell on a very familiar book on a small end table nearby.

The Valor of the Seas.

He picked it up without thinking, turning the book over in his hands, his sweater forgotten. A little piece of paper fell out and he quickly picked it up.

A receipt.

The date was a few days before, a vendor from the Midnight Market.

He wondered...had she...did she...

It was hard to imagine really.

It was terribly romantic, it was exactly the sort of thing he would do.

But...no.

There was no way. Not Wren.

The formidable and dazzling Captain Wren buying a book because...she'd seen him reading it?

The door opened with a creaking sound and he looked up.

Wren was opening it carefully with a plate piled high with rolls and a mug in her hand.

"Morning," Tristan said.

She jumped a little and turned to look at him.

"You're up," she said with a half-grin. "Glad to see it. How are you feeling?"

"Exhausted."

"About last night...what do you remember?" she asked, setting down the food and not meeting his eyes.

"Not much," he said. "I was um, doing the Starlight in the storm, and then..."

"Do you remember...saying anything?" she asked, her voice barely a whisper.

"No, I don't remember anything after I fell down on the deck. I think someone helped me down here, but I'm not sure."

"Oh." She said quietly. "Well, I'm glad you're..."

Her sentence trailed off as she caught sight of the book in his hands.

"What are you doing with that?" she asked sharply.

"How far along are you?" Tristan asked breathlessly, not noticing the edge to her voice. "Have you got to the part where Alexander confesses his–"

"I haven't read it!" she said hastily, snatching the book out of his hands and clutching it tightly to her chest. The receipt fluttering to the floor like a flower petal in the wind.

"It's very late, or, early or whatever," she said, her tone going icy. "Now that you can walk again, you should get back to your room and stop poking around in mine."

"Oh, right, yes, of course, I'm sorry, thank you," he said, speaking so fast he wasn't really sure what he'd said.

He grabbed his cloak and backed out of the room quickly,

momentarily stunned by her strange behavior. He staggered down to his cabin, shielding his eyes from the harsh sunlight and going over what had just happened.

He kept coming back to her face when she'd grabbed the book and the way she'd looked at him. He didn't know what to make of it, but he knew that right now it didn't matter. Right now, he only needed one thing.

Sleep.

Chapter Sixteen

When Tristan woke again it was nighttime. Thankfully, there was no horrible bell today, but instead there was a gentle knocking on the door to his room.

"One second," he called out, looking around frantically to see if there was anything he needed to clean up. The room was a little messy, but when he sat up and felt the shooting pains up the taut muscles of his stomach he knew he wasn't going to bother with putting away some piles of clothing.

His head was swimming. Everything ached, and the idea of even walking across the room to open the door felt almost impossible. He had fallen asleep in his undershirt and trousers, so nothing to worry about there either.

"Come in," he called.

The door opened and Bonnie and Wren walked through. The Majesteria followed closely behind, scrambling up onto the bed to look at him with scrutiny. He thought he saw Wren looking around his room with curiosity as well, peering into his trunks surreptitiously.

"You're right Wren, he doesn't look well," Edwina said, shaking her head.

"He won't make it through another night like this," Marigold agreed.

"He's tired," Chica said, poking him with her paw. "I would know."

"Ahem," Wren said. "Good evening Tristan."

"Is this a meeting about how sick I am?" he asked.

"Not exactly, dearheart," Bonnie said. She gave him a gentle pat on his arm and he winced in pain. Wren raised an eyebrow but didn't say anything.

"We already had that meeting," Edwina explained.

"When Wren told us how you couldn't walk or stand last night we realized that your body was in worse shape than we thought. Truthfully, our previous experiments with this spell have been too small to really see how they would impact a human Starlight conduit over a sustained period."

"It's quite disheartening really," Edwina said with a frown.

"I'm sorry to have such a disappointing body," Tristan said.

"Oh no, it's not your body that's the problem," Marigold said seriously. "It's a perfectly fine specimen of a human body, very muscular and well taken care of, with excellent force of willpower."

Wren's eyebrows shot to her forehead with this description and she looked like she was putting in some effort not to laugh.

"Um, thank you," Tristan said with a tone of bewilderment.

"If I had to put my paw on it I'd say the problem is one of the spellwork, it just requires too much Starlight. If we had more time we could work on crafting a more streamlined spell–"

"And that's certainly something we'll be looking into when we get home," Marigold added.

"Too true," Edwina agreed. "But with this limited timeline, we can't create a new spell. After a bit of academic debate earlier we arrived at the conclusion that a curative method was our only realistic path forward."

"Unfortunately, the magnitude of this kind of healing is way beyond our capabilities," Marigold said. "As you know, healing has always been something we've struggled with learning to a satisfactory degree. So we turned to Bonnie, who is a most capable and talented healer, to provide us with a workable spell."

"Thank you, dearheart," Bonnie said with a nod of her head.

"No, thank *you*, Bonnie!" Marigold said cheerfully. "Your spell is very well-made and should work wonderfully for our purposes. There's just one problem, the spell requires quite a lot of fuel, for lack of a better word."

"We just don't have enough power, and the only way to get more is, well...*you*," Edwina said.

"There's only one solution we've been able to come up with," Wren said. "We're going to use the Royal Cinderflower."

"WHAT??" Tristan said, gasping.

"We're gonna do the funky flower magic on ya!" Chica said cheerfully, before flopping over onto her belly on the bed.

Wren hazarded that it was safe to laugh at this time and gave a little chuckle before she said,

"As Chica said, yes, we're going to use the Royal Cinderflower to do magic. But only a very, very small amount."

"So insignificant you wouldn't notice it if you weren't looking for it," Edwina said.

"The clipping will be as small as a wisp of hair," Marigold confirmed.

"Even so," Wren said, her voice taking on an authoritative tone, "this is still...*treason*. There's no getting around it, this is absolutely against the law and we should not be doing it."

Tristan leaned back, his mouth falling open.

"What are we going to do?" he asked.

Wren unfolded a piece of paper and laid it carefully on the bed, smoothing the wrinkled edges. Tristan picked it up and scanned the words quickly, it was written in the looping script he recognized as Edwina's.

It was a Binding spell.

"Do you still have your necklace vial of Starlight?" Marigold asked. "Have you filled it up?"

Tristan nodded numbly, undoing a button of his shirt to reach inside and pull out the vial. It glittered with white light in the dimly-lit room.

"I filled it up on the first night," he said. "Just in case."

He took the vial off and set it down on the bed next to the Majesteria where it glowed brightly. The light was faded a bit but it was still strong enough to use for most spells.

"What is this spell for?" he asked.

"To make sure we all take this secret to the grave," Wren said.

"No, I'm sure I'll be fine," Tristan said, shaking his head. "We don't need to be so dramatic, I'm just a little tired."

He got out of bed and stood up to prove his point.

Well, that was the plan anyway, but his legs had other ideas.

As soon as he tried to put weight on them he could feel just how battered his body was, how his muscles protested with every movement.

He scrambled to grab onto something and not fall to the floor.

Bonnie caught his arm and gently helped him back into bed.

"Come on Tristan, don't be ridiculous," Marigold said. "Your body may be much bigger than mine but Starlight drains us all."

"On that note, we are planning to have a few drops of the healing potion as well," Edwina said. "The casting has been hard on everyone."

"We should give some to Wren too," Tristan said, noticing for the first time how sunken her eyes looked and how carefully she was leaning against the wall of his room. She made it look like she was just being casually cool, but if he really focused he could see she was hiding a lot of pain.

Her eyes flared.

"No, I'm fine, we have to prioritize-" she said.

"I mean, only if we have any to spare," Tristan cut in. His voice was gentle but firm.

She locked eyes with him for a moment, challenging him.

Finally, she nodded her agreement.

"Fine, but the mages come first."

"Of course, but we need our Captain too," he said.

Wren didn't say anything but the corners of her mouth turned up in the hint of a smile, the type of smile that made Tristan's heart leap.

Edwina picked up the spell and started mumbling an incantation while Chica unscrewed the lid of the Starlight vial and began to pull out the threads of glowing light, winding them around her paws.

"Okay everyone," Marigold said, "please put your hands together in a pile."

They did, first Bonnie, then Tristan, and Wren. Next the mice each placed a paw on top of Wren's hand.

With their spare paws Chica and Marigold began to wind the glowing white threads of Starlight around the stack of hands while Edwina kept mumbling and squeaking her incantations.

When they reached the end of the Starlight they tied the ends carefully in a bright white knot of light, and at that moment Tristan felt something move through him. The Binding spell was complete and he felt a tiny pinching in his heart. It was impossible to explain, but he knew now that he could never tell this secret to anyone, even if he wanted to.

He met Bonnie and Wren's eyes and saw that they felt it too.

"That's some powerful magic, dearhearts," Bonnie said with a bit of a shiver.

"Good." Wren said firmly, "This secret never leaves this room."

And that was that. They all filed out of his room, leaving Tristan alone to rest while they worked. He gently rolled over, ignoring the shooting pains in his torso, and settled down to read *The Glory Of The Storm* by the warm glow of the lantern.

About an hour later Wren knocked on his door.

She came in carrying a small cup of glowing orange liquid. She looked bright and energized, as fresh as the first day he'd met her, and just as magnificent. He was momentarily stunned by her dark, brooding eyes and shimmering bronze skin.

"I see we had enough for you too," he said.

Wren laughed, "Was I really looking that bad?"

"You always look beautiful," Tristan said before he could stop himself.

There was a dead silence in the cabin which suddenly felt very small and full of bed.

"I mean, I wasn't..." he trailed off, looking anywhere but at Wren's face.

Wren set the drink down on the bedside,

"The potion actually made a lot more than we expected. We all had a bit, and Bonnie is going to have Basel mix some into the strawberry lemonade so the crew can all have a little as well."

"Is there any special way I need to take it or anything?" he asked.

"Not that I know of, I had mine like a shot of whiskey," Wren said with a shrug.

"Thank you," Tristan said, trying to ignore the moonlight falling across Wren's face in alluring shadows.

"Of course," Wren said turning to leave. Halfway to the door she stopped, her gaze falling on the linen shirt he'd bought at the Midnight Market. "Nice shirt," she said, not turning around.

And then she was gone.

The potion was, in fact, not any worse tasting than a shot of whiskey. Tristan had tried quite a few potions over the years, and this one was undoubtedly one of the better tasting ones. But it was made from the Royal Cinderflower, so it made sense when you thought about it.

Far more interesting than the flavor, however, was how it made him feel.

At first, he felt like he was floating on a cloud. All the pain poured out of his body like a river and he felt light as air. He jumped out of bed and noticed that in fact he *was* light as air.

He was floating a few inches above the floor. He let out a small, involuntary yelp of delight as he floated across the room. He spun around and drifted back to the floor. He held his hands up in front of him, they were sparkling. He turned them side to side and held them up to the moonlit window, admiring the beautiful effect of the magic until it faded away. Soon his hands resumed their normal color, although his tattoos still crackled with glittering warmth.

He stretched with a big grin and began to dress for the day.

He changed his trousers and reached for a new shirt, and stopped. His gaze lingered on the linen blouse. Why not?

He put on the shirt and looked at himself in the mirror.

The healing potion had done him a world of good, the grey look was gone from his face and his cheeks had a warm glow again. His eyes looked bright, the dark hollows had vanished.

As for the shirt, well, it looked fabulous.

The voluminous sleeves, the soft delicate fabric allowing for ease of movement, it suited him.

But something was wrong.

He added the silver dangling earring he'd bought at the Midnight Market. It helped but he still looked...not quite there.

The earring looked great, so did the shirt but...his hair!

That's what it was.

Braided and tied carefully behind his back to keep it out of his way, in the traditional style of Teakley mages.

He remembered when he was a teenager and he'd first started wearing his hair that way. He'd been excited to dress like one of the Junior Apprentices who all looked so smart with their capes and brooches, marching through the hallways of Teakley, their chests bursting with pride.

But...part of him had hated it too. He missed running through the gardens with his hair flying out behind him, or whipping across his face on a cold and windy night.

He hadn't really thought about it in a long time. He'd just accepting being who Teakley wanted him to be because he wanted to be a mage, he wanted to work with magic and become a Majesteria Handler.

It didn't seem fair now.

He pulled the ribbon out of his hair and unwound the braid

with his hands, letting his long wavy hair, with its shades of light brown and blonde, cascade down and land softly on his shoulders.

He smiled to himself, it just felt right.

MAYBE IT WAS the effect of the Royal Cinderflower, or perhaps it was his unkempt new hairstyle, or even his newfound confidence from doing meaningful magic. Whatever it was, as he walked onto the deck Tristan was filled with what could only be described as... swagger.

Very possibly for the first time in his life.

He jogged across the deck with renewed energy, waving to the sailors and feeling the unbridled delight of his hair flying in all directions. He wasn't the only one, the whole crew was renewed. The night was bright and clear, not quite warm exactly but it wasn't snowing anymore. The crew were hanging the lanterns and humming cheerfully, putting up the freshly sewn sails and pulling ropes tight.

With a light heart and a bounce in his step he clattered up the little staircase to the small deck with his magical toolkit. Wren was standing there alone, overseeing the crew as they prepared for the night's hard sailing.

She caught sight of him, the moonlit wind blowing through his tangled hair. He noticed, with some satisfaction, that the little gold coin stopped moving in her hands as she stared at him.

"Evening," he said, casually.

Wren shook her head, seeming to remember who she was again.

"I see you...had the, um, the...the...potion," she said, stumbling over her words.

Tristan fought to keep the smile off his face.

"Mhmm, did me a world of good," he said.

"I...I can see that," she said. She hastily looked away and began searching for something in a nearby crate.

He turned to his countertop and was busy setting up his instruments when she appeared at his side, a bottle of rum in her hand.

"Want some?" she asked, her gaze lingering over his flowing hair and dangling earring.

"Ask me again when we get to the Evarian Sea," he said, gesturing to his array of magical instruments.

"Right, of course," she said, looking out at the sea.

She took a big gulp herself and said,

"That shirt...it suits you, I like your hair wild like that too. You look...more like yourself."

Tristan decided he was never, ever going to wear another shirt again.

A LITTLE WHILE later he came down to deliver the first batch of Starlight and saw Edwina brandishing her sword at a few bewildered sailors who were doing their very best not to laugh.

"Really? No one?" Edwina said. "Fine then, your loss!"

She turned around and rejoined the other mice who were nibbling on a large slice of mushroom quiche.

"What was that about?" Tristan asked them.

"She beat five people at Cherry Basket and now no one wants to play with her," Marigold explained.

"Cowards!" Edwina said, shaking her head.

"In their defense you are quite a formidable opponent Edwina," Tristan said amiably.

"I'll take that as a compliment," Edwina said decisively. She put her sword away and looked at him curiously for a moment. "You look different."

The other mice turned to look at him.

"It's Adventure Tristan!" Marigold said with a happy squeak.

"What?" he asked.

"Well you see, when we first got on the ship...we did something a little reckless," Edwina said.

"You mean when you snuck out in the middle of the night?"

The mice, as one, gasped.

"How did you know?" Edwina asked.

"You weren't exactly subtle, you left pawprints all over the hall-way," Tristan said with a shrug. He flipped his hair out of his face and grinned dashingly, it felt good.

The mice were stunned.

"But humans never notice," Marigold said quietly.

"I guess I'm just different," he said.

"I like it!" Chica declared.

"Anyway, please continue Edwina," he said, picking up a grape and popping it into his mouth.

"Well, when we snuck out," she continued, giving him a slightly suspicious squint, "Marigold was leading the charge. She explained that she was in fact Adventure Marigold, who is more bold and courageous."

Marigold bowed dramatically.

"Now we have Adventure Tristan too!" Marigold squeaked.

Tristan laughed, "I like that. What about you two?"

"I'm *always* Adventure Edwina," Edwina said, pulling out her tiny sword and holding it up to the sky dramatically.

"I'm *always* ready for a nap," Chica said with a yawn.

He watched the Majesteria do their spells for a while, and then he returned to the upper deck to begin his next round of Starlight casting. Wren was gone and Emyr was at the wheel, he nodded to Tristan amiably. Tristan returned to work, laying out the channelling batons and warming the spindle as he looked out at the deck below. The bright lanterns swinging in the wind, the sails flapping, the night sky an endless expanse of glittering lights.

Doing magic out here, like this, it felt different. He felt impor-tant, like what he did mattered. Back at Teakley it was all quiet scrib-blings, magical experiments and intellectual debate. It was all *theoretical*. Here, magic was a living breathing thing that could make a ship fly across the sea, could fight off an evil pirate, return strength to a battered body. It was powerful, and meaningful, and it filled him up in a way he didn't know it was possible to feel. He realized being on this ship, with these people, was starting to change him, and he had no idea what to do about it.

～

IT WAS a beautiful night and things were going well, after taking the magical Cinderflower potion everyone's abilities and morale had improved. After carefully mapping the stars Wren had determined they would be arriving at the Dragon's Neck by morning, everything was looking good.

But of course, the Otherwilde Sea wasn't done with them just yet.

It was about halfway through the night when the Sea Serpent arrived.

Tristan was about to start pulling threads of Starlight when a massive tentacle thumped onto the deck with an ear-splitting crack. He jumped back and then gripped the counter as the ship began to lean sharply towards the monster.

He turned his eyes to the sea and gasped in horror.

The monster's head was rearing out of the water, the roiling seas crashing around it in white-crested waves.

The head was like that of a dragon, covered in shimmering aquamarine scales, it's eyes glowing yellow with a mouth hanging open to reveal its rows of sharp, pointed teeth.

But its body was made of slimy grey-green tentacles, each one as a big as a tree trunk. The tentacles plunged through the water violently, reaching for the boat as Wren scrambled to pull it away.

The Serpent roared with a horrible sound, shrieking its violent fury across the turbulent seas. More tentacles appeared at the sides of the ship, ripping and tearing away at the sails and anything that wasn't nailed down.

Tristan stumbled forward as the ship stopped moving with a

shuddering jolt, as one massive tentacle squelched across the middle of the deck and tried to pull the ship towards it. Wren was trying desperately to steer the ship away, but the monster's grasp was already too tight.

"THE WEAPONS! GET THE WEAPONS!" Wren screamed across the deck.

But Emyr was already running for her office, his deep brown skin a streak in the dark night.

"What is that??" Tristan asked, gripping the counter tightly. "Is it a Kraken?"

Wren looked up at the strange almost dragon-like face with its yellow serpentine eyes.

"No, Krakens don't have heads like that, but…"

She looked down at the giant tentacles wrestling with the ship.

"I don't know what it is, honestly," she said. "But it doesn't matter, it'll kill us all no matter what we call it."

"What do we do?" Tristan asked, shouting to be heard over the screams of the crew and the horrible cracking of the ship's railing.

"We fight it. We've dealt with Krakens and Sea Serpents before, usually a good stabbing gets them to leave, they don't like prey that fights back," Wren called out. "But *you*, you need to get downstairs and stay safe. NOW!"

"WHAT? WHY?" Tristan shouted.

"You're a guest!" she called back, her hands gripping the wheel tightly.

"Are you serious?" Tristan said, stunned.

"YES! GET DOWNSTAIRS!"

"*NO!*" he shouted, staggering across the deck to argue with her. "After everything we've been through, you can't seriously tell me I need to run inside like a fucking guest! I'm going to fight that thing with the rest of the crew!"

"You're not a bloody sailor Tristan, you *don't* belong out there," she said, stepping closer to him.

"Does everything I've done mean nothing?" he shouted, waving his hands in the air. "How can you say I don't belong here?"

He stepped closer to her, their faces only a few inches apart, anger blooming in his chest. His eyes met hers and he saw something he hadn't expected; she was terrified. He wondered if she was worried something might happen...to him.

"That's not what I mean!" Wren shouted.

"What *do* you mean then?" he asked, searching her eyes, willing her to say that words that had been haunting his dreams for weeks.

"Dammit Tristan, I just..."

She let go of the wheel and put her hands on his shirt, pulling him close until he could feel her breath on his lips. He wondered for a moment if this was real life, if this was really happening. If the most incredible person he'd ever met was really about to kiss him while a giant monster of the deep roared with rage beside them.

And then it was happening, and she was twisting her fingers into his tangled hair, pressing her lips against his and pouring all her emotions into that kiss.

He reached his arm around and pulled her waist towards him, wrapping her wet shirt in his fingers as he kissed her deeply, trying to put all of his yearning and passion into a single moment. The kiss was filled with magic and electricity, but not from the Starlight still flickering in his body; it was her kiss that made the wild sparks light inside his heart.

She released him, and returned to grasp the ship's wheel with both arms.

"You're not allowed to die, you hear me?" she screamed over the roar of the Sea Serpent. "And take this bloody rum," she said, tossing him the bottle. "You'll need it."

"AYE CAPTAIN!" Tristan shouted, drinking the rest of the rum in one massive gulp and throwing the bottle over his shoulder into the sea.

Chapter Seventeen

TRISTAN RAN down the deck with a fire in his belly and a song in his heart. One of the large, slimy tentacles was gripping the deck tightly, trying to pull the ship towards it and eventually under the water. The grey end of the tentacle sought for purchase among the ship's sloping decks, searching for something to break the balance in the Serpent's favor.

But the crew were gathered around the tentacles and taking up arms. Swords, axes, bows, even kitchen knives were wielded to hack, saw, and stab, fighting to break through the tough, glistening appendage.

"Can anyone give me a weapon?" Tristan called out across the deck.

Birdy threw him a sword.

It was a battered old thing, with notched sides and a slightly rusted handle. He hefted it in his hand and took an experimental swing which knocked him slightly off balance.

"Do you have an axe maybe?" he shouted over the squelching sounds of the crew hacking away at the monster.

A nearby sailor stopped their stabbing and ran over to him.

"Trade?" they said.

He nodded and traded the sword for the axe.

He felt the weight of it in his hands, it was familiar and comfortable. Within moments he was swinging it around with confidence. He'd barely ever touched a sword but he'd chopped a lot of wood back at Teakley.

The monster was bellowing ferociously now, its slimy, muscular sinews rippling and bucking on the deck as the crew continued their assault. The roaring was deafening, drowning out even the shouts of the sailors and the endless noise of angry waves crashing against the ship in the turbulent waters.

The ship began to lean sharply towards the Serpent, the crew running to stay upright as the deck tilted below them.

Tristan very quickly discovered that chopping wood is absolutely nothing like hacking a squishy sea-monster tentacle on a furiously careening ship. He tried to saw at the slimy thing while he fought to remain standing on the swaying deck, but the axe mostly slid down the side of the slithering mass.

He had only just broken the surface of its strange, smooth skin before the ship tilted again and he tumbled backwards with the rest of the crew.

He staggered to standing and hefted the axe in his hand, approaching the monster again to pound at it fruitlessly with his axe. His lack of experience was frustrating, he was used to solving problems with magic not axes. He wondered if there was something he could do, some way to use Starlight against the monster. The Majesteria would know.

He stopped hacking and looked to the awning in front of Wren's office, searching for somewhere out of the way where the Majesteria would be hiding.

But they weren't hiding.

Just like him, the Majesteria were ready to fight for *The Snapdragon*.

He saw a small bright light flickering under the awning. It looked like they were huddled in front of their boarding trunk attempting to create a spell.

Tristan realized as he saw the small light glowing brighter that they had barely any Starlight to work with. They had used up the last batch on the sails already, which meant the Majesteria were trying to pull down Starlight themselves for their spell.

It wouldn't be enough.

He knew their capacity for catching Starlight was small and would severely limit them in what kind of spells they could produce. It didn't seem worth the risk of their safety.

"Majesteria! Get into the office!" he shouted at them.

"*NO!*" Edwina shouted back, "We're doing a spell! We're going to help!"

"You can't get enough power!" he called. "Get yourselves to safety!"

"Why don't you help us then?" Marigold yelled.

"FINE!" he shouted, knowing their infinite capacity for stubbornness. He turned away from the monster to run towards the Majesteria.

But it was too late.

The other tentacle crashed down in front of him, splintering the boarding trunk and sending the Majesteria flying wildly into the air. He watched with horror as their tiny bodies flew out over the crew, the sails, the railing, and dropped into the roiling sea.

His axe clattered to the deck, forgotten, as he skidded across the hardwood to the railing. Wren almost beat him to it, her eyes wild and hair flying everywhere as she ran up to him

"Did I just see the Majesteria fall into the sea?" she shouted, her face a mask of horror.

"There they are!" Tristan shouted by way of answer.

He could see them, all three were bobbing up and down in the sea, flailing their little paws and trying to spit out the salty water before they swallowed too much. Every now and then he would see a small spark of light as they attempted to do magic but the ferocious waves were too much for them. The sparks went out almost as fast as they came, the strong currents pulling them under again before they could finish calling out their spell. It was all they could do to stay afloat and not get sucked under the ship.

Tristan looked out at them with grim determination.

He began to climb over the railing.

"What are you doing?" Wren shouted.

"I'm going after them!" he said, swinging a leg over the side and trying not to think about the terrifying fall.

"What! Can you even swim?" Wren asked.

"Yes!" he said.

This was, technically, true. Of course, doing laps in the relaxing natural pools of the mountains outside Teakley was perhaps not the same as leaping into a roiling abyss of furious waves.

"I'm coming with you," Wren said, clambering up onto the railing too.

"What? No!" Tristan shouted.

Then Wren was at his side, looking into his eyes with the same ferocity he felt.

"They're my crew too," she said.

He nodded.

"BIRDY! GET US A ROPE!" she shouted.

Then she put her hand in his and they jumped off the ship.

They crashed into the freezing ocean a few seconds later, dipping their heads below the surface in a chaotic splash of bright green water. The force of the fall knocked them apart and when Tristan surfaced he couldn't see anything but white foam and crashing waves.

He struggled to stay upright, his muscles complaining as he pushed back against the violent water.

After a moment he finally spotted the mice and he wasn't far away. He pushed forward, his strong muscular arms propelling him through the water as he fought his way towards the struggling mice.

He saw Marigold first, her witch hat already lost somewhere in the sea.

He scooped her up and held her gently but tightly in one hand.

Next was Edwina, her miniature sword still at her side. He picked her up, her tiny body shaking with violence as she tried to spit water out and cast a spell at the same time.

He looked around but Chica wasn't there. He couldn't think clearly as panic gripped him.

"*CHICA!!*" he screamed.

"I've got her," Wren yelled nearby, holding up the tiny bundle of wet fur and glittery dress.

"I'm wet!" Chica shouted.

Tristan was too panicked to laugh at this, he just held onto Edwina and Marigold as they continued spluttering the sea water out of their lungs. He held them as high as he could while trying to tread water. Already his legs felt like they were made of lead, but he barely noticed, he was too full of adrenaline and blind terror.

A moment later the rope descended from the ship like a ladder from the heavens. Wren grabbed it deftly and hoisted herself up with one arm while she held Chica carefully.

"Throw me!" Chica said cheerfully.

"What!" Wren said.

"Yeah, just chuck me over, it'll be fun!"

"NO! You're crazy," Wren said, shaking her head and putting the protesting mouse on her shoulder so she could reach out a hand to pull Tristan in towards the rope.

Tristan struggled over, holding the two mice above the water as best he could. He handed Edwina to Wren who put the mouse on her shoulder next to Chica. Wren held out her hand and he grabbed it, hauling himself onto the rope. Moments later Wren was climbing up the side of the ship, the mice clinging to her soaking wet linen blouse.

Tristan put Marigold on his shoulder and she scrambled to hold the wet fabric as he began the ascent up the knotted rope onto the ship. It took him quite a bit longer than Wren, the going wasn't easy and his feet kept slipping on the slimy rope. Marigold clung tightly to him as he pushed himself up the swinging rope, while the ship was still being violently rocked by the Sea Serpent on the other side.

Finally, he made it to the railing and clambered awkwardly over it, gasping and spluttering. He stood up, his soaking wet clothing dripping puddles on the deck, and heard a cheering from some of the nearby sailors, who'd paused their assault on the Sea Serpent to applaud their Captain's safe return. But the joyful cheers were quickly drowned out by the roar of the angry monster, still battering the ship.

He saw a new tentacle flailing in the direction of the deck and realized that despite the daring rescue of the Majesteria, they weren't out of the woods just yet. Wren must have had the same thought because she was already halfway to the stairs, carrying Edwina and Chica. He ran after her, ignoring the chaos of the sailors and the Sea Serpent. All he could think of was getting the Majesteria to safety.

A moment later he was barrelling down the stairs and through the hallway, close behind Wren as they ran towards the kitchens and Bonnie's quarters. The ship shuddered with the force of the Sea Serpent still gripping it tightly as the crew battled its tentacles.

They arrived at Bonnie's quarters, her door was already open with bandages and poultices prepared on the table. She was clearly ready for the eventual deluge of sailors needing healing salves once they beat the Serpent. Wren and Tristan rushed into the room and set the Majesteria down gently on a towel.

"I need to return to the crew, will you be alright?" Wren asked them.

Edwina and Marigold nodded their heads affirmatively, even though they were too shaken to speak.

Meanwhile, Chica looked positively cheerful.

"Go get 'em Captain!" Chica said.

Wren smiled and with a quick nod to Bonnie, ran out of the room.

Tristan heard the pounding of her boots as she ran down the hallway and it matched the hammering in his chest. The adrenaline was still coursing through his body as he hurriedly sat down on a chair near the Majesteria and looked them over.

"Do you need anything?" he asked anxiously. "What can I do?"

"Let me do *my* job first, dearheart," Bonnie said with the kind firmness of a professional healer. She stepped to the table, gently nudging him out of her way so she could bend over the Majesteria carefully.

"I don't have much experience with animals, but it would appear you have injured your paw," she said to Edwina.

Edwina nodded as she lifted one soaking wet paw limply, wincing in pain.

"I wonder if I could use the same method to bandage it as I use for humans. Perhaps if I just cut the bandage very small?" Bonnie mused to herself as she took Edwina's tiny paw delicately in her hand, looking at it carefully with an expert eye.

Tristan caught Marigold's eye while Bonnie examined Edwina. He saw her making an expression he'd never seen her have before... fear. He'd never seen the Majesteria be afraid of anything or anyone, but she was clearly shaken by what had just happened.

He understood how she felt, he was rattled too. It wasn't just the memory of the Majesteria flying across the deck or flailing in the sea that chilled him.

It was the feeling of total helplessness, how completely unprepared the four of them had been to deal with the situation. He had always thought the Majesteria could do anything, with their powerful magic he figured they could take on any monster and easily win. It was a comforting thought, but he was starting to realize that it wasn't actually true. He wondered if Marigold had just noticed the same thing.

"I think a bandage should work just fine," Bonnie said, setting Edwina's paw down gently. "But first let's get you some dry clothes and a little bit of cheese, eh?"

"I'd prefer a lot of cheese," Chica said. She seemed entirely unperturbed by the whole incident and was lying belly-down on the towel, her paws buried happily in the soft fiber.

Bonnie laughed, "A lot of cheese then, dearheart."

"I'll get you some dry clothes," Tristan said.

But before he could leave the room he heard the sound of pounding boots in the hallway again. Everyone looked to the door with worried expressions.

A sailor he didn't know by name, a young man with nut-brown skin and curly hair was panting at the doorway.

"Tristan!" he said between breaths, "Captain needs ya!"

"Me?" Tristan asked, surprised.

"NOW!" the sailor said, turning around to run back down the hallway without even waiting to see if Tristan was following.

Tristan looked at the mice, wondering what to do. The idea of leaving them right now felt awful, but he was sure if Wren was sending for him it was important.

"What's wrong with you?" Edwina scolded. "*Run* Tristan! Captain needs you!"

Tristan suddenly found his legs could work again and he nodded once to the Majesteria before bolting down the hallway.

THE SCENE on the deck was terrifying. The ship was quaking as the serpent crashed against it, with furious white-capped waves spraying water high into the air. The Sea Serpent's head was thrashing violently as it fought with the ship, trying to pull *The Snapdragon* into the deep. The Serpent roared with frustration as the ship refused to budge in its murderous grasp.

The dark blood of the monster was everywhere, soaking clothes and seeping into the deck, making it slippery. The frantic crew kept hacking away at the undulating tentacles but even as they did so more were coming. As soon as one injured tentacle would pull away, another would take its place with no respite for the weary crew.

He ignored the gruesome sight before him and turned to the stern where Wren was hanging on to the wheel tightly. Emyr was nearby, ready to help as needed and shouting orders to the sailors.

He knew she wouldn't have sent for him if it wasn't important so Tristan ran up the deck and said,

"I'm here, what do you need?"

"We can't get away from the Serpent," Wren said, speaking loudly to be heard over the sounds of the beast and the ocean, its surging waves crashing against the ship with a thunderous roar.

"I see that, what can I do?" he asked.

"It's the magic," Wren explained, nodding to Emyr who seamlessly took the wheel from her so she could step away and talk to Tristan while the strong winds whipped her dark hair across her face.

Tristan looked up at the sails, he saw the Majesteria's spell was still there, working feverishly to fill the sails to capacity and send the ship flying across the sea at high speed. He saw the sparks of light in the wind all around him, the spell must have been so powerful that bits of it were leaking out and creating small gusts of wind all over the ship.

But the ship wasn't flying across the sea. It was stuck, held in place by the angry Sea Serpent, its tentacles pulling the ship ever closer to its home in the dark depths of the sea.

"I don't understand," Tristan admitted.

Wren nodded, "I need to be able to pivot quickly, in the opposite direction of the wind. In order to escape the Serpent I would need to do a very fast maneuver, turning the ship in the few seconds before the monster strikes again. But every time I try to twist the ship away, the magical wind is pushing it in the opposite direction. It's so powerful, I can't point the ship any direction except where the spell wants it to go. Can you diffuse the spell? Or weaken it or something?"

Tristan felt that same horrible feeling he'd felt when he looked at Marigold a few minutes before. That awful helplessness, the lack of knowledge or skills. For a second he wondered why they'd never taught him any of this at Teakley, wasn't it supposed to be an academy of magic? But they only cared about academic theories and magical ideas. Most of which wasn't any help to him now.

The reality was, he couldn't diffuse the spell.

Well, maybe he could, if he had a few weeks to study books, poke around theories, and design a good plan.

But now? Right *now*? No.

He had no idea how to do that, and he hated it.

But that wasn't worth thinking about right now, that wouldn't help anyone.

"I'm so sorry, I don't know how to do that," he admitted reluctantly. "I believe the Majesteria would say the same. We could do it... but not fast enough, the earliest would be a few hours."

For a moment Wren looked upset, but then she set her jaw and nodded her head sharply.

"Alright, thank you. I guess we'll have to go with the reckless, dangerous option."

And with that she was gone from his side, returning to the wheel and giving a quick command to Emyr which sent him running across the ship to yell orders at the crew and calling out to Birdy for her assistance.

For a moment Tristan wondered what the dangerous plan was, but soon enough all was revealed. Within a few minutes he saw some of the crew assembling into a group to assist Birdy as she climbed the rigging with a large cutlass in hand. As she approached the top of the sail he realized what she was planning to do and called out to stop her, but his voice was lost on the wind, and she probably wouldn't have listened anyway.

It was reckless and dangerous, and she already knew that.

But what else could they do?

Birdy cut the sail loose and the large ball of spinning magical light exploded onto the deck, knocking many of the sailors to the ground and sending Tristan staggering backwards towards the railing. The blast of wild, uncontained wind magic around them took his breath away. He was blown back against the rail, his hair flying out behind him, eyes watering from the sharp sting of the wind.

The sparking winds went everywhere, tearing at clothes and

sails, breaking apart barrels and crates already battered from the Sea Serpent's assault. Sailors were being flung across the ship in all directions, grabbing desperately onto anything stable so they could stay standing.

The Serpent pulled away from the powerful magic, its strange serpentine eyes narrowing as the magical winds blasted its gaping maw. It sniffed the air and recoiled, its bloody tentacles slithering away from the ship.

Wren was ready as soon as the Serpent pulled away, she was somehow holding her ground in the strong winds and gripping the wheel tightly. She pivoted the ship quickly, turning it on its axis away from the thrashing monster. But the turn was frenzied and uneven in the fierce winds, causing the ship to careen sharply, almost dipping into the sea. Wren was grappling with the ship, desperately trying to get it stable. Tristan was so focused on her fight he didn't notice anything else was happening until he heard people screaming.

He looked up and saw Birdy go flying, her body like a ragdoll carried on the high winds. She sailed over the deck, her limbs twisting unnaturally in the magical wind.

There was a horrifying thump and cracking sound as her body landed on the deck, followed closely by a scream. Ginger's howl could be heard by everyone on the ship as she ran across the deck to kneel down beside Birdy's limp form. Everyone else soon joined her, crowding around the body while Basel tried desperately to push the sailors back.

"Come on now, give her some room! You there, step back," Basel boomed, shooing the sailors aside so Ginger had space to maneuver around Birdy. She leaned over her, whispering to her as some of the other sailors tried to lift her sagging, limp body. Eventually, Birdy opened her eyes and tried to stand up. She quickly saw she couldn't stand, she could barely move at all, but...she was alive.

The crew carried her downstairs, Ginger at the lead, her normally bright cheerful face full of fierce determination and worry.

It had all happened in the space of a few minutes. Tristan felt the ship lurch again as he watched the sailors carry Birdy away while the rest of the crew was thrown around in the magical wind storm. He fell down hard against the deck, gripping the rail with one hand as Wren yanked the wheel and pulled the ship further away from the Sea Serpent and the whirling winds full of bright sparks of magic.

He struggled to his feet in the fierce wind, wishing desperately that he knew some kind of spell to help them, to make this situation any better.

But he didn't.

He knew the names of hundreds of plants.

He knew the theories of every notable mage for the last ten centuries.

But he didn't know how to stop a spell that he had started.

He felt the sinking horror of his lack of true magical knowledge deep in his bones as he watched helplessly while the crew struggled to re-attach the sail and Wren deftly maneuvered the ship to stability again.

He watched as the Sea Serpent, bereft of its prey and distressed by the magical winds, began to swim away in the opposite direction in search of easier food to hunt.

He looked around him at the wrecked, bloody ship and the exhausted sailors struggling to help each other recover.

It was an image he wouldn't soon forget.

ONCE THE SHIP was sailing comfortably again Tristan walked on unsteady legs down to Bonnie's quarters to check on everyone.

The hallway was full of sailors, most of them trying to peer into the room where Birdy was lying on the bed and the Majesteria were sitting on a blanket eating snacks and chatting with people.

"Oh yes, it was terrible, I saw my whole life flash before my eyes," Marigold was saying, her paws up in the air dramatically.

"It was mostly cheese," Edwina said, which caused a laugh from the sailors.

"Mmphggh," Chica said. Tristan saw that someone had provided the mice with overflowing plates of cheese, small mushroom pies, scones, and strawberries.

Someone tapped his shoulder. Basel handed him a woolen blanket and a steaming mug of tea.

"Thank you," Tristan mumbled, still in a daze from the evening's events. He took the warm mug with shaking hands.

"You'll be alright Froggy, but maybe you should sit down, eh?" Basel said.

"I'm alright," Tristan said, but even as he said it he realized his legs were wobbling and his hands wouldn't stop shaking, causing some of the tea to slosh out of the mug. Basel noticed too and stepped in front of him.

"Outta the way for Froggy!" Basel boomed, pushing the sailors back to make room for Tristan to go into the room and sit down on the bed. "Let 'em through!"

The sailors parted hastily and Tristan walked into the warm, cozy Healer's quarters, his eyes sharply focused on the very inviting bed next to the Majesteria. He sunk into the soft pillows gratefully, curling his legs up under him and putting his hands around the mug, its gentle warmth radiating into his cold bones. He knew the night wasn't done yet but for the moment, he could finally rest.

Chapter Eighteen

It was about an hour later when Wren came down to discuss their next move. Tristan had chatted with the Majesteria, drank his tea, and eventually napped for a little while on the cozy beds in the Healer's Quarters.

Tristan looked over and saw that Ginger was keeping watch over Birdy while she slept in the other bed. She looked a little nervous to be there, she kept standing up, looking at the door like she was thinking about leaving, and then sitting back down again.

Tristan realized that he'd never seen the two of them be very public about their relationship, and perhaps they didn't want to be. Maybe it wasn't that serious, although the look on Ginger's face suggested otherwise.

But really, he didn't know how sailors lived or had romantic entanglements; perhaps they were all like Emyr.

As if she knew what Tristan was thinking, Ginger stood up apprehensively when Wren came in. She looked around anxiously, as though hoping there was a convenient door she could slip out of before Wren noticed she was holding vigil at her lover's bedside.

For her part, Wren ignored Ginger's behavior completely and addressed her as she would any sailor.

"How is she?" Wren asked somberly.

"She's going to be alright, broken quite a few bones Bonnie says," Ginger replied. "She needs to sleep for a while, then Bonnie is going to redress her wounds and give her some splints for the broken bones."

"That's good," Wren said, looking down at Birdy with a soft sigh of relief.

"Do you...do you need me on deck, Captain?" Ginger asked timidly.

Tristan saw a hint of a knowing smile cross her face as Wren said,

"I think you're most needed here, would you mind watching over her?"

"Not at all!" Ginger said, a little too quickly.

"Thanks Ginger," Wren said, turning her attention to the other side of the room where Tristan and the Majesteria were resting.

Tristan felt a quickening of his pulse as she turned her piercing gaze to him.

He suddenly remembered their kiss on the deck and felt his body flush at the memory. But she wasn't looking at him any differently than any other member of her crew. Right now all Wren was thinking about was the ship and getting them all to safety.

"How about the rest of my crew?" Wren asked, looking down at the Majesteria with a smile.

"We're feeling much better," Edwina said.

"Thank you for the daring rescue, Captain!" Marigold added, with a dramatic bow.

Chica was snoring.

"And you?" Wren asked, turning to Tristan.

"I've had a good rest and I'm ready to get back on the deck," he said. "I'm still feeling very good from the, um...drink I had this morning."

He felt a strange prickling feeling on his tongue as the pact bound him from mentioning the Cinderflower potion, even if he'd wanted to.

"That's good because I think we'll need you again shortly,"

Wren said, casually pulling up a chair from nearby and turning it around so she could sit on it backwards, her arms draped over the side casually.

There was something about the movement that Tristan found unreasonably attractive, and he found the heat returning to his cheeks. But maybe he was just remembering that kiss again. He wondered if it meant something to her, or perhaps it was just a passing pirate fancy; perhaps it didn't mean anything at all. He knew that either way it paled in comparison to the crew's mission to get the Cinderflower to the Coronation, but even so, his mind kept straying to thoughts of kissing the Captain again.

"I mapped our location with Emyr just now," she was saying, completely oblivious to the teenage dreamy-eyed romance happening inside Tristan's head. "It's generally good news. The burst from the...*drink* you had this morning was significant. The wind's power was way faster than even the first few days, and we didn't lose much time to the Sea Serpent. Additionally, it's a very windy night so we are being propelled at a good speed, even without magical support. I believe we'll arrive at the Dragon's Neck in the morning."

"That's good to hear," Tristan said, finally getting himself to focus on the seriousness of the situation again, even if he didn't have anything very useful to contribute.

"Since we have the natural wind at our disposal, I'd like to make use of it," Wren went on, "Everyone has had a rough night and I'd like to give us all a rest if I can. The magical sailing has been a strain on the whole crew."

"I hadn't considered that," Marigold said thoughtfully.

Tristan guessed she was wondering what could be done to design a spell in the future to make wind spells easier for sailors. He suspected she'd have a few scroll's worth of notes before the journey was over.

"My question is this," Wren said, "would we be able to have Tristan make some of the Starlight spindles tonight and then store them to use in the morning after we enter the Evarian Sea?"

"Hmm," Edwina said.

"Wake up Chica," Marigold said, nudging the snoring mouse.

"Huh? Why?" Chica's sleepy voice said.

"We gotta do important mage stuff," Marigold said.

"Ack! I don't wanna, you do it," Chica said, putting her head back down.

"Please, Chica! You're making us look bad in front of the Captain," Marigold said, kicking the sleeping mouse lightly.

"You could've mentioned the Captain was here!" Chica said, sitting up and wiggling her whiskers to appear more awake.

"I don't see why not," Edwina said finally. She had been completely absorbed in her thoughts about the wind spell and had not noticed the situation with Chica at all.

"Whatchu need Cap'n?" Chica asked with a yawn.

Wren smiled just a little, Tristan could tell she was trying very hard not to laugh.

"The Captain is wondering if I could fill up a couple of spindles now, but you wait until morning in the Evarian Sea to use them," he said. "That way, the crew could get a bit of a rest, and you could go back to sleep."

"I'm in!" Chica said. "If it gets me sleeping, it's a good idea."

Marigold glared at her. "Despite whatever Chica's reasons are, I'm actually in too. I expect the amount the Starlight would fade in that amount of time to be minimal, especially after the um, extra support from the um, thing with the, the, the...you know."

Just like Tristan, she couldn't mention the Cinderflower potion. The prickling on your tongue was a strange sensation, he wondered if he'd ever get used to it.

Wren nodded, "Yes, I thought that might make this a little more likely to work. Alright then, the only question left is if you're up for it, Tristan."

"Absolutely, Captain," Tristan said. Deftly avoiding saying the next thought that entered his mind, which was something along the lines of, 'I'll do anything you want me to.'

~

Despite the exhausting night he'd had already, the Cinderflower's magic was still tingling in his veins and Tristan found he had a surprisingly light step as he bounded up onto the deck to finish his work for the night.

The wind was strong, but not that bothersome after the storms they'd had, and it felt good running through his long hair. When he got to the deck he saw some of the crew who weren't already in the crowded Canteen finishing up the recovery effort from the Sea Serpent. All the splintered and broken items had been put in a big heap in one corner, where a few of the sailors were throwing another shattered crate. Someone else was nearly finished mopping up the serpent's blood and was busy wringing it out over the side. A few more people were tying sails, re-knotting rope, and assessing the damage to the railing. For the most part, everyone looked untroubled and generally relieved to not be barrelling through the sea at breakneck speed or fighting a sea monster.

His hair whipped around his face joyfully as he headed up the stairs to the little deck with the steering wheel. Wren and Emyr were there already, she was steering the ship and he was leaning over the side of the railing, staring out at the horizon with a bottle of rum in his hand. They looked relaxed, which was a beautiful thing to see after the last few days.

Tristan nodded to her and their eyes caught briefly.

The look was different than when they'd spoken downstairs.

It had a little bit of fire to it.

The good kind.

Tristan turned away from her and began to assemble his tools for casting, noticing as he did that his hands were trembling ever so slightly.

He wondered why.

He questioned what was happening to make him so anxious,

and after a careful inventory of his thoughts, he realized it was Wren. But that couldn't be right, he thought, he'd just been talking to her, they'd spent plenty of time together. Why was he suddenly trembling with nerves?

He realized it was because after the kiss, it all felt different.

It felt like maybe it could be...real.

All the things he'd been bottling up, all the feelings that had been growing inside him since the very first moment he'd met her. What if she'd felt something too? Something real, something more than a chaotic moment of panic about a Sea Serpent.

In that moment he knew he was going to have to find out.

He needed to know if their kiss had been just a strange impulse in the heat of the moment or if it was something more.

He resolved to talk to her after he'd finished casting.

Somehow, with a lot of effort that took way longer than usual, Tristan managed to stop thinking about Wren's dark eyes and focus on pulling down shimmering threads of blinding light and winding them around the large metal spindle. He had finished the first spindle and was taking a moment for his body to recover when he saw Wren break away from the wheel and pass it over to Emyr who gave her a smile and a nod of the head.

Tristan felt his palms begin to sweat and his heart race involuntarily as she walked cooly over to him, her sensuous eyes meeting his with that same fire he'd seen earlier.

"I'm done for the night," she said, leaning up against the counter next to him, her favorite gold coin spinning in her fingers. "Emyr has kindly offered to sail us through the Dragon's Neck. How are you doing?"

Tristan heard a tone in her voice, a yearning huskiness he hadn't heard before, and it made his skin tingle like wildfire.

"I'm halfway there, just finished one," he said, pointing to the brightly glowing spindle.

"So you're feeling...*good*?"

Somehow he felt like that wasn't what she was really asking.

"I'm feeling *very* good," he said, leaning slightly closer to her. He felt the warmth radiating from her body washing over him, stark against the coldness of the windy night.

"Glad to hear it," she said, her voice still low and hoarse. "I was wondering, after you're done here, could we...talk?"

"Sure," Tristan said. He was consumed with the sight of the moonlight dancing across her bronze skin in shimmering waves.

"Privately," she added abruptly. She broke their gaze and looked away.

Suddenly the sensual energy of the moment drained out of Tristan and he was filled with frazzled nerves again.

What did she mean? Was she upset about the kiss earlier? Did she want to make it clear she wasn't interested in him romantically?

If that was true...why was she looking at him with that hunger in her eyes?

All these questions and more were screaming inside him, but all he said was,

"No problem, I'll knock on your door when I'm done here."

"Thanks," she said, and disappeared into the night.

THE SECOND SPINDLE was a beast to finish. Tristan lost his focus and snapped the Starlight threads three times and had to carefully tie them together with needle and thread so he didn't have to start over. It wasn't infuriating, he hadn't snapped a Starlight thread since he'd been a Junior Apprentice. But he just couldn't hold his focus.

The dual emotions of the wild sensuality of Wren, and the mounting fear that she'd never want to kiss him again was just too much. He'd barely managed to get the Starlight to flow at all when he first started, his mind was so full of racing anxieties.

But at last it was done, and after saying goodnight to Emyr and safely storing the spindles in a crate on the deck, he packed up his toolkit and slung it over his shoulder. He made his way down the stairs and onto the deck, it was peaceful and quiet now. Only a few sailors were still up, keeping watch while gently nudging the sails and rigging to make sure they stayed on course.

When Tristan arrived at Wren's office it was dark. He didn't see a light anywhere through the mottled glass windows. That was puzzling, but he decided to knock anyway. His hands were sweating and shaky as he rapped on the door softly, some part of him hoping she wouldn't open it at all and he could just go back to his quarters and go to sleep.

Maybe they could just forget about the kiss.

Well, forgetting was very unlikely for a kiss like that, but at least they could pretend that it had never happened.

There was no answer.

He knocked a second time, a little louder.

The door remained firmly shut and for a moment his heart flip-flopped between relief and misery.

Then, he was flooded with a warm, yellow light.

He looked up. The door of Wren's personal quarters was open and she was there, her eyes burning bright.

"In here," she said, opening the door wider for him to slip inside.

His heart was fluttering like a bird as he walked through the door into the inviting living space.

And...bedroom.

The bed, with its big fluffy white duvet and mess of pillows was very loud in his mind suddenly. It felt almost like some kind of Eldritch presence, dominating the space and invading his thoughts.

She turned away and walked towards a shabby wooden cabinet with a small door, which she slid open. There were bottles of alcohol inside, she talked over her shoulder as she sorted through them.

"How are you?" she asked, in that same husky low voice she'd used on the deck. It sent shivers up his spine in the best possible way. "The other night you were very...strange, after you'd been doing magic all night."

The glow of the candlelight shimmered across her warm bronze skin, her shining dark hair floating in waves down her back. She looked relaxed and comfortable, Tristan saw her moving through her room and the space suddenly made so much sense. He could feel her presence in the choices of furniture, the silver jewelry scattered about haphazardly, the piles of black clothing slung over the sides of chairs. It was the comforting room of a busy person who usually had more important places to be, but wanted to feel good when they were here. Somehow, it made him feel safe.

"I'm feeling fine, actually," he said, surprised. "The Starlight hasn't been affecting me like it usually does, I think because of the... special drink. The biggest problem was how distracted I was."

She stood up and looked at him with that sharp, inquisitive gaze. A bottle of rum and two glasses were in her hand.

"Distracted? By what?" she asked.

There it was again, that deep, sensuous tone to her already commanding voice.

"I just, um, I was very, well, you know, it was..." he stammered, trying to find the words.

"Rum?" she asked, holding up the bottle.

"Yes, I think that would be perfect," he said, relieved to no longer be on the spot.

She set the glasses down and casually poured a large amount of the amber liquid in each, sloshing a bit over the sides.

"What was that?" she asked, holding out a glass to him. "Why were you distracted?"

He took the glass and their fingers touched briefly, though he felt like she held hers a little longer than was necessary.

"It was just...I kept wondering...I'm so...I keep thinking...well, why did you ask me here?" he said finally, taking a sip of the liquor with a barely contained grimace. Perhaps it was the rum, giving him that infamous 'liquid courage,' or maybe he just found the strength within himself, but either way he decided to plunge ahead, even if it was rather uncertainly.

"I figure it's got to be about the kiss right?" he said, taking a sip of the rum and beginning to pace softly across the plush rug, "I mean we're working together, right? It's not exactly proper. But then, well, you're a pirate, so who cares about impropriety, I suppose. But you're not a pirate really," he continued, pacing faster across the room, lost in his ruminations. "I'm sorry, I didn't mean to call you a pirate, I never actually found out if that bothered you or if you were just joking. I certainly don't mean to compare you to someone awful like Mad Richard. But you know there are a lot of lovely pirates, certainly some of the fictional ones, so maybe it's not a bad thing. Captain Santiago comes to mind, he's certainly charming. I mean, lots of people like pirates don't they? They wouldn't write so many books about them if they didn't–"

"I don't mind being called a pirate," she said, a dangerous smile playing across her lips. "But I fear you've gotten rather off track, weren't you talking about the...*kiss*?"

The way she said the word kiss made Tristan stop his pacing immediately. Somehow she managed to put all the yearning and passion in his heart into just that one word.

"Right...I...yes," he stammered. He ran his hand through his long hair and shook it out, the silver earring making a soft tinkling sound. "If you...um, well, I guess...Really...I'd just like to, yes."

"Like to?" she asked, her eyes dancing playfully, lit up with the fiery glow of the candles.

"Do it again," he said, finally. "Kiss you, I mean."

"See? That wasn't so hard," she said, setting down her glass with a loud clink that sent Tristan's nerves racing.

"I suppose not, it's just that...well, I just thought, I don't know if you want to, and I have just been feeling so many things I wasn't expecting to, you know, I was just supposed to just go to the Coronation and..."

And then she was there, her body heat racing across his skin, her fiery eyes inches from his face, her leather-clad hips melting into his.

"Tristan, maybe we can do less talking tonight, what do you think?" she asked, biting the corner of her lip and sliding her rough, callused hand down his face.

"Mhmm," he said, not daring to breathe as she leaned forward, her lips meeting his in a kiss that started out questioning, soft, and gentle. Then he was weaving his hands into her dark tangled hair, and she was pulling him close against her chest and the kiss was transformed into the vibrant, fiery passion of deep desire left too long unfulfilled.

After a moment she pulled back, breathing heavily, her face flushed. She looked over at the bed which suddenly seemed to have a magnetic pull to it.

"What do you think then? Would like to stay?" she asked.

"There is literally nowhere I'd rather be," Tristan said breathlessly.

And then her lips melted into his and everything else faded away.

TRISTAN WOKE up the next morning under a fluffy white duvet with bright sunshine streaming through the slanted windows above him. For a moment he forgot where he was, and then it all came back to him and he shivered with delight. He spotted Wren across the room, it looked like she hadn't been up for long.

She was wearing a rumpled linen blouse and nothing else, sitting on an old wooden chair with her bare legs folded up. She looked relaxed, reading a book he thought he recognized. After a moment's examination he realized it was *The Valor of the Seas*.

Tristan sat up on his elbows, his long, unkempt hair falling softly on his naked shoulders.

"Morning," he said.

She looked up with a small smile and his heart beat faster. Her already tangled mess of hair was wilder than ever and something about her disheveled appearance was just breathtaking.

"These are highly inaccurate," she said, shaking the book at him with a cheeky grin.

"It has been just getting more accurate everyday for me," he said, waving his hand around Wren's bedroom.

She laughed, "Fine, but these scenes with the sails, they're completely wrong. That's not how you wind the ropes at all!"

Tristan just kept staring at her, the morning sunlight falling on her bronze skin, her bright eyes looking down at the book with an adorable frown. He realized he wanted to wake up here every morning.

"Why are you looking at me like that?" she said, grinning.

"You just look beautiful," he said simply.

She stood up and moved towards him, her grin widening.

"You look rather good yourself," she said.

She had almost made it back to the bed when there was a hammering on the door.

"CAPTAIN! WE NEED YOU ON DECK!" Emyr called.

She froze, the smile fading from her face.

Instantly, the bubble was popped and they were sent careening back to reality. Tristan suddenly felt a chasm growing between them. Who they were, their responsibilities, the unlikeliness of their relationship.

She turned away and started looking for her clothing, throwing things on quickly. She put on her pants without ever turning around, then grabbed her hat and stopped, not looking at him.

"You could stay..." she said, very quietly.

For a moment he stopped breathing.

He didn't know what to say or do.

He wanted to, *so* much. He wanted to stay in this room, in this moment, forever. But his job, the Majesteria, *magic*...

"I have so many responsibilities," he whispered, more to himself than to her. He was trying to figure out what to say, but when he looked at her he saw that he'd already said the worst possible thing.

Wren had immediately shut down, the cold and strong captain had returned, all the sweet softness washed away like waves on a beach.

She grabbed his clothes from the floor and threw them at him

"Forget I said...anything. I have to go," she said.

"Wren, wait–" he started to say but she was already out the door.

"Captain," Emyr said as soon as she stepped out of the cabin, "we spotted Mad Richard's ship patrolling the waters between here and Fairefeux. I believe he's been waiting for us, he knows our destination and intends to cut us off on the way. I saw we were near Granite's Crag island and was able to steer us out of view behind its rocky cliffs, but we can't keep hiding here if we want to make the Coronation in time. I think we'll need the mage's help, I suggest we wake up Tristan and–"

Emyr raised an eyebrow as he saw Tristan quietly slipping out of Wren's door while trying to put his earring back on.

"I see you've already got that covered," he said with low chuckle.

"*Focus*, Emyr," Wren said tartly. "How far away is he?"

Emyr handed her a spyglass and pointed out at sea.

She looked through it and then turned to Tristan.

When she spoke it was as a Captain, any trace of the glittering smile he'd seen a few minutes ago was gone.

"Can you bring the Majesteria to my office immediately?"

"Of course," Tristan said, nodding sharply and running down the stairs.

But even as he jogged through the corridor, rushing to get his friends and help the Captain, his mind was still clouded over with thoughts of Wren.

You could stay...

Chapter Nineteen

When Tristan returned to the deck with the Majesteria, he immediately felt something was amiss. As soon as he stepped onto the deck he felt a strange presence in the air, high up in the clouds above him. Something like a twinge of magic, but very different than his own. He stopped walking and peered up at the fluffy white clouds drifting across the bright blue sky.

"Do you feel that?" he asked, but the Majesteria weren't paying attention. They were scurrying ahead to Wren's office, already debating their opinions on the best possible course of action.

The pull of the strange magic got stronger for a moment and then suddenly it was gone. Like a cord snapping, the feeling of magic had vanished as quickly as it had come. He looked around for the source of the magic but nothing was there, it was a phantom on the wind.

"Are you coming Tristan?" Edwina called. The mice were standing impatiently at the door, waiting for him to open it for them.

With one last look at the sky he nodded and said,
"Of course."

Wren's office was cool and dim, protected from the bright

morning light by the mottled glass windows. Wren and Emyr were hunched over a map of the Evarian Sea and she was drawing a line with her finger while he scribbled calculations into a small notebook.

"How can we help ya Cap'n?" Chica said cheerfully as the mice clambered onto Wren's desk.

Wren spared a smile for the mouse as she leaned back from the map.

"Good morning," she said, "I'm afraid we will once again need your support in order to get the Cinderflower to the Coronation in time. Mad Richard is hunting for us, he's patrolling the waters between here and Fairefeux."

"We were just exploring the possibilities of alternate routes," Emyr said with a frown, "but I don't think we'd make it in time, even with magical winds."

"Our only option is to sail past him," Wren said grimly.

"Won't we be casting wind spells?" Tristan asked. "Can we not just outrun him?"

"I doubt it," Wren said. "As you know, he has mages onboard too. I've heard rumors about him arriving at destinations far before he was expected to, and now I finally know how he did that."

"Oh."

Tristan felt a strange aching in his heart to think that other mages would be helping Mad Richard. In his mind, magic was meant for good.

"I think really what we need is a head start," Wren explained. "Once we're in the port of Fairefeux he won't dare to attack us, the place will be swarming with Royal Mariners on alert for threats to the Coronation. If we can get past his ship and start casting wind spells before he does, we could beat him to the port and get the Cinderflower to safety."

The cabin was quiet for a while as everyone thought very hard about how they might accomplish this.

A few times someone opened their mouth to share an idea but quickly shut it again. The silence grew longer and louder, and

Tristan was just starting to really worry when Chica stood up and cleared her throat.

"The ship wants to help!"

Wren paused with a mug of coffee halfway to her lips.

"I'm sorry?" She said.

"Your ship is magic Captain," Marigold said with a dramatic bow. "It's got...a personality, you could say."

"I'm aware," Wren said with a wry grin, "I suppose it makes sense that you would have noticed. But she doesn't usually *talk* to me."

"She doesn't talk to us either," Edwina said, "but we can get a sense of what she wants."

"We are very in tune with magic of all kinds," Marigold explained.

"Plus, she's really loud," Chica said.

Wren raised an eyebrow.

"Is she now?"

"Magically speaking, yes," Marigold confirmed, then added, "when she wants to be."

"I see, and she...wants to help?"

"Aye Cap'n!" Chica said.

"What exactly would that entail?" Wren asked.

"Not sure, let's find out!" Chica said, jumping down from the desk with Marigold and Edwina close behind. The humans peered down at the huddle of mice as they put their paws to the floor carefully and closed their eyes. They talked to each other in small, quiet squeaks. Eventually, they nodded agreement and clambered back up onto the desk.

"Her capabilities are very limited, she doesn't have much magic she can use," Edwina said.

"But she's very loud," Chica added.

"Yes, she is, we'd have to study her more to understand the extent of the magical possibilities," Marigold said sagely.

"But, we have settled on an idea," Edwina said cheerfully.

"Really?" Wren asked.

"She can change color," Edwina said.

Wren sat back in her chair, eyes wide, "What?!"

"Yes, she should be able to change the color of the wood all over the ship," Edwina replied.

"We think if we work with her, we could construct a small Glamour to disguise the shape of the masthead as well," Marigold added.

"Although that is risky if Mad Richard's mages can sense the magic," Edwina said.

"We're hoping it won't be too noticeable from afar, not the way something big like the wind spell will be. What do you think, Tristan?"

Tristan was surprised to find every eye in the room looking at him. Wren's look in particular was appraising and complex, he found himself deeply yearning to escort everyone else out of the room so they could just be alone for five minutes.

You could stay...

The words hadn't left his mind or his heart since she'd spoken them, they rattled around begging him to pay attention to them.

But now was not the time.

He looked away from the deep dark pools of her inquisitive eyes and focused on the task at hand. After a moment's contemplation he said,

"Glamours are very risky, they rarely last long and a well-trained mage can see right through them. But it's worth a shot, at the very least it should confuse them long enough to give us a head start. I'd say we'll want to have the Majesteria on deck with all the wind spells prepared and ready to launch at a moment's notice, though."

"Do we have enough Starlight for that?" Wren asked.

Tristan nodded, "I did two spindles last night before I...went to bed," his gaze darted between Wren and Emyr as he said the words. "It should be enough to get us to Fairefeux."

"Well then, I guess we'll try," Wren said. "Emyr, can you notify the crew?"

"Of course, Captain," Emyr said, before darting out the door.

"What now?" Wren asked the Majesteria.

"Let's go to the deck," Marigold said, hopping off the desk.

"Time to give this ship a makeover!" Chica said with a twirl of her sparkly dress.

The bright sunlight beat down on them as they emerged, blinking, from Wren's office. The crew were listening as Emyr explained the situation, Tristan saw many raised eyebrows and whispered conversations. He didn't know what their adventures usually entailed but he imagined this week must have been a very unusual one to be a sailor on *The Snapdragon*.

The Majesteria formed a huddle on the deck in front of Wren's office. They put their paws to the wood and after a few moments Tristan felt a surge of magic all around him, coming up from the wooden floor. It was warm and comforting, and he recognized the feel of the magic as one he'd been living with for weeks, an ambient background noise of tranquility. He felt the ship's magic surging around him now, stronger and louder than he'd realized it could be. Chica was right, *The Snapdragon* was loud when she wanted to be.

And then...it began to change. It started as little splotches on the deck, like dripping paint, bright pools of red edged with glowing white lines began to form around the Majesteria's paws, flowing outwards in rivulets across the beams of the deck and over the sides of the ship. Everywhere that was painted deep green became a bright, vibrant red. The dark oak planks of the deck became a light birch wood, and the masts were colored red to match the sides of the ship. Even the sails, battered as they were by their trip to the Otherwilde Seas, got a transformation and turned a vibrant cherry-red color.

The crew gasped and ran to the railings to look over the sides at the ship as it changed color, the waves of gold-rimmed red cascading over the dark green and enveloping the sides of the ship.

"Now, for the Glamour," Edwina said. "Tristan, can you get the Starlight?"

"Of course," he said, running along the ship to the stern as the decks changed color beneath his feet. He brought the large, glowing metal spindles down to the deck and set them before the Majesteria.

"We should hide these when we sail past Mad Richard's ship," Wren said thoughtfully, "if someone looks at us through a spyglass they would be very conspicuous."

"Understood Cap'n!" Chica said cheerfully.

She unwound a small length of glowing magic from the spindle and snipped the thread with a pair of tiny bronze enchanted scissors from her toolkit. Once the Majesteria were satisfied they had enough magic for the Glamour, they nodded to Tristan who moved the spindles into Wren's cabin.

Edwina and Chica worked on the Glamour while Marigold had enlisted some of the sailors to help her draw the symbols for the wind spell across the expanse of the deck.

"Once we cast this Glamour we should start sailing immediately," Edwina said. "It won't last long and it will wear thin quickly. As soon as we set the Glamour to the masthead we will begin crafting the Wind casting spell from within Wren's office, waiting as long as we can to infuse the Starlight into the spell lines on the deck."

"I'll make sure everyone is ready to sail," Wren affirmed, quickly moving across the deck to speak with Emyr.

They rounded up the sailors, who had not stopped admiring the bright red ship, and within moments everyone was back at their positions, setting the sails in place to start moving as soon as the Glamour was in place.

"All clear," Wren called out to the Majesteria with a tip of her hat, before running to stand at the wheel, ready to steer the ship out of the shadow of the craggy rocks and into the open water.

Marigold kept drawing lines across the deck while Edwina and Chica twirled the ball of light that was the Glamour spell between their paws. Tristan saw Edwina struggling to hold the Starlight due to her injured paw, but she kept going with grim determination.

Compared to the Wind spells, the Glamour spell was just a slip of a thing. A small wisp of Starlight curled into a glowing ball, infused with whatever things Edwina and Chica were whispering to it in hushed squeaks.

"It's ready Tristan!" Edwina called. "Bring us to the Masthead."

The mice did not usually like to be picked up by humans, but on rare occasions where it was simply the easiest method of travel, they allowed Tristan to carry them. He knew how particular they were about this, so when he knelt down to pick them up he asked,

"Do you want me to carry you?"

"Yes, and hurry!" Edwina said, carefully stepping onto his outstretched hands while keeping hold of the hovering ball of light. Chica followed closely behind, and then Tristan stood up ever-so-carefully and walked to the front of the ship with the mice standing on his hands.

When he arrived at the pointed end of the deck he asked,

"Is this close enough?"

"I think so," Edwina said. Chica nodded her agreement.

Tristan stood with hands outstretched and waited while the mice whispered their final incantations for the small spell, and then lifted their paws high, throwing the tiny orb into the air.

The whirling ball of light expanded and shifted shape, spreading out bigger and thinner like a pancake, transforming from a small sphere into a large net of gossamer threads of Starlight. The net flew up and over the beautiful merwoman on the masthead and wrapped itself around her. A moment later, Tristan saw the net shimmer and shake and a new shape emerged.

The Glamour did not fool his eyes, as a well-trained mage who knew the masthead had been glamoured he could still see its true form. But he also saw a second, shimmering shape outlined around it. A bright red dragon's head, not unlike the Serpent from the Otherwilde Seas.

He heard a gasp from nearby. He looked and saw many of the sailors pointing in awe at the new masthead, which undoubtedly looked entirely solid to their untrained eyes.

He quickly set the Majesteria down on the deck, and they scurried back to join Marigold to finish drawing the wind spell on the deck as Wren quickly began to move the ship out of the shadow of the craggy rocks. A few minutes later they were heading out into the open waters of the Evarian Sea and Tristan was running to Wren's office with the Majesteria.

And then they were sailing, their bright red ship with its Serpent masthead was picking up a strong wind and heading for Fairefeux, with everyone onboard desperately hoping the pirates in the distance wouldn't notice they had three Majesteria and the Royal Cinderflower onboard.

It was quiet for a long time while they sailed through the Evarian Sea. Tristan and the Majesteria had done their best to prepare the wind spell for casting, but soon there wasn't much left to do except sit with the spindles and wait. The ship sailed on and the crew called out directions to each other in somber tones. Eventually, Edwina suggested they play Cherry Basket with a pack of nearby cards. Marigold agreed, but Tristan knew better than to play Cherry Basket with Edwina. Chica fell asleep on top of a map on Wren's desk.

Finally, there was a soft knock on the door.

"Dammit, I was about to win!" Edwina said.

Tristan chuckled and opened the door while Marigold nudged Chica to wake up.

"It's time," Emyr said, before darting off across the ship to issue orders to the sailors adjusting the rigging.

Tristan picked up the large glowing spindles of Starlight, and the Majesteria began to transport the beginnings of the Wind spell they had crafted in the office. The threads of Starlight wound over and under their paws as they moved it across the deck, laying it down across the chalk symbols and feeding the light into the large circle.

While the mice did their work on the quiet ship, Tristan looked out to sea, hoping to see the mad pirate's ship. It wasn't hard to spot, they were still very close to the ship; so close he could even make out the people standing on it, some of whom were looking at them through spyglasses.

"Should we cast the spell so soon?" he asked.

Emyr, who had just stopped nearby to wind a rope said,

"We don't have a choice. The Glamour is already beginning to fade on the Masthead and they are still watching us closely. We're just going to have to hope the head start was enough."

Tristan wasn't sure it would work but he couldn't disagree. His gaze fell on Mad Richard's ship, its dark shape loomed on the horizon, its distinctive horse-shaped masthead casting black shadows across the sea. The ship was very dark, almost black, and over its flapping sails he saw the cutlass flag on full display. There was no attempt at a false flag this time, Tristan realized that was probably because Mad Richard *wanted* them to feel the inevitability of his presence. He was saying: no matter where you go, I will find you. A chill went down his spine at the thought.

Then he felt the magic of the Wind spell rising in the air behind him, and he quickly put out a hand to steady himself on the railing. He turned around to see the Majesteria watching with some satisfaction as the spell ascended above the ship and instantly filled the sails with wild, sparking magic winds.

And then they were off again, flying across the deep blue waters with unnatural speed. He looked back at Mad Richard's ship and saw he had wasted no time. The dark ship was already following them, although it lagged far behind their magical speed. Now, all that remained was to see how long it took their mages to get their own spells up and running.

As it turned out, not very long at all. He had barely been standing at the railing for five minutes before he saw the mages cast their magic. But they were not casting wind spells like the Majesteria, instead he saw a greenish ball of light in the water at the back of the ship, swirling and twisting with magical energy, propelling the ship forward. The magic was of a type he didn't recognize, the same bright green color as the catapult flames they'd shot at the Straights of Stormrock.

Soon enough Mad Richard's ship was speeding up and following them closely. But as expected, the head start was enough to keep them out of his range, for now anyway. There was nothing to do but keep going and hope he didn't catch up.

~

THEY WERE SAILING with magical winds like before, but everything felt different now. It wasn't just the bright afternoon sunlight bearing down on them, or the deep blue of the Evarian Sea. The crew, all of the crew, had been changed by the experience in the Otherwilde Sea. The sailors were struggling without Birdy climbing up the rigging to fix the sails. Everyone felt the absence of Ginger's cheerful smile and bright blue curls bouncing across the deck since she'd barely left the healer's quarters after Birdy's injury.

The Majesteria were different too. Edwina hung back, mostly shouting orders and casting as little as possible due to her injured paw. Marigold looked not like herself without her witch hat, and there was something very uneasy and tentative about all of them; they were not the same mice they'd been on Appleton Island. They had been out in the world and found themselves woefully unprepared. He could see that it weighed on them just as it did him.

And of course, there was Wren.

His heart fluttered at the thought. He knew he wanted to talk to her, *needed* to talk to her. He wasn't even sure what he wanted to say, but it didn't matter, something had to be said.

It was hard to keep it out of his mind.

You could stay...

The idea of getting off the ship at Fairefeux and never seeing her again was unimaginable. But so was leaving the Majesteria behind and quitting his job at Teakley. No matter what, he knew he needed to talk to her.

After making sure the Majesteria had everything they needed, he ran up the stairs to the wheel where Wren was steering with fierce concentration.

"Do you think Emyr could take over for a moment?" he asked. "I'd really like to talk to you about, um, things."

"Now is not a good time Tristan," Wren said, her voice tight and clipped. She barely spared a glance in his direction.

"Yes, I know, and I'm sorry, but we're going to be arriving at Fairefeux today and I–"

His sentence was interrupted by a crashing sound in the water right beside the ship. Tristan ran to look over the railing and saw bright green flames hitting the water only a few feet away from them.

"Take this and tell me what you see," Wren said, throwing him her spyglass.

He peered through the metal contraption and saw the ship chasing them with its vibrant green energy ball, the magic's eerie glow reflected in the deep blue sea. Mages in protective armor were standing on the deck preparing bright green balls of fire for their catapult.

"They're shooting fire at us again!" he said. "I don't know how they can manage to do that and chase us at the same time. How many mages are on that ship anyway?"

"A lot," Wren said grimly. "Is there a chance the Majesteria can make us go any faster? If he can get close enough to land a few of those, it won't be pretty."

Tristan handed her back the spyglass as he thought about it. But his thoughts were suddenly interrupted by the return of that strange feeling; the weird magic high in the sky. It was distractingly loud this time, he felt his skin tingling and almost burning.

"What are you looking at?" Wren asked as Tristan craned his neck back to try to see something, anything, in the blue expanse above that would be causing his skin to tingle like wildfire.

All at once he felt something else, something bigger, a horrible wave of magic crashing over and around him. It was bright, light, heat, energy, and compressed sound all fighting for his attention, overwhelming his senses. He leaned over, hands covering his ears as he tried to block out the explosion of magic around him.

It felt wrong, like a jumble of polarizing energies mixing together. It disturbed his senses and made him want to vomit. The Majesteria came running up the deck, their paws over their ears, trying desperately to avoid the waves of chaotic magic.

"WHAT IS IT?" Tristan shouted over the nauseating white noise corrupting his mind.

But before the Majesteria could try to answer, it became clear.

Snaking across the water like rivers of bright white heat were ropes of twisted magic. They weren't coming from Mad Richard's mages, but from the direction of Fairefeux. Skittering and weaving through the waves, the ropes of magic were heading right for *The Snapdragon*. Before they even had a chance to react the thick, hideous ropes of chaotic magic were lassoing themselves around the ship, pulling tight on the masts and twisting around the masthead.

"Tristan, what's happening?" Wren asked, her eyes wide with fear. "Do you know?"

And then they *pulled*. Once the ropes had the ship in their grasp they yanked the ship towards Fairefeux with a furious drag that made the ship shudder and jolt. The cords pulled it quickly across the ocean, out of reach of Mad Richard and his catapults. Immediately they were racing across the sea, their speed increased exponentially by the dense magical cords.

After a moment Tristan felt his initial panic abate as he got used to the strange soup of magics surrounding them. The nausea passed and he could remove his hands from his ears, though he was still on edge. It felt like something was crawling up his spine and he never wanted to look at the magical ropes again.

Unfortunately, that was exactly what he needed to do.

He went up to the nearest cord and examined it. The harsh ropes of bright light were as unyielding as steel cables, pulling and yanking at the ship without concern for anything or anyone. He wondered briefly just how many mages were involved in creating this spell. When he looked at the ropes closely he saw they were not one thing but dozens of strands of light, all different colors, braided together. No wonder it was making him feel sick, so many kinds of magic all in one place, it wasn't right.

Where or how could you even make a spell like this?

"It's Blanchard," Edwina said firmly, her mouth set in a frown. "I'm sure of it."

"Oh, definitely," Marigold said, scrambling up onto the railing to touch one of the ropes with a paw. She yanked it back quickly like she'd been burned.

"I felt something in the sky a little while ago, before the ropes appeared, did you feel that?" Tristan asked them.

"*Scrying*," Chica said, shaking her head with a scowl.

"Scrying?" Tristan gasped. Most forms of scrying were forbidden at Teakley and they considered them to be a serious offense to the laws of magic.

"Absolutely, I felt it too," Edwina confirmed.

Marigold hopped down off the railing to stand next to the other mice.

"I don't like it, but it seems like there's nothing to do," she said. "Blanchard is bringing us to Fairefeux whether we like it or not."

"At least it gets us away from Mad Richard," Tristan mused, as the ship lurched forward with another shuddering jerk. He felt the nausea rising in him again and stepped as far away from the amalgam ropes as he could.

"Can someone tell me what the hells is going on?" Wren asked, stepping closer to them as Emyr took the wheel. She carefully touched the nearest magic rope and then pulled her finger back with a small cry of pain.

"Probably best not to touch those," Tristan said with a frown, "we should tell the rest of the crew as well. They're made from...a mix of different types of magic. It's a dangerous spell to put it mildly."

He looked at the ropes and shuddered. To his mind it was an abomination to twist together so many magics this way.

"What are they doing? Where are they taking us?" Wren asked.

Tristan looked into her worried eyes and felt an aching of guilt, he had brought so many problems into her life. He sighed and said,

"We're pretty sure it's Lord Blanchard, my superior. He's been spying on us magically and decided to bring us in to Fairefeux...a little faster. I suspect he's very anxious to get the Royal Cinderflower."

"Spying on us...magically?" Wren raised an eyebrow.

"Yes," Tristan with a grimace, "he's been *scrying*," he spat the word. "It's illegal, well, maybe not, but it's definitely against the rules and I can't imagine the Headmaster would be pleased if she knew."

"Just like Blanchard to only follow the rules when it suits him," Edwina said, shaking her head.

"Has he been spying, or scrying, or whatever, for the whole trip?" Wren asked.

"I don't believe so," Tristan said, "I don't think he could access us in the Otherwilde Seas. He probably started searching for us after we disappeared into the portal."

"I see," Wren said, gazing out on the water, the deep blue waves marred by the twisting magical ropes.

ABOUT AN HOUR later they saw the bright island of Fairefeux come into view and began their ascent into the harbor. It had been a fast but tumultuous journey. Being pulled through the sea by Blanchard was not at all like being propelled by the Majesteria's spells. The world was a blur of blue sea and green blobs of islands in the distance and they whizzed through the sea, barrelling towards the port of Fairefeux at unimaginable speed. The creaking and cracking of the ship's wood as it strained under the pressure was terrifying to listen to, and he saw the looks of worry and fear on the crew around him.

Not that Blanchard would care about that.

He probably wouldn't care if the whole ship sunk to the bottom of the ocean as long as he got the Royal Cinderflower.

It was strange watching the port of Fairefeux get closer. They had spent so long worrying and thinking about this moment, the day they finally pulled the ship into the docks with the Royal Cinderflower safe in the cabin below. The idea of arriving at Fairefeux had taken on an almost mystical quality, which was only amplified by the powerful magic reeling them in to the port.

After everything they had been through there was something tremendously odd about seeing the normal, busy docks full of hundreds of ships, the port crammed to capacity with guests for the Coronation. It was so busy, in fact, that the sight of a large ship careening into the docks at high speed, pulled by magic ropes, barely seemed to catch anyone's attention.

But Tristan barely had time to think about that, because they were going so fast that almost as soon as he saw the gleaming city come into view they were already arriving, watching as a few dozen mages yanked and pulled their ship to the docks.

Within moments Blanchard and more than a dozen mages in Teakley robes were swarming the ship, shouting orders.

"WHERE IS TRISTAN MULBERRY'S ROOM?" Blanchard bellowed.

"I can show you, Sir," Ginger said meekly, jangling her keychain in front of his angry, stoat-like eyes.

He nodded his agreement and the mages flooded down the stairs in a wave, Tristan trailing after them helplessly.

"Blanchard, Blanchard!" He called out, trying to get the man's attention.

"Who the hells are you?" Blanchard demanded.

"What? It's me, Tristan!" He said.

Blanchard stopped his march to look at him with shrewd eyes while the mages ran ahead with Ginger.

"You're not Mulberry," he said, frowning.

"Of course I am," he said.

Blanchard scrutinized him for a moment.

"What are you wearing? You're not even wearing a cloak! You can't wear that."

"I don't see why not," Tristan said.

"You're a *Teakley Mage*!" Blanchard said.

"So? Why can't I dress how I like?" Tristan asked. "I'm still wearing the brooch."

"Decorum! We need to look like proper mages or we won't be taken seriously," Blanchard said, resuming his march down the hallway.

"With all due respect sir, our Headmaster has the head of an owl," Tristan said.

It was true. A few years back Professor Bramblebranch had left on a trip to the Mountains of Morgravia, and when she came back her human head had been replaced with that of a large owl. She was otherwise the same and no one had been courageous enough to ask her what happened. Everyone just pretended it was normal.

There was a frosty silence while Blanchard glared at him.

"Are you trying to equate yourself with our esteemed Headmaster?" Blanchard asked, his tone laced with danger.

"No, but I–" Tristan tried.

Blanchard cut him off. "When you have bested every mage in the Evarian Sea, authored more than two dozen textbooks, and fought your way across the Mountains of Morgravia like our glorious Headmaster, then perhaps you can dress however you like. But *today* you are a Majesteria Handler, which means you answer to *ME*."

With that, Blanchard turned on his heel and marched into Tristan's quarters.

They arrived to a room in chaos. The mages were piling Tristan and the Majesteria's belongings into trunks haphazardly. They were throwing ink bottles and sweaters in with no regard for their condition, only how quickly they could remove them from the ship.

The largest cluster of mages, however, was huddled around the Royal Cinderflower's trunk, which they were peering into with interest.

"*WELL*?" Blanchard asked, looming over them aggressively.

"It's alright, Lord Blanchard," one of the mages said, standing up and bowing to his superior. "Although a little on the droopy side."

Blanchard glared at Tristan.

"Anything else?" he asked.

"It appears to be missing a large chunk out of one leaf," another mage said with a worried expression.

"WHAT?!" Blanchard bellowed.

Tristan's eyebrows shot up and he looked at the Majesteria, realizing with horror that the 'imperceptible sliver' of the Cinderflower they'd taken for their healing potion may have been a little more than they'd admitted.

For their part, the mice looked rather sheepish and put their arms behind their backs while looking at the ceiling.

"EXPLAIN THIS, MULBERRY!" Blanchard screamed, his face turning the color of a beetroot.

"I–I–Well, Sir, it was a long trip and–and–" Tristan babbled as he tried to think of something that would satisfy the furious mage.

"Ahem!" Edwina said, stepping forward to speak in her most imperious voice. "The specimen in question had root rot, which caused a browning on one of the leaves. We had to remove a tiny bit of the tainted leaf or risk it spreading to the rest of the plant. There was nothing for it, it will grow back with time."

Tristan realized with some surprise that the mice must have been planning to lie about what they'd done to the Cinderflower to make the healing potion since the beginning.

Blanchard looked down at the mice with loathing.

"*With time*? WITH TIME?!? The Coronation is at DAWN you insolent fools!"

Edwina reached for her sword but Marigold held her back, shaking her head.

"As one professional to another, I'm sure you can understand that we did what we had to in order to ensure the Cinderflower's arrival at the Coronation in the best possible condition. We have a plan, of course, to help the Cinderflower look its best for the big day," Marigold said, walking slowly up to Blanchard dramatically. She continued,

"We'll cast a Glamour on the leaf for the day of the Coronation. It's not ideal, but it's good enough, and I'm sure you'll be able to explain the situation to the Crown in a satisfactory manner. You are, after all, a Liaison, are you not? Now, as for *your* behavior," Marigold had the attention of quite a few of the mages now, "I truly believe you only had the best interests of Teakley in your heart when you decided to insult the three Majesteria entrusted with protecting the Royal Cinderflower. With that in mind, I am going to let this indiscretion slip, but in future I would remind you that *your* position, good sir, is as a Liaison to the Grand Majesterium. It is in everyone's best interests to keep our interactions civil and friendly. I would hate to think how Headmaster Bramblebranch would feel should The Grand Majesterium have to withdraw our collaboration with Teakley Academy due to the mistreatment of their Majesteria."

Blanchard was steaming, but you didn't stay in middle management as long as he had if you didn't know how to back down from a fight you couldn't win. He stepped back and bowed deeply, his hands trembling with barely contained rage.

"My sincerest apologies, Your Grace," he said, through gritted teeth.

"You can call me Marigold," the mouse said cheerfully.

"Thank you, Marigold," Blanchard said coldly. He turned to Tristan as the mages began parading their trunks out the door.

"Mulberry, you will escort the Majesteria back to Ivylane Manor while we take the Royal Cinderflower to the representatives of the

Crown." He looked around the room a moment and said, "Where is their Boarding Trunk?"

"Um, it's gone," Tristan said.

"What?"

"It was destroyed by a Sea Serpent," Tristan replied with a sigh. It really had been a very long journey.

"We can walk," Chica said cheerfully.

Blanchard looked down at her, frustration and anger threatening to overwhelm him.

"Ugh, *fine*," he said, "but all of you will have a *very* thorough assessment of your conduct on this journey when we get back to Teakley, believe me!"

Before Tristan and the mice had time to think Blanchard and his mages were surrounding them, hurrying them up the stairs and towards the ramp to the shore. Tristan knew Blanchard would pitch a fit if he tried to talk to Wren or say goodbye to the sailors. The thought of saying goodbye to them was awful, he wasn't ready. He didn't know what he wanted, but he knew he couldn't leave without saying anything.

They emerged on the deck, and Tristan saw Wren standing by her office door with her arms folded, her dark hat tipped over her eyes.

He glanced at Blanchard, who was stomping across the deck, yelling at the Junior Apprentices to walk faster.

It was now or never.

He peeled off from the mages and ran across the deck to Wren.

There were so many things he wanted to say, but with so little time, all he could say was,

"When can I see you again? How long will you be here?"

"About a week," she said, her tone not giving any emotions away. "We've got a lot of repairs to do."

"I'd like to–" he began, but he was cut off by a shout.

"MULLLBERRRYY!!" Blanchard hollered impatiently.

"I'm sorry, I've got to go," Tristan said, hoping Wren saw the pain in his eyes.

"Duty calls," she said, nodding her head.

He never saw her eyes, he never knew if she was furious or miserable or didn't care at all. But he didn't have a choice; he had to go, so he turned around and ran.

But with every step he felt his heart break, and soon he heard her words echoed across his mind, over and over.

You could stay...

CHAPTER TWENTY

TRISTAN STUMBLED through the port with its colorful array of people, pushed along in a sea of Teakley mages, their capes fanning out behind them. He tried to look back at the ship, but it was already melting into the scenery. He felt like he couldn't breathe, like he was losing everything that mattered to him, like he was careening down a hillside and he didn't know how to stop.

He wanted to turn around and run right back, but he didn't. He couldn't. But Wren and the crew weren't the only thing causing the panic surging inside him, another thought kept bubbling up to the surface and demanding to be heard...Mad Richard.

He'd looked behind the ship while they whizzed across the sea to Fairefeux, and Mad Richard had never stopped following. Blanchard's horrifying spell had moved the ship fast enough to get them away from the pirate ship, but he was still following, still out there, looking for them.

It was a terrifying thought. Wren thought he wouldn't come into Fairefeux, and Tristan believed her, but something was prickling in the back of his mind.

He thought about what kind of person would do things like capture mages and torture people, what might drive someone like that to action. Why, he wondered, was Mad Richard waiting for them when they came out of the Otherwilde Seas? Why had he gone to all the trouble to find them again? Why would he be patrolling the seas, waving his cutlass flag?

That wasn't the behavior of someone who just wanted to seize some Majesteria because he'd heard they were valuable. He wasn't behaving like someone who was afraid the Royal Mariners would catch them any day now. If that had been the case, he'd have disappeared after the whirlpool.

But when he thought back, Tristan remembered the look on Mad Richard's face after the Majesteria attacked his ship: he was furious. Mad Richard was the type of man who wasn't used to people fighting back. Tristan ventured to guess he *definitely* wasn't used to people damaging his ship. So that was it then, his pride was hurt. That's why he wanted them to see his flag, to know he was coming for them.

He wanted them to be afraid.

And in Tristan's case it was definitely working.

He stopped on a nearby dock and turned around to look out across the sea. His heart was hammering in his chest as he squinted out at the horizon, hoping he wouldn't see that dark ship in the harbor. Hoping he was just being paranoid and dramatic. He hoped, but in his heart he just didn't believe that Mad Richard was the type of person to let them go that easily.

Unfortunately, he was right.

There it was, lurking out at the edge of the port. Although the ship was flying the Queen's Flag now, Tristan recognized that dark ship with the horse's masthead. He watched the brooding ship lingering in the distance for a moment, and then he saw a small dinghy detach from the ship and begin to make its way to the docks.

He turned around with wild eyes, searching for Blanchard.

"Lord Blanchard!" he called out, running to catch up with the boorish mage.

"What?" Blanchard snapped, his attention entirely focused on

the mages gingerly lifting the Cinderflower into an ornately orna-
mented cart.

"Mad Richard, the pirate who was chasing us, he's here!"
Tristan said breathlessly.

"Where?" Blanchard asked, peering around at the thronging
crowds.

"He's on a dinghy, coming into the port," Tristan said, pointing
out to the harbor.

Blanchard rolled his eyes, "Who cares? Let the pirates sort out
their own drama."

"No, but Sir, he's after the Majesteria!" Tristan said. "He
kidnaps mages, I believe that's why he was chasing us."

Blanchard turned around and folded his arms, glaring at
Tristan.

"And how, pray tell, does this mad pirate *know* about the
Majesteria? I believe I was exceedingly clear when I sent you on this
trip that you were *not* to reveal the Majesteria's existence to anyone,
certainly not dangerous pirates!"

"That doesn't matter–" Tristan began.

"It matters to ME!" Blanchard said, "And *you* answer to *me*,
you'd do well to remember that Mulberry."

"I'm sorry, Lord Blanchard," Tristan said quickly, "I simply
meant that how he knew about the Majesteria wasn't the priority
right now, of course I will answer all your questions later. But at the
moment we really need to make sure he doesn't come after the
Majesteria."

"Why?"

"I'm sorry, Sir?" Tristan asked.

"*Why* do we need to make sure that some foolish pirate doesn't
try to find the Majesteria? Are they not some of the most powerful
mages in the realm?"

"Well yes, Sir," Tristan said, "but they're not exactly trained in
combat and–"

"They shouldn't need to be trained in combat to take on a

stupid pirate!" Blanchard said, shaking his head. "We are Teakley Mages! They will wither under our might!"

"Sir, with all due respect–" Tristan tried again.

Blanchard held up a hand.

"I don't have time for this Mulberry," he said. "If it'll get you to shut up, I'll have a Junior Apprentice go and tell the Royal Mariners about this little situation."

Tristan felt a sinking feeling as he remembered the sight of the Royal Mariners leering at him while they extorted Wren. But he recognized the look in Blanchard's eyes and knew that in his mind the matter was finished and he would get no further with him.

"Yes, Sir, thank you, Lord Blanchard," he said wearily.

Tristan knew then that if Mad Richard was following them to Ivylane Manor, they were on their own.

A LITTLE WHILE later Blanchard and the rest of the mages piled into an assortment of carriages and carts to escort the Royal Cinderflower to its destination, leaving Tristan and the Majesteria in the care of one very nervous looking Junior Apprentice who'd been entrusted with leading them to Ivylane Manor. Tristan watched the cart with the small trunk he had fought so hard to protect rolling through the crowd, and he felt a mix of emotions as it disappeared in the distance.

Their job was done, it was all over. They'd done it, they got the Royal Cinderflower to Fairefeux in time for the Coronation. But there had been no parade, no hero's welcome, not even a thank you. He thought back to all the pain and agony he'd gone through, *everyone* had gone through, to get it there...and it was like it didn't even matter. Blanchard had dismissed the entire crew of *The Snapdragon* like they didn't exist, and now Tristan and the mice were alone in a crowd of people, without their crew.

The thought hit him like a knife to the gut.

He loved the Majesteria, he loved being a mage, he even loved Teakley in its way, but...he had never felt like he *belonged* there in the way he did with the crew of *The Snapdragon*. He'd never felt like he was fully himself, or even like he knew who he *wanted* to be until he was casting Starlight in the Otherwilde Seas.

These thoughts swam through his mind as he trailed along behind the Junior Apprentice through the crowds of revellers. After some subtle encouragement from the Majesteria, he began to notice the world around him as they walked through Fairefeux, and it was, in fact, quite a sight.

The Coronation would be at dawn's first light the next day and the air was fairly buzzing with excitement as they walked through the crowded city, eating their spiralled potatoes on a stick they had bought for too much money from a curly-haired dwarf with a small cart. Everywhere they turned there was something interesting to look at; fire breathers, jugglers, wandering bards carefully strumming classic folk songs. Vendors selling sparklers and fairy sticks, maps of the city and candies shaped like the Royal Cinderflower. The food was just as mouthwatering; the garlicky scent of mushroom kabobs roasting over an open flame, the vibrantly colored platters piled high with chopped fruits to be served in a small wooden cup with a dollop of whipped cream, chocolate crepes, and spinach pastries. Food, drink, and trinket vendors were crammed in along the streets in every available corner, and nearly everything looked interesting or delicious.

It was easy to see why the vendors had crammed the streets for Fairefeux; thousands of visitors from all walks of life had descended upon the gleaming city for the Queen's Coronation, from high-born nobles and foreign princesses to rural farmers and wandering bards. Most people were somewhere in between; merchant traders and middle class tourists from the surrounding islands and nearby countries, excited to be able to tell their grandchildren that they'd been there when Princess Poppy had become the Queen.

For its part the city had gone all out, decorating every available surface with bunting and flags, posters depicting Princess Poppy, fresh flowers, and various interpretations of the Royal Cinderflower. Tristan saw the flower everywhere; you could buy it on spongey lemoncakes, rings set with gems, hand-carved pocket-watches, commemorative daggers and mugs, and more than a dozen paintings and illustrated scrolls.

As they stopped for the second time so Chica could get Roasted Chestnuts from a small rolling cart, a movement caught Tristan's eye. Across the street a small carpet with a half dozen people sitting on it was ascending into the air above the city.

He looked at the building below and saw a big sign advertising that tourists could take a short carpet trip around the island to see everything from above. The sign felt familiar somehow, and then finally he remembered.

It was The Great Magick Carpet, he recognized their logo as the same company he'd seen at the Midnight Market. He stared at the sign quietly for a moment, lost in his memories of the day he'd seen all the other guests on the ship leave to take The Great Magick Carpet to Fairefeux, and Wren had flirted with him, her gold coin spinning in the bright afternoon light.

It felt like he was looking through a window to another time. He wasn't the same person who'd watched the guests leave that day. He was so far removed from that version of himself it was hard to believe that had been him.

"Mmpgh!" Chica said.

"What was that?" Marigold asked.

"I said, let's go!" Chica replied, before somehow stuffing three Roasted Chestnuts into her mouth at once.

"Tristan, are you coming?" Marigold asked.

"Huh?" he said, returning from his hazy reverie.

"Come on, we're almost at Ivylane Manor," Marigold said.

"Oh, right, of course," Tristan replied. He took one last look at the Magick Carpet sign before turning his back on the past to hurry after his friends.

~

WHEN THEY ARRIVED at Ivylane Manor, the large estate that had been loaned to the Academy for their use during the Coronation, it was like stepping into a different world. After weeks of briny decks and creaking wood, being on dry land was strange enough but the opulent halls of Ivylane Manor were a lot to take in.

They walked through the big double doors, opened by two butlers in matching perfectly-pressed crisp suits. There was a Senior Apprentice he didn't recognize standing at the foot of the stairs waiting for them. Tristan squinted at her brooch and saw she was from Teakley South.

"Tristan Mulberry, Majesteria Handler?" she asked suspiciously.

"Mhmm," he said, barely paying attention as he looked around the glamorous entrance hall. Velvet curtains descending from vaulted ceilings, vibrant orange trees sat in large golden pots; even the curving stairway's bannisters were inlaid with abalone flecked with gold.

She looked at him for a moment, taking in his billowing linen blouse, tangled blonde hair, and dangling silver earring. She gave him a look of scrutiny and a whiff of disdain that reminded him how high-strung everyone could be at Teakley.

"*You* are a Majesteria Handler? Where are the Majesteria?" she asked primly, as though he was perhaps not who he claimed to be.

"We're right here!" Edwina said, with a tone Tristan recognized as annoyance.

The Senior Apprentice jumped back. She looked down at the mice.

"Oh, but you're...I thought you'd be carrying them!"

"We can walk perfectly fine by ourselves," Marigold said.

"It's just that all the other Majesteria I've met..." she trailed off as she saw Edwina reaching for her sword. "Alright, anyway, is there anything else you need?"

"I don't think so," Tristan said, "just to be taken to our rooms."

"Ahem," Marigold said, stepping forward imperiously. "I would like a witch hat if you can find one."

"Excuse me?" The Senior Apprentice said, raising her eyebrows.

"I need a witch hat, you know, black, pointy, wide brim?"

"In...In...your size?" said the confused Senior Apprentice.

"Of course, what other size would I want it in?" Marigold replied.

"Right, yes, of course, Your Grace," she said wearily.

"You can call me Marigold," she replied cheerfully.

"Of course, Your Grace, I'll see about that right away," the Senior Apprentice said, leading them up the grand staircase. "Please follow me to your rooms."

The hallways were just as luxurious as the entrance hall, with sumptuous wallpaper and intricately woven carpets. He caught glimpses of lush gardens and kitchen staff bent over warm ovens through the windows as they went upstairs and around to the third floor where most of the Teakley delegation were staying.

"I believe you will be sharing quarters, they should be stocked with refreshments, but Junior Apprentices are available if you need anything else," she said as she pulled out a silver key and handed it to Tristan before hurrying away down the hall.

Their quarters matched the lavish decor of the rest of the estate, with rich velvet furniture and fresh flowers in every room. Much like their cabin on *The Snapdragon*, their quarters at Ivylane Manor was two rooms, a living space with a hearth, and a small bedroom, though it wasn't nearly as cozy. Their luggage had been placed haphazardly in one corner of the room without care for its condition.

Tristan immediately went over to the trunks and began to sort through them while the Majesteria ran to the small coffee table where a platter food had been provided with a large pile of cheeses, fruits, and bread. They snacked on the small feast while Tristan carefully sorted through their possessions, folding sweaters and gently rolling up scrolls, piling the Majesteria's things on one side and his personal items on the other.

After consuming a generous portion of the cheese, Chica plopped down on the rug in front of the fireplace, and immediately sat up again.

"Ew, this rug is all scratchy," she said with the a frown.

The floors were shiny dark hardwood with large throw rugs laid on top. The ornate rugs had tight embroidery interwoven with scratchy metallic thread. The effect was beautiful and looked quite luxurious, but it wasn't very soft.

"Let me see," Marigold said, hopping down from the coffee table. She laid down next to Chica.

"Ugh, that's dreadful," she said, shaking her head.

Edwina joined them and gave her agreement.

"These rugs are bad," she said, before climbing back on the table for more cheese.

"Fine, I'll say it," Chica said. "I hate this place."

Tristan looked up from the collection of small quills he was carefully returning to their cases.

"Pardon?" he said.

"I hate it here," Chica said, folding her arms and glaring at the offending rug.

"Why?" he asked.

"I like the pirates!" Chica said.

Marigold sighed, "Me too."

"Mhmm," Edwina nodded her head around a mouthful of cheese.

"Even the cheese isn't as good," Marigold said mournfully.

Tristan looked at his friends and saw the same sadness he felt.

"I don't like it either," he said quietly. "I miss the rocking of the ship."

He missed a lot more than that, but it was all he was prepared to admit.

"But...we're not really cut out for the adventure life, are we?" Edwina said, hopping off the table to help Tristan sort the scrolls.

"What do you mean?" he asked.

"I mean, we messed everything up," she said darkly.

"It's true," Marigold agreed. "Did you see Birdy when she came into the healer's quarters? She was barely moving. That was our fault, we didn't know how to stop those spells."

"I remember," Edwina said woefully, looking at her bandaged paw. "I'll never forget the look on Ginger's face as long as I live. We should have been more prepared."

Tristan remembered the bloody deck after the battle with the Sea Serpent, the torn and twisted sails. He felt it too, the fear, the worry. What if they returned to *The Snapdragon* and ended up hurting them again? What if something even worse happened?

"Maybe you're right," he said in a small voice. But something inside him rebelled at the thought; something was telling him he belonged on that ship. Before he could figure out which part of him was right, there was a knock at the door.

He stood up and opened it, looking at a gaggle of Junior Apprentices carrying glittering bundles of fabric.

"Good Evening, Your Grace," a curvy girl with red curls said in a dramatic formal tone, bowing stiffly.

"Emma, it's me Tristan," he said. "What are you doing?"

She looked around the room nervously, like she was worried Blanchard might jump out at any moment and scold her for impropriety. For a moment, she dropped her formal tone and far more cheerfully said,

"Sorry Tristan, but Blanchard insisted we call *everyone* Your Grace while we are at the Coronation, he said it makes us seem more regal. Nice earring by the way!"

"Thanks Emma," Tristan said with a friendly grin, "do you guys have the Coronation robes for us?"

"Yes, Your Grace," Emma said dutifully as the rest of the Junior Apprentices filed into the room behind her.

Tristan winced at the formality but decided not to push the issue, he certainly didn't want to be responsible for anyone getting yelled at by Blanchard. The young mages began carefully placing the jewel-encrusted garments on the tables and over the furniture in the sitting room. They set everything down safely, and then Emma turned to Tristan and said,

"Do you need anything else, Your Grace? Will you be requiring assistance with your garments?"

"No, I can definitely dress myself, thank you," Tristan said with a laugh.

She nodded "Of course, Your Grace. Lord Blanchard, Senior Liaison to the Grand Majesterium, has requested that you and the Majesteria have your final fitting tonight. You'll need to try on your garments to be sure that no additional alterations will be required for the big day."

"No problem, we'll make sure to let you know," Tristan said, glancing briefly at the glittering array of clothing.

"We were also able to fulfill the Majesteria's request," she said, producing a small item from somewhere. She held up her hand to him, on it was resting a very small black witch's hat. "Although Lord Blanchard, Senior Liaison to the Grand Majesterium, requested that I make sure to let you know that she should not to wear the hat to the Coronation."

Tristan took the hat carefully with a gentle smile. Although it felt like his world was falling apart, it was nice that at least one thing was going right.

"Thank you Emma, er, sorry, Your Grace?"

Emma stepped back with a shocked look on her face, a few of the Junior Apprentices giggled.

"No, Your Grace, you may refer to me as Junior Apprentice or Miss," she said with a grand bow. "Do you need anything else Your Grace?"

"I don't think so, thank you," he said.

Emma looked at Tristan for a moment, his sea-water soaked linen blouse, tangled hair and weary, dirty face. Her gaze travelled to the luxurious bespoke Coronation attire, and lingered over the jewel-encrusted doublet. She coughed politely and said,

"Would you perhaps like us to draw you a bath, Your Grace?"

Tristan had to admit that was a rather good idea.

~

HE SUNK his tired body into the warm water with a sigh. He knew the Junior Apprentice had only suggested a bath because she'd feared he was too dirty for the fine fabrics of the Coronation attire, but he was grateful nonetheless. He took the lavender scented soap and washed the grit of the sea out of his hair, feeling the stress and worry of the last week drain out of him.

At least, that's what should have happened.

And he tried, he really did.

But he just couldn't relax, ever since he'd left *The Snapdragon* he'd felt a tension growing inside him, like he couldn't be the person Teakley wanted him to be anymore. He stepped out of the bath and pulled the dressing robe around himself, shaking out his dripping hair and brushing it with a comb inlaid with abalone. He pulled out all the tangles and then lay down for a moment on the pillowy soft bed and began to try to sort through the complex emotions he hadn't had time to figure out.

He started by allowing himself to dream.

To dream of a life aboard *The Snapdragon*, a life as a pirate.

Not a silly fantasy of a pirate novel but a *real* life, living on *The Snapdragon*, sailing across the world...with Wren.

He remembered that island he'd seen from afar in the Otherwilde Seas with the little blue bulbous houses, and imagined finally finding out who lived there. He dreamed of swimming in warm seas, of standing at the prow and looking out over the deep blue water, of sleepy mornings with Wren's tousled hair resting on his chest.

But he felt a nagging pain that soon dissolved his perfect dream. He was not a sailor, he was a Majesteria Handler. He was proud of his job and he loved it, and that had become all the more clear from his journey. Helping the ship's crew with the Majesteria had filled up his heart in a way he didn't know was possible. It made him feel useful, powerful, important. He couldn't imagine doing anything else, nor did he want to.

But he couldn't let the dream of *The Snapdragon* die that easily either.

He wanted to be a Majesteria handler and travel on *The Snapdragon*, he wanted to use his magic and learn more about it.

He wanted both.

With nothing resolved and no answers forthcoming he put on his undergarments, braided his hair tightly and began to dress in the Coronation garments. His outfit was all bespoke, custom made for him to wear to the Queen's Coronation. The pants were silver-gray velvet pantaloons that ballooned outwards, not really his style but they were fine. The doublet on the other hand was something else entirely, the shimmering metallic silver fabric was scratchy and coarse, worse yet was the copious volume of beadwork, embroidery, and inset glittering gemstones that covered the thing, weighing it down til it was as heavy as a suit of armor. It was blindingly bright, reflecting every shaft of light tenfold. He struggled into the doublet, its stiff form constraining his movement at every turn. After nearly wrenching his shoulder to button up the back, he finally stood up, breathing heavily, and made his way to the mirror.

The reflection he saw confused him. Inside this strange, stiff, glittering garment was a person he didn't recognize. His eyes, his face, he was so different than the person who had left Teakley Academy. He thought of his linen blouse floating on the breeze as his hair whipped around his face, and then looked at this confining prison of a garment and sighed.

He just couldn't do it anymore.

He couldn't follow all the rules, he couldn't be this formal, obedient person everyone wanted him to be. He had to be himself, whatever that meant.

And suddenly, he knew what he had to do.

He realized all this time he had only been thinking of talking to Wren, that she would be the only person who could help him figure out what he should do. But she wasn't the only person who held a piece of his heart.

He had to talk to the Majesteria.

He opened the door of the small bedroom and walked into the sitting room, ready to tell the Majesteria that he couldn't live like this any longer.

"We want to leave Teakley and travel on *The Snapdragon*!" Marigold announced as soon as he walked in.

"We need to get back on that ship!" Edwina declared.

"I hate these rugs!" Chica added.

The Majesteria were standing on the top of the sofa wearing their Coronation outfits. They had originally requested to wear traditional ceremonial Majesteria robes, deep blue gowns with glittering celestial designs. But Blanchard had insisted that everyone from Teakley needed lavish, bespoke attire for the Coronation, including the Majesteria. After a few very heated meetings, Blanchard had won and the specialty clothier he'd requested from the Mainland had designed the elaborate gowns the Majesteria now wore.

They were made of layers upon layers of shimmering silver fabric, with huge poofy sleeves and skirts that ballooned out like a lotus flower. The clothier had said the design was to emphasize the Majesteria's importance in spite of their size. Tristan was pretty sure it was just supposed to make them look bigger.

The three glittering puffballs jumped off the couch, and tried to run across the floor but instead fell flat on their faces, tumbling over each other. He crouched down near them and said,

"Are you alright?"

"Ugh, it's these stupid dresses," Edwina said, scrambling to her feet in a tangle of silver brocade.

"We keep tripping over them," Marigold said.

"I hate this!" Chica exclaimed, not even bothering to try to stand up again.

Tristan chuckled, "I don't like my outfit either, it's beautiful but...it's not me."

"Yes, because you're Adventure Tristan now!" Marigold declared.

He smiled wryly, "I think you may be on to something," he said. Then he looked at his friends, took a deep breath and said earnestly,

"I want to go back to the ship."

"Oh thank the Stars," Edwina said.

"We do too!" Marigold exclaimed, "But we didn't know if you'd want to."

"Oh gods yes I do," Tristan said with a relieved sigh. He sat down next to them and began to struggle out of his heavily bejeweled doublet. "This all feels so wrong, I just keep thinking...isn't there some way we can still be Teakley mages but be sailors on *The Snapdragon* too?"

"Duh," Chica said. "We already have a plan."

Tristan finally wrenched himself free of the doublet and fought every instinct to throw it across the room, instead setting it down carefully next to him. He wasn't quite ready to break the rules *that* much.

"You have a plan? Really?" he asked.

"Of course," Edwina said, lifting her snout in the air proudly. "We're going to be Field Researchers, writing books about far-off lands, learning about new types of magic, searching for undiscovered plants and creatures!"

"We discussed it and I believe we shouldn't have much trouble getting Teakley to agree to it," Marigold said, "they should be willing to fund our journeys too. We'll be able to research and discover all kinds of new magic, which will be wonderful for the Academy. It seems like a win for everyone, really."

"Except Blanchard," Tristan said with a laugh. "I don't know why he'll hate it but I'm sure he will."

"Even better!" Edwina said.

Chica raised her hand

"Um, yes Chica?" Edwina asked.

"Will there be new types of cheese?" Chica asked.

"Oh yes, so many I'm sure," Marigold said wistfully.

"I vote yes then," Chica said. "That means I want to go," she added.

"That settles it then," Marigold said. "We will talk to the Headmaster after the Coronation, and then we'll sail off across the Evarian Seas!"

"But what about earlier, when you said we weren't made for adventuring?" Tristan asked.

"It's true, we haven't learned everything we need to," Marigold said somberly. "But I believe we are capable if we put in the effort, I know we can do it.

"We're just going to have to work harder to be the Majesteria the crew needs us to be," Edwina said with determination.

"We just need more books," Chica said.

"I can't disagree with that," Tristan said with a grin. "Tea?"

"Oh yes, please!" Marigold said.

"But no Midnight Delight," Edwina said with a laugh.

"It wasn't that bad," Chica said.

Marigold and Edwina gave her a horrified look.

"What? It wasn't," Chica shrugged.

Tristan reflected on this exciting turn of events as he brewed them some Chamomile tea, carefully pouring the steaming liquid into the Majesteria's tiny teapot. He was delighted by the Majesteria's idea but there was one more nagging fear that he couldn't get out of his head.

He brought the tray of tea over to the Majesteria by the hearth and sat down on the couch nearby. He held his hands around the mug, but its warmth brought him no comfort as his mind was clouded with dark thoughts.

"What's wrong Tristan?" Marigold asked.

He looked at his friends and somehow found the courage to ask the scariest question of all.

"What if...what if they don't want us back on *The Snapdragon*?"

It wasn't that hard to imagine. After all, they had brought little to the ship besides danger and destruction. Not to mention how cold and stoic Wren had been after they'd spent the night together.

Everyone was silent for a while, sipping their tea and contemplating this idea. Finally, Marigold said quietly,

"I, for one, would still like to travel. I believe *The Snapdragon* is where we belong but I feel in my bones that no matter what, I need to explore. I want to see the world, feel the wind in my fur, see that hazy horizon fade into the distance."

"Here, here," Edwina said, raising her mug.

Chica murmured her agreement and raised her mug too.

Tristan smiled and nodded, joining them in a toast to their proposed future.

But privately, he wasn't so sure.

He couldn't imagine himself being okay anywhere but on *that* ship, with *that* crew, with...that Captain.

Chapter Twenty-One

UNSURPRISINGLY, Tristan couldn't sleep. He missed the creaking of the ship, the subtle movement in the water, the sounds of the crew on the deck above. Everything was all different here, and he was finding it hard to adjust to solid ground. He tossed and turned in the bed, his thoughts soon turning to a fear that had been lurking just below the surface of his mind all day...Mad Richard.

Earlier in the evening he had discussed the pirate with the Majesteria and they'd assured him he was, in fact, being paranoid and dramatic.

"We made it here just fine, no Mad Richard in sight," Marigold had said.

"Maybe the Royal Mariners caught him," Edwina had added.

"Maybe he gave up," Chica had said with a shrug.

"Maybe..." Tristan had agreed, letting the matter drop.

But the prickling worry had continued to nag at the back of his mind for the rest of the night, the memory of that little dinghy sailing in to port kept returning to demand his attention.

While he lay in the bed unable to sleep, he started to formulate a plan. He remembered having read a book once called *Casual Magic for Hearth & Home*, which had contained many small and easy spells, including some for simple protection and warning. He wasn't very good at spellwork but they were simple enough he thought he could manage it by just taking a little Starlight and twisting it into the right shapes. Then he could put the spells on the doors and windows, totally out of sight. No one would ever know they were there, but if someone came through with ill intent they'd make a sound. It would be just enough to give a little warning if any unwanted visitors decided to make an appearance in their quarters, but mostly it would give him peace of mind.

It was actually a rather good plan, one that would have been quite useful.

If only he'd thought of it earlier.

Mere moments after he had made the decision to create the house magic spells was when he heard the sound. At first he was sure his mind was playing tricks on him; his paranoia had gotten the better of him, and now he was hearing strange thumping sounds from the sitting room. But as the sounds continued and were followed by muffled, whispered conversation, he quickly knew he wasn't imagining things.

His heart started beating frantically in his chest and his breathing became shallow as his panic grew. Thoughts were whirring through his mind, was it Mad Richard? What were they doing? Why didn't he hear the Majesteria?

He searched around the room in a frenzy, trying to figure out what to do. All he could think of was the brass candlestick on the table nearby. He blew the candles out and quickly set them down on the table before running towards the door, his heart hammering in this chest.

He threw open the door of his room and was instantly blinded by the bright green light engulfing the sitting room. He shielded his eyes and turned away, trying to peer through the strange magical light to see what was happening.

The green glowing light permeated everywhere, lighting up the room with an ethereal glow. After his eyes adjusted to the brightness, he saw the light was most concentrated in the middle of the room by the fireplace. He stood up, blinking, and saw there was a half dozen dangerous-looking men in the room, all of them wearing black and holding weapons, their metal blades gleaming in the moonlight. One of them was holding a small crystal and whispering incantations as he held it up towards the middle of the room, the crystal was bright green and glowing as brightly as the North Star.

Mad Richard was standing right behind the dark mage, watching with pride as the man raised his hands and Tristan saw what was contained within the brightly concentrated light in the middle of the room.

The Majesteria.

The three mice floated in the air, motionless, held in stasis within the luminous orb of light created by the mage's spellwork and his channelling crystal.

Tristan felt the air knocked out of him by the sight, but somehow he managed a mangled scream.

The pirates turned to him and he saw a look of deep satisfaction in Mad Richard's eyes.

"Guards! Blanchard! Anyone! HELP! They're taking the Majesteria!!" Tristan screamed before charging at Mad Richard with the brass candlestick in his hand.

He almost made it.

He was only a few feet away when everything went black.

TRISTAN WOKE up with his face on the floor and a throbbing ache in his temples. His first thought as he opened his eyes was that Chica was right, the rugs *were* scratchy and unpleasant. A moment later he sat bolt upright and said,

"CHICA!" as he remembered how he had ended up on the floor.

He looked around the room but the Majesteria, and Mad Richard's gang, were nowhere to be found. Instead, a handful of Senior Apprentices had just finished breaking down the door and they were running inside with Blanchard behind them, wearing his nightcap and looking tremendously irritated.

Tristan looked around the room frantically and took in the scene. The tables and some of the vases of flowers had been knocked over, the window was wide open with its white curtains streaming out into the sitting room in the strong winds from the sea. One of the end tables near him had been broken, and on the floor near the window...was Marigold's new witch hat.

He felt like his heart would break in two and his hands were shaking with panic as he staggered to his feet to address Blanchard.

"Well, Mulberry? What happened?" Blanchard asked, folding his arms while the Senior Apprentices fanned out to search the room for clues or additional information.

Tristan quickly relayed the what he'd experienced before the pirates had knocked him out while Blanchard listened with a blank expression.

"We have to go after them!" Tristan finished, his hands still trembling as his eyes darted wildly around the room, some part of him thinking that Mad Richard might still be hiding behind one of the curtains.

"We *have* to do no such thing," Blanchard said sternly.

Tristan's mouth fell open in shock, he wanted to respond but he couldn't comprehend what the man was saying.

"We're...not going after them, Sir?" one of the Senior Apprentices said, surprised.

"What did I tell you about calling me Sir, McLean?" Blanchard replied.

"I'm sorry, Your Grace, Lord Blanchard, Senior Liaison to the Grand Majesterium and Collected Mages," she said, bowing deeply.

"That's better," Blanchard said haughtily. "In answer to your question, no. We will not be running around Fairefeux on a wild goose chase a few hours before the Queen's Coronation. No other mages were harmed in this incident and nothing else was taken or damaged. Of course, we are *devastated* that these three mice have been so *violently* taken from us, but we must remember the bigger picture. What really matters to Teakley; we need to think of the *whole* delegation. How would it look if we *all* missed the Queen's Coronation because we were running around looking for some foolish pirate?"

"WHAT THE HELLS?!?" Tristan shouted, "you're just going to...to...let them...go?"

Blanchard rolled his eyes, "Don't be so dramatic Mulberry, of course we're not just going to let them go, that would be ridiculous. But I'm also not going to go galavanting off to gods-knows-where trying to find a needle in a haystack. I've called for the Royal Mariners, we'll be letting the professionals handle this."

There was a knock at the door and a Senior Apprentice slipped inside, tapping Blanchard on the shoulder.

"See? That's them now," Blanchard said, sweeping out of the room with Tristan following close behind. "Is the Headmaster here? Can I talk to her?" Tristan asked as he followed Blanchard down the grand stairway to the entrance hall.

"Don't be absurd! *You* will not be speaking to the Headmaster, if you have any questions I'm sure our esteemed colleague from the Royal Mariners can answer them for you," Blanchard said as they arrived at the bottom of the stairs.

Tristan somehow knew exactly who he'd see when they got downstairs, but it didn't make it any better when he saw Lieutenant Fisk's greasy hair and sneering grin standing in the doorway with his gang of oafs behind him.

"Well, well, well," Fisk said, stalking into the room like a cat with its prey. "Looks like the fancy mages have got into a spot of trouble, eh boys?"

Some of his troops chuckled.

"Sir, I would strongly council against working with the Royal Mariners, I would suggest we work with the crew of *The Snapdragon*. If we brought all our mages we could–" Tristan said, but Fisk wagged a finger in his face, cutting him off.

"I don't think your girlfriend needs to get involved," Fisk said with a smirking grin. There was more tittering from his gang.

Blanchard turned to Tristan with a raised eyebrow and folded arms.

"Is there something I need to know, Mulberry?" he asked.

Tristan felt his cheeks burning but he didn't take the bait. He couldn't let these stupid bullies get the better of him, he had to focus on the only thing that mattered: getting the Majesteria back.

"Lord Blanchard, if you would please consider how it would look to not have the Majesteria at the Coronation. I think it would be a terrible mistake," Tristan said, trying to steer the conversation towards something useful.

"Ohhh, now you're questioning my leadership decisions?" Blanchard said hotly, "When *you* are the one who brought these vicious pirates to our door?"

"With all due respect, Sir, it was your idea we take this method of travel, I was opposed to it," Tristan said, trying to keep his temper in check.

Blanchard glared at him and said, "You didn't answer me Tristan, is there anything I need to know about your little *adventures* at sea? What exactly did you get up to out there? *Where* did you go for so long?"

"There is nothing you need to know, Lord Blanchard, what matters now is finding the Majesteria," Tristan said, gritting his teeth to keep hold of his rising anger.

"Really? I should think I would need to know if you were breaking the rules, wouldn't I? We already know that your pirate friends were aware of the Majesteria and they were doing magic on the ship, what *other* rules were you breaking?"

Tristan stepped forward, his hands balling into fists at his sides.

"You want to talk to me about rule breaking? *How* did you know that the Majesteria were doing magic? Was it because you were *scrying*? And don't even get me started on those ropes you used to reel us in, does the Headmaster know you did that?"

"Now, now, let's all keep our heads on," Fisk said, strutting between them, his thumbs slung through his belt loops, "this really don't concern any of you, the Royal Mariners can take it from here, boys."

"Don't listen to him Sir," Tristan said, panic rising as he looked at Fisk's scheming grin. "They won't fix anything, they are corrupt liars."

Blanchard, who was still looking rather stricken by Tristan's revelation about his scrying said, "Those are some strong accusations from someone who is himself a well-known liar. What is your evidence? Can you actually prove anything?"

"Well, not exactly, but I–"

"Then I'd suggest you keep your *political* opinions to yourself," Blanchard said sternly. "I'm sure the Royal Mariners will do a *fine* job of finding our mice."

"Fine then, if you won't listen to me, I'm leaving," Tristan said, turning away from the cruel men and heading for the door. He was so upset he hadn't even noticed that he was only wearing his pajama shirt.

But it didn't matter anyway, because he wasn't going anywhere.

There was suddenly a strong hand on his arm, holding him in place.

He looked up into the face of a tall and menacing Senior Apprentice from Teakley South.

"You are expected at the Coronation, you *will* attend, and that's an order," Blanchard said firmly.

"You can't be serious!" Tristan said, wriggling in the man's firm grip. "You sent a dozen mages in some twisted amalgam of magic to reel in our ship so we could get here a little faster, but now our own Majesteria have been captured and you're just going to make us all go back to bed like nothing happened?"

Tristan tried to wrench his arm free from the large man, but his giant hands were like an iron clamp, gripping him tightly. Tristan pushed and pulled, but he was as immovable as a tree.

"Let me *GO*, Blanchard!" he shouted, twisting desperately in the man's grip and trying not to look at Fisk's smirking face.

"Calm down Mulberry, stop being so dramatic," Blanchard said, rolling his eyes. "Huntley, take him back to bed."

"I'm taking this to the Headmaster," Tristan said, fuming, "*you are completely out of line, Blanchard.*"

Blanchard stepped closer to him and squinted his beady eyes to look at him with careful scrutiny.

"Who *are* you? This isn't the Tristan Mulberry I know," he said.

Blanchard looked into his eyes and saw in them the smoldering spark of Tristan's growing rebellion.

"Hmm, no you're not the same Mulberry, are you?" he mused. "Why don't we station a few mages outside your door, just to...keep you safe," he said, nodding his order to the hulking Senior Apprentice, who murmured his agreement.

Fisk and his crew waved cheerfully as the Senior Apprentice turned Tristan around and marched him towards the sweeping stairway.

"Don't worry pretty boy, we'll find your little mice, they probably just ran off to look for some cheese," Fisk called out as Tristan was pushed up the stairs by the Senior Apprentices.

The sounds of Fisk and his gang's laughter echoed down the hall as Tristan returned to his room, his head bowed in defeat.

FOR THE FIRST fifteen minutes after Tristan returned to his room he just paced, muttering to himself and punching the air with his fists. He had never been one for violence or uncontrolled anger, but Blanchard was certainly pushing him to his limits.

But after a while he started to calm down and began to grudgingly accept his situation. After a quick peek out the door to make sure that Blanchard had kept his word, Tristan finally returned to his bed.

He lay down and pulled up the quilt, wondering what he should do.

Part of him, the part that had always followed the rules, was trying to convince him that he should accept things as they were and make the best of it.

That was, however, becoming a rather small part of him.

The rest of him was screaming that there had to be something he could do, some way to make Blanchard help him.

He sat up and began to look at things logically, thinking about all the times he had fought with Blanchard, and when he'd managed to make the hard-headed man see reason. After thinking it through he soon realized that he would not be getting Blanchard's help to rescue his friends, the man was impossible.

He flopped back down in bed and sighed.

There was nothing to do, the voice in his head said, you should just give up and accept things as they are.

At that moment he suddenly remembered Captain Wren, sitting in her office on that sunny morning outside Strawberry Island, telling him something her old Captain used to say. Truthfully, he couldn't quite remember the quote, it was something about if the rule is rotten, throw out the whole basket? No, that wasn't it.

Whatever, it didn't matter. What mattered was the idea, the idea that sometimes breaking the rules was the *right* thing to do.

Tristan had followed the rules his whole life and where had it got him? The Majesteria were missing, *The Snapdragon* would be sailing away without him,

and all he was supposed to do was put on some pretty clothes and stand around eating canapés.

He jumped out of bed and said,

"FUCK THIS!" before running out of the room.

Despite his bold exclamation he didn't make it very far because he had to run back to put his clothes on and make a plan. But by the time he had laced up his boots he'd already figured out what he was going to do. First, he put on his rather dirty linen blouse, fastened his silver dangling earring, and pulled his hair out of its braid, shaking it out dramatically.

Next, he pulled all the sheets off the bed and tied them together. Then he went out to the balcony, carrying the large bundle in his arms. He looked over the side and his stomach dropped as he saw how dizzyingly high up he was. But he quickly pushed past his fear; he was riding a wave of emotion now and he was going to let it carry him all the way to the Majesteria.

He carefully knotted the rope around the metal bars of the balcony before heaving the pile over the side. He took a deep breath and clambered over the railing, grabbing onto the swinging sheet with shaking hands.

Tristan marveled at himself as he clung to the sheets and slowly made his way down from the third-story window. The version of Tristan who left Appleton Island would never have dreamed of disobeying a direct order from Blanchard, let alone dangling by a bedsheet thirty feet in the air.

But that Tristan was gone.

He was pretty sure he had died somewhere in the Otherwilde Seas.

Adventure Tristan was here to stay, and he was prepared to do just about anything to save his friends.

The journey down the bedsheets from the third floor wasn't nearly as hard as he'd expected it would be. All those strong arm muscles from cutting wood back at Teakley had really paid off, and he shimmied down the sheets with ease, jumping the last few feet to land in a crouch beside the backdoor of the kitchens.

He paused for a moment, adrenaline coursing through his veins, and looked around to make sure no one had spotted him. Once he saw the coast was clear he jogged around the elegantly cultivated gardens of the estate towards the main entrance.

He was almost at the gates when he spotted a large wood pile. He turned and darted over to it, searching the area til he found what he was looking for. At last he saw it, and with a sly grin he grabbed the axe and slung it over his shoulder before he left Ivylane Manor for good.

Mad Richard was about to learn why you should never, ever, piss off a Majesteria Handler.

Chapter Twenty-Two

He realized almost immediately that the axe was a bad idea. Not because he wasn't willing to take up arms to defend the Majesteria, he absolutely was, but because the streets were by no means empty. Despite the late hour the streets of Fairefeux were packed with revelers who were twirling sparklers, dancing, laughing, and singing. He looked down at the axe gripped tightly in his gloved hands and realized he might give the wrong impression as he ran through the bustling crowds to the docks.

In his experience, crowds tended to be alarmed by people running through them with axes.

So, a few streets away from the Manor he turned down a side street and leaned the axe gently against a wall before returning to the main boulevard and readying himself to jog through the swarming masses as fast as possible.

It occurred to him that Mad Richard had likely brought the Majesteria immediately to his ship and sailed out of the harbor, which meant that every moment he hesitated, they were getting further away. He had no time for the partying crowds in the streets of Fairefeux; they were only an obstacle on the way to his true destination, the one place he knew he could find help.

The Snapdragon.

He bobbed and weaved through the jubilant crowds, trying his best not to bump into people. He didn't always succeed, and a few times had to shout apologies over his shoulder as he sent someone's roasted chestnuts skittering across the cobblestones. His racing paid off and this journey through Fairefeux was a lot faster than the walk to Ivylane Manor had been. Soon he followed the swelling crowd around the corner from the main boulevard and out to the busy port. He looked around with wild eyes, assuming he'd see *The Snapdragon* immediately. But the deep green ship was nowhere, at least that he could see because there were ships *everywhere*.

The port was massive and packed to capacity for the Coronation with ships of all shapes and sizes, from huge passenger ships to small fishing boats and everything in between. Even though the Coronation was less than six hours away, there were still new ships pulling in to port with clusters of people hurriedly disembarking. Carriages and wagons were pulling up to the ships and carrying away people, luggage, and crates of cargo. Everywhere he turned he saw sailors, pirates, tourists, ships, and boats.

He stopped dead in the middle of the busy cobbled street, his hands trembling with panic and adrenaline. How was he ever going to find *The Snapdragon* in this chaos? He looked around frantically again but he didn't recognize any of the ships.

But suddenly, he felt something.

Magic.

It wasn't any magic he recognized, it was a small spark that touched his senses at the back of his mind. He looked around and saw the source of it, a nearby street performer, a young woman with long pointed ears was performing a magic display for the crowds. She lifted her hands into the air and created a swirl of magic sparks in the shape of the Cinderflower, and he felt that little pulse again.

This time, it gave him an idea.

The Snapdgragon had a very distinctive magic, one he'd come to know well in the time he'd spent on the ship. If he could focus his senses and reach out for that pulsing tranquil feeling of *The*

Snapdragon's magic. If he could find that feeling, he'd be able to find the ship. The difficult part would be getting himself to focus.

He took a deep breath and held his body still, ignoring the crowds swarming around him as much as possible. He tuned out the shouts, laughter, chattering, and drunken singing. He looked inside, feeling for those threads of magic that permeated the air around him, the ones he pulled from when he brought Starlight magic down from the stars above.

Soon he started to feel more little pulses and ripples of magic than just the street performer. He realized with surprise that there were dozens of mages scattered among the crowds. He also felt other, stranger kinds of magic. The subtle hum of the magic carpets stored for the night, the street vendors selling magicked sparklers. He felt quite a few magical animals, and even a few other magical ships. Strangest of all was a deep, heavy, oscillating rhythm of some very old magic entity buried far below the ground.

This was going to be harder than he thought.

But still, he knew he could pick out the feeling of *The Snapdragon*, even in all these different types of magic, he could find it. He was sure of it, he had to be.

So he sorted through the magics, trying to turn away from the ones he knew weren't right, focusing in on the ships. He even started leaning his body subconsciously towards the sea as he tried to feel the magic in the air.

At last! That was it!

It was just a whisper for a moment, but when he focused on it, the feeling got stronger.

The tranquil pulsing of *The Snapdragon* was laced with kindness and warmth, it was a feeling he knew he'd recognize anywhere.

The more he focused, the strong the feeling got, and then he was running, bolting through the crowds to the source of the magical feeling that he now felt there was only one word to describe...home.

He didn't remember when he'd started running, it was just happening, it was involuntary. He just had to get there and he was beyond thought, the only thing he could do or feel was to follow that magic as fast as he could, the ship's magic was calling out to him like a lighthouse in the night.

He ran and ran, no longer remembering to apologize if he spilled someone's chestnuts, no longer remembering that there as anyone else there. It was just him, the cobblestones under his boots, the wind in his hair, and that magic beckoning him home.

At last he saw the bright green of *The Snapdragon*'s sails tucked in between two much larger ships in the darkened end of the port. Most of the ships down here looked like they'd been docked for a while, no one was getting on or off. This was a place to dock your ship if you intended to stay for more than a few hours.

As his racing feet brought him closer to the ship, he saw the lanterns hanging in the rigging and he felt hot tears welling up inside him. He was overwhelmed by the sight of those lanterns' warm glow waving in the breezes from the ocean. He hadn't realized just how adrift he'd felt until he saw his destination in sight. It was going to be okay, surely the crew would know what to do.

As SOON AS he arrived at the ramp to the ship, he knew something unusual was happening. He had expected a few sleepy sailors, maybe someone moving some cargo or poring over some paperwork. But it wasn't like that at all.

A few dozen people, many of whom he didn't recognize, were crammed onto the ship's main deck. The sounds of laughing, singing, and upbeat folk music wafted down from the ship. He realized that some part of him had imagined that life on *The Snapdragon* had stopped when he'd left, but he saw now that it definitely hadn't.

Not at all. In fact, it was quite the opposite.

They were having a party.

It made sense, really. Who wouldn't want to relax and have

some fun after the journey they'd had? But still, some part of him felt...weird. Sad? Jealous? Hurt?

Something like that.

It's not that he expected the whole crew to be sitting around crying that he'd left, but...still. However, he spared no more than a moment for these thoughts. His personal feelings could wait; finding the Majesteria was all that mattered.

Well, there was nothing for it, this was just another crowd of revelers he had to fight through to find the Captain and get her help. He ran up the wooden ramp and onto the deck.

When he got there he saw tables laid with an array of Basel's delicious foods and crates of rum and ale. Sailors danced, drank, twirled and laughed, while in the bow of the ship a small band of bards played jovial folk music.

Some of the sailors in the crowd recognized him and called out to him cheerfully.

"Hooray! Tristan is here!" someone called.

"Wahey! Tristan!" someone else said, raising a wobbly glass of rum in the air with a clumsy toast.

"Tristan?!? Where? Did he bring those adorable little mage mice?" he heard someone say as he pushed his way through the dancing drunken sailors. He waved to a few people as he frantically searched through the crowd for that streak of black leather with a glittering gold coin, but she was nowhere to be found among the revelling sailors.

Eventually, he started asking people.

"Have you seen the Captain?" he asked breathlessly of a young brown-skinned man he remembered as a member of Basel's kitchen staff.

"Hey, it's you, Star Magic Guy!" the man said cheerfully, clapping him on the back. "Want a drink?"

"Not right now, have you seen the Captain?" Tristan asked again, this time a little impatiently.

"Uhhh, I don't think so, maybe try Emyr?"

"Good idea," Tristan said, spinning around to search for the well-dressed First Mate. After a moment of searching the deck he spotted him.

Oh.

Well, so much for that.

Emyr was...unavailable. In perhaps the least surprising thing that had happened all day, Emyr was very busy with an incredibly handsome man Tristan didn't recognize. Of course he was. But he didn't have time to ponder how on earth Emyr had already found a new lover in only a few hours, so he continued asking people where the Captain was until finally a red-haired woman said,

"I think I saw her head that way with a fresh bottle of rum a while ago," before pointing towards the little deck above the Captain's quarters.

Whatever he had been expecting to find when he saw the Captain again, it certainly wasn't this. Wren was sitting in a dark corner, far away from the party, her knees up and arms rested over them. She had a pained look on her face, a sullen look of defeat, and if Tristan didn't know better her puffy red eyes would make him think she'd been crying. She held the remains of a large bottle of rum lazily in her hand.

"Wren!" he said breathlessly, leaning over to catch his breath, feeling the relief wash over him at the sight of her.

Her eyes went wide when she saw him and she scrambled to her feet, running her hands through her hair and looking around frantically for a place to stash her bottle of rum. She wiped her mouth with her shirt and straightened up, in a rather poor attempt at assuming a cool, casual stance, leaning against the railing.

"Uh, Tristan, what are you, um," she stumbled over her words until she saw his expression. Instantly her demeanor changed completely, she was no longer a nervous person pretending they hadn't been drinking away their misery. She was a capable Captain ready to lead the charge to save whoever needed saving.

"What happened?" She said, her tone sharp and steady.

Tristan let his shoulders down as he breathed a sigh of relief.

Finally, he knew it was going to be okay.

~

"My best guess is that he's going to that little town in Red Moon Cove, there's a tavern there where pirates and smugglers trade," Wren said, pointing at a small island on the map before her.

It was fifteen minutes later and they were gathered in Wren's office, the sounds of the merry folk band muffled through the mottled glass panes of the windows. After he had explained the situation to Wren, she'd suggested they get Emyr and go to her office to make a rescue plan.

While they'd been trying to explain the situation to a rather intoxicated Emyr, with an *exceptionally* handsome man clinging to his arm, Basel and Bonnie overheard and immediately insisted that they be included in the meeting.

So now Tristan was standing in Wren's office with a very tipsy Emyr, an extremely worried Basel, and steadfastly determined Bonnie. Wren had been looking at maps and muttering to herself for the past few minutes but she was finally ready to start making plans.

"Red Moon Cove is located here," she said, pointing at the map. "It's halfway between Fairefeux and the Gaffwyn Pass, which is a common route for traders, pirates and some of the more...unsavory characters you might encounter in the Evarian Sea. I'm guessing he'll want to get rid of the Majesteria as quickly as possible to avoid any complications. If he's looking for a buyer, I believe that's where he'd go to find one."

Tristan felt his chest get tight when Wren discussed 'finding a buyer' for the Majesteria. Even in his loose linen blouse he felt like he couldn't breathe when he thought about the Majesteria being sold like sacks of grain.

"With that in mind, I think we can expect to find his ship along the eastern route out of Fairefeux," she continued, drawing her finger across the map. "My guess is he'll be heading that way, and fast."

"So what now?" Tristan asked. He realized he hadn't considered any sort of plan besides finding Wren and begging her to help.

Wren pondered the question, "Well, we have two obstacles," she said. "One, we need to catch up to him, he's got a head start of a few hours and mages who can push his ship faster. Two, we need a plan of attack once we get there. He's got us way outnumbered and he's likely got far more weapons and experienced fighters than we do. Also, most of our crew is drunk."

"I think...I can...um, I mean give me a coffee and I'll probably..." Emyr said, stumbling over his words as he tried to get his head in working order.

"We'll get you coffee, but we still need a plan," Wren said, frowning.

"Can't you cast a wind spell like you did before, Tristan?" Bonnie asked.

"No," Tristan said, "I don't create spells, I'm just a conduit. Starlight is a very delicate and difficult to manipulate magic form; what the Majesteria can do is far beyond my capabilities. An easy way to think about it is that I can get a lot of clay, but the Majesteria can sculpt that clay into a piece of pottery."

"What can you do with a lot of clay?" Basel asked.

"Not much," Tristan said darkly.

"Darts!" Emyr said suddenly.

"What?" Wren asked.

"Darts, we shoot 'em with darts!" Emyr said, only slurring his words a little.

"Emyr may be as drunk as a skunk, but he's got a point," Basel said. "He's got that big dart collection, and he's good at throwing 'em too, when he can see straight."

"Perhaps I could make a sleeping poison," Bonnie suggested, "we could dip the tips of the darts in it and shoot them at the sailors. That way we could sneak onto the ship and avoid a confrontation altogether, what do you think dearheart?"

"An interesting idea," Wren said, "but that couldn't work out on the open waters, the only way we'd be able to sneak onboard unnoticed is if the ship was anchored, and if we wait for him to dock it might already be too late. Which brings us back to the question: how could we get close enough to shoot them? Surely Mad Richard's mages would be able to fire at us with that catapult long before we could put anyone to sleep with a poisoned dart. No matter how good a shot Emyr is."

"And that's assuming we can get Emyr sober enough to do it," Tristan added.

"Some of Basel's special Blackest-Black Black Coffee will do the trick, doncha worry Froggy," Basel said, clapping Emyr on the back with a giant hand.

"And *that's* assuming we could somehow even catch up with him," Wren continued, "without the Majesteria's wind spells I don't see how it's possible."

But it *was* possible, it had to be.

And suddenly it all came together in Tristan's mind, the whole plan.

"I think I may have a solution," he said. "We can't beat them by ship, there's just no way. They've got us beat in every way if we try to sail after them. So I say, if we can't beat them by ship, we don't."

"What do you mean?" Wren asked.

"We won't sail there, we'll *fly* there."

"EVEN THOUGH WE'RE hoping not to be seen I still think we should bring some sailors more experienced at fighting, and some weapons," Wren said thoughtfully as they sprinted through the hallway to the Canteen. Basel ran into the kitchen to get their special Blackest-Black Black Coffee for Emyr and snacks for the Majesteria, after insisting 'with all they've been through those little dumplins' are gonna be hungry when we get 'em back!'

While Bonnie, Wren, and Tristan went to the healer's quarters so Bonnie could work on her sleeping poison.

Tristan walked in first and saw Birdy sitting up on one of the beds, knitting furiously while Ginger sat on a chair nearby reading a book.

"Oh, hello Tristan!" Ginger said, "I heard you had left the ship and Wren was really upset about it– Oh, hello Wren," she finished with an awkward cough.

"What's wrong?" Birdy said suddenly, after taking a look at their somber faces.

"The Majesteria have been abducted by Mad Richard, so we're about to go steal a Magick Carpet and sneak onto his ship to rescue them," Wren said as though this was the most natural thing in the world.

"*Borrow*!" Tristan said quickly. "We're not stealing it, we're *borrowing* it. We're going to return it and Teakley will pay them later."

Wren rolled her eyes, "we're breaking in to *borrow* a Magick Carpet."

"I'm coming with you," Birdy said quickly. "You'll need my skills–"

"No, you're not," Wren said, shaking her head, "you have multiple broken bones and I'm not even sure you can stand up."

"I'm coming with, you can't stop me!" Birdy said, struggling to get off the bed.

"But I can," Ginger said severely, pushing her back onto the pillows.

"Ging, we *have* to go! It's the Majesteria, they need our help!" Birdy exclaimed.

"You can't walk because of the last reckless and dangerous thing you did, now you have to wait before you get to do another," Ginger said tartly. "And I'm staying with you to make sure you don't do something else stupid."

Birdy groaned.

"Fine! At least take Graves, Netty, and Brynn, you should have good fighters with you just in case things go sideways and they're the best on the ship."

"The *best* fighters?" Wren asked with a raised eyebrow.

"Besides everyone in this room, of course," Birdy said hurriedly.

"Alright then," Wren said. "We'll see if they're sober enough to come with us before we leave. How's that potion coming Bonnie?"

"Almost finished, dearheart," Bonnie said over her shoulder as she carefully ground the smelly concoction with her mortar and pestle.

"Then it's almost time to leave, let's hope Basel has figured out a way to get Emyr sobered up," Wren said with a sigh.

As they hurriedly made their way through the spirited crowds the small group of pirates chatted with each other and discussed possible plans of attack when they reached Mad Richard's ship. Only Wren was notably quiet and distant, keeping all her thoughts to herself.

Tristan started to worry. Well, that's not entirely accurate. Tristan continued to worry, as was his nature. He'd been so concerned with the Majesteria's safety that he'd barely considered the impact this rescue mission might have on the crew. Until now.

He started to wonder if this was even a good idea, and suddenly all his worries came spilling to the surface.

"Are you sure you should do this?" he asked her. "You don't have to, I was just so scared and I didn't know who to turn to, but maybe there's some other way. It's just so dangerous for you all to get involved, you'd be making an enemy of Mad Richard, and helping me steal this carpet could get you into trouble with the Royal Mariners–"

Wren held up a hand,

"They're my crew," was all she said.

But it was enough. Everyone knew what it meant, everyone felt the same. Tristan realized, his heart filling with love and admiration for his new crew, that he felt the same about everyone on *The Snapdragon*. They were all his crew now too, and if something bad happened to any of them, he would fight tooth and nail to help them.

This was, unsurprisingly, Tristan's first time breaking into anything. He looked around nervously, his mind whirring with fear and anxiety as Wren carefully picked the locks of The Great Magick Carpet's building.

But he needn't have worried, any Royal Guards around were far too busy with the crowds of partying revelers to notice a handful of sailors casually standing around at the shaded door of a Magick Carpet shop.

It took a lot less time than he would have expected; less than a minute and the door was swinging open into the darkened shop and they were scurrying inside, shutting it behind them.

The closed door muffled the sounds of the party in the streets, leaving them in the hushed quiet of the closed shop. Tristan felt a wave of worry and guilt rising inside him. Breaking the rules was one thing, but *breaking and entering* was another. Immediately, he knew he had to put these feelings aside. Borrowing a Magick Carpet for a few hours just wasn't a big deal, not in the grand scheme of things. Not compared to the Majesteria's safety. He suddenly realized maybe he needed to start thinking differently.

He needed to start thinking like a pirate.

Wren moved through the building like a cat, gracefully agile, peering around corners carefully before ushering the rest of the crew towards the back door, which opened onto the Magick Carpet yard.

Immediately Tristan was hit with a wave of magical energy from the dozens of stored carpets around him. He stumbled backwards, tripping over a crate on the ground. He steadied himself against the doorframe and took a breath, focusing hard on pushing the overwhelming magic to the back of his mind.

"You alright?" Wren asked, her inquisitive eyes fixed on him sharply.

"Mhmm," he said, "it's just...a lot of magic."

"From the carpets?" she asked.

He nodded, "Yeah, they're all saturated with magic, it's overwhelming. Let's just get one and get out of here."

"Sounds good to me," Wren said.

There were rolls of carpets lining the walls and in the middle of the courtyard there was a small wooden platform. The whole area was open to the sky so the Magick Carpets could take off from right the yard. Wren looked over the carpets quickly, reading their carefully marked labels, which cataloged how many people they could safely carry and how far they could be expected to travel. After a moment she selected one of a medium size that she surmised would be large enough to hold everyone.

She brought it over to the platform, untied the ribbons holding it shut, and unrolled the large, plush carpet. Everyone held their breath as she dramatically laid the ornately patterned carpet out across the platform.

And then...nothing.

The carpet just sat there like, well...a carpet.

It didn't move or shake or hover.

To Tristan's eyes the carpet was buzzing with magical energy, but to everyone else it just looked broken.

"Now what?" one of the sailors asked.

"I don't know, I've never ridden a flying carpet before, have you?" Wren said. Everyone shook their heads.

"Let me try," Tristan said, approaching the carpet gingerly. He placed his palm on the thick fabric, closing his eyes. He felt a friendly hum from the carpet, like as though it wanted him to do magic with it. He opened his eyes and saw that the carpet had two golden ropes attached at one side. He realized the ropes were probably reins for steering the carpet through the air, and most likely the entry point for magical energy.

He clasped the golden ropes and felt a surge of magic soar up his arms. Immediately, he felt the ropes' connection to the rest of the carpet, and in his mind's eye he could see the strange spiderweb of magic interwoven through the thick fabric.

He sat down cross-legged on the carpet, holding the reins tightly.

He focused his mind, trying to sense the carpet's magic, willing it to move.

He pulled the reins up and...

Nothing happened.

"Is this going to work?" Emyr asked, grimacing as he took another sip of the flask of Blackest-Black Black Coffee Basel had given him.

"Probably not," one of the sailors said with a chuckle.

Wren glared at them, "Give him a second," she said sharply.

For his part, Tristan was lost in thought, trying to remember all of the magical experiments he'd done with the Majesteria back at Teakley and how they'd gotten magical objects to respond to them.

After a moment he said,

"I think it needs more magic, I'm guessing the mages who operate these infuse them with fresh magic when it's time to go."

Wren nodded her understanding and watched with interest as Tristan pulled the vial of Starlight out from under his shirt, its bright glow illuminating the dark carpet yard. He unstoppered it and pulled out a few small threads of Starlight, winding them around his leather-gloved hands. He then carefully wound the threads around the golden reins, pushing the magic into the fibers with his fingers.

The effect was almost instantaneous.

The carpet started to hover, bucking and flapping a few feet above the ground. It moved almost like some kind of wild animal, and when Tristan closed his eyes he could feel the web of magic pulsing underneath him frantically.

The carpet wanted to fly.

He pulled hard on the reins, pushing his attention towards the magic in the carpet, willing it to stay still. It wasn't easy, especially with all the other carpets in the yard trying to pull his focus.

"Hurry up, this thing wants to fly, I can't hold it for long," he said.

Wren wasted no time, she grabbed a step stool sitting near the platform and quickly ran up to jump onto the carpet next to him. To his surprise the carpet held her weight easily; it didn't even buckle when she sat down. After seeing their Captain climb onto the carpet the rest of the crew hurried up the stairs and situated themselves behind Tristan, eyes wide with awe as they hovered above the ground.

Tristan took a deep breath and willed the agitated carpet to start rising into the air. It was easy, far easier than keeping it still, because the carpet longed to fly. It leapt into the air, tossing the passengers around while Tristan frantically yanked on the reins until he found a tension that worked to keep the carpet steady.

Finally, he found a balance to stabilize the carpet, and then they began to ascend, soaring up and over the city's glittering lights, flying off across the night sky.

CHAPTER TWENTY-THREE

THE ISLAND GOT SMALLER and the air got colder as Tristan pulled the carpet higher into the night sky. The experience of flying a Magick Carpet was exhilarating to put it mildly. Even in the midst of their stress, everyone was excited to be flying through the sky at high speed. The pirates looked over the side, pointing at things and waving to some of the revellers in the street before they flew too high to see them.

Soon, they were lost in a sea of clouds.

Puffs of white and grey dissolved into wet, clammy mist as they flew through the veil of clouds and over the Evarian Sea. Eventually they dipped down again to coast above the water as they started charting their course to find Mad Richard's ship.

Wren was sitting near him holding a map while Emyr looked through a spyglass at the coastline below, calling out landmarks to her. She would look at the map and make sure they were on the right track, occasionally pointing Tristan in a different direction.

Tristan was relieved to have Wren and Emyr handling the navigating because keeping control of a Magick Carpet wasn't easy. The carpet struggled and pulled at the reins, trying to go faster or higher, or sometimes just turn in a different direction entirely. After less than an hour in the air Tristan's arms were aching and his shoulders were sore with tension. But he kept going, his eyes watering in the cold winds as they cruised along in a blustery air current somewhere between the clouds above and the sea below.

There was something magical about navigating the skies together. Of course the experience of flying through the night sky was already majestic, but even more than that, he enjoyed working together, figuring out where they needed to go, supporting each other.

He wished he could have enjoyed it, flying through the night sky with his crew under a full moon.

But he was too tense, too afraid, too worried.

Because it wasn't really his crew.

Not without the Majesteria.

After the initial excitement of flying, the group had settled down to planning their mission, discussing possible ways to strike, and how to stay out of sight. They had the advantage of surprise; Mad Richard's crew would be on the lookout for another ship, not a flying carpet. But that advantage would only get them so far. So, they talked through possible strategies, what to do if there were mages on deck, how to disarm opponents.

The conversation didn't make Tristan any less worried.

The more they talked the more anxious he became, it didn't sound like people planning to quickly grab some mice and fly away into the night.

"Tristan?" Wren said.

"Hmm?" he asked, rousing from his brooding to look at her sidelong.

"Will you be able to keep the carpet in the air while we search the ship?"

"I'm going with you!" he exclaimed, horrified.

"But what about the carpet? We're going to need to make a *very* fast escape," she said.

"I'm getting on that ship and finding the Majesteria," he said with unwavering, iron-clad determination.

"Okay, then how do we keep the carpet flying?" Wren asked, her tone cross. "Can someone else hold the reins?"

Tristan realized he didn't know, but he didn't think it was likely. "I...I'm not sure," he admitted.

"Should we try it?" she asked, putting out her hand.

Tristan looked at it nervously for a moment, then nodded and handed her the reins. As soon as the reins were out of his hands the feeling of the carpet's magic shrunk in his mind. It was still there, but it was a soft humming underneath him, he could barely see the spiderweb of magic threads coursing through it.

But he didn't spend much time thinking about that because the carpet was wobbling and dipping, already pointing downwards and leaning sharply to one side as Wren struggled to pull the reins up.

She quickly handed them back to him and he pulled the carpet up sharply, breathing a sigh of relief as it levelled out.

"I guess it's got to be you then," she said.

"Let me think about it, I may be able to come up with a plan," Tristan said.

"Fine, but we are going to need this thing ready to fly as soon as we get the mice, there's no other way we'll make it out of there alive."

"I'll make sure it's ready, you can trust me on that," Tristan said firmly.

As they got closer to the area where Wren guessed Mad Richard's ship would be they began to finalize their plans. Unfortunately, they couldn't really know what they were going to do until they saw the ship because there were just too many unknown factors. Bonnie's potion had only made enough for a handful of darts, so the biggest concern was how many pirates were on the deck.

Ultimately, their chances of success all came down to how arrogant Mad Richard was. If he was worried that people were hunting him down, he'd have dozens of pirates on deck; mages would be at the ready with spells for their catapult. But if he was more confident that the Royal Mariners wouldn't find him, he'd likely be in bed and the ship would be manned with a skeleton crew of lookouts and only a few guards.

As it turned out, Mad Richard was exceptionally arrogant.

When they finally saw the dark ship's horse-shaped masthead in the distance, Tristan immediately followed their plan and angled the carpet up into the clouds to give them cover, his heart racing.

"What now?" he asked as he tried to slow the carpet's progress through the sky. After a little bit of wrangling, he finally managed to convince the carpet to hover in the air with a faint humming motion.

"Can you dip down quickly for me to look over the side and then pull back up into the clouds at my signal?" Wren asked as she started to inch her way gingerly towards the edge of the carpet.

"What's your signal?" Tristan asked, panicked.

"I'll whistle," Wren said, barely paying attention to him. She was already angling herself to lie on her stomach with Basel holding onto her so she could lean over the side of the carpet with her spyglass in hand.

The sight of Wren's head disappearing over the edge of the carpet sent Tristan's heart leaping into this throat but he tried not to think about it and focused his attention on maneuvering the carpet. As soon as Wren was in position he nudged the carpet down with his mind, willing it to sink just below the bottom of the clouds.

Tristan's view was mostly white and grey fog as he waited for Wren's signal, his sweating hands nearly slipping off the golden reins. He waited and waited, it felt like forever but it was probably only a few minutes. Finally, he heard a low whistle float across the wind. He jerked the reins quickly upward, pulling them above the clouds a little too quickly. The carpet leaned and some of the crew tumbled backwards, frantically grabbing onto the tasseled end of the carpet.

"Everyone alright?" Tristan called.

"We're all alive at least," Wren said sardonically.

Tristan was too wound up to laugh.

"Well?" he asked. "How many?"

"There's only a few sailors on deck," Wren said, her tone surprised. "He must be exceptionally confident that no one is chasing him. Honestly, I'm starting to wonder if he's bribed the Royal Mariners."

Tristan thought about this for a moment.

"You know, based on everything I've seen, it seems pretty likely," he said. "Is there anything we can do?"

"What?" Wren asked, confused.

"About the Royal Mariners, can we prove they're corrupt and get them arrested or something?" Tristan asked.

Wren gave him a quizzical look and said, "Maybe someday. But I think *right now* we should really focus on rescuing the Majesteria. Is everyone ready? Emyr, are you ready to shoot the darts?"

"Aye Captain," he said, holding up his nearly empty flask of Blackest-Black Black Coffee, "I'm as sober as I'll get."

"Alright then," Wren said. "Tristan, bring us down."

The pirates readied themselves, crouched and tensing on the carpet as Tristan took a deep breath and plunged the carpet down, turning it in a big sweeping arc across the night sky towards the ship's stern. As he got closer he saw a shadow at the wheel, a dark hat silhouetted against the night. But Emyr was ready, throwing his dart, a whizzing red streak in the darkness. The dart hit its mark and a moment later the man crumpled onto the deck, flat on his face. Tristan's heart leapt at the sight but there was no time to celebrate their success, he immediately brought the carpet around in an arc towards the front of the ship where a few pirates were sitting on crates playing cards.

As the carpet wheeled out of the sky, one of them stood up and pointed, but before he could shout to his comrades he was already falling over. The others looked around to see who had knocked him out, but it was too late.

Wren pointed to the last two sailors, guarding the door of the

Captain's Quarters, swords at the ready. Tristan nodded and pulled the carpet up alongside the ship, Emyr leaned over and quickly took care of them.

And then it was quiet.

The dark night enveloped the ship, the only sounds he heard were the waves hitting the side of the boat, the subtle rustling of the carpet, and his own pounding heart. Wren pointed down and Tristan nodded, angling the carpet back towards the middle of the ship where he brought it down low to hover a few feet above the deck.

While the rest of the crew dismounted silently onto the darkened ship, Tristan remained on the carpet. He pulled the vial of Starlight out from under his shirt, its bright glow lighting up the deck like a beacon. He pulled all the remaining Starlight out of it in one long thread, winding it carefully around his leather-gloved hands. Then he tied the end of the thread around the golden ropes of the carpet, pushing it in with his fingers and willing the carpet to hold its place. For a moment it seemed to shimmy around as though in agreement with his request.

Well, there was nothing for it.

He took a deep breath and jumped off the carpet onto the deck.

He spun around and saw the carpet was holding steady a few feet in the air, rippling slightly. The power of his makeshift Starlight lead seemed to be enough for him to keep the carpet afloat, even if he wasn't sitting on it. He breathed a sigh of relief and began to follow the rest of the crew, who were furtively making their way across the deck. He unwound the bright glowing Starlight lead behind him, making sure it was always keeping him magically connected to the Magick Carpet.

"I think they'll probably be keeping them in the Captain's Quarter's," Wren whispered, pointing to the office at the other end of the ship. Tristan looked and saw a familiar bright green glow coming from the windows.

"I recognize the glow, that's the one I saw when he captured them," Tristan whispered.

Wren looked at him and then glanced dubiously at the Starlight thread Tristan was trailing behind him.

"Will that really work?" she asked him quietly.

He nodded, "Yes, as long as I keep my focus it won't break. This way I'm still connected to the carpet and I can keep it in the air."

"Are you sure–" Wren began.

"There's magic in there," he said, pointing to the glowing green light, "you might need me."

She raised an eyebrow but didn't say anything, she just turned around and motioned to the rest of the crew to head for the Captain's Office.

The sound of their boots on the deck felt deafeningly loud, or at least it felt like it in the empty stillness of the ship. Tristan had never realized before how loud boots could be, but even as they tried their best to step lightly it felt like every creak in the deck was echoing across the night. The crew moved quickly across the deck and arrived at the cabin, its bright green glow illuminating their tense faces.

The pounding in Tristan's heart got louder as he carefully stepped over the snoring bodies of the two sailors who'd been stationed to guard the office. He looked over his shoulder nervously as Wren crouched down and pulled out her lock-picking kit, the shiny metal glinting briefly in the moonlight. He held his breath as he waited for her to pick a lock for the second time that night, his mind split between holding the carpet aloft and listening for the sounds of pirates coming up behind them.

Click. Whirr. Click.

The door swung open and Wren put the kit away, ushering them into the cluttered office. Tristan came last, trailing his little thread of Starlight carefully behind him, constantly checking that he was still connected to the humming carpet.

And then he saw them.

The office was, in many ways, similar to Wren's. A little less tidy, a lot more weapons, but full of maps and paperwork, rum and brandy, telescopes and spyglasses.

There was, however, one very notable difference.

On top of the desk, next to a half-empty bottle of rum were three golden cages, each containing one of Tristan's best friends, held motionless in a ball of glowing bright green light.

He gasped, and let out a small cry of horror.

Wren put a finger to her lips and he mouthed the word '*sorry*'.

She nodded and very carefully closed the door behind them, taking care to wind the thread of Starlight underneath it. Once the door was closed, they all relaxed a little and began to assess the situation.

"What's wrong with them?" one of the sailors asked.

"Oh, dearhearts! They look so small and helpless, it's dreadful," Bonnie said.

"Not even a wedge of cheese, it's a disgrace," Basel said, shaking their head. "What do we do Captain?"

Wren turned to Tristan, "What do you think?" she asked.

But Tristan wasn't listening. He was already crouched down by the Majesteria's cages, his hands shaking as he fumbled desperately with the doors. The small doors swung open easily, they weren't even locked. Why would they need to be? The cages were just ornamental. The magic was what was really holding the Majesteria prisoner.

For something so powerful the magic was...surprisingly quiet. It buzzed with a sort of organic energy, like a waterfall or roiling river. His body wasn't repulsed by it like Blanchard's amalgam ropes, it was just...strong, and steady.

And he had no idea how to destroy it and free his friends.

"I don't know what to do," Tristan admitted, standing up, his eyes never leaving the Majesteria. "I've never encountered magic like this before."

"It looks like the magic is connected to that crystal," Wren said, pointing. Nearby there was a small glowing crystal on a velvet pillow. Tristan hadn't even noticed it, he'd been so focused on sensing the magic that he'd barely used his eyes.

Underneath the crystal's pillow was a spell, a shimmering circle of green light and occult symbols sketched on the table. Now *this* one was a spell Tristan recognized.

He hurried over and bent down to examine the complex web of symbols.

"It's a locking spell," he said, breathlessly. "I've seen many spells similar to it before."

"Do you know how to break it?" Wren asked.

"I think so," he said. "Does anyone have a Pixie Match?"

One of the sailors handed him a leather tobacco pouch. Inside he found a metal case with a few small pixie-dust-infused sticks in it. He took one out, striking it on the case to make a flickering, pink-tinged flame. He closed his eyes, putting his mind towards the match, infusing it with his magical intention. Then he blew it out and set the smoking end on the outer ring of the spellwork. Immediately the shimmering lines and symbols of the spell began to to shift and waver, soon they dissolved and disappeared into the smooth wood of the table.

Everyone gasped quietly as the spell disappeared, and as one their heads swivelled to look at the Majesteria's cages.

But nothing changed.

The Majesteria still hung in the air, frozen like statues.

The green glowing light still filled up the room, buzzing with strong natural energy.

Tristan carefully picked up the crystal, holding it in his hands. He felt its strong, steady power but nothing had changed. He moved it around the room a little, holding it up to the sky and down to the floor, to no effect.

He set it back down and stepped back, looking from the Majesteria to the crystal, unsure what to do next.

"What now?" one of the sailors asked.

Tristan looked down at the Majesteria, their tiny bodies not moving at all as they floated in their air, frozen and vulnerable.

He wanted to scream, to punch something, to cry.

They'd come so far, it wasn't fair.

But instead he said, "I'm...not sure."

"What if we smashed it?" Wren asked, thinking quickly. "Do you think that would harm the Majesteria?"

Tristan thought about it for a moment. He was deeply aware that their safety and options were trickling away like sand in an hourglass. They had to get the Majesteria out of there immediately. So even though he wasn't totally sure, he knew he had to make a decision.

"I don't know if it will work but I doubt it would hurt them," he said, "Certainly not beyond anything we couldn't fix with a good healing poultice."

"I've already got one ready, dearheart," Bonnie said sweetly.

"Alright then," Tristan said, stepping back from the crystal.

"You heard him," Wren said, giving Basel a sassy look.

The cook stepped forward, a large cast-iron frying pan gripped tightly in their hands and a gleam in their eye.

Basel brought the frying pan down hard on the crystal. The sound was ear-splitting, it reverberated not only in Tristan's ears but in his brain, his soul, his very being. He crouched down as the crystal splintered into a thousand tiny sharp pieces, shooting out in all directions, slicing the skin of his arms and neck.

Instantly, the light went out of the room and the Majesteria dropped to the bottom of their golden cages. But Tristan didn't notice any of that because there was a surge of magical energy, like all the potent magic from the crystal was pouring out into the air around him. He fell to his knees as the wave of powerful magic overtook him. Some part at the back of his mind felt the thread connecting him to the Magick Carpet snap as his being became consumed by the magical energy from the crystal.

It didn't feel bad exactly, but it was completely overwhelming. It wiped all thoughts and emotions from his mind, leaving him a blank canvas.

For a few moments he didn't know...

where or...

who or...

what...he was.

And then he was back, crashing into his body, feeling and remembering everything all at once. All the potent magic had left the darkened room, but it had been replaced by confusion and chaos.

Everywhere someone was bleeding and woozy from the shards of crystal and wave of magic. He heard a loud thump as the now untethered Magick Carpet crashed onto the deck. The sound was followed closely by shouting and scuffling boots from outside. Around him the sailors were readying themselves; Wren began directing the small group for how they would fight their way across the deck.

"We only have a few darts left so we'll need to fight now and save the darts in case the mages come out," she said, to agreement all around.

Meanwhile, Basel was scooping up the Majesteria into their arms gently.

"Are they alright?" Tristan asked, his voice hoarse.

"Aye, the dumplins' are sleepy but they're alive," Basel said tenderly.

"We won't be able to say the same if we don't get the hell out of here," Wren said.

Then she wrenched open the door and ran out onto the deck shouting.

Tristan stumbled after her and the rest of the crew as they struggled across the deck, battling with the pirates. It was only a few sailors so far; no one he recognized, and no mages. They had a chance.

But not if he didn't get the Magick Carpet flying again.

Tristan dodged around the fighting pirates, trying to find a pathway to the carpet with the sound of clashing steel ringing in his ears. Basel followed closely on his heels, holding the three mice carefully in their massive tattooed arms. Tristan dodged under a swinging bat and twisted his body to avoid being hit.

He arrived at the carpet, now quiet and still. The magic was still there, he could feel it humming, but it wasn't ready to fly. He pulled out his Starlight vial to get more magic.

It was empty.

He cursed the gods above and below.

Frantically, he yanked at the golden reins, willing the carpet to leap into the air again. He pushed and pulled, trying in vain to infuse his will into the limp, lifeless ropes. It didn't work, the carpet remained flat and unresponsive. What could he do? If he couldn't get more Starlight they were going to be stranded in the middle of the ocean with a ship full of pirates who wanted them dead.

"Are the Majesteria awake?" he asked Basel desperately. Tristan was sure they would know what to do.

Basel shook their head, "Barely, I don't think they'll be talkin' for a minute Froggy. What's goin' on?"

"I'm out of magic to launch the carpet," Tristan said, his hands shaking as the sounds of sword fighting behind him got louder.

"*TRISTAN!*" Wren screamed as a few more sailors barreled up the stairs, from the lower decks. "We need to go, *NOW*!"

"I'm trying!" he called back, but he didn't even know what that meant.

Trying implied he had a plan, mostly he was just panicking.

"Can't ye get more magic, Froggy?" Basel asked, "I thought you got the clay? Ain't that all you need?"

Right. Tristan gets the clay, the Majesteria make the pottery.

That was all he needed.

He just had to get more Starlight.

With no toolkit, no channelling batons, and no ability to focus due to the fact that almost everyone he cared about was currently in mortal peril.

Easy.

"Right, I'll get more Starlight," he said shakily, hoping that if he said aloud that he could do it, it would become true. He took the gloves off of his trembling hands, willing his heart to slow down enough to let him focus. There was still a bit of the night left, enough that when he revealed his star tattoos they began to glow faintly.

He took a deep breath and against all his body's instincts, he closed his eyes. Somehow, that only made everything worse. He had hoped closing his eyes would block out the fighting so he could focus better, but instead it only amplified it. The sounds were all the more terrifying when he couldn't see what was happening.

His eyes snapped open and he tried instead to look up, focusing on looking at the sparkling stars above, building his emotional connection to them. He felt a faint whisper of Starlight, he saw a few threads in his mind but they fizzled out as quickly as they'd come. Every time he started to get close, the fighting or fear would distract him and he'd lose the threads again.

He felt tears pricking at the corners of his eyes as he began spiraling into fear and despair. What if he couldn't do it? What would they do? His hands were shaking violently now as the anxiety gripped him, compounded by the pulsing adrenaline. There was no way he would be able to catch Starlight like this.

And then, someone took his hand.

A strong, steady voice said

"It's going to be alright, you can do this."

She really was an excellent Captain.

He looked at Wren's hand grasping his tightly, and felt her willing that cool head under pressure into him.

She stood in front of him, her voice low and strong as she locked eyes with him.

"Hey. Tristan. You can do this. Look at me, focus only on me."

"Alright," he said. His hands were shaking but he looked into her eyes. If there was anyone who could make him forget the rest of the world it was Captain Wren Hawthorne.

She squeezed his hand and he felt himself relax a tiny bit. He almost forgot all the noise and chaos and fighting around them, letting himself believe it was just the two of them and the stars above.

Suddenly, he could see the Starlight threads in his mind, plucking them out of the air with one hand while clasping Wren's hand with the other. It was so easy, he was perfectly focused. He could see the Starlight all around him but when he focused on her touch, their intertwined fingers, he could return to his body without any struggle.

Because there was nowhere else he'd rather be.

He had almost finished winding the threads around his hand when he heard a loud, menacing voice call out across the deck.

"Well, well, if it isn't the *timid* Majesteria Handler! I believe Fisk owes me a gold coin," Mad Richard said with a sneering laugh.

"Ignore him Tristan, focus on the carpet," Wren said. She dropped his hand and unsheathed her sword as Mad Richard made his way towards them. His matted dark hair swirled around his cruel eyes, his cutlass glinting in the moonlight.

"Emyr! NOW!" Wren shouted.

Emyr was ready. He threw his darts quickly with perfect aim, each one landing squarely in the chests of the oncoming mages, and one more for Mad Richard himself.

The mages staggered backwards but...nothing else happened. They did not collapse or fall asleep.

"Oh, were you expecting something else? Maybe a little nap?" Mad Richard jeered with a cackling laugh.

He ripped open his shirt, revealing tight leather armor underneath.

"Don't come on a pirate's ship if you're not prepared for a *real* battle," he said. Then he ran forward, rushing towards them with his sword drawn, glinting in the moonlight, his vicious eyes squinting in fierce determination.

"Tristan, we need to GO!" Wren said, shouting to the rest of the crew to pile onto the carpet as Tristan quickly wound the Starlight threads around the golden reins.

He looked around for Basel and saw to his relief that they were sitting on the carpet while still ferociously holding the Majesteria in their grasp. Tristan did not doubt they would keep them safe, and fiercely defend them if it came to that.

Mad Richard was shouting to his crew to surround the Magick Carpet as he made his way across the deck, sword in hand. His mages were busy behind him, frantically preparing their spells.

Tristan hurriedly picked up the golden ropes, once again feeling the spiderweb of magic laced through its fibers. Now that he'd pushed the threads of Starlight into the reins the carpet barely needed more than a suggestion to leap into the air, rippling on the wind.

The pirates surrounding them leapt back as Tristan yanked the reins up, willing the carpet to fly into the sky. The Magick Carpet started to move, but instead of soaring upwards it twisted, struggling as it tried to obey his command. The violent motion sent some of the sailors tumbling backwards, yelping loudly. He looked around and saw that something was holding the carpet in place. It was, of course, Mad Richard.

The vicious pirate was grasping the corner tightly, his cutlass held between his teeth with a wicked gleam in his eye. Tristan barely had time to realize what had happened before Mad Richard was leaping onto the carpet and charging at him, removing his sword from his teeth and pulling it down in a sweeping arc.

But he never even got close.

Wren was there, sword in hand. She lunged between them, blocking his advance as their swords met with a clang, throwing him off balance on the rippling carpet. Mad Richard grimaced and stumbled back towards, trying to regain his footing. He swung at her head, but Wren ducked just in time, the wind from his blade whipping her hair across her face. Their clashing swords rang out in the night as she advanced, parrying his every move until she finally got the upper hand.

With a definitive push and a hard kick to the groin she sent him flying backwards off the carpet. He landed sprawled across the deck with blood dripping down his face.

Tristan wasted no time, pulling on the reins to send the carpet careening into the sky, arcing around the ship and away.

"Don't think I won't get you!" Mad Richard shouted as Tristan spun the carpet around and up into the clouds.

"Not if I get you first!" Wren shouted back. "These mice are *MY* crew and *no one* steals my crew!"

She fell back onto the carpet and said,

"Get us out of here!"

He didn't need to be told twice. Luckily the carpet was finally eager and ready to soar, more than willing to send them high into the clouds. Tristan's blood was pumping in his ears and his hands were shaking uncontrollably as the carpet rose higher into the night.

They heard a whizzing noise followed by a loud splash behind them

"They're shooting at us with the catapult!" one of the sailors said.

"Oh gods, they're going to shoot us out of the sky!" someone else said.

But it was just a parting shot. It was too late for Mad Richard and his mages, because they were already gone.

They soared up into the clouds, the dark, ominous ship and glistening ocean waves shrinking below them as they ascended into a big, open sky full of stars.

And then...they were free.

And Tristan could finally breathe again.

~

"How are they?" Tristan asked worriedly, glancing over his shoulder at the Majesteria who Basel had, rather reluctantly, lowered gently onto the carpet near them.

"What's going on?" Marigold asked.

"Mad Richard, he was in our room with these weird mages and..." Edwina trailed off as she looked around her in surprise. "Was that a cloud?"

"This rug is niiiiice," Chica said.

Tristan felt his shoulders finally relax and his heart soared with joy when he heard the chipper sounds of his friends.

The sun was just starting to paint the sky shades of bright pink and warm umber as Wren explained what had happened to the Majesteria while Tristan navigated the skies and began to let his nerves finally unwind.

The Majesteria were quiet for a while after Wren had told them the tale of their rescue.

"But...where is everyone?" Edwina asked, looking around as though a dozen angry Teakley mages might materialize in the sky.

"Where's Blanchard?" Marigold asked.

Tristan felt pain and anger welling up inside him again as he tried to figure out a way to tell them what had happened at Ivylane Manor.

"I brought ye some snacks dumplins'," Basel said, opening a large leather bag and pulling things out to set on the carpet. "The strawberries are a little crushed but I promise the cheese is still good."

The mice ignored Basel.

Tristan knew it was serious if they were not even distracted by cheese.

"Tristan? Where's the mages?" Marigold asked again.

"I...Um..." he sighed. It was so unfair. After everything Blanchard had put him through now *he* had to be the bearer of bad news to his friends too.

"Blanchard told me to not to come after you."

"WHAT!" Marigold said, shocked.

"Because he was going to come after us himself, surely?" Edwina said, looking out across the skies again.

"Um, No."

"Wh...wh...what do you mean?" Marigold asked in a small voice.

"He said I wasn't allowed to follow you. When I refused he... locked me in my room with mages standing outside the door," Tristan said.

"How *DARE* he! He threatened violence against you by our *own* mages?"Marigold was seething.

"But...how did you get here then?" Chica asked.

"I, um, well...I made a rope out of sheets and climbed out the window," he said, a little shyly.

"Yeahhh, Adventure Tristan is a bad ass," Chica said.

Wren raised an eyebrow. "I must admit, I'm impressed," she said.

In spite of himself, Tristan smiled.

The mice were silent for a long time after that, and soon everyone on the carpet went quiet too. Bonnie tended to people's wounds, but the mood in the air was somber as the Majesteria tried to come to terms with everything that had happened. Eventually, Chica took some of the cheese, thanking Basel with a little curtsy.

When it felt like the silence had truly become too much to bear and Tristan was on the verge of saying something Edwina suddenly stood up, raising her sword to the sky and said,

"*FINALLY!*"

"I'm sorry?" Tristan said.

"You don't know how *long* I have waited for this day," she said, her voice taking on a vengeful edge Tristan wasn't used to. "We've been trying to get rid of Blanchard practically since he arrived. We have brought many inquiries against him, but he always managed to find a way to wriggle out of it. But not this time, oh-no! We've *finally* got 'em."

Marigold stood up too, her eyes shining.

"You're so right! Why didn't I think of that? We can finally get him thrown out! This is a glorious day indeed."

"Can we get Muggward back? I liked him," Chica said.

"I doubt it, that man is happy as a clam, he loves his mollusk research," Edwina said.

"I didn't know you were trying to get rid of Blanchard," Tristan said, surprised.

"We've been trying to get him dismissed for ages!" Edwina replied, "but this time he finally took it too far, I can't wait to tell the Head of the Grand Majesterium about this. Believe me, Finnrake will *not* be pleased. Blanchard is going to be in a world of trouble when we get back to Fairefeux."

"What if this creates a problem for *The Snapdragon*? It may take us a little longer than a week to deal with all this, you know how bureaucracies are," Marigold said.

"Ohh, I hadn't considered that," Edwina said thoughtfully. "Would that be a problem for you, Captain?"

Wren looked at the Majesteria, utterly confused.

"Would, um...what, exactly, be a problem?" she asked.

"Delaying the ship's departure, of course!" Edwina said cheerfully.

"Why would that delay our departure?" Wren said, looking at Tristan with a hitch in her voice.

"Does that mean ye comin' with us dumplins'?" Basel asked, their eyes turning misty.

"Oh, I do hope so, dearhearts. That would be so lovely!" Bonnie said.

"Why...would it delay the ship's departure?" Wren asked again, her dark eyes sharply focused on Tristan.

Tristan looked at her and everything else faded away. All he saw was her questioning eyes and the emotions written all over her face. Fear, excitement, worry...hope.

Tristan felt himself blushing and nervous suddenly.

"I...I was going to talk to you...later, after everyone was safe," he mumbled.

"You...you're planning to come aboard *The Snapdragon*?" she asked.

"Well I just, I mean, we discussed it, yes." Tristan said, feeling himself careening off into a nervous ramble again. "The Majesteria wanted to become Field Researchers, travelling across the realm, and I...well...you said...*you could stay*. But, but...um, if you've changed your mind, or didn't mean it, I think, you know, I could, well, um, I don't know. I can't imagine being anywhere else, really, it feels like my home, like my..."

"We're you're crew," Wren said, breaking into a huge smile.

"Yes, that's the perfect way to put it," he said, relief washing over him.

"Welcome aboard, Tristan Mulberry," she said, sparks dancing in her eyes.

She leaned forward til her face was so close to him he could feel her breath whispering across his skin, her eyes asking permission for a second before their lips met.

This kiss was different than the ones before, it wasn't quite as full of wild hunger and desperate longing, although that was still there. But mostly, it was soft and tender, full of deep emotions and the promise of tomorrow.

As he lost himself in the world of Wren's lips and her soft hair caressing his skin, Tristan felt like he was falling. The wind rushed through his hair and it felt like he was flying down towards the deep blue sea to drown in the dark pools of her eyes.

"AHHHH! We're falling!" Chica screamed.

"Tristan! The reins!" Marigold shouted.

Wren and Tristan broke apart and he was startled to realize that he was, in fact, *actually*, falling. He had been so lost in the wonder of kissing Wren that he'd let the reins drop and now they were careening swiftly towards the sea. He frantically pulled up on the reins and after a few moments of chaos they were stabilized and horizontal again.

"Er, sorry about that," Tristan said with an embarrassed cough. "Is everyone okay?"

"Please focus on flying," Edwina said sharply. "You two can canoodle later, *I* don't want to crash into the sea and miss the Coronation!"

Tristan looked at the sky, the bright light of dawn was already painting the horizon with its crimson hues.

"I'm so sorry Edwina, but I think you're going to miss the Coronation anyway," he said.

"What!? Why?" Edwina said.

"It's at dawn," Marigold said sadly. "It's already started."

"I didn't even think of that," Wren said with a frown. "We were all planning to go as a crew and sit in the cheap seats at the back."

The rest of the sailors murmured their disappointment.

"Oh, I *so* wanted to see it," Edwina said, beside herself. "Isn't there some way we could get there in time?"

"Not if we have to go back to Ivylane Manor and change, I'm sure the rest of the Teakley delegation has already left anyway. But I may have an idea, it's not perfect, but it *is* fun," Tristan said mischievously.

"What are you going to do?" Marigold asked.

"You'll see," Tristan said with a wink.

"Ohhh, Adventure Tristan is sneaky, I like it!" Chica said cheerfully.

Tristan urged the carpet onwards while the Majesteria settled into the ride by having a lively theoretical debate about the magical workings of the Magick Carpet and how the spellwork might be scaled down to make a carpet designed for a mouse.

Less than an hour later the Magick Carpet sailed over the city of Fairefeux and up the sloping hillsides towards the amphitheatre. The Coronation was being held in a large open-air amphitheatre constructed in a natural bowl on the side of a massive hillside. There were tens of thousands of people there, everyone from the highest born nobles and royalty to merchants and peasants.

Tristan smoothly brought the Magick Carpet to a hovering stop at the outer rim of the amphitheatre, high up on the top of the sloping hillside. They looked down at all the cheering people and the stage below, where an orchestra had just started to perform a bombastic rendition of the National Anthem.

"Oh my stars!" Marigold said, standing up to get a better view of the immense amphitheatre and its wildly cheering crowds.

"I thought, if we can't attend as guests, maybe we could at least see the Coronation from up here," Tristan said.

"This is wonderful!" Edwina said, clapping her paws in delight.

"Thank you, Tristan," Wren said with a warm smile.

"Is that the National Anthem?" Chica asked.

"Let me fly closer so we can get a better view," Tristan said, lifting up the golden reins.

"We'd better not," Wren said, putting a hand on his arm. "Best not to call attention to ourselves with a stolen Magick Carpet."

Borrowed," Tristan corrected. "We're returning it right after this."

"I doubt the Royal Guard will make that distinction," Wren replied.

"Alright, we'll stay here then," Tristan said leaning back a little to get more comfortable.

He let his hands relax on the reins, just enough to keep the carpet flying but allowing himself room to stretch out his legs and converse with his friends. After a little while he found he preferred watching the Coronation from the back anyway. Although the stage was far away and tiny, the view of the amphitheatre was spectacular, and there was something truly special about watching the whole event from high up in the sky, with the sunrise bursting over the horizon and casting its shimmering light over the crowds below.

Soon Basel pulled more foods out of their leather bag; squished breads, slightly crushed pastries, soft cheeses, and smushed fruits.

Basel passed them around to the everyone, and no one dreamed of complaining. When you're hundreds of feet up in the sky watching the Queen's Coronation any food is a welcome delight, even if it's seen better days.

Wren pulled out a flask of rum and handed it to Tristan.

"It's just past dawn! Isn't it a little early for rum?" he said.

Everyone looked at him like he was mad.

"Umm, we're *pirates*?" Emyr said flatly.

"Didn't those novels teach you anything?" Wren said, with a laugh. "Besides, you didn't even go to sleep."

"Still..." he said.

Wren shrugged, "More for me then. But if you're coming aboard *The Snapdragon*, you'd best get used to the taste of rum."

"And strawberries!" Marigold added with a giggle.

The food and the rum flask were passed around the carpet as they listened to the orchestra playing a long, vaguely familiar symphony while dazzling firedancers wheeled across the stage.

Wren and Emyr pulled out their spyglasses and everyone took turns looking through them to get a closer look at the spectacle on the stage below. Acrobats that looked more like birds whirled down from the rafters in brightly feathered costumes, a troupe of Dragonlings and their keepers performed an elaborate firedance before swooping over the audience to blast puffs of flame above the jubilant crowds.

When it was his turn with the spyglass Tristan found himself drawn to looking out across the audience. He enjoying seeing everyone's fantastic outfits and joyous faces, clapping and cheering for the performers.

In the front of the amphitheatre, closest to the stage, the nobles and dignitaries stood calmly in their glittering regalia. Looking at the outfits of the courtiers Tristan saw that actually the bespoke outfit Blanchard had picked out for him would have fit right in. But...he wouldn't have. Tristan knew now that he belonged out here, with the crew on *The Snapdragon*, travelling across the seas, exploring and adventuring and sailing off into the starry night.

Chica laid out across the rug with her chin in her paws while the Queen's Mages cast the first round of sparkling, wheeling pixie-dust fireworks to dance across the sky to the delight of the enraptured crowds.

"I could get used to this," she said. "Can we keep this rug?"

"*No*," Tristan said firmly. "It's *borrowed*."

"I wish more rugs were woven with magic in them, it's so cozy," she said, sighing and wiggling around on the carpet. "Much better than those stiff rugs at that hideous Manor."

"I'm so happy we got to travel on the Magick Carpet after all," Marigold said, lying down next to her and kicking up her feet. "Now if only we could see the Ruins of Ahmet!"

"We still might, who knows where the high seas will take us!" Edwina said.

"Maybe even somewhere *more* exciting than the Ruins of Ahmet," Tristan suggested.

"Let's not get carried away," Edwina replied.

After a row of satyrs wearing blooming flowers dancing in unison to a merry folk tune left the stage the orchestra changed to a slow, dramatic rendition of the National Anthem and a hush came over the crowds as it became clear Princess Poppy would be the next to take the stage.

Everyone leaned forward to get a better view of the tiny person far away, squinting to try to see her face as she marched regally onto the massive stage. Tradition dictated that the Crowning Ceremony had already taken place at midnight in a grove of ancient dryad trees, so the new Queen was already wearing her glittering crown when she arrived on the stage to a huge wave of thundering applause.

Princess, nay, *Queen* Poppy was a tall, broad shouldered woman with kind eyes and big, voluminous hips. She had long white hair, woven through with small pink flowers, and she wore an iridescent white-silver dress embroidered with thousands of crystals, reminiscent of the glittering first snow of winter. On her back she wore faux wings of gossamer and silk, shimmering like sunlight on a cold sea.

She was followed by a few dozen handsome men with rippling muscles, glittering headdresses, and very little clothing. Emyr whistled loudly, cheering and clapping for the brawny, half-naked men. Next, a dazzling golden cart with a red velvet pillow was carefully wheeled out onto the stage by a rotund dwarf in a long cloak embroidered with flowers. Sitting on top of the velvet pillow was a very special gilded cage that Tristan knew all too well.

There it was...

The Royal Cinderflower.

The Majesteria gasped and clapped their paws when they saw it, and Tristan was overcome with a deep sense of pride as the dwarf carefully presented the Royal Cinderflower to Queen Poppy and she picked up the cage, lifting it high into the air. The crowd went wild, the orchestra immediately launched into a bombastic salute and the mages sent bright sparkling fireworks up into the sky which exploded in the shape of the Royal Cinderflower.

Tristan looked down at the Majesteria and saw they were feeling the same thing he was. The world may not have known they were heroes, there hadn't been a parade, or even a thank you, but they knew. They knew that without them Queen Poppy wouldn't be holding that gilded cage and waving at her thousands of cheering citizens.

They did that.

And they knew, everyone on *The Snapdragon* knew what they'd done.

And surprisingly, that was enough.

Wren gently snaked her hand into his, weaving their fingers together. Her skin was rough from hard work at sea, and the feel of it made his heart hum with joyful expectation.

She looked at him with a crooked smile, "We did it, I'm proud of us."

"Yeah, we did," he said, "I'm proud of *all* of us."

Tristan knew later there would be fighting with Blanchard, intense discussions with the Headmaster, and at least one formal inquiry. They'd have to bring the Magick Carpet back and hope they could be forgive for borrowing it. There was a world of drama and paperwork ahead of them. But right now, none of that mattered. For now they had this perfect moment watching Queen Poppy holding the Royal Cinderflower, their hearts swelling with pride knowing it could not have been on that stage without them.

After the Royal Cinderflower was set down carefully on its pillow and the mages launched another Cinderflower-themed fireworks display, the strapping men carried a huge bejeweled throne onto the stage, and Queen Poppy perched upon it theatrically, her long glittering gown trailing out across the stage. The brawny men fanned out behind the throne, their rippling oiled muscles shining in the morning light as the nobles and dignitaries lined up to present Queen Poppy with gifts from their cities and countries.

Tristan was admiring the view of the muscular men and beautiful new Queen through the spyglass when he heard the Majesteria whispering in little squeaks next to him.

"I think we should tell him now!" Edwina said.

"But what if the Headmaster says no? I don't want to disappoint him!" Marigold said.

"But telling him now would be *FUN*," Chica countered.

"Tell me what?" he asked, handing the spyglass back to Wren.

The mice looked at each other a moment and Marigold shrugged.

"Guess we don't have a choice now," she said.

Marigold stood up, taking on the dramatic tone and theatrical movements that Tristan recognized as her 'professional' voice. He sat up a little straighter as the mouse cleared her throat and lifted her paws to the sky.

"After our experiences with Starlight magic at sea, we have come to a conclusion which we plan to discuss with Headmaster," she said. "Due to the nature of Starlight magic the need for your assistance in our work is far greater than we originally realized. Thus, we have come to the conclusion that you should no longer be a Majesteria Handler, but should be instead classified as a Majesterial Assistant. Your work is too vital and necessary not to be recognized. And compensated, appropriately."

Tristan raised an eyebrow

"A promotion?" he said. He was both surprised and touched.

"*And* a raise," Chica said pointedly.

"Assuming Professor Bramblebranch agrees," Marigold added.

"I'll *make* her agree," Edwina said, raising her sword into the air.

"Are you threatening violence against our Headmaster?" Tristan said with a laugh.

"Uh, no," Edwina said, putting her sword away hurriedly. "I'm just excited and got a little carried away."

"I can certainly relate to that," Tristan said, smiling. "Well, thank you, all of you. I really appreciate it, I would be honored to become your Majesterial Assistant."

"We would be honored to have you," Marigold said, bowing with a dramatic flourish.

"*And* you're gonna get a raise," Chica reminded him. "Think about all the cheese you could buy with that!"

"I think I have enough cheese as it is," Tristan said with a laugh.

Chica looked shocked.

"Don't be ridiculous, you can *never* have enough cheese!"

-FIN-

✦ About The Author ✦

Corwynn Rosewood (They/She) is an Atlanta based writer, performer and artist. They are the Creator and Writer of the narrative fiction podcast All Vampires Are Gay.

They grew up in the wild misty woodlands of the Pacific Northwest, and they identify as Bisexual and Non-Binary Genderqueer.
Besides telling stories they love reading fantasy books and watching supernatural tv shows and movies.
Some of their other interests include listening to pop music, experimenting with fashion, herbalism, cozy gaming and embroidery. They love tea, coffee, dancing, dressing up and rainy days. Especially rainy days.

Instagram: @corwynnrosewood

I *love* hearing from fans! If you want to
make my day, send me an email:

hello@corwynnrosewood.com

I also love hearing from fellow authors,
and I read books way too fast so I'm
always hungry for more stories!

author@corwynnrosewood.com

If you'd like to send me snail mail
the address can be found on my website:

www.corwynnrosewood.com

ALSO FROM CORWYNN ROSEWOOD

STREAM ON: 

All Vampires Are Gay is a queer supernatural campy adventure audiobook-style fiction podcast with ambient soundtracking.

It's a supernatural action/adventure story with a sassy side dish of rom-com! If you're looking for an exciting and comforting show about magical & paranormal adventures, you've found it.